LET THIS PLACE BE FILLED WITH
WITH DEATH AND LIFE, WITH HUMANS AND NON HUMANS,
WITH UPHEAVAL AND CHANGE.

THESE ARE THE THINGS WE NEED FOR THE TELLING.

THESE ARE THE THINGS OF MY STORY.

In the void of time, Kurangaituku, the bird-woman, tells the story of her extraordinary life—the birds who first sang her into being, the arrival of the Song Makers and the change they brought to her world, her life with the young man Hatupatu, and her death.

But death does not end a creature of imagination like Kurangaituku. In the underworlds of Rarohenga, she continues to live in the many stories she collects as she pursues what eluded her in life. This is a story of love—but is this love something that creates or destroys?

Kurangaituku *is a contemporary retelling of the story of Hatupatu from the perspective of the traditional 'monster'—bird-woman Kurangaituku. For centuries, her voice has been absent from the story, and now, Kurangaituku means to claim it.*

KURANGAITUKU

KURANGAITUKU

WHITI HEREAKA

First published in 2021 by Huia Publishers
39 Pipitea Street, PO Box 12280
Wellington, Aotearoa New Zealand
www.huia.co.nz

Reprinted in 2022

ISBN 978-1-77550-656-0

A catalogue record for this book is available from the National Library
of New Zealand.

Published with the assistance of

ARTS COUNCIL OF NEW ZEALAND TOI AOTEAROA

Hey you little hōhā,
keep questioning and
keep pushing boundaries.

ACKNOWLEDGEMENTS

I feel like this is a story that I have carried with me since I was a child. My whānau would spend a lot of time driving between Taupō and Rotorua, and we would always stop at Te Kōhatu o Hatupatu in Ātiamuri. I would leave my koha in the rock and shiver thinking about Hatupatu hiding there from the terrible bird-woman. Being a hōhā kid, I always wanted to know more about *her*—the bird-woman.

I acknowledge Te Rangikāheke, whose work inspired the book of Māori myths I read as a child, and the other storytellers from Te Arawa—I hope that my work can contribute in a small way to our mātauranga Māori.

I also mihi to my tīpuna and whānau.

I have been writing this novel for almost a decade, so there are many people and organisations that I am grateful to for their support over that time. Thank you to the NZSA Auckland Museum Research Grant and the very helpful librarians at the Auckland Museum in particular, who guided my initial research. To Creative New Zealand for their ongoing support, especially Haniko Te Kurapa (you can stop asking me how the novel is coming along now!). I worked on this novel during my residencies at the Michael King Writers Centre and at the Roxby Downs Community Library supported by Writers SA.

I am also a bit overwhelmed thinking about the many people whose work has inspired me or whose presence in my life unlocked a bit of this novel. Thank you to the many writers I know who have listened to me talk about this book for almost a decade and who have been, perhaps, a bit bamboozled by my jazz hands as I talk about it.

Thank you Witi Ihimaera for very gently suggesting that perhaps I was trying to write more than one book at once—you were right! You said this to me when I needed clarity, and to be honest, a boost in confidence to keep going. Ngā mihi ki a koe, e te matua.

Another special thank you to Pip Adam, a writer and reader (and human) I admire very much who very generously read this novel for me before I submitted it and let me know that my ambitious idea for the format of this novel actually worked.

Thank you to the team of people at Huia Publishers, who have been supportive and, let's be frank, patient with me! Thank you for the inciteful and incisive editing, Liz Breslin, Jane Blaikie and Bryony Walker. Ngā mihi to the reo Māori editors Kawata Teepa, Brian Morris, Pania Tahau-Hodges and Mairangimoana Te Angina who wrangled my enthusiastic but very basic understanding of te reo Māori into sentences that actually make sense! Thank you to the design team, Te Kani Price, Christine Ling and Camilla Lau; your work is consistently beautiful and does so much to support the story. Thank you Waimatua Morris, Claudia Palmer, Michaela Tapp, Brian Bargh and Eboni Waitere for taking my story from manuscript to book, from my hands into the world.

And finally, I mihi to Kurangaituku. The challenge of writing your story has tested me as an author and as a human, but I think that I am better for it. Although I remain a poor vessel for your voice, I am forever grateful for the chance to try and capture it. Forgive me my mistakes.

TE KORE

Kurangaituku

My story, my name, me.

My name tells a story.

Perhaps a story familiar to you.

I have waited so long for you to return to me. I mourned the loss of you for a while, convinced that you would not return. Had I imagined our connection? Did you not feel the same pull on your wairua when we were separated? You had forgotten me, forsaken me. The memory of you haunted me. I doubted my mind, my heart, my reality. How could I have been so wrong?

I sent miromiro to find you. Whisper a charm to the miromiro and he will sing to your errant lover—

Tihi-ori-ori-ori.

Bring her home. She is lost to me.

The sweet call of the miromiro winding the intentions of love into your heart.

Miromiro, a conduit for messages between lovers separated by the forest, by lands far away. The thoughts of your lover whispered from the shadows of the forest—you cannot see your lover, but you know that they are thinking of you, calling you back to their arms.

I whispered my love for you to the small bird and sent him to find you— across the forest, across mountains, across time. Did you hear my yearning for you in his melody? Did you think of me?

Tihi-ori-ori-ori.

A hum of recognition.

And you are here. Perhaps you thought we had been apart too long, that our bond had been severed. But we are entwined, aho twists over and under whenu. We are the fabric of each other—our lives must intersect. I have missed you, and I welcome you back with love.

I have a gift for you—a black sphere, almost perfectly round. I place it in your hand; it sits in your palm, your fingers must cradle it so it does not fall. It is lighter than you expect; it is not a dense mass of stone but something else, something yielding. The sphere feels warm in your hand; it is wet to the touch like a pebble pulled from a river—glossy obsidian, with flecks of white. It seems like the entire night sky has been captured within it. Hold it to your eyes. Through it you see everything—the black, the dark, the nothingness. Open your mouth, and place it on your tongue—it is too large for you to close your mouth, and I can see the panic in your eyes. Surrender to the feeling. The sphere changes—no longer round, the mass in flux, pooling on your tongue—it spreads out from your open mouth over your face. A scream enveloped by darkness. The dark invades your body through your eyes, your nose, your open mouth. It is the air in your lungs, the blood in your veins, the marrow in your bones. Let it invade you, colonise you, assimilate to it, until your body is no longer anything—it is part of the darkness. There is something in the dark, unseen, but known. Every instinct whispers *monster*. It is not the monster that is frightening—it is the dark.

I am dead.

Am I dead?

The world is dark and all that is left is darkness, a black void blankness. Let it be blank. Listen to the blank, the black, the dark. Blank is different from nothing. Nothing suggests, well, nothing. No. Thing. But blank is possibility —it may be filled, it may change, or it may remain. Blank.

Te Kore,

endless Te Kore, the void that stretches forever because there are no boundaries, no time. There is just Te Kore.

Te Kore,

endless Te Kore, the void that has no substance. There is nothing to perceive. There is nothing, just Te Kore.

Te Kore,

endless Te Kore, the beginning and the end. All the things that have been and will be, but cannot manifest in—

Te Kore,

endless Te Kore.

Everything, every possible thing, is enfolded together so very tightly that enormous heat is generated. It is the heat of creation, the blank feeling its potential.

And in the infinite void of Te Kore there is a hum, a hum of recognition, a prediction of change. We have started something. It is a beginning and in less than a second everything expands into—

Te Pō.

The darkness at last a presence, there is no longer an empty void. There is the night that stretches on.

Te Pō.

And in the darkness, the hum grows stronger. It is the hum of many voices, of infinite voices. It is all that has been, that will be, finding its form. Finding its will to be.

Particles combine and divide—the ripples of their coupling and divorce spread out and become great waves. Everything has changed.

Te Pō.

The darkness envelops. It invades. It is you and me and we are darkness.

Te Pō.

The darkness is complete, oppressive. It defines and shapes our form. It pushes down, and we push back.

Te Pō.

The darkness is our comfort, yet we continue to repulse it. The darkness that had defined our form has been replaced with space.

Te Pō.

The darkness is now an absence of light. We have perceived this. Our eyes have opened.

Te Pō.

And in the darkness, we listen for the hum. It is both within us and without us.

Te Pō.

The darkness is a womb—it has nurtured us, but we cannot stay within its confines forever.

Te Pō.

And in the darkness we realise that we are not alone. We are many who dwell in the darkness of—

Te Pō.

The darkness, o the darkness that has nurtured us, that has oppressed us and defined us. The darkness that is us must inevitably arc into light.

Ki te whaiao, ki te ao mārama.

A pinprick of light. It is the seed of potential. It is minute in the great void, this particle of light. I am tempted to say insignificant, but because it holds your attention, it *is* significant—you have imbued it with importance. Thus, this tiny speck has become the centre.

Watch as it continues to grow—the heat and light increase at a rate impossible for us to fathom. To our slow senses it is as if we are witnessing a great explosion. One moment we can hardly see the light, the next we are surrounded by it.

Meet me here at the centre. The centre of all that is known, all that will be.

We will create a world here from a few words, we will make a place where you and I will be comfortable. Let us first build a whare where we can share a story. A whare tapere, a house of storytelling and games. A pātaka kōrero, a storehouse of language. Dig foundations in the light, holes for posts—four. Our whare will be a simple rectangular shape; symmetry soothes and pleases. From afar, our whare shines in the blank, it is a tiny speck in the great abyss of Te Pō. It carries you and me. It is so small in the vastness, so vulnerable. How is it not crushed by the black? Be comforted by the thought that eventually night arcs into day.

We must continue. Walls. Plain for now, but by the end of our telling they will be carved by words and deeds—life, if you'd call it that, frozen in the moment. Past, present, future simultaneous. As it is; as it should be.

Below is the blank, the black—a floor is a necessity. Let us throw a mat on the floor. It is finely woven from flax fibre. The warp and the weft are tight; none of the blank shows through the minute holes, the pinpricks, the specks. Not a particle of blank shows through. The floor supports and yields. It is comfortable sitting here, perhaps even lying here, letting my words lull you to sleep.

Above are ridgepole and rafters, the backbone and ribs of the whare that envelopes us. Do you imagine yourself the heart? Keeping the rhythm of the place, letting the whare live. The kōwhaiwhai patterns have yet to be painted on the rafters and ridge—they too are blank, waiting for their story to begin.

What more do you need to be comfortable? A roof overhead, thatched as they were in old times. A window to let in some air. A door so that you can leave this place when it is time. Across the window, we will place a sliding panel so that we might shut out the world if we choose to. I will borrow it from a whare carved by expert hands long ago. Or perhaps, from this point of time, that whare has yet to be built. Perhaps it is our whare that will inspire the carver—his dreams are of our pare and our door. The door will depict a likeness of me. On the window, the likeness of Hatupatu.

The whare, now whole, must be blessed so that we may dwell together. I take water into my mouth, let it drip from tongue to beak to hand, and cast the drops into the corners. The water both cleanses and nourishes the seeds of potential here—we stand at the beginning and the end of a journey. I open a path so that my words might be fruitful, so that you may hear them and be satiated. I welcome you to this place that we have created. I welcome those whose lives I will invoke here—or at least, the part of their lives that I have glimpsed.

Let this place be filled with the things that we will need for the telling— a frayed taupō unpicked by my curious claws hangs in a corner; the pelts of two kurī, one black and one white, stretched out on drying frames; the fine cloaks and weapons that Hatupatu stole propped up against a wall—things I would have given freely, if I had been asked. A miromiro sings—*tihi-ori-ori-ori*—a lament for a lost lover.

Let this place be filled with love and betrayal, with death and life, with humans and non-humans, with upheaval and change.

These are the things we need for the telling. These are the things of my story.

Stories live through you and you through them.

A story does not live until it is told; the initial thought in the storyteller's head is a quickening, it is the spark of something, it is the beginning.

I will try to share my story with you, but these shapes and groups that you think of as words cannot convey the experience. They are an approximation. Is it truly possible for anyone to understand the life of another? But I will tell you my story anyway—it is enough for you to have a taste, to run your tongue along the edge of my blade.

It is a privilege to be heard—and one not many are allowed. There are always those who will speak for others, to take control of the narrative. In my absence Hatupatu told *his* story; my voice was erased entirely. I found myself clothed in a character that wasn't familiar—skin that had been pulled and stretched to fit another idea of me. I became an adjunct to his story, a character to be played against so that he might learn bravery. The fact that he is a thief and a murderer is glossed over. The truth is forgotten.

Ah, the *truth*. The tūī sings a different song to that of the kākā. But both sing the truth.

This story does not dwell within me but in the space between us. I cannot hold this story too tightly to myself. To live, it must have room to grow. Remember the story of how the gods separated the sky father Ranginui from his wife, Papatūānuku—the earth mother. Rangi and Papa held each other in such a tight embrace that their children could not thrive. It is only when Tāne-mahuta forced them apart that life could flourish. Is it not the same for a story?

It lives in the telling.

I live in the telling.

But that is telling.

I am a creature of words. I am a creature of imagination. I live on the edges of dreams and the margins of thought. I live in the whisper of the page. It is selfish then, this story. I want to be heard. I want to exist again, at least in your mind. I need to tell you this story so that you'll let me in and I can breathe again. I was hatched in the imaginations of many. I slipped into the minds of the flock, generation after generation. I was a mutation that helped them adapt to their niche. I was a thought that was passed on to their children and grandchildren. I was woven into their nests and burrows. I was in their flight patterns and mating calls. I boomed in the night and trilled in the day.

And eventually I *was*. What is a body, but a collection of carbon atoms held together—in my case—by will. Is it not true that the mind is part of the body and therefore a body can be imagined?

My body, in the beginning, was that of kōtuku, the white heron, a bird who lives on the margins of water and land, on the margins of the natural and supernatural, a conduit between Te Ao Mārama and Te Rēinga. The bird who is rarely glimpsed—he kōtuku rerenga tahi; the bird who stands motionless in wait of its prey—he kōtuku kai whakaata, a kōtuku that feeds upon its reflection.

`He tohu, a hum of recognition.`

A pattern is emerging on the ridgepole above us, pinpricks of gentle bluish light, like the stars through leaves. If we speak too loudly, the light disappears only to return when we are silent once more. Look up at the twinkling light— perhaps you can see constellations in miniature above you.

When I first dwelt in my cave, I could not stretch my mind to make a simple metaphor, glow-worms into stars. To me, stars were stars and pūrātoke were pūrātoke—each beautiful, but quite different from one another. I had no innate gift for storytelling, no need then to tell my story, to have a voice. This need, this *want,* is a gift from humanity. Your gift to me.

Events slide in and out of view. The endless repetitions collide with one another and create a pattern that is reflected upon itself. I have trouble keeping all I've experienced in an order that you expect and understand.

Beginning.

Middle.

End.

Middle.

Beginning.

Te Kore.

Te Pō.

Te Whaiao.

Te Pō.

Te Kore.

So this is where we start. It is at once a beginning, a middle and an end.

Through these pages, through these words, I live. Unread, these pages are my burrow buried beneath the ash and debris of a violent eruption—here I wait for the return of beings that create me. I am bound and unbound—in this form I can exist in many places, in many minds at once. I am physical, yet I can fly again without a body—I can fly to places as yet unimagined, see new wonders through your eyes.

Through you I am renewed. How will you remember me? The creature without a body, the collector of taonga, the betrayed lover? A contradictory creature—attractive and repellent. A liar, a thief, a murderer.

A giant. A monster. An ogress.

A monster who killed the birds of her flock and consumed them—not out of hunger, but out of curiosity. Through their flesh I could see their life experience. I could see where they had flown, taste what they had eaten, hear the sounds of their flock. I would suck the sweet brains from their skulls, tainted by the surprise of their own death, later with the fear of the monstrous creature that had killed them.

You too are a curious creature, hungry for experience—I recognise myself in you. Look at the book in your hands, the leaves opened, the spine cracked. The words on the pages are like a pulsing heart—you can see life here. You can feel it in your hands. A life waiting to be consumed. Through stories you glimpse the world of the other. One hundred lifetimes or more able to be lived by a single being. Past, present, future—all able to be lived and felt. The lives you can live within a story are endless. The lives I have consumed are countless.

Do these words that we share make you think that I am whispering to you? Is it my voice that you hear in your head as the shapes of the letters, the meaning they hold, fire up your neurons? I have borrowed your voice;

I am clothed in your accent. You may imagine that my voice is harsh like the screech of a kārearea, or the trilling sweetness of a korimako, but in truth I have never had a voice of my own. Even when I finally managed to become corporeal, when I had learnt to push blood through my body with a heart, had contained my mind within the fleshy confines of a brain—I didn't learn how to manipulate vocal cords and air to make sound. It was easier for me to communicate in other ways—to use the thoughts of others to communicate.

See now through my eyes—let my words fill your mind, let me weave for you my story.

A bird who cannot sing. A ridiculous creature.

It is sad indeed to be a creature who is unable to sing its own song.

This story, then, is my song.

Strike from the page all that has been written before. Let the words and letters slip from your mind; pile them upon one another, obliterating their meaning—their ink bleeds into the white spaces: they become pōngerengere, dark and suffocating.

See now through my eyes. Let my words fill your mind. Let me in.

How can I live without thee, how forgo
Thy sweet Converse and Love so dearly join'd,
To live again in these wild Woods forlorn?

John Milton, *Paradise Lost*, Book IX

TE AO MĀRAMA

CHAPTER ONE

KUTUKUTU AHI

We started something.

A quickening, the spark of something.

We made fire.

I stood on the soft māhoe as he rubbed with his kaikōmako stick. I stood with my back turned to him, trusting that he would keep the sparks from my wing tips, trusting that he would not burn me. My trust was freely given then.

Even though I could not see him, every other one of my senses was attuned to his presence—as if without my eyes I could see him more clearly.

The change in the air between us as his arm and hand moved closer to me. I breathed in the smell of the veins in his forearms engorging with blood. I held the breath until my head felt light, not wanting to lose this small part of him and me to the atmosphere. I could feel the pressure he exerted on his kaikōmako as he thrust it deeper into the groove of the māhoe, the rhythm working its way up from my feet to my spine, and it took all my self-control to stop the feathers on my back ruffling with pleasure.

The knot of tī kōuka leaves caught alight, and he brought the flames to life with his breath. Ka hā ia.

'I first met you by the fireside,' Hatupatu said. This was not true. We had met in the forest, long before we had made fire together. I tipped my head back, my long neck curving to the sky, so I could look him in the eye while my back was turned. It was a risk. Sometimes it was hard to predict his reaction to me, and my body. There were times when he despised me for reminding him that I was something not human. Times when the space between us was too great for our minds to meet, and in those spaces his fear would easily tip into violence. He laughed. I chattered my beak—*explain*— and he laughed harder.

'Turn around and look at me properly,' he said. Why did he think that I could not read him upside down? That his way of seeing was the only way? Still, I let his words move me. I turned and let my neck rest in the front of me, hiding its inhuman length in its curve. I cocked my head and looked at him. He made me wait. I watched him as if he was the kōaro I stalked in a swift stream—he was just as elusive. The ripple of firelight across his face thickened the shadows around his mouth—was he smiling?

'In stories. I first met you in stories.'

A hum of recognition, a hum of prediction.

I had preyed upon the Song Makers in their dreams—seeking the cracks in their subconscious where I could seep into. I invaded their thoughts, pressed the thought of me into the air around them—a fearsome creature, a great white bird stalking them in the forest. I was the something lurking in the corner of their eye, the something that whispered into that ancient part of their brain that still thought of itself as a small mammal— the part that makes skin goose-pimple in fear, that makes the heart beat faster in the presence of a predator.

I made their stories, and they had made me. He made me.

He told me my story, the story told by his father and brothers. The story that made young boys scared to become hunters. The korimako that had been sacrificed to make his voice sweeter must have been a prodigious bird. His words bewitched me and nearly undid me—I could feel the borders of my reality fraying. Stitch by stitch he was unpicking me. The idea of me warped by his story, by his imagination. I could feel the shift in my mind and in my flesh.

Aho twists under and over whenu.

I felt weak against him, but I had to hold the thought of me together. I pushed that thought out into the dreams of the birds that roosted above us—the tūī, the miromiro, the pīwakawaka. Amplified by their dreams, the thought spread further and deeper into the forest to the kererū, the kākā and kōkako. The idea of me was so thick in the air that the night birds had waking dreams of me—the calls of the ruru, the whēkau and the kiwi were a litany of me. Strengthened by my flock, I could face him again.

'Kurangaituku,' he said, and I was undone again. His voice twisted my name around me, binding me to him. And my heart betrayed me—beating as if I was the prey and he the hunter. Hatupatu smiled, 'Come, let me tell you a story.'

We started something.

A quickening, the spark of something.

We made fire.

Before the birds, I was nothing. No. Thing. Incorporeal. Can I ever explain what it was like? Perhaps it is akin to describing light—that it can be two things at once, that it can embody two behaviours at the same time. I was both particle and wave—here and non-existent. Most beings experience the world through the body. Every sensation—sight, sound, touch, taste, smell—builds how they conceive the world. You exist as a body and you die as a body, and when you have finally rotted away and your bones have turned to dust, you will no longer exist. Being incorporeal is more than being free of flesh and the forces that act upon it—time, gravity, hunger—it means perceiving your self entirely differently as well.

Someone, somewhere, tells a story about you. In that act of storytelling, that person is not just talking about you but has actually created a you that exists in their story. You exist in this plane and in the world created by story. Both instances are you and exist independently, and more importantly, *dependently.* What is that idiom? Are your ears burning? The burning of your ears is the *awareness* of your other. Push it further—you are not only aware of your other and your other of you, but you *are* the other. It is as if you are many and one at the same time.

You and your other experience their lives individually—what you do in this plane does not dictate the actions of your other in theirs—but also collectively. You lead, as one of your phrases goes, a double life. They are both you—individual and part.

Can you imagine that? Two of you living separate but connected lives, each instance of you informing and enriching the other's view of the world. Now take those two lives and double it in your mind. Double it again and again, beings upon beings created, splitting from one another like cells dividing—until the entire world is populated with you.

You are here and there and aware of both.

We became aware of each other—the birds and me. Until they perceived me, I had never thought about myself. And it changed how I thought of myself. My identity was defined in relationship to the other—the birds became my negative space.

The birds were the first to recognise me—they called me down from the mist and I was formed by their song. At first I was mutable, every bird remade me in their image. A ruru sang of me, and I would fly the night sky with him hunting for wētā. At dawn, the notes of the korimako would evoke me, and I would dart amongst the treetops looking for nectar. I flew and ran and swam with my flocks for centuries. And the thought of me grew stronger with each generation, their songs binding me forever to the corporeal world.

And then the world changed.

The birds knew that something was awry. Of course the birds knew. They had felt the tremor within the earth for months, weeks, days. Some had only known the earth like this—so short were their lives. But they recognised the change that was coming. A hum of recognition. Whatever it was, the birds *knew*.

The flock flies, or swims, or runs. And if some survive the blast they are not those in its path—those in the forest that hadn't taken flight, those in the forest that *couldn't* take flight, have no chance of survival.

High above the rimu canopy, a kārearea soars. The shock wave hits the forest. Looking down, the kārearea sees the mighty trees felled in an instant. Ancient trees that have blocked the sun from the forest floor for centuries, maybe more, topple, rip from the ground like a weak sapling in a spring storm.

An eruption so tremendous that it colours the sky on the other side of the planet, and rips apart the centre of this island.

Our kārearea stays steady, as if tethered to the spot by a line we hold. How long must he stay here? In our minds we can make this moment stretch out forever—he will be frozen on this page as if he is caught in the ignimbrite flow. A kārearea-shaped stone defying gravity because we will it so. He looks to the crater that has opened up from the earth. A huge column of debris rises above the earth. We can take our time describing what he sees. We can slow down the process, which would have happened in the blink of your eye, or rather, the boom of the shock wave. Had he been looking down to the forest our kārearea would have missed the column. We can imagine him looking at two places at once. It is the prerogative of the storyteller—we could justify it. Imagine that he looks down briefly and back up again so that it makes sense—although in 'reality', in the time it took to glance down and up again, the column would have already collapsed. And so, we freeze the column too—to give us time to describe it, to give us time to imagine it.

The column is made up of ash, pumice and lava. It is bigger than any of the buildings that you have engineered, or will engineer. It glows with the heat of the earth, expands with the gases that are created by the heat. Within it a storm rages—lightning rips through the column. If there is thunder, it is drowned by the roar of the earth as it pushes out more and more debris.

And then it collapses. We will slow time. Compare its fall to that of a building imploding, filling the city streets that surround it with dust and the atoms of the people it has crushed. The bottom of the column spreads out pulling the top towards its centre. The weight of the material pushes it across the land so quickly that it reaches the top of this island in a quarter of an hour. It is tempting to think that the boom preceding the fire cloud was a sort of warning, a siren for all living things to take cover. There is no point in playing the childhood game of counting the seconds between the flash of lightning and the clap of thunder to guess how far away the storm is because it is already here. It is a trick of our imaginations—that because we've slowed down time, we've allowed some life to escape. We have written in a space between the shock wave and the fire cloud that really didn't exist. If their bodies had survived the boom, if their organs had not been liquefied, if their lungs survived to take their next breath, it would have been one of fire and poisonous gas. They would have been obliterated from inside and out as the heat of the debris, as the force of it, bore down on them.

It is impossible not to admire a force such as that. It would be easy to attribute such force and destruction to a malevolent god, a god who must be bound by powerful magic to the mountain he inhabits so that he cannot consume the earth again. With every rumble of the earth—the worry that his ropes had slipped, that he might rise again, this slumbering giant.

The flock has no thoughts of gods, no worries about what they may have done to cause this. The flock doesn't attribute the workings of the world to their existence—it will be, whether they are or not. Survival is the only thing the flock thinks about, although the chance of survival is slim. The boom of the flattened forest spreads up into the air, knocking a few to the ground. How high would they have to fly to escape the cloud? The great tsunami of gas and pumice? Heated air usually provides uplift, but this air is so hot that feathers and wings disintegrate. Gas burns out the lungs of those still in the air. Do you imagine their bodies dropping to the ground, pillowed and preserved in the ash? In this death their bodies do not succumb to gravity—their carbon is rent in mid-air.

What of our kārearea? Our stoic kārearea who witnessed this all for our greed for knowledge? Do we leave him tethered to the spot to be battered, shredded, consumed by the fire cloud that engulfed him? Does he manage to fly away to safety? Does it matter? He has served our purpose and our thoughts are elsewhere, our thoughts are not high above the cooling ignimbrite but below it.

The crater that is left is the shape of a human heart, and will eventually fill with water, the source of many awa that run like arteries across the landscape. Around this huge crater the forests of rimu, felled and burnt by blasts, are unable to re-establish in the new soils rich in pumice. In their place matai and tōtara will grow, and in these forests I will eventually hunt the birds that my beloved desired. In these forests I will be betrayed.

This landscape is utterly devoid of life, blanketed as it is in the now solid fire cloud. Ash still hangs in the sky making the light from the sun murky, like the canopy of the forest is still intact. But of course it isn't. The ground that had once been the forest floor is buried under this new land. If you imagine the tallest trees from the forest—taller than the trees you think of now as giant, the trees that are grandfather to those you presume to call ancient—if those trees were still standing, if they hadn't been consumed by the cloud, then you could imagine that the ash and rock would cover the tips of their newest leaves many times over.

And beneath all of this, I am curled in my burrow.

I am dead.

Am I dead?

Life when it is trapped will attempt escape—tree roots will crack rock, animals will test their traps, perhaps maiming themselves to be free.

The first song that birds dream is of escape. You can hear them sing it just before they hatch—a muffled prayer.

Escape, escape …

… this place is too small for me. Body folded, wet with albumen, yolk sack absorbed. Egg tooth pierces the air cell and I breathe for the first time—hā.

Egg tooth chips at the shell—light rushes in and I can taste the air.

And so it was for me.

The life I had so carefully pieced together, the body made up of dreams, borrowed from nightmares, had to be free from the bonds of the earth. I was stuck. The limitations of a body, of a life starkly apparent. I couldn't stay in this burrow forever. What was once a home was now a prison—both burrow and body. I needed to be free. I could dig with my claws and find my way back to the surface, but my claws were like the raindrops above, wearing down the rock over generations.

There was no longer a forest above me, nowhere for a flock to make its home. How would I be sustained without them? How could I live on in their memories if I could not implant myself in them? Even if I spent years digging my way to the surface, would my body just cease to exist as the memory of me faded, as the flock renewed itself generation upon generation and as the few that had known me died? Would they still sing of me?

There was no longer a forest above me, nowhere for a flock to make its home. If the birds' imagination had given *me* form, then what would become of me lying beneath the earth for centuries? Would my body cease to exist as the memory of me faded?

My burrow, large enough to accommodate me, small enough to keep the warmth in, deep enough to preserve my life—or at least my body. It had been buried deeper by the debris—although not as deep as the tallest tree in the forest, just a sapling of two or three summers.

And I was frightened of my demise. Frightened that as I had attained life, that as I had rejected myself as incorporeal, I would die. That this would be the end of my existence. In the midst of the fear then was joy, because I *had* attained the life I sought, because I knew what it was like to be alive. Life is the fear of mortality. Life is the fear of the unknown world of the dead. Life would rather rip itself apart to try and survive than to lie in wait of death. And so it was that I clawed at the earth, at first with a desperation that wore my claws down to nubs, that broke the tip of my beak. It was frustrating and fruitless, but still I continued.

Before the eruption, there was life around my burrow. Microbes, insects, worms. In the rich soil above me I could feel the weight of them, the writhing millions above me. I could hear them, the worms, the invisible of the forest, tunnelling through the soil, eating and excreting the leaf litter and turning it into food for the trees. This reason alone should exalt the worm. Later, much later, I had another reason to honour the lowly worm and its role in our world and another.

Even the worms had gone. I was alone. The cooling rock above me had no dreams. I succumbed to the comfort of the dark, of nothingness. Above me was death. Below me was death. I was surrounded by it. How easy it would be to surrender to it.

To learn what it was to be extinct, what it was to no longer exist. Te Ngarohanga.

But life is tenacious. Life returned to me. Perhaps it recognised itself in me. Wind brought leaf litter from surviving forests. The microbes upon the leaves—bacteria and fungus—broke them down until at last there was enough matter to sustain a small colony of worms. When we consider the forest, it is easy to look at it in parts, focusing on the birds or the trees. It is more difficult to consider the whole, that all creatures that dwell in the forest do not just live there, but they make up the forest. The forest does not exist without every one of them, even down to the earthworms. There is love between the plant roots and the earthworms—they feed each other, without one there can be no other. They are bound, they are joined. It is like storyteller and audience—both are dependent on the other.

Life returned. Earthworms moving as one mass—a knot of creatures curled around each other alone and as one—colonised the forest again. I pushed the thought of me through the rock, I was the rotting leaves for the earthworms to gorge on. The meagre thoughts of the worms were like a feast to me. And I am made in the image of those that dream of me. I am soil and segment. I am moisture diffusing through skin. My limbs were no longer covered in muscle; the fibres twisted themselves into thousands of writhing worms knotted together to form me.

The forest regenerated above me and the flock returned. I could feel their thoughts above me—I could *taste* their thoughts. I slipped into their minds, a half-forgotten dream, a passing thought. Year by year my strength returned.

I dreamt of escape. My burrow was too small for me.

The rain wore away at the ignimbrite above me. Water froze on the surface, cracking the shell around me, forcing it apart millimetre by millimetre. There came a time when a crack became big enough to change the light in my burrow. I could taste the air again. I could breathe again—*hā*.

Hhhhaaaaa.

Hhhaaaa.

Hhaaa.

My bonds had been broken, and the world could creep back into my consciousness.

A tōtara seed became lodged in the crack. Its roots would force the crack apart as the tree grew. My burrow expanded as water dripped in, wearing the rocks and rotting my feathers away. It was many more years until the crack became a hole big enough for me to squeeze my body through. And finally I was free to roam the forest again.

I emerged from my burrow, my skin naked and raw like a newly emerged hatchling. It was very different—the world had changed over the centuries it took for the forest to renew. The forest had returned, but the trees of the forest had changed. The species I had once walked under could no longer survive the mixture of ash and pumice in the soil, and new trees had taken their place. The trees were filled with the chatter and song of the birds that were so familiar. It was good to hear them again after all my years underground.

Far off I heard the call of a bird I had never heard before. A slow, mournful song, punctuated by a bass pulse underneath the melody. A new bird, a new flock. A new mind to add to my collection. It sounded to me like one great creature, a bird of many throats singing in the forest.

The tōtara above my burrow had grown to full height. Its trunk was at least twice my height in diameter. I climbed it, the rotted feathers making my wings useless. My curiosity urged my weakened body further and further up. I had to find where the new flock lived. In the tree I had a good vantage point—I could see the changed plateau that I had been part of for centuries. I could see a clearing, smoke rising from it. It would seem the fire of the eruption still burned in some places, perhaps creating mud pools and geysers like the ones that lay to the north. I scanned the canopy before me for the mystery bird.

Where was that haunting song? Where was the creature that made it? I closed my eyes to listen for it, as if I could sharpen my ears if I blocked the distractions of the world of light. I felt impatient to find it—me who had waited in my burrow for hundreds of years, now could not wait a few minutes. Why had it stopped? Why did it no longer sing?

You can probably guess the creature who had made the song. It was a song made by bone and wood and gourd, not by the flexible vocal cords of a bird. It was not a bird I had sought, nor a creature who was supernatural—although at the time I did not know this.

And then the low notes pulsated; the mournful song I yearned for began anew. I compared it to the birds I knew, the birds I was familiar with.

Such a song must be made by a creature who has the ability of the tūī to sing two songs at once. It must use the landscape to amplify its song like the boom of the kākāpō from its bowl on a ridge. I concentrated on that sound and only that sound, letting it reverberate around my head and ignite my imagination. I moved my head in its direction and opened my eyes. The new song was coming from the clearing. Perhaps a bird had adapted to the landscape of fire, although it hardly seemed possible having only these centuries to evolve. But it was a better explanation than magic, that perhaps this new bird had been created by the eruption itself. A fire-bird who lived on ash and sulphur, who made its nest in the cooling lava flow.

At the edge of the clearing I saw them, the new creatures. I had never seen beings like them before; to my eyes they were just as monstrous as the taniwha in the Song Makers' stories. They stood upright like moa and were almost as tall. They were sparsely feathered like newly hatched chicks and draped themselves in dried leaves and the feathers of my flock. They had surrounded the clearing with young trees, stripped of branches and leaves, the ends sharpened. They had planted the trees closely together, forming a barrier against—I couldn't think what. They had built nests upon the ground, entirely enclosed like that of the riroriro but created in strange rigid shapes, the tops pointed to the sky like the tops of volcanoes. The earth was still active here—hot pools and mud pools boiling from the magma beneath were dotted near the clearing, but the smoke did not come from those sources. The creatures had found a way to trap fire, tamed in small pits outside, or remarkably, within their nests. Perhaps they *were* creatures made from the eruption, creatures who did not seem to fear fire like the rest of the forest did. A fire-bird, of sorts.

They refused the limits of their own voices, creating instruments for song when their own voices could not create the sound they wanted. To me they seemed magical. They had the ability to make the inanimate sing— music created from stone, bone, shell, wood and plants. A tūī has two voice boxes, but the Song Makers could have many, not only the instruments they played individually, but the voice they created when they sang together. When they sang in unison, the different tones of each voice would blend to make songs that I had never heard before.

I did not know that their real talent was the ability to shape reality to their will—to create objects and dwellings from trees and stone, to shape the land around them, to grow the food they needed, to hunt and store for lean times, but most of all to tell stories. Everything they did told a story, the lines etched into their bodies, the lines etched upon the land.

The world had changed. Changed around me, changed without me. I was no longer the apex of these islands. I had been usurped.

CHAPTER THREE

SONG MAKERS

I called them Song Makers—they made the world around them sing. Their language mimicked the songs of the birds around them—I could hear the birds' notes in every word. Later, when the Settlers came, the Song Makers would embrace the word for ordinary as their identity.

I watched the Song Makers for years, in the shadows of the forest, in the lee of their barrier. My years, my centuries, my millennia on these islands of birds left me unprepared for the arrival of the Song Makers. The birds were unprepared too. They had never encountered a predator like the

Song Makers before. They overpowered the moa. Against four or five Song Makers, the impressive stature of the moa seemed insignificant—a riroriro in the clutches of the kārearea. The Song Makers hunted them and feasted upon their large bodies until the only place that moa lived was in the stories that the Song Makers told. The moa, all of the moa, gone. The scraps of them in middens or the bodies of the clumsy forgotten in tomo. The moa was kin to me now—a bird of legend, a bird of the imagination.

The Song Makers enthralled me. Their language was unintelligible to me for at least a season. But I was determined to learn their language because it is an act of love to learn a language, an act of becoming.

When I finally grasped their notes I was amazed to find that some of their chatter was about things that didn't exist, speculation on how the world was formed and histories of their ancestors. They took pleasure in both the telling and in listening to them. These were creatures of the mind and I allowed myself to become enamoured by their words. I bound myself to them, as I've bound myself to you.

I gorged myself watching and listening to the Song Makers. I wanted to feast on the endless stories they seemed to possess. I wanted to possess such imagination—the ability to see this world anew through their eyes. Consume their thoughts and absorb their imagination. I would use their imagination against them just as they had used the moa's body against itself. I would invade their thoughts, just as I had done with the flock—become part of their minds, part of their homes.

Ah, but the Song Makers resisted me. I had not encountered minds that were closed to me before. I could slip into the dreams of birds easily— they had called me to them, evolved with me in their niche. But the Song Makers had barriers I could not scale.

I had learnt from the tōtara seed. I would find a crack.

There were a few individuals amongst the Song Makers who were open to the unseen, matakite. I preyed upon them in their dreams, and while they slept I took root in their subconscious.

By and by there were hints of me in their storytelling. At first I was a kōtuku—the bird that flies between realities. But they recognised that I was rarer than the kōtuku, a bird seen perhaps once in a lifetime. I was kin to the kōtuku, but something *different*—a great white bird that stalked the forest looking for Song Maker prey. In their stories they called me giant, and my stature grew with each telling. I nurtured the idea of me by lurking close to their village. My presence in their midst did not go unnoticed. There were times when I pushed my mind so hard against theirs that one would pause and shiver. I allowed one or two to glimpse me amongst the shadows. Soon they would hesitate when I was present in the dark. I was the something lurking in the corner of their eye, the something that whispered into that ancient part of their brain that still thought of itself as a small mammal, the part that makes skin goose-pimple in fear, that makes the heart beat faster in the presence of a predator.

I fed on their stories of me, this monstrous bird who lurked in the forest forever hunting. A bird with a taste for Song Maker flesh, who would eat the souls of the unfortunate.

I fed on their idea of me, allowing it to divide my cells and rebuild my body. I was malleable, like the red clay from Kurawaka, hewn by Tāne to create his daughter-wife Hineahuone.

Before he created Hineahuone, Tāne's urge to procreate was strong. He fathered the trees in the forest, the birds and the lizards. It seemed that this did not slake his appetite, and for a time he contemplated mating with his own mother. But Papatūānuku told him to take the red clay from her pubis to create his bride. From the Kurawaka clay Tāne shaped his wife. Before he breathed life into Hineahuone, Tāne made love to her inanimate body—where he spilt his seed became the mucus of her nose, the wax in her ears, the saliva of her mouth and the tears of her eyes. Eventually, he breathed life into her. She sneezed and he proclaimed, 'Tihei mauri ora!' At least, that is what has been told.

The changes to my body were violent, an eruption of imagination. I let their stories absorb into me. I curled around the story and let it curl me.

I opened myself up to it—the story and I were no longer separate. The Song Makers' stories of me evolved quickly, and their storytelling tore my body apart—my bones grew longer and heavier, ripping apart the muscles and tendons, bursting through the thin skin that covered them. To say that this transition was painful seems laughable and useless. What else could the reformation of skeleton and musculature be but painful? It was not just that I was growing bigger, I was growing differently. Somewhere in the telling the story changed—the Song Makers introduced humanity to a story that was not human at all. I was no longer just a bird, I was becoming more like my *creators*, the humans I desired. They did not grant me a wholly human body, just parts of it. Somehow this mixture of bird and woman made me more fearful in their stories. Perhaps it reminded them how close they actually were to the natural world they believed they ruled. Perhaps they thought themselves like moa trapped by hunters, that part of their brain still whispered *predator,* over and over again.

Because of their words I became more like the Song Makers—the shape of my legs changed underneath the shaggy down of my feathers. The muscles in my thighs lengthened, flaring out softly to my knees, which turned from the back of my body to the front. My feet were sturdy, large like the moa and able to cross the forest floor, the rocky coastline, the tussock of the volcanic plateau, easily.

My wings were like the Song Makers' arms although they were feathered and much longer, almost twice the length. At the end of their span, where there were once elegant wing tips, the Song Makers had gifted me their hands, at least the shape of them. My fingers were elongated and made even longer by the claw-like fingernails at their tips. I spent some time making a fist and then stretching my fingers out.

This body was foreign to me—I no longer knew its parameters. My torso had changed. The down on my chest and belly gave way to skin. It was pale, far too pale for a Song Maker; it matched my feathers—white like the kōtuku. Sitting high on the chest were breasts, globes of fat that hung from me. My breasts peaked into the bud of a nipple, that most mammalian thing. The breasts seemed to serve no purpose, did not keep my heart and lungs warm at all. Later, I would see them used to feed the very young Song Makers. Later still, I would find that they gave pleasure as well.

Why would an animal evolve so that their vital organs were so vulnerable to the elements? I shivered whenever it was cold. I had not known such cold as that first winter without my feathers. My skin was so vulnerable to the cold and the wind, not only did it shiver, but it also became chapped and raw. The nipples on my chest cracked and bled, and some days the heat from my body attempting to repair itself was the only warmth I felt on my skin.

They had made me woman.

I lay in the forest unable to move my broken body, waiting for my flesh to grow and heal. It worried me to be that vulnerable, for as much as the Song Makers feared me, I feared them. They were the apex predator of these islands now—they had already wiped out a slew of species. I invaded the minds of the birds around me, the nest builders and the chick feeders, suggesting that they nurture this strange creature I was becoming. And so a nest of twigs and leaves and mud and spit was built around me. I concentrated my mind on making proteins and cells come together, on making the idea of me stay together. When I was strong enough, I followed the pekapeka to their cave and made it my home. Away from the Song Makers I would no longer be at the narrators' mercy. I could rest and let my body become whole and stable.

And so for a while, months or years I could not tell you, I lived a life you would think of as hell. Hurt and alone in the cave, my broken and mutilated body repairing itself as I became used to its parameters. I let the pain define me. Sometimes I would stretch my limbs and claws just to feel the pain crackling through the fibres of my muscles. It was a strange kind of pleasure. It confirmed that this body was mine, that I inhabited it, more than I felt that I had inhabited my former self. Because of the pain, my mind and my body were as one. I could only think of my body, my being, when the pain was at its greatest. There was no room for plans or strategies or experiments. There was just being and being in pain. I lay on the floor watching the constellations of pūrātoke fade and change over the generations. Their extinguishing light was not something to be mourned but a new phase of their life. A new phase of my life.

For most of the time I was alone in my cave while I recovered, but sometimes I had visitors—the birds who had fed and protected me as I lay in the forest ventured into the cave to find me. I had not realised how strong my suggestions had been, but I was visited with beaks full of water or tiny insects. I would allow the birds, so tiny now in comparison to my new body, to feed me their offerings. In reality, their drops of water would do little to aid my recovery, but their presence was comforting to me. They would continue to accept me no matter what I had become. Eventually, some decided to dwell in the cave with me, even though their bodies were not suited to the gloom of it—in the deep of the cave they would fly blindly, relying on my thoughts alone to guide them. Later, I would move closer to the mouth of the cave as a courtesy to those who chose to dwell with me, so that they could fly freely in my home without me. So that they could make it *their* home, and they did, raising their chicks in nests made in the hollows of the walls, drinking water from the dips in the ground.

When the pain subsided, I moved my limbs, lifting up my legs, stretching my wings and opening and closing my claws, reminding my muscles that they had work to do. The pain was exquisite and overwhelming—the first time I tried my limbs I blacked out.

Te Kore, endless Te Kore.

The darkness must inevitably arc back into light.

I woke, pain pulsating in time with my heartbeat. I moved again, lifting my legs and stretching my wings. This time I found myself wet, even though there was no drip from the cave above. The moisture had sprung from the skin that covered my chest and face. It rolled down my forehead and stung my eyes as if it was sea spray. It settled on my body, and when I stilled my limbs it cooled me down, and then I was shivering with cold. It was an odd sensation, the seeping and oozing of my skin. I imagined it to be like the ice and snow on top of mountains, that I was melting in the spring sun. And that thought shook me. And that thought pleased me. It was a poor metaphor, but one that had sprung from my mind. This new form, part bird, part Song Maker, had changed my perception. I could see beyond the actual. I could create realities of my own.

The gnawing desire to see the Song Makers again possessed me. It fuelled my daily exercises, made it possible to stand on these new feet and take my first steps as a bird-woman. My limbs were still weak, just standing made my whole body shake. I found it difficult to coordinate my limbs, their new proportions strange. It was exhausting both physically and mentally—each step was a challenge.

Once I was mobile, my strength returned quickly. I would roam the forest at night, running on my new legs, using my claws to climb to the tops of the trees. I edged closer each night to the Song Makers' clearing, but held back. My body was still in flux—it could change at the whim of a careless storyteller. Perhaps night would be safer. I was vulnerable when they were awake, but the Song Makers were vulnerable when they were asleep. Over time, I would whisper my image into the minds of the matakite. I would let a Song Maker glimpse me in the forest, and by and by the descriptions of me would meld and agree.

I tried to fly, to beat my wings and lift into the air, but the wings were useless for flight. I could no longer swoop through the air, but I could use my wings to glide if the updraught was good, but I needed height to try.

I found a tall tōtara and had to rest underneath it, my breathing heavy and my skin slick with sweat. I rested until I felt my skin chill and goose-pimple. I climbed up the tree, using the claws on both my feet and hands to pull me upwards. I opened my wings and surrendered to the air, falling more than flying—a fledgling from the nest too soon, crumpled on the forest floor.

CHAPTER FOUR

RARANGA

Stories, stories, stories. They twist under and over each other—stories within stories, chaos, until a pattern finally emerges, an abstract representation of a life. Geometric and symmetrical, it soothes and pleases.

It is a warm, sunny day. Follow me outside, walk with me to the river. It is not the water we seek, but the harakeke that grows along its margins. When the flowers are in bloom, the tūī will drive the korimako away, to hoard the nectar for themselves. The tūī will wear the golden pollen on their heads—a bright crown on their iridescent feathers.

Let us gather harakeke—be careful not to cut the rito, the heart of the harakeke. Take the outer leaves, mātua, the strong parent and grandparent leaves. Breathe the air—astringent now with chlorophyll. Help me carry the leaves back to the whare, let your hands and arms become sticky with sap.

The sun is high now, let us take shelter in the mahau while I prepare the harakeke. I scrape the outer layers of the leaves with my beak—staining my tongue with its bitter tang. The pale muka inside is revealed, and I pile the fibre at your feet. Ply the muka together—roll the strands up and down between the palm of your hand and your thigh. I will roll them on my chest. The fibres intertwine to become strong thread—some for the weft, aho, and some for the warp, whenu.

Bundle the fibres together, and I will patu the muka until it is soft and pliable. Before the day cools, let us go down to the river to wash the muka clean. Bring the scraps of harakeke—we will give them back to their whānau to nourish the next generation.

I wash the muka as you plunge beneath the water, it is cold: the river is snow-fed from the mountains that loom above us. You hold your hand out to me, try to tempt me into the awa, but I am a wading bird, so I stay close to the bank.

The muka dries in the afternoon heat. Some of the fibre will be left pale and shiny, and some will be dyed—plunged into the iron-rich mud called paru for black, steeped with raurēkau or tānekaha bark for yellow, brown or red.

Although it will be many days until I can start the tāniko, I show you the pattern I intend to make. I sketch the pattern on the ground in front of you, triangles within triangles—negative shaping positive. Aronui, the pursuit of knowledge, one of the kete brought down from the realm of Ranginui. The kete of philosophy, ritual and poetry.

A hum of recognition, a hum of prediction.

Perhaps if I wasn't so inquisitive, if I didn't have a need to accumulate knowledge, perhaps, perhaps, perhaps. The negative shapes the positive.

When I first learnt to weave I was illiterate. I did not know that each pattern the Song Makers created was a story in itself. I did not recognise my whanaunga. Perhaps if I had learnt my craft from a kaiako instead of stealing it, I would have known this. Perhaps if I had grown with the stories wrapped around me, I could have read the shapes easily. Instead, my first attempts, although eerily accurate, lacked the wairua to make them true art. I had observed, but I had not seen.

A kākahu was the first taonga I brought into my cave, although if Hatupatu had seen such a humble garment he would not have regarded it as such. The taonga he came to covet would take years to acquire. But value is relative. This cloak was to me the finest thing that the Song Makers had wrought, except for, of course, their stories and me.

It was not the taonga I had been seeking that night. It was cold midwinter, just before Matariki was to rise. I had decided that I was strong enough, stable enough, to seek the Song Makers once more. In the evening when I would roam, the Song Makers would retreat to their shelters. A few ventured into the forest. I pushed the thought of me out into the trees. Drank in the smell of their fear, saw the hair on their skin rise up. I would stand still in the shadows and watch them. Even if they couldn't see me, they seemed to know that I was there. Sometimes, they would call back to their friends at the clearing, to let their people know that they were safe, or perhaps just to make themselves feel safer. It would be difficult to take one. It would seem that the entire flock would notice if one went missing.

I followed one who seemed oblivious to my presence. Perhaps it was because he was bundled up in a cloak, pulled up to his ears to block out the wind, his skin unable to sense me under the layer of clothing. I closed my claws around his shoulders, and he screamed when he turned and saw my face. I should have broken his neck right away, but I wanted to savour the moment, and in my hesitation to strike, he got away. I was left holding his kākahu, and at the time I thought it a poor consolation prize.

Once I had put on the cloak, I forgot about the disappointment of losing him. In the cold of that night, his kākahu was far more valuable to me than his life. The cloak was still warm from the Song Maker's body, still reeked of him. I tried it on. It was too small for me to place over my shoulders as he had—my back was broader than his and to wear it as he had would pin my wings to my body. Instead, I wore it over my chest so that my wings were free and my skin was finally warm. My chest looked like that of a fat kererū, my human chest covered with something that looked familiar. I smoothed my palms over the kākahu as if I was preening my lost feathers.

I sat with the cloak wrapped around me in my cave and under the soft light of the pūrātoke above, I examined it. I felt the bumps of weft with the pads of my new fingers, marvelling at both the texture and my ability to feel it. The band around my neck was deep, almost my hand width, probably a Song Maker's easily. Here was a design that seemed to emerge from the fabric itself, like the different coloured feathers of the birds in the forest. A flash of red from the underside of the wing of the kākā, the shifting blue-black on the back of the tūī. The patterns were the tight, regular shapes that I had seen at the Song Makers' clearing—the way they set out their dwellings, the patterns of their gardens. I had only seen geometry like this in nature amongst the insects, perhaps the Song Makers were like bees—gathering nectar to transform into honey. Here, they had gathered flax and other plants to dye it and created something extraordinary.

There was a faint scent of the plants that made up the cloak through the human scent. The fine strands of flax stripped of their hard outer layers were smooth and pale—they had a subtle lustre in the glow-worm light. The pattern of the band was made of more flax fibre, but some had been soaked in the bark of tānekaha so the flax became a rich brown, and some dyed with raurēkau to turn it golden yellow. At that time, of course, I did not know the process of dyeing, nor the stripping of flax to reveal the soft muka fibre within. At that time, I sat and tried to puzzle out how such familiar smells, familiar species, had become unrecognisable.

The flax was woven more finely than any nest I had seen. What fine beaks had made such a thing? How many seasons would they have spent creating this cloak? Had the Song Makers trained some strange creature from their homeland to make such things? I doubted that the Song Makers could have made such a thing themselves. I looked at my hands—so clumsy and inelegant. How could these things create a cloak as fine as this?

Over many nights I studied each centimetre of the cloak. I loved the slight irregularities—a change in tension, the fibre thickening slightly in places, the colour patchy and fading. I used my claws to unpick the bottom, unravelling the weaving and fraying the edge. I preferred it that way; it reminded me of my lost feathers. At this time, I thought I had acquired a specimen of the highest artistry. It did not occur to me that this was an everyday garment—why would such work be put into the mundane?

That strikes me as funny now. Looking back on my life as we are, it would seem that my entire existence has been in pursuit of the mundane. The energy and time I have spent on the everyday experience, and I had thought that this object was above it. To think that in a few short years I would regard this treasured object with disdain, call it 'ordinary', as if ordinary is something to despise.

Aronui, aronui. What drives us to pursue knowledge? What makes us climb up into the heavens, willing to risk the fall back to earth? Even before the Song Makers arrived I had been acquiring and pursuing more knowledge than one being should surely need. I was driven by the need to up the sensations I felt. I was driven for the need of more. Perhaps it is a quality that has been present since before existence. Would Te Kore have evolved into Te Pō without the potential for more? Isn't the relentless pursuit of more akin to the growth of the universe? The concept of Te Kore, of an endless void, depends on its contrast with the wealth of material in the universe to exist.

But such thoughts only serve to slow down my story. They are loose threads that if pulled upon will fray my existence.

In pulling the cloak apart I had shortened its life. The fibres, once free, were delicate and would shed as if I was in moult. But there were no replacement fibres lying in wait—the cloak was disintegrating every time I wore it, every time I moved. Even if it had lasted until the end of that winter, until the strong winds that herald spring died into the calm of summer, I would have needed a new cloak in autumn.

There was a whare, much like ours, in the middle of the Song Maker clearing. A whare tapere, a place of storytelling. Imagine me then, a frayed dishevelled cloak looped around my neck, covering my chest with light, feathery fibre. The eaves of the whare were low, so I crouched and crawled to tuck myself under them like a frightened kurī shuffling on its belly, keeping its body and head low. In the shadow, in the night, no one would see me and if someone did happen to glance my way, they could fool themselves into thinking that I was just a collection of leaves and feathers against the side of the whare. Which, I suppose, I was.

But what was the story? What was the story? We are all eager to hear. You and the Kurangaituku of the past, crouching in the shadow of the whare. What was the story? What was the story?

It would be a great coincidence if, on the first night I crept into the shadow of the whare, the story I needed to hear was being told. It is almost impossible that it would happen this way. But the rules of story allow for such miracles to happen. It is a happy coincidence that I happened to be searching for that very story on the night that I was present to hear it. We can call this sleight of hand fate, or destiny if you like.

That night, there were visitors from another settlement. I had thought that this flock were the only Song Makers on these islands. It was foolish of me. Of course there would be other flocks in other forests—had I not seen the same amongst the birds? And like the tūī whose songs differ from place to place, so too the stories of the Song Makers.

The storytelling begins. It begins with another race of people who lived on these islands. It is a mistake of the Settlers to regard these people as human. The people, who some say were here before the Song Makers, are more akin to me than you. The Song Makers called them patupaiarehe, which the Settlers would later translate to fairies. I know that now people regard fairies as benign creatures, small and pretty and clothed in petals and leaves. Patupaiarehe demanded more respect than that from the Song

Makers. These 'fairies' lived as the people—they worked, they sang and they fought. Sometimes they acquired a person, to take as a lover or perhaps to kill them for their trespass, or worse, for sport.

I listened keenly—these were creatures that were kindred to me. Creatures that preferred the night, the shadows or the mist to dwell in. Creatures who were ancient and had much knowledge. Creatures that humans ought to be wary of, ought to pay respect to. The patupaiarehe had taught humans to weave. That is, the humans had tricked the patupaiarehe to weave well into morning, and when the patupaiarehe had discovered the trick they fled, leaving their work behind.

In this story a patupaiarehe woman, Hinerēhia, had married a Song Maker. For a time they were happy together, and she bore many children with him. She brought with her great knowledge of weaving—preparing harakeke and dyeing the muka, knowledge on how to weave the garments she wore and the mats underfoot. She worked at night. The Song Maker women in her adopted village wanted to learn her techniques, but Song Maker eyesight is poor in the dark—they needed the bright daylight to see how she worked.

At this point in the story, the listeners all hummed in recognition, as if the storytellers had revealed a great truth. It would take listening to many more stories about the patupaiarehe for me to understand the hum of the audience that night. Patupaiarehe do not just prefer the dark, it would seem that their magic is undone by the light. If they use their skill during the day then it is lost to them, their lives with humans are lost to them. Foolish humans who want to see their fairy lovers during the day, who want to reveal their secrets under the light of the sun, only succeed in driving them away. The patupaiarehe will flee back to their home, leaving husbands, wives and children behind.

And so the hum was one of prediction. That to gain the knowledge of Hinerēhia, the Song Maker women would have to trick her into working into the day. The Song Maker women would have to condemn a family to being ripped apart, that to gain the knowledge of Hinerēhia, her children would forfeit life with their mother. These women then, who hid in the shadows of the whare of Hinerēhia, watching her work as the sun rose higher, were like the pīpīwharauroa chick taking over the nest and destroying the eggs that it already held.

Once Hinerēhia had discovered that she had been tricked, that she had worked into the bright morning, the skill left her hands. Weaving, the skill that belonged to the night, had now been claimed by the day. And so it was that women gained the skill to weave—but they must only do so in the daylight for if they weave at night the skill will leave their hands and become part of the night once more, claimed back by the patupaiarehe.

I would steal the Song Makers' knowledge of weaving as they had done from Hinerēhia. I would trick them into teaching me. I would hide in the shadows and learn.

I could not be kanohi kitea—my presence would frighten the Song Makers, and I was frightened of them. Instead I needed a kanohi kē, a mask to hide me. I chose the miromiro. A small, unobtrusive bird that could sit in the eaves above the weavers and watch. I used the eyes of the miromiro to observe the Song Makers as they worked during the day.

It was miromiro that followed the women to gather harakeke, that watched them scrape the muka clean with mussel shell or chips of obsidian, that followed them to the swamp to gather paru.

> Mate kanohi miromiro—to be found out by the
> sharp-eyed bird.

I could argue that at the time, it was just a whim I could try to separate my life from this fiction, but we already know that my life *is* this fiction. And so I understand if you are incredulous of my claim that I simply picked the miromiro. Of all the birds I could have picked, I chose the miromiro.

Through the eyes of the miromiro I would learn much.

The miromiro would sit near the women as they wove. Two women sitting side by side with their work stretched out between two poles in front of them, creating the beautiful geometries of the bands that they called tāniko, twining the whenu around the aho with their fingers. When the light began to fade, the women would pack up their work and hide it from the night-time, from whatever patupaiarehe may be lurking. They would return to their work the next day as surely as the sun.

As the shadows lengthened the small miromiro stirred from its daytime perch to find its roost for the night in the forest nearby. And I waited for it, hungry for my daily lesson. The miromiro would not see the moon or the sunrise—its last day on earth was precious to me, and I sipped on its mind carefully and fully. I practised my weaving in my cave, the pūrātoke my weaving companions. I had gathered my own harakeke, taking the long parent leaves from a stand far away from where the Song Makers had gathered theirs. It took some practice to be able to scrape the leaves enough to reveal the fibre within, without breaking it into unusable lengths. I could not roll the fibre against my thigh as the women had done. My thigh was still covered in feathers and the attempt I made in copying the Song Makers had been painful—the twining thread pulled out my feathers. But the skin that I had been given on my chest, the patch that stretched from under my chin to just below the ridiculous dip of my navel, was at last useful. I rubbed the itchy fibre against the sensitive skin of my breasts until the fibre was soft and strong.

I found the same dyes the women had used and prepared baths of them in the small dips that pocked the cave's floor. It was a wonder how the fibre took the colour up and held it fast within itself. It was a wonder that the Song Makers had discovered these secrets, secrets that made the world into an image that was agreeable to them. These creatures had learnt how to manipulate plant and mineral, and I would discover later animal, to comfort and protect their own vulnerable bodies. I had admired the birds who had adapted to their niche in nature, but the Song Makers could adapt the world to suit their needs. They had adapted the ability to adapt. It was dizzying in its audacity.

I found two strong branches and stripped them of their bark, smoothed their surface, so that the fibre would not snag. I decided to work at the mouth of my cave under the moonlight. It was fanciful of me, but there was a small part of me that thought that if I wove in the open that I might be able to catch the attention of a passing patupaiarehe. Perhaps I could weave them into existence as I was weaving my first kākahu, using the Song Makers' descriptions of them as my aho and whenu. I would think of them as I worked, knowing how powerful repeated dreams can be.

The ground at the mouth of the cave was soft so I could bury the ends of my branches to create my loom. I set the branches apart wide enough to accommodate two or three women, even though I'd be working alone, my long arms comfortable in the span. I set up my weaving as my borrowed eyes had seen, struggling at first as my fingers were hobbled by my long claws. That first night I thought my claws to be a hindrance, as I tried to weave as the humans had with the soft pads of their fingers. I thought of the other weavers I had seen in my life—the birds who used their beaks as needles, pushing and pulling moss or leaves through twigs to bind them together. I decided to try to work with my hands and not against them. My claws could be just as nimble as human fingers, or a beak. Over time, as I became more adept at the art of weaving, my claws would allow me to make finer fabric, tighter twists, than a human hand could ever make. I would sharpen the ends of my claws to fine points for my weaving, although some would later think I did it as an act of aggression—that my sharpened claws were things of destruction not creation.

That I am a thing of destruction and not creation.

My first cloak was clumsy, but serviceable, made entirely from muka like the cloak that I had first stolen. But still I sent more and more miromiro to spy— perhaps this year there would be a new technique to learn or a new fibre to use. It shouldn't have surprised me that the Song Makers would use feathers in their weaving—who would not want to be clothed in feathers? I was impressed by their resourcefulness, that they could take a by-product of their appetite for bird flesh and make things that were beautiful and practical.

I too could use the by-product of my own appetite for knowledge, and so I kept the feathers from the tiny bodies of the miromiro that served as my eyes. If I told you that I was able to make a full cloak of their black feathers, speckled here and there with their white breast feathers, would that shock you? The number of birds that I killed to learn to weave? The number of birds that gave their lives so that this cloak could exist? I used their eyes and I used their feathers. It is what it is.

The cloak suited my purposes. It kept my frail chest warm. It covered the skin that was still offensive to my eyes. It was strange, but sometimes I felt as if in wearing it, I became like the miromiro—hiding in shadows and observing the world with my ever-watchful eye. I wore the kākahu until the feathers fell out of their muka sockets, until the muka disintegrated from the sweat that seeped into it from my skin. The miromiro feathers had been useful beyond the lives of the birds they belonged to.

And then I made another.

Although that would make you think that I had given up weaving entirely while I wore out the miromiro kākahu. I did not. It is one thing to acquire a skill, but to master it is another thing entirely. I continued to weave, continued so that my muscles learnt the movements, so that it became as natural as flying had once been. Once a skill is that ingrained in your body, your mind is free to push the skill further, to create finer, more delicate and intricate work, to work faster and more efficiently, to stretch the material to its limit.

The cave became a repository of my work, a gallery if you insist. My first crude mats covered the floor until they were covered by finer work, and then those were replaced in turn. I made several cloaks at a time—some for different weather, light for summer and heavy for winter, some for the challenge of their creation. Almost all were covered in feathers. Some I acquired by killing the birds, some by simply waiting until the birds had moulted and collecting each stray feather. Some were made from my own moults—and if I was impatient, missing a bundle of feathers to complete a row, I would pluck from my body, sucking the small beads of blood from their ends so they would not stain the muka.

Does this paint a picture of me content to observe and learn of the Song Makers from afar? That perhaps I had given up my ambition to take one, to experience humanity through their eyes? No, I had learnt that the successful grab opportunity would present itself—the seed finds a crack in the barren ground after an eruption, a bird adapts to a niche. Observing the humans and their ways was essential—it was a way to find a crack.

Binding feather and muka, twining whenu around aho, I wove myself to the Song Makers. Playing at being a Song Maker did not sate my curiosity; it just made it keener—it sharpened the edge of my hunger.

I was not content to learn only the women's work—I sent my eyes to watch the men construct eel traps, bird snares and their carved weapons. I used my superior strength and height to construct an object based on an eel trap—a cage big enough for a human. It amused me that I would entrap a Song Maker with a device sprung from his imagination—the cage and I were kindred in this way.

CHAPTER FIVE

KUTUKUTU AHI

I folded myself to sit beside him, tried to rearrange my body so that it would be proportionate to his. Tried to make myself more human. Let his words caress and invade me.

The fire we made flickered before us.

I knew him through the stories he told, the tales he told of his short life and the people within it—his mother, his father and his brothers. In this way we were kindred, the sum of the stories that we had told, the stories told of us.

'Kurangaituku,' he said, and I watched the shape of me in his mouth. His breath gave me life—the purr of it as it rolled over and into the sigh of *ngai*, back up into the staccato of *tuku*. His voice was as lilting as any of the birds in my flock. More beautiful than any of them because it was his.

'Kurangaituku, bird-woman, loathsome and feared ...' Was he as skilled with a taiaha as he was with his words? Knowing where to land the blows?

He looked at me and smirked. It was a test—I had thought we were beyond those games. But he was always testing me. Always trying to find the boundaries.

'Or so they say. Perhaps when I return I will tell them a different story?'

Kura the Soft. Kura the Loved. Kura the Fool.

'Perhaps I will tell them that Kurangaituku found a boy in her forest, left for dead by his brothers. And instead of killing him she made him her ...'

Husband. Lover. Whaiāipo.

But he won't say those words. He would never admit what I was to him. Not even to me.

'This is how I came to be in the forest, Kura. How you came to find me.'

All of the threads that came together for us to meet in the forest. All of the decisions made over aeons that put me in his path. All the lives that had to be lived so that I could have him, for a time, in mine.

I am afraid that if I run my hands over them too often they will fray and disintegrate.

CHAPTER SIX

PENEI ME TE PĪPĪWHARAUROA

A tale of two birds, a mother and a mentor. Riroriro and pīpīwharauroa, two small birds common to the treetops of the forests. So common, most would think them insignificant. The small, grey riroriro—so small that its wings would barely span the outstretched hand of a Song Maker, grey like the lichen it picks for its nest. The most striking thing about the riroriro is its discerning eye—red against grey.

The riroriro is a collector—her nest made of roots, moss, grass, lichen and spiderwebs, woven into a dome high up in the trees. You could say she has an eye for things. Yet, season after season she fails to see the cuckoo's egg, fostering a stranger in her nest. How does pīpīwharauroa do it? How does she trick another to raise her eggs? Is it the nature of riroriro to accept a changeling? A tiny bird raising a comparative giant. Perhaps having raised two or three broods already, the riroriro is just too tired to care anymore, too tired to notice. Perhaps it was nothing but an act of kindness—an urge to nurture and protect a being abandoned by its family in the forest. How would riroriro know in that moment how her kindness would be repaid?

The pīpīwharauroa is showier than the riroriro—banded feathers of white and bronze on its breast, iridescent green and bronze on its wings and back. It is almost twice the size of the little riroriro. The pīpīwharauroa waits until the sun warms the earth again to return to these islands. The pīpīwharauroa builds no nest of her own, instead she finds the nest of the riroriro. The pīpīwharauroa chick has assassin instincts—the first act it performs, before it even opens its eyes, is to throw the riroriro's eggs from the nest. The cuckoo demands much of its adopted parents—its begging is incessant. They fly further and further away from the nest to feed the pīpīwharauroa's appetites. I hope they are spared the sight of the murder of their clutch by the intruder—no parent should come home to find their young slain by a creature they have gone out of their way to help.

It is betrayal. And yet, the next season the riroriro will welcome another pīpīwharauroa as if the betrayal never happened. Are they better creatures than I? Do they turn a blind eye? Or are they foolish and blind?

As people are fond of saying—love is blind. Blind to the dangers love poses, to your inherent vulnerability.

I should have learnt from my observations of riroriro. I observed, but I didn't see. I should have learnt the lesson of the pīpīwharauroa and the riroriro. But I didn't have the foresight of a storyteller then. I didn't know that the experiences of others could teach me about my life. I didn't have a life then. Perhaps with the eyes of a hawk I would have seen Hatupatu as just prey. Perhaps with eyes that were not so welcoming I could have left the boy starving in the forest. Cuckoo he was, yet I welcomed him to my nest.

I welcomed him to my heart.

Aho twists under and over whenu.

Call it fate, call it destiny, call it will.

One day he was there, in the forest. Hatupatu. In the tradition of many a love story our meeting is one of coincidence and of fate. Truth be told, I'm not sure if I found him or if he found me, if I had twined his story into mine, or if he had twined my story into his. For a time the story did not belong to either of us exclusively—for a time it was *our* story.

It was hunger that brought us together. Not just his literal hunger, although that played a part, but his hunger for adventure, for his part in the story, that drew me near.

Monster, giant, predator.

Did his spear meet my fingernails or my beak in the small bird we both hunted? It doesn't matter. He ran into the forest, and forgetting his feet, he tripped over the roots there. Perhaps Hatupatu thought that I was his punishment from Tāne made corporeal—Tāne had sent the terrible bird-woman to exact his revenge. How little he knew me then, as if I could be directed to do anything by god or man. Although, that just shows how little I know of myself.

It was cowered underneath the fronds. I picked Hatupatu up. He fainted, his body limp in my grasp. For a moment I thought I had lost my opportunity—that the boy had died. I cradled his head in my claws, unsure if I had the strength to twist it off like the miromiro's skull. I felt his breath on my fingers and held him to my breast. I could feel the beat of his heart against my own chest. I took him to my cave. I had prepared for this day, the day I caught a Song Maker, but I never really believed that it would happen. I put him in a cage like he was an addition to my collection. The favourite, the spoiled mōkai.

It was perhaps a later embellishment to his story that made Hatupatu my mōkai. A mōkai to the Song Makers did not have the same connotation to the audiences who would read his tale many centuries later, who would imagine his role as 'mōkai' much like that of their own indulged animals, a cat by the fire, a dog on a leash. They had translated it to mean 'pet', but as I understood it back then it meant *captive*. The first audiences to hear the miraculous story of Hatupatu would have caught the reference, a hum of recognition.

The idea of a human mōkai would have been horrifying to the Song Makers, who would have made the connection between the capture of Hatupatu and the bird-woman's greater plan—to hunt and feast on them all. Hatupatu was kept not as a pet, but as a tool, a tamed creature to be used by a skilled hunter to lure its kin to their snares with its cries. It is one thing for a dumb creature like a tūī to be a mōkai, quite another for a human being.

If *only* our relationship had been hunter and mōkai. If only. The truth of our relationship, if there is any truth to any relationship, is that it was ever shifting and complicated. Kidnapper, nurse, patient, mother, son, victim, teacher, student, rapist, lover, enemy, thief, murderer, corpse—we played all roles.

Our relationship was too complicated for the hero narrative of Hatupatu. It would have damaged his reputation to admit to caring, at least in part, at least for a time, for me. That the creature that would horrify and disgust most of humanity had been loved by him. If forced to admit his feelings, perhaps he would say that I had enchanted him, that I had forced his feelings for me. The blame for our relationship and his actions within it would fall at my claws. He could excuse himself from responsibility because no one would believe that a hero would debase himself with me. He had a legacy to protect, and perhaps a young wife to impress. How could he live his life if the people knew what he had done—how could he live with their sideways glances and whispers?

He told his story—he took control of his life and future. In his story I was the hunter and he was the mōkai, and so it became reality.

If only.

It did not occur to either of us, Hatupatu or me, that he would be my mōkai. It would have suited us both to cast him in that role, a bargain struck between the equally desperate. It would have made an exciting scene—I capture the young Hatupatu and spirit him away to my lair. He awakes in a cage, and I have my back turned to him. He sees my massive wings, and his eyes follow the feathers up along the span of the wings to the end where my human-like hands appear. He sees that I have a patu in my hands, and is both terrified as to his fate and impressed that I own such a fine patu made from the pounamu that can only be sourced in the far-off island to the south. He has only a few seconds to think, from when I grasp the weapon and when I turn towards him, the full weight of my body behind the imminent blow. But his shout stays the blow. His proposal that I spare his life so that I can take many more intrigues me. I listen to him with my head cocked to the side, the quick movements of my head as I listen to him like a pīwakawaka flitting to catch insects on the fly. I spare his life, but damn many more—the Kurangaituku in this scene thinking that those lives will be human, the dramatic irony being that it will be her birds' and her own.

`If only.`

In this telling, I waited for him to open his eyes. If I was an adept storyteller, perhaps I would describe how the moon rose and stretched across the sky as I waited, that it was with the rising sun that he stirred. In the darkness I watched him, in the dim light I watched him. Until the time he opened his eyes and he watched me.

He looked at me side on. He moved slowly in his cage, seeing himself reflected in my eyes—Hatupatu lost in the dark of them: he, a tiny speck in the middle of Te Pō. Finally, he was upright, seated in his cage with his back against the wall. He looked at me head-on, his head tilted back slightly so that he was looking down at me. His arm rested on his knee as if he was at rest, but I could see that his leg strained against the cage wall, testing its strength.

And in a breath, that was no more than a sigh, I was named.

Kurangaituku.

How easy it would have been to snap his neck and scoop out his brains. I could have killed him when he opened his eyes, slit his throat in that moment, but I hesitated and let him speak just one word. He named me *Kurangaituku*.

And I was undone.

A name is the start of a story. When strangers meet they tell each other their names and over time their names become intertwined with how their new friend sees them. It is linked to their appearance and temperament, associated with memories and judgements, becoming a stand-in for the actual being. The image of the person will be able to be conjured by people telling a story far away from them—those people can now change the story, ascribe their own truth to the name that you have given them.

Many, many years later, after I returned to this world, I heard that some humans believe in an ancient magic—that if you know the true name of a creature that you will have dominion over it. In those stories, creatures take care that their names, their true identities, are never revealed, but somehow, the hero of the story always finds out their secret.

That is the power of a name.

I will not claim that it was not a sort of magic that stopped me from fulfilling my goal of experiencing a human mind. It was not the kind of magic that would curse me or send me back to the place where I had been made. But it was enchanting, to be named. I had never had a name before—it is not something that birds do; they do not have to assert their lives in that way. They exist and are acknowledged without the need to be *someone*. Although I had heard this name before in the stories that were told of the terrible bird-woman, I had not been *given* it.

It was his gift of a name, his koha to me, that saved his life that day. It was a gift, this name, 'Kura of the claws'. It was more than just a novelty to me to be named—it seemed as if this was the beginning of experiencing what it was to be human. It made me think of what more I could learn from him if I allowed him to live.

It *was* magical then, my name. He did have power over me because of it.

I left him in my cave that day. If I was to keep him then he needed to be fed. I tried to remember what I had observed the Song Makers eating. I had seen their gardens so it was safe to assume that they would eat plants, but I had also seen them hunting birds. I had caught this one hunting kererū, so they were meat eaters as well. I headed off into the forest followed by my new name, 'Kurangaituku!'—he howled it now. The sound of it, the syllables of my name, *my name*, twined with fear and frustration and anguish made me giddy. I ran faster with the joy of it, and his howls became indistinguishable from the howls of a far off kurī.

Kura-ngai-tuku!

Kura-ngai …

Kura …

Auau auau!

I had a name, the sound of it running over and over in my mind. The force of the thought was hard to contain, and I thought that I could hear strains of it in the song of the tūī who fed nearby. My name would become a new melody in the dawn chorus, sung in exultation of the new day for the rest of time. Perhaps the Song Makers had gifted me an ego with this new body, because I felt pride in the thought of my fame. This human had given me a wondrous gift on the first day that we had met—what more could he give to me?

And then I realised that he had given me my name, but he had not given me his. Of course to you it would seem that I already knew his name then—I've mentioned his name many times already in this narrative. It would seem that I knew his name before I had ever picked Hatupatu up from under those fronds. Stories can be tricky like that.

But on that first day, the day that I was named, I was ignorant of the name of my manuhiri, and I would remain ignorant of it for many days afterwards. For the first week or so of our relationship, the boy would only utter my name when I was present. After a few days I thought that perhaps I had caught an untypical specimen, a child whose mind had been addled by some malady or hereditary mishap. I began to doubt that he had named me at all—perhaps this *Kurangaituku* was the only call he knew, perhaps he was incapable of speech or deeper thought. I pitied myself then, and the luck that I had. My first attempt in capturing a Song Maker resulted in a cloak, and my second in a being who seemed just as inanimate.

It hadn't occurred to me that the boy was protecting himself. That he was so frightened of me that he would hold his words and thoughts close to himself. I had thought that he would chatter to me as I had seen the Song Makers chattering to each other, that I would be accepted as part of his flock. One day, lingering close to the mouth of my cave I heard the boy singing. It was a surprise to hear his voice in song—it was clear and sweet. The words he sang did not have the same edge as when he said my name—

Kura … Ngai … Tuku.

I realised that he was taking pleasure in these words, he was enjoying their shape in his mouth. There was a joy in this song that was never present when he said my name. I waited a while, until he had finished his song, before I made my presence known. I let my feet fall heavily on the ground as a sort of courtesy to him, so that we could both pretend—that he hadn't been singing and I hadn't been listening. I left at the foot of his cage the birds that I had caught for him and removed the birds that had begun to rot and stink. He was not eating the birds. I tried to help him—his fingernails seemed unable to rip the meat from the birds. I used mine to cut down the breast of a bird, its blood staining the white feathers of its chest and its intestines popping out as the pressure of the skin was released. I offered it to him as a mother bird offers food to her chicks, but he had turned his head from me— his stomach seemed to be clenching, making his whole body convulse. Later, I would recognise this as his body attempting to vomit, that regurgitation in humans is a sign of illness, not a way to nourish the young.

He seemed determined to let his life slip away, and I was determined to save it. I would find something that he would eat, something to restore him to health.

I had brought him other food from the forest—also left untouched and to be cleared away. Even though he did not eat the birds, he would diligently pluck them clean of feathers. He seemed to spend his days sorting the feathers into colours and lengths as if he was preparing them for weaving, although I had never seen a male weave. It was obsessive—he would sort and resort the feathers as if he could make sense of his life from making sense of them.

It is easy when retelling a story to put more emphasis on a decision made in a moment. To make it seem that in that moment I realised the decision would be a turning point in our story. That I had known what consequences my decision then would have on our lives. Although it seems to me that any decision that I have made has had consequences in my life.

I could tell you that the decision I made to weave him a cloak was an act of compassion or kindness. Perhaps it was—the days were becoming shorter and colder and the boy had little to protect his vulnerable skin. I thought that since he seemed to find comfort in the kererū feathers he had collected, he would find comfort in the kākahu if I used the same feathers.

I set up my loom at the mouth of my cave as I always did—the branches buried in the soft earth far enough apart so that I could work comfortably. From his cage in the cave, Hatupatu would not see me work. To him I set off to hunt as I had always done, leaving him alone for hours. When he thought that I was far away, he would sing. I wove and listened to his voice, weaving the muka and his words into the cloak, whenu and aho, melody and meaning. It took little time for me to finish the tāniko. Perhaps this image of me in your mind is a loving one. A woman creating a garment as her sweetheart serenades her from afar. In hindsight, perhaps this is true, but at the time we were just living.

Hatupatu was only just living. He was weak from hunger, his body having already used what little reserves of fat that it had. His ribs were showing and his eyes were sunken. There was little point in keeping him caged— he would be too weak to make a break for it. I broke the bindings of the cage and noticed that he had tried to break them himself—the fibres were a little frayed, probably from his teeth. He made no move to escape from the cage. I tried to pull him from the cage myself, but he retreated further into it as I tried to take hold of him. I decided that he would come out of the cage eventually and let him be.

Opening the cage had disturbed his carefully sorted piles of feathers. I scooped the feathers into a pile and took them from him. He sat up, as if he would try and snatch them from my claws, but instead he spat my name at me.

'Kurangaituku.'

How quickly the sound of my name lost its ability to fill me with joy. I now knew what the difference in his tone meant, that some words can be used as weapons. I was learning much from him.

I sorted his feathers into piles, taking as much care as he had done to separate them into colour and length. The monotonous task was oddly soothing, calming the buzz of thoughts that crowded my mind, allowing it to become clear and focused. And that's when I noticed that he had stopped singing. At first I thought that perhaps he was sulking that his feathers had been taken from him. Then I thought that perhaps he was resting, or drinking water to soothe his throat. I didn't think of anything more serious until I had worked a number of rows and the cave was still silent.

He had crawled out of the cage, but the effort had left him unconscious. I scooped him up and pressed my palm against his chest—his heart was still beating, although it was weak and his breath was shallow. I lay him down on a mat and took a small amount of water in my beak. I let the water dribble from my mouth to his. He coughed—the water seeming to do him harm when he lay flat on his back. I took some more water in my beak and sat down with his head propped up on my legs. I bent my head down, my beak forcing his lips apart, and let the water drip. I could not see his face from that angle, but I could feel his breath on my beak. He was still breathing.

He needed more than water to sustain him. The blood in the birds that I had caught for him had already become thick and congealed. I needed a fresh kill, but I did not want to leave him alone in this state. Although by now the cave was hardly lonely—there were birds that had known no other home for generations, lizards that crawled on the floor and climbed the rough walls. I could reach out from where I sat and capture one of the many creatures that called my cave home, so I did.

The Song Makers did not hunt the riroriro, the bird too small to bother with. The riroriro in my hand did not struggle, but I could feel its heart beating. This tiny bird's heart seemed to beat stronger than that of the boy at my feet. I held the bird in one hand and pierced its breast with a claw of my other. I did not want to prolong its death by swallowing it whole and alive, letting it drown in my saliva, or be crushed by my gullet.

Once the small life had been extinguished then I swallowed the bird. I did not pluck it clean as the boy had done. I crushed its feathers and bones in my gullet, mixed its flesh and blood with my saliva, and regurgitated the slurry, letting it slowly drip into the boy's mouth.

`Once again the riroriro feeds the pīpīwharauroa.`

He slept for days. I spent my time feeding and cleaning him and weaving his cloak. When it was finished I wrapped him in it, swaddling him in kererū feathers. I sat at the mouth of my cave, letting the sun warm my body. I heard movement in the cave—I cocked my head to listen. He was awake, I was sure of it, but I stayed where I sat. The boy seemed frightened of me and afraid that he might lose consciousness again at the sight of me.

Later, when he recounted this time to me, he said that when he awoke he was surprised to find himself wrapped in a kākahu of kererū feathers, a kākahu he had once imagined his mother would weave for him. He had crawled to a puddle on the floor and lapped the muddy water like a kurī. He had pushed himself up onto his feet and supported himself against the wall, clinging to it when he rested, pushing against it to propel himself to the mouth of the cave. And when he finally got to the mouth I was there.

Kurangaituku.

When I had put my hand to my breast it confused him—it was almost human. 'It was as if you had claimed the name, as if you understood me,' he told me.

I thought it was the gestures that he read as human that softened Hatupatu towards me, just as my gestures towards you have established our relationship. In hindsight, perhaps it was the cloak that I had wrapped around him. Hatupatu would tell me it was the finest cloak that he had seen. He believed I had acquired it from some traveller, some other human who was not as lucky as he. I suppose in some way he was right—I *had* acquired the knowledge from humans, but looking back on it, it irks me that he believed that I was not capable of such artistry, that only humans were capable of such feats.

Ignoring the nest builders and spiders whose fine work is never a boast of their superiority. It just is what it is.

Perhaps I am being too judgemental myself, letting the lens of my later experiences with him colour my early memories. But memories are never discrete—they cannot be held separate from later experiences. You can only revisit them from a later point of view. Each time they are conjured, they are layered with new experiences—they can never be pure and unadulterated.

In the early days, Hatupatu had stayed because of the cage. Later, he stayed because he was too weak to go. Once he was strong enough, he stayed in my cave and I did not think to question why he did so. If I had, perhaps then I would have thought that he stayed out of friendship, and later still I would have thought that he stayed out of love. It is only now that I suspect his motives to be driven by greed. It is only now that I suspect he had a motive to stay at all. I was still naive to the workings of a human mind.

Why had I abandoned my original plan? I could have snapped his neck.

If only.

I'm not sure if it was just physical exhaustion or the shock at my reaction to my name, but the strength left his legs and he slid down the cave wall to his knees. I lifted him up and held him to my breast. He relaxed in my arms and allowed me to take him back into my cave. Allowed me to place him on a sleeping mat. Allowed me to envelop him in my wings.

This time he said my name without fear or malice or anger, 'Kurangaituku', and I placed my hand on my breast again.

He put his hand over his heart as well and said, 'Hatupatu'.

CHAPTER SEVEN

WHAKAMĀTAU

He underestimated me.

'I'm thirsty,' he said and I handed him a calabash. As he reached for the gourd he realised what had happened—the start of a crude kind of communication between man and beast. He drank the water without taking his eyes off me. Hatupatu would later tell me that he wasn't sure if I had understood him or if my actions had been a coincidence. That as he drank he was thinking of ways to test me.

Ah, his arrogance. It is one of the characteristics that made Hatupatu and me kin to each other. Neither of us thought of the other as our equal.

We both thought of ourselves as superior to the other. I thought then that he was no match for my intelligence. And here I make that same mistake again—thinking I can outwit you by using the past tense as a disguise. I still believe I am superior to him, even though he outwitted me.

    I underestimated him.

I want to colour my past feelings by saying that I had let my guard down around Hatupatu, but that would be a lie. I never felt threatened by him— I could have easily overpowered him, I could have easily crushed him. I was secure in my superior strength and size. At that time I did not know that Hatupatu could crush me. I had faith in my physical prowess—it did not occur to me that I could be bested emotionally.

    Hatupatu had the innate talent to manipulate emotion—his and others. I mean this with no malice—it is not a judgement. I think that I will never master my emotions, because I think of them as other than me—a sort of parasite in my being. When I say that Hatupatu had a talent to manipulate emotions, I think of the skill of the weaver manipulating the muka into a fine garment. Hatupatu had the talent to see the whenu and aho in emotions, he had the skill to weave them together to create what he wanted. As a fellow weaver, it is a skill that I admire, even if, ultimately, it would be used against me.

    When he spoke before, it was not to me, or the birds. I think in the early days he spoke to comfort himself, a reminder that he was a Song Maker. He needed the familiar syllables of his people to quiet his mind. His voice had not yet deepened to what it would be, what I remember now as the sound of his voice. Some of the later stories would cast Hatupatu as a young boy, his voice thin and pitchy, but the boy I had taken was on the cusp of being a man—he had attained most of his height but was like a reed. He needed a few more seasons to fill out.

    In the beginning, I doubt he thought that I could understand him—he did not attempt to conceal his voice as he had done when he was trapped in his cage. He would chatter away, mostly narrating his actions and marking the passing time. He knew I was listening, but didn't know I could understand him. It was that simple gesture—handing him the calabash—that revealed me.

And the tests Hatupatu created revealed more about him than they did me. First, he made loud noises to see if I would scare and take flight like the small birds. When I stood my ground, he reasoned that I was more intelligent than the riroriro or pīwakawaka. His next test was a snare—would I put my head through a noose 'hidden' by leaves? I would not. He concluded that I was more intelligent than a kākā or kererū. The next test was fit for a kurī, a great leap up from birds in his mind. He would name an object and I would fetch it. I indulged this game, as I suspect the dogs do—they get food and shelter, and I got an afternoon's diversion. The next test Hatupatu devised, he thought, was sure to stump me. He drew a simple shape in the ground at the mouth of the cave and shrugged at me. He asked me to copy the shape, which I did as crudely as he had shaped his own. What amused me about this test was how it proved nothing. Had I not understood his language I could not perform the task—I needed to have enough intelligence to understand his instruction, to learn the shape he had drawn, and to use a tool to replicate it. What if I had understood his instruction and could recognise the shape, but did not have the motor skills to replicate it? He would have dismissed me as a kurī.

So we continued.

For the next test, Hatupatu gathered a number of objects—stones, feathers and leaves. Would he test me on the size, shape or colour of the objects? Would he ask me to group like with like, even though it could be argued that at many levels each object was alike—they all hailed from the same area, for example. They were all chosen by him.

No, it was a simple memory test. Hatupatu would arrange the objects and have me look at them for an absurdly long time, a minute or two. He would then have me turn away and he would move an object from its position or, more difficult he thought, remove it all together. My role was to replace the object where it had once been—in the arrangement that is, not the forest, although I am confident that if asked I could have done both. But to the task that was in front of me.

The poor boy and his limitations. He had set the test according to his parameters, expecting, for instance, that I needed a minute or two to memorise the positions of objects, that it would take that long to train the synapses of my brain to lock in the relative position of stone to feather, leaf to stick—like his slowly plodding brain. I moved my head slowly around in a circle, as if I was examining each object in turn: the spotted breast feather of a ruru curled down to a dried kōwhai seedpod—I hovered my finger above it, almost touching the brittle skin, and ran my hand down each bump so he would think that I was counting each of the eight puku pregnant with seed, the tip of the seedpod nestled in the small, spiky leaves of a kānuka twig, the resiny leaves—plump and green—a visual contrast to the desiccated brown pod above it, the scent of the kānuka coiled around and through the pores of the koropungapunga across from the twig, the off-white of the stone looked a dirty grey next to the tiny white fluff of a miromiro feather, so small that I wondered how Hatupatu with his clumsy hands could have placed it so delicately beside the kōhūhū leaf made holey by some hungry ngārara—the edges of each meal an oxidised red brown, slightly darker than the piece of rahoto behind the leaf, the heavy stone made redder by the tail feather of the pīpīwharauroa above it, the shimmer of the iridescent green evoking the call of spring from its long-gone owner, the song mirrored in the deep black of a shard of obsidian: the piece Hatupatu used to shave the hair from his face—a few specks of his hair and skin cells lodged into the miniscule cracks of the sharpened edge—I let the smell of his sweat and blood fill my nostrils until I could taste him at the back of my throat and then my circle and ruse were complete. The performance was part of the game for me. At a glance I could perceive the objects and the space in between them, I could perceive the objects and the space that they occupied. When Hatupatu moved or removed an item, say the koropungapunga, I could perceive all of the spaces that the stone occupied from the start through the movement until he released it again. If he had known to ask me, I could have told him how quickly he had moved the stone, what angle he had held it at, how long he held his hand above it before deciding that it would be that object that he would move. But I was a creature as dumb as a kurī, or perhaps as clever as a small child, if I was successful at his test.

I used the time allotted for my memory to observe Hatupatu. Another limitation of the boy—he assumed that my eyes worked the same way as his, that if my head was pointed toward the objects, they would encompass the majority of my field of vision. He did not wear a mask, what you might call a poker face, during this time—I could watch his facial grimaces as he counted the time and speculated with himself about the outcome. When I performed my task, head down, focused on the difficulty of a task set by a creature of far greater intelligence, I watched as the anticipation grew on his face—would I fail? Would I succeed? And what would either outcome mean?

It would be fair to say that I played up to my role, letting my hand stray over the miromiro feather that had not moved and watching his eyes grow a little wider, then letting my hand hover over the koropungapunga that he had moved and hearing his heart beat just a little faster. Sometimes, if I lingered a little too long over the kōwhai seedpod, he'd have to bite his lip so that he wouldn't give the game away. If I could have heard his thoughts, he surely must have been thinking, *No! Not that one!*

The most interesting reaction was during the few times that I had decided to fail, a decision made partly to conceal the ease with which I had mastered this test, and partly to see the contortions of his face. And they were glorious, a mixture of disappointment and triumph. My failures reassured him of his place in the world, of his species' place in the world.

He concluded that I had the intelligence of a small child, estimating the age in reference to his own perceived mastery of the set task. I believe he overestimated his own intelligence as a six-year-old child—judging from his behaviour I would have put his mastery of such a task at perhaps ten years. And what if the tables had been turned? What if I tested him according to *my* limitations? Such a test would doom him to failure, but if I were feeling kind perhaps I would compare him to a fertilised yolk in an egg, and if cruel then I'd compare him to a stone on the ground.

But, because I thought of him that way, I never saw him as a threat. Although I could perceive the relative positions of the objects before me, although I could perceive their positions in an infinite number of scenarios, I was blind to the relative positions of us—Hatupatu and me. In our relationship, I could not predict how he would move and how I would shift in response. I think of myself sitting across from him, smugly observing his face, thinking that I knew all the possibilities.

CHAPTER EIGHT

REO

Let me in. See now through my eyes. Let my words fill your mind. This is how I communicate, then as now, mind to mind. Perhaps you think of this as extraordinary— it is the stuff of stories and a skill held by the monstrous.

This monster. This giant. This ogress.

I have never had a voice of my own, not the screech of a kārearea, nor the trilling sweetness of a korimako.

82

A bird who cannot sing. A ridiculous creature.

It is sad indeed to be a creature who is unable to sing its own song.

I have never had a voice of my own—I use the thoughts of others to communicate. I clothe myself in their accent, cadence and language.

Listen now to the voice I used with Hatupatu. He would remember my words—eerie, disembodied, the words sharpened by the metallic rasp of my vessel's voice. This is how I found my voice.

'You don't speak,' Hatupatu said to me. 'Not my language, not the birds'. But you understand me, nē?' He spoke slowly and deliberately. I cocked my head to the side as if observing a worm, to show him that I was listening, that I understood.

'Can you make any noise at all?'

How else to respond to such a question but to beat my wings and stamp my feet?

Hatupatu sighed, closed his eyes and pinched the bridge of his nose between forefinger and thumb.

'I mean from here.' He touched his chest and throat. 'Can you make any noise?'

I opened my beak and pushed the air from my lungs out, but there was nothing more than a sigh.

'Tāne gave all the birds their songs, each has a voice of their own. It's so strange that you have none.' His hands were just as active as his voice when he spoke, as if Hatupatu was trying to shape his thoughts in the air. 'You are a child of the forest, you are cloaked in their feathers, yet you have no voice, no song. Perhaps you are not a child of Tāne?'

If only his mind was open to mine he would have heard my reply, *I am a child of my own creation. I am a child of will and imagination. I am a child of tāne, that is, man—not an atua.*

'How am I to learn about you without language?'

Observation. Patience.

If I could have made a sound, perhaps I would have laughed, contracting my diaphragm over and over until I was doubled with pain. From what I had observed of Song Makers, their consumption of other beings yielded little more than sustenance. Even if Hatupatu had cracked open my skull and eaten my brain, he would have had little insight of me. He would, perhaps at best, have had a satisfying meal of sweet brain. I would like to think that my brain would still have unsettled his stomach.

Of course, from your point of view you know that Hatupatu and I found a way to communicate, but at this point in our story, we sat across from each other in silence. I could be dramatic and say that we sat this way until we found a solution, that we sat staring at each other for days until the idea finally came. That is what characters do in stories—their life comes to a halt until a solution presents itself. But life doesn't seem to respect dramatic pauses. I had birds to catch to satisfy my guest's hunger. He had bodily functions that demanded his attention. We went about our ordinary business while the idea of language sat like a seed waiting for a crack.

At dawn the tūī would sing. Despite the darkness of the cave, the birds always seemed to know when the sun was about to rise. I heard Hatupatu sigh—he would often complain about the birds in the cave. That morning he whistled, trying to capture the song of the tūī on his own lips. Did its song make him think of the mōkai? He sat up on his sleeping mat.

'The tūī, Kurangaituku.'

I cocked my head at him. I rarely caught tūī—he seemed to prefer the fat kererū to the svelte songbird. In one stride I was standing near the bird and I silenced its song with my claws. I dropped the dead bird on his lap. He wasn't pleased by the kill—he looked troubled by it. I cocked my head at him again.

'I didn't mean that,' he picked up the dead tūī and threw it on the floor before him. 'You see there is a tūī in my village, a *special* tūī.' As he looked at the tūī at his feet, there was a tension in his upper lip. So slight that if I didn't know his face so well, I wouldn't have seen it. Pity. Disgust. I had seen it directed at me so many times.

'The tūī was raised by a tohunga—it sings *our* songs instead of the songs of the forest.'

Ah, and that's why it's special.

'It used to scare me—to hear the voice of a man coming from the throat of a bird. I thought it was the most eerie thing in the world, until I met you.'

A diversion, the tūī.

The Settlers named them parson birds, their cravat of white feathers and coat of black—at least from a distance—like the raiment of the clergy. Or perhaps it was their drunken stumble from harakeke flower to harakeke flower, their heads dusted in pollen.

Honeyeater, honey-tongued tūī.

When I dwelt in the forest, I could pick an individual just by its song—the trills and clicks and creaks reflecting where the bird had been, who they had become. They sing songs for the turn of season, songs for their mates, songs of their home. Sometimes, when the moon is full, they sing songs for the darkness, songs for the heavens.

Silver-tongued tūī.

Their talent for mimicry was exploited when the Song Makers arrived, mōkai tūī tethered at the base of a bough reassuring the other birds who came to eat that the food provided so abundantly had no strings attached. Apart from the nooses they stuck their heads through. Much later, when forest had been replaced by towns and cities, the tūī learnt the urban songs of machinery, jackhammers and sirens. Their mimicry of your world still delights, although most of the sounds of the tūī are wasted on you—your ears are too blunt an instrument. The song of the tūī is only truly appreciated by their fellow subjugated species—leaving you to wonder why your dog has picked up his head and ears.

And then the Song Makers decided to teach their songs to the tūī. The Song Makers taught the tūī their words, poems or recitations. Later, the

Settlers would teach them scripture—so they would truly be parson birds, perhaps spreading the gospel in the forest.

The youngest male of a clutch was taken to train, isolated from his flock, from all other birds. From an early age he only heard the voice of the tohunga—the only notes he would learn were those of the Song Makers. When the tūī was strong enough, his tongue would be split and the fine hairs of it shaved off to give his new Song Maker voice clarity. If a year had passed and his words were still muddy, his tongue would be split again. His education would be painful and bloody.

The village of Hatupatu was not far from the cave. Perhaps a day's walk for him—significantly less for me. My plan was to set out for his village as the sun set. I left Hatupatu with a few extra birds to eat in case I was not back by the morning. I wasn't sure if he'd understood my meaning—he just took the clutch out of the cave and dressed the birds as his brothers had taught him.

I left Hatupatu to cook his birds and eat his fill before it became too cold for him in the chill of the winter's night. I don't know what he made of me leaving that night. I didn't have a way to communicate my plan to him, and even if I did, I doubt I would have let him know where I was going. I could not lose him before I had found the conduit to allow real communication between us. At least, what I was willing to give away.

I walked into the forest a short distance before climbing up into a tree. In those days I preferred to travel up in the canopy, gliding from treetop to treetop in a poor imitation of flight. Sometimes if I caught an updraught I could glide for such a time that I could let myself believe that with a few short flaps I could fly again. It was nice to be away from the cave and alone with my thoughts. I spent a good amount of time composing our first conversation— what I would say and his answer in return. I supposed the first topic would be how I acquired my voice. A thought halted my progress—what if Hatupatu recognised the bird? He would know that I had visited his village. What if he demanded that I take him home? What would he do when I refused? I fretted as if Hatupatu held all the power, as if it would matter that he found out I had visited his village. If needs must, I decided, I would snap his neck and be done with it and hope that the tūī would teach younger generations the Song Makers' tongue while I waited for a new specimen. It was foolish for a creature such as myself, clearly superior to Hatupatu, to worry about his reaction. I doubted that he was observant enough to tell the difference between one tūī and another.

I had thought from the story that the Song Makers had only the one bird, not the half a dozen or so tethered near their masters' dwellings. It was impossible to tell which bird had the humans' language when they were at roost, so I took them all. I found a kete tucked close to the door of a dwelling. Although it was not as fine as those made by my hand, it would do for my purpose until I returned to the forest. A kurī greeted me at that first dwelling and insisted on following me from place to place, watching as I cut the birds' tethers with my sharp claws. I cut closely to the knot at the branch and kept their leashes long. I gently held each bird in my free hand and once I knew that they had settled, I placed them into a kete while I moved about the village. In my mind I projected *quiet*—not the word, which would not have been understood by the birds, but the state of being, the concept. Even if it would have made my task easier if they all sang, I did not want to disturb the sleep of the Song Makers. I was sure I could subdue one human, but I wasn't sure of a whole village.

My projection was stronger than I had thought; every creature in the village was quiet that night. The snores and whimpers of the Song Makers' dreams were silenced, no babies woke fretful for their mothers. Even the wood in their structures halted its contraction under my command of *quiet*.

Quiet as I freed each tūī.

Quiet when I decided to take the kākā as well.

Quiet as the kurī followed me to the edge of the village and bade me farewell with a lick.

I climbed a tree and leapt from treetop to treetop. It must have looked comical, a bird-woman leaping from tree to tree with a kete full of tūī in one hand and a kete full of kākā in the other. I stopped on a treetop that was as far away from the village as it was from my cave. I emptied the kete of the birds and let the baskets drop into the branches below us. I gathered the ends of the tethers in my hands and wound them around my palm. I urged the roused birds to fly and I continued my journey gliding across the forest canopy with my hands buoyed by tūī and kākā.

When we reached the mouth of the cave, once again I projected *quiet*. I let go of their tethers and the birds found roost around the cave. The beating of their wings did not disturb the dreams of the boy amongst them. I will describe them with an image that will be familiar to you but wholly foreign to the experience of Hatupatu. The birds were like balloons gathered on the ceiling of a surprise party. And like a surprise party, I kept the birds quiet until the perfect moment.

At dawn I rescinded my *quiet* projection and replaced it with *ata mārie*. Hatupatu awoke in the middle of a crowded dawn chorus. The tūī and kākā that I had freed that night, the birds that already made my cave home all sang 'ata mārie' in their own tongues. The glow-worms were swayed by my projection as well—lighting their trails even in the din of the birdsong. Amongst the noise of the birds, Hatupatu and I heard his own language, 'Ata mārie', said over and over again, albeit tinged with a strange metallic tone.

I found the bird and pulled it gently from its roost by its tether. Now that I had found the bird, I could stop projecting my thoughts so widely. The rest of the birds' songs quietened down to the odd trill or screech. The glow-worms retreated into the shadows.

I pushed my thoughts into the mind of this bird only.

'Kurangaituku,' it said, and I placed my palm on my chest.

'Hatupatu,' it said, as I pointed to my human companion.

'Ata mārie.'

I had finally found a voice, and Hatupatu appeared to have lost his. I repeated the same words, *Kurangaituku, Hatupatu, ata mārie,* again and again. Hatupatu just sat there looking at me and then at the tūī and back again. I felt impatient with him, his mind seeming to take an inordinate amount of time to process this new reality. He spent a lot of time shaking his head as if he had to realign his thoughts about the world physically.

And then finally he spoke.

'How?'

I wasn't sure if the tūī could form entire sentences. Up until that point I had only pushed isolated words into its mind. What if something as complex as a sentence pushed the mind of the bird too far? Although it frustrated me to speak in a halting, simple manner, I thought it wise to build slowly so as not to burn the creature out entirely.

'Found.' I pointed at the bird. 'Bring.' I opened my arms out to indicate the cave.

'No. How are you talking through it? The tūī only knew a few phrases— it did not understand them.'

I resisted the urge to lecture him on how much the tūī *actually* understood and how little Hatupatu and his kind understood of the tūī.

I tapped my head, 'Thoughts.' And then I pointed at the tūī again, 'Voice.'

'But, how?'

Even if I could use the tūī to explain, I doubted that Hatupatu would understand. I chose a simple demonstration. On the ground I gathered some pebbles and made a pile. A short distance from that pile I dug a small shallow hole. I touched my forehead to symbolise my thoughts and touched the pile of pebbles. I touched the head of the tūī and then the shallow hole. I pushed the pebbles one by one into the hole.

'How.'

Hatupatu nodded. He looked as if he was trying, with difficulty, to evacuate his bowels. He leaned in close to me and picked up the pebbles. He dug his own hollow in front of himself.

'If these are your thoughts,' he held a pebble between his thumb and forefinger and shook it at me, as if it was measuring the rhythm of his idea. 'And this,' he touched the hollow, 'is my mind, then why not ...' Hatupatu pushed the pebbles into the hollow as I had done earlier.

How to explain to a child that I had practised this skill on the tūī for centuries, millennia? That I had become an element of their niche that they had evolved to embrace. That I had evolved with them. That I had studied the intricacies of their minds and brains, so I knew the shape of them both figuratively and literally. I knew where to push my way into their minds. That Hatupatu and his kind were too new to me—I did not know his mind as intimately. I did not know how to enter his maze. Yet.

I could not tell him all this, and so instead I chose flattery.

I pointed at his forehead, 'Strong.'

That pleased him and he smiled. It surprised us both when the tūī began to laugh, a coughing sort of bark. I had not heard my laugh before. I did not know that I had one.

Hatupatu laughed too.

I cocked my head to the side, and he laughed louder.

'The look on your face!'

Which is an odd thing to say.

'Eyes. Look?'

He circled his hand around his face. 'No, how your face looks to me.'

'Funny?'

'Yes. It's funny.'

I tried to find comparisons in my catalogue of experience, a million thoughts at once. The tūī let out a low growl—there was too much for it to articulate.

Hatupatu stopped laughing. 'Are you angry?'

I shook my head. 'Thinking.'

'What are you thinking about?'

'What. Funny?' The tūī growled again.

'Do you mean what makes me laugh?'

'No. Me.'

'Haven't you ever laughed before?'

'No.'

'You found something funny. What made you laugh this time?'

'You.'

And not surprisingly he took that to be a compliment. He was the type of man that thought the whole world was laughing *with* him.

His estimation of my intelligence went up. I had listened to his story and understood it. That made me at least as intelligent as any woman he had known, but still well below his own mind.

From that conversation on, we talked with the help of the tūī. Hatupatu insisted that I let the bird perch on my arm or shoulder—it helped the illusion that the words were coming from me. When I was away from the cave, the tūī could rest. I did not know that when I left to hunt on that first day, Hatupatu had tested the bird to see if it was the prodigy, but all he could evoke from it was the stock phrases it had learnt from its former master. He knew then, from that first day, from my first word, where I had taken the tūī from. Yet he did not confront me about it. Was it then he planned my destruction? Did he plan to silence me from the very day that I found my voice?

Once the door was open between us, Hatupatu and I spoke together often and greedily. In the early days it was frustrating to me to distil my thoughts into words and sentences, to follow one thread of an idea at a time. The low growl of the tūī punctuated many of our early conversations, as I learnt to reign in my thoughts, to think narrowly. Hatupatu assumed that the growl meant that I had not quite grasped what he had said and needed time to figure it out. He thought the growl was proof of my inferior intellect. Perhaps I could have shown him—pushed hundreds of pebbles into the shallow at the same time, but it suited me that he thought himself superior. It left him open to me.

CHAPTER NINE

WHATU

'Your eyes,' he said, 'are like nothing I've seen before. They are not human, nor bird, nor any other creature that I have seen. Your eyes are like the night sky— not just stars, but constellations. I could navigate the world with your eyes.'

He was not flirting, his words not an overture or foreplay. There was no heat, no desire, no passion. The idea of seducing me had not occurred to him, my being repulsed him. I was truly monstrous in his eyes. He had not planned to make our relationship ... How would you like me to phrase it? Euphemistically, as physical or intimate? Or bluntly, as sexual?

His words were nothing more than an observation and I took them as such.

It may seem strange to you, but up until this point I hadn't thought to look at myself, that is, to look at my face. The rest of my body I was familiar with. I could see my limbs and wings, my chest and because I was still partly bird, I could turn my head around far enough to see my back. I could see the tip of my beak, but I had never seen my face.

Have you thought about your face? The part of you that you think distinguishes you from all others. Is it strange to you that you've never really seen this part of yourself, this part that is tied up so closely with your identity? You have only seen yourself in reflection or in photographs but not in real life, not with just your eyes. Is that why it is so jarring to see your reflection? It is not how humans are meant to be seen.

I wanted to see my face, my eyes. Perhaps you may have conjured a picture of me gazing at myself in the stilled waters of a lake. If you are happy with such a benign image of me, then perhaps you don't want the truth of how I came to see my face for the first time. Perhaps you should look away while I see it for the first time.

It should be of no surprise to you now that when I wanted to look upon my face, it would be an act tinged with blood. Why look upon myself in still waters—wraith-like and drained of all life and colour—when I had a better method at hand? And so, at dawn I went hunting in the forest, looking for the eyes that would see me best. That day I caught several birds. For the last minutes of their lives I held each one in my hand firmly. I made each look into my eyes, cradling their body in my hand like a Song Maker cooing to her baby. I waited until their heart had slowed down, waited until their bodies had stopped shaking, waited until my face held their attention, and then I snapped their necks, twisted off their heads and sucked out their brains.

I could see my face through their eyes—the kererū, the tūī, the kākā. I could see my face in their eyes—the riroriro, the miromiro, the kōkako. Each version of my face was slightly different, but each was true. I could make a composite of myself through their eyes, complicated and nuanced, unlike your reflection in a mirror. I saw that my eyes were like he had said—black with streaks and spots of shining white, just like the night sky.

And then I plucked one of my own eyes out and held it between my claws—looking at myself, looking at my eye. There was a gaping void where my eye had been as if there was nothing to me but the facade.

This ogress. This giant. This monster.

I was a creature trapped somewhere between bird and Song Maker. My face was covered in the same pale skin as my chest. The feathers on my head started high on my forehead, mimicking the hairline of my Song Maker creators. I kept the beak of the kōtuku, but the position of my eyes had changed—forward facing like the Song Makers.

Was I hideous or beautiful? I had never asked myself that before, but now I couldn't stop the thought. Until that moment, I suppose I had no ego. At least no idea that my curiosity ought to be focused on myself.

Before, I wasn't concerned with my own image. It was the influence of Hatupatu—he gifted me that obsession. Until he reacted to my presence I didn't care what I looked like. I wasn't curious about it. But then ... I wanted him to look at me like ...

I wanted him to look at *me*.

I pulled my other eye out, and held them both in my palm. I had thought they'd be like pebbles from a river—solid and dense. There ought to have been weight to them. There ought to have been mass. I crushed them and for a moment I felt them yield, like they would pop and fill my hand with jelly. But they just didn't exist anymore. There was no blood or gore or even dust staining my palm when I opened it. My hand was empty, just like my eye sockets.

I walked home. I would not be without my eyes for very long. As soon as he heard me approaching, Hatupatu conjured me in his mind. I could smell the thought of me in the air. I closed my eyelids over empty sockets and opened them. My galaxy eyes had returned just as he remembered them.

I took home the bodies of the birds to my cave to feed Hatupatu. He never seemed to question why the birds I gave him had no heads. Perhaps he thought that was just how I killed them. Perhaps he didn't care, one less task in the job of cleaning them after all. I wondered if he would be able to taste the image of my face in their flesh, if the thought of me would work its way from stomach to flesh.

Much, much later I learnt one of your sayings, *The way to a man's heart is through his stomach*. I was foolish then, as it has been foolish of women who have heeded this advice.

The way to a man's heart is through his chest.

I say that now to amuse you, but I did think of killing him then. Of twisting off his skull and eating his brain. To hold his eyes in my claws as I saw what he saw in my mind. To see how he truly saw me. But I was afraid of the truth.

'What have you seen, Kura?'

I wasn't sure how to answer him—had he discovered my spies? Did he know that I had seen this world through many eyes and not just my own? I cocked my head at him.

Hatupatu laughed. 'You've been in this world longer than me. Surely you've seen amazing things.'

Well, of course I had. I didn't know what to say. In all our time together Hatupatu had never asked me what I thought of the world, had never asked for my stories. I stood up to fetch the tūī from its roost, but stopped when he started to speak again.

'You may have seen the many wonders of this world, Kura, but I doubt you've seen beyond that.'

Ah, it wasn't the start of a conversation. I sat back down. His posture and cadence shifted. It was to be a whakataki—it was his own voice he wished to hear, not the metallic rasp of my proxy.

'Only Tāne has climbed to the realms above Rangi. Birds have never soared as high as he.'

The Song Makers had conceived of their world, their *worlds*, like the layers of sediment in rock, each layer stacked upon one another. There are the worlds above the sky of Rangi; the earth of Papa ruled by her son Tāne; beneath her, the soils where the gods of kūmara and fern root rule; and then there are the realms of the spirit world Rarohenga.

'It is said that when we die,' Hatupatu said, clearly not including me in his definition of 'we', 'our spirit enters the Underworld. First to Te Rēinga where we live as many years there as we walked on the earth.'

I must have looked incredulous, because his voice became insistent.

'You doubt the word of our most powerful tohunga? Men who have walked the path of the dead while still alive?'

I couldn't contradict him. I had no voice. Whether he took this silence to mean I agreed with him I do not know. In truth, I don't think it mattered to him.

'From Te Rēinga we travel down through seven more realms. Until Meto.'

Meto—to become extinct.

'It is a journey each spirit must take, a journey to learn how to be alone, to learn how not to exist.'

I thought that perhaps the pressure of the worlds above crushed a spirit into oblivion, like the thin line of stone that once was metres of ash. I was impressed by the Song Makers' idea of impermanence—that everything eventually erodes, mountains, bodies and souls alike. It is an observation unexpected of creatures who live such short lives.

I read nothing more into his stories of the slaying of taniwha and the Underworld of Rarohenga, other than a way to pass the time. How would it have been possible for me to know that these stories were a way for him to refine his plan? He would tell me how taniwha were tricked into cages or nooses to be killed. I felt flattered when he'd say that I was far too clever to be beaten that way.

I did not know that his descriptions of Rarohenga were a test to see if I had heard of the place. My rapt attention as he described the lake surrounded by hills, to which the spirits would descend to find their family, must have confirmed to him that my kind did not dwell there. He would be safe, even in his afterlife, if he murdered me.

It is easy to say now that if I had known I would have sent Hatupatu to Rarohenga during his stories. But I'm not sure if I would have. Although I can't say that we were happy, I thought that we were content, and I couldn't have imagined life without him.

CHAPTER TEN

WHAKAMOEMOE

I wanted the truth. I wanted Hatupatu to be truthful. It was time for us to stop pretending. I wanted him to make a fire with me.

A hum of recognition, a hum of prediction.

I knew he wouldn't show me if I asked him directly. I doubt he would have admitted to lighting fires if I confronted him. I would have to force his hand. So one day I decided to stay near our cave, rather than spend the daylight hours waiting in the forest. Hatupatu was agitated—his morning meal had been delayed by me. He fidgeted, wringing his hands together.

'Are you ill?'

I shook my head.

'What's wrong?'

I shook my head again.

'Are you hunting today?'

Again I shook my head.

Hatupatu groaned. It reminded me of the growl of the tūī—I had frustrated him.

Hatupatu walked out of the cave and sat in front of where he would normally make his fire. I had followed him out into the open air and sat opposite him. He had a stick in his hand that he used to prod the ground.

'Are you going to stare at me all day?'

I shrugged.

'You could at least talk to me.'

I shrugged again. We had never used the tūī outside of the cave. Hatupatu threw the stick at me, not hard enough to connect with me but in my direction. It landed at my feet. He rolled his eyes and left for the cave. After a minute or so he reappeared with the tūī lashed to his hand. The eyes of the tūī were no longer used to the sun—the only light it had seen for a while was the blue of the glow-worms. The poor bird, cursed because of its talent. I am ashamed to say that at this time I had come to regard the bird as my voice—not as a being in its own right. I had come to think of myself as its owner, that it would love me for the utility I had found in its life. I thought that it had become as dependant on me as I had become on it. But the lift of its head that morning as the breeze picked up, the stretch of its short wings in the wide open space of our clearing, reminded me that it would escape if it were not tethered to me. I would have to make sure that the fibre of its leash remained true.

If only I had been vigilant with all my tethers.

If only, if only.

Hatupatu handed the tether to me, and I felt the strength of the cord as I wound it around my hand. The bird was secure for today at least.

'Why are you still here?'

Well, that is a question that can be pondered on many levels really, although I knew he just meant today and the change in routine.

'You.'

'What do you mean me?'

'Talk.'

'We talk all the time.'

'No.'

'We do. You have to understand it's frustrating for me to talk to you. It's like talking to an infant.'

Grrr. This time the sound was full of frustration and rage. *Grrr.*

'And there's that. You don't know how irritating that noise is.'

'Same.'

'What does that mean? "Same?"'

I decided to push the tūī—perhaps by now the bird would be able to form more complex sentences. My simple prompts seemed to elicit simple replies.

'Talking ... to ... you. Like ... an ... infant.' They were faltering, stuttering sentences, but they were sentences all the same.

Hatupatu looked at me and narrowed his eyes, 'Why haven't you spoken like this before?'

'Afraid ... of killing,' I stroked the breast of the tūī—its breathing had become fast and shallow as it struggled with my thoughts.

Hatupatu laughed.

'What ... is funny?'

'You, Kurangaituku, are afraid of killing?'

'Only ... this.' The bird's voice had a metallic edge to it that made my words cut through his laughter. Hatupatu was silenced, and he stared at me across his empty fire pit.

I cocked my head and looked at the ground rather than directly at him, a move to make him feel more comfortable. To him it would seem I no longer had him fixed in my gaze, and if my eyes were human this would be true.

'Not … hungry?' I could hear his stomach rumbling.

'No.'

'You cook. Eat.'

'You know about the fire? How?'

I tried not to push my amusement out into the tūī. Hatupatu wore a face of disappointment. He had thought he tricked me by concealing the remnants of his fire. I could tell him that I saw smoke rising from this place every morning, that I knew he kept a store of firewood. Instead, I tapped my claw on my nostrils.

'You could smell it?'

I nodded.

Hatupatu sat for a minute as if he was processing this version of reality.

'Why didn't you tell me?'

'Why … didn't *you* tell me?'

He wasn't sure if I was copying him or not, like a parrot or in our case, a tūī. 'I thought—' He paused. 'Aren't you afraid of fire?'

I shrugged in reply. What was his fire compared to the fire I had seen? His people had not yet witnessed an eruption, still too new to this land. I'm not sure if they had yet made the connection between the volcanoes and the hot pools and boiling mud near their home.

Hatupatu gathered his firewood and stacked it near his fire pit, placing it in order of size. He placed two other pieces of wood next to the fire pit—a pointed stick of hard kaikōmako and a flattened branch of māhoe. The māhoe had a groove worn in it from the kaikōmako that was tinged with the mark of fire. Next to these Hatupatu placed some dried moss. He then tied dried tī kōuka leaves into a bundle, placed that next to the moss, and then looked at me. 'Are you sure you want to be here?'

I nodded. Hatupatu picked up the kaikōmako stick and began to rub it in the māhoe groove. He rubbed so quickly that the māhoe branch flipped over before he could get it smouldering. Hatupatu placed one of his feet on the end of the māhoe, and rubbed again with the kaikōmako, but his awkward pose robbed the swiftness from his arms, and again the māhoe failed to smoulder. I wondered how he was able to make a fire by himself when I was not here to help him. Perhaps the change in our routine had thrown off his skills.

'Takes all day?'

Hatupatu groaned at me. 'You're making me nervous.'

I nodded, it is always harder to perform for an audience when you are accustomed to doing something by yourself. I stood up and pushed him aside. I placed my foot on the māhoe, careful to place the majority of my weight on my other foot so that I did not snap it.

Hatupatu looked up at me from where he was kneeling. I could see the heat coming from his face. It was strange—he had not exerted himself enough for his face to colour or his breath to become so uneven. I cocked my head at him and he averted his eyes. He rolled the kaikōmako between his fingers, instead of rubbing it deep into the groove of the māhoe.

'Make ... fire.'

Hatupatu shook his head. 'I can't.'

'I hold. You can.'

He looked up at me again. His face seemed to be burning with colour. There was something wrong with the boy.

'Make ... fire.'

'This is not a promise.'

The tūī growled.

'You don't understand. To make fire like this, a man and a woman make a fire *like this* when they are to be married.'

'What is married?'

'When two people have only each other.'

'Then we are married. Make fire.'

'We're not married. You're not a person.'

'I am person.'

'No, you're not.'

'What is person?'

'I am.' Hatupatu stood and touched his arms, his legs and his head, as if these features were exclusively human. 'I am a person.'

I echoed his movement, touching my arms, legs and head. 'I am person.'

'No. I have thoughts and dreams and ideas.'

'Same, same.'

'No. We are not the same.'

His logic and reasoning were poor. He refused to make fire with me because it was a sign of marriage. He explained marriage as a relationship between two people. He said that I was not a person for some undefined reason—from what I could glean, his criteria were based solely on the fact that I looked different to him. Even if these arguments were true, he should have no qualms in making a fire with me. 'Not same. Not person. Then make fire.'

Still he hesitated before plunging his hard kaikōmako stick into the soft groove of māhoe, as if a part of him knew that I was a person, that it was a commitment according to his own tikanga. He held the kaikōmako in his two fists, using his body weight to push deeper and faster. A spark glowed near my foot and he sprinkled the dried moss on it to feed it. He blew gently on the small flame engulfing the moss, sprinkling more on it so it grew bigger. Once the flame had strengthened, he placed the tī kōuka bundle on top, careful not to smother the flame. When at last the flame had worked its way into the tī kōuka, he placed the bundle in his fire pit. On top of this he placed his smallest twigs and watched as they caught alight.

He did not thank me for helping him. Whether he wanted to admit it or not, we both knew that I had taken him as a husband.

This is what marriage is—sitting across from him one night watching the light from the flames picking up the high points of his face, his forehead and cheekbones. It looked like the flesh had been stripped away from his face and all that was left was his skull—his eyes and cheeks in shadow. Marriage is imagining the time when he will be dead and I will be alone.

Hatupatu sang a song about lovers separated by responsibility and geography. He had not talked about love before.

'What is "lover"?' I asked, the tūī struggling with the words as it longed to be left alone to sleep. I had begun to use it more and more as Hatupatu spoke more freely with me.

'A person you love,' Hatupatu blushed, 'and who loves you.'

'What is love?'

'A feeling of joy and sadness that makes you want to be with a person.'

'Mating? For offspring?'

He blushed again, 'Sometimes. If you're lucky. But it's not just about children, it's greater than that. Sometimes there is love between man and man and that would never result in a child, but it is love all the same.'

Of course I had seen this in flocks—birds who mated with a member of their own sex. I had thought it was a way to control both a surging population and hormones. I did not know if the birds practised this out of love.

'You and me? Love the same?'

He looked as if he had smelled something rotten, 'No. It's not the same.'

'Why?'

'Because ... because it's not. We've been through this before, Kura. You're not a person. You're ...'

An ogress. A monster. A thing.

I shook my head and waved my hand as if clearing the air. We sat in silence for a while, Hatupatu avoiding my eyes. I'm sure he would have spent the evening in happy silence, amusing himself by burning small twigs in the embers, but I wanted to know more about his idea of love.

'Do you love?'

Hatupatu threw one of his twigs into the middle of the fire. It caught alight and twisted around and in on itself. 'You shouldn't ask me that.'

'Why?'

'It's private.'

I made a show of looking around as if looking for other people. I looked at him and shrugged. 'No one else.'

'I meant that the thoughts are mine to keep.'

It seemed at odds with what I had observed of Hatupatu and the other Song Makers—it seemed to me that every one of their thoughts was shared. It was as if their thoughts were not real until they had voiced them, that they could not trust their own minds without having sought a second opinion. It made me wonder what other thoughts might be locked up in his mind. It tempted me to go to the source of his thoughts and to gorge myself on them.

'I'm not going to tell you, Kura.'

I cocked my head. The words held one meaning but his tone another. I thought he was looking for an excuse to tell me, a way in which he could hold me to blame for opening up. He was asking me to force the truth out of him.

I straightened my head and pulled my shoulders back. I opened my wings so quickly that they made a deafening clap. Dust and smoke from the fire blasted at Hatupatu, and he pushed himself away. He watched me as I settled back down again. I cocked my head and waited for the story.

'Fine. I'll tell you. What difference does it make anyway?'

I found his petulance charming. Even now thinking back on it, thinking of all the things that came to pass between us, I still find it charming. It is some sort of madness that has taken root deep inside of me. This is what love truly is—insanity. Driven at first by a chemical imbalance and kept aflame by nostalgia for that initial feeling.

Hatupatu did not love me. He had fallen for a girl who was betrothed to one of his brothers. I forget which. There are times in my mind when Hanui and Haroa are interchangeable at best, one and the same at worst. Did this girl love Hatupatu back? It is hard to say without consulting her. It is fair to say that as a storyteller Hatupatu was prone to exaggeration. It makes for a better story if both Hatupatu and the object of his affection were madly in love. With each other, I should add.

'Ātaahua,' he said and I mistook it for her name, but apparently it is what she was—*beautiful.*

'If I could talk to her I would whisper these words: Ko Hinetītama koe, matawai ana te whatu i te tirohanga.'

> *You are like Hinetītama, a sight that causes the eyes to glisten.*

Hinetītama. The child of Hineahuone, the wife Tāne made from clay. Tāne fathered Hinetītama and left Hineahuone to bring her up alone, while he attended to his other children in the forest. When he returned, Hinetītama had grown into a beautiful woman and he took her as his wife. He fathered many children with his daughter-wife, but when she found out his true identity she ran away to the Underworld and became Hinenuitepō.

Ah, Hinenuitepō. I remember the sight of you and my eyes do glisten. But that is another story.

His love, his Ātaahua, was a couple of years older than Hatupatu, ready to be married off. If she had been of lower birth, she and Hatupatu could have had a dalliance, but she was of a chiefly line and her offspring had to be assured of their heritage. The youngest son of four was not good enough for that marriage. Not only that, but Hatupatu was still considered a boy, not ready for marriage, although most mornings I had witnessed that he was physically ready to mate.

'Ready?'

'To take on responsibility, to leave behind childhood. The hunt my brothers took me on was to be my first step to adulthood. Then I would wear tā moko.' He traced swirling lines on his cheeks with his finger.

I had seen older Song Makers with these marks—the males with their faces almost entirely covered, the females marked on their chins or brows. I had thought it was their adult plumage, just as many a fledgling loses its fluffy down or the dull brown feathers that blend with their nest for the bright colours of sexual maturity. It made sense too that the male of the species had the showier markings—it is after all the female who must be choosy with her precious clutch of eggs.

'When?' I touched my own cheek. 'After moult?'

Hatupatu squinted at me for a moment as if smoke was in his eyes. I cocked my head at him and he laughed.

'We don't grow it. What did you think? That we woke up one morning with tā moko in place?'

I don't know why he would laugh at me. I had seen such transformations in many creatures—birds, insects, frogs. Why would I think Song Makers were any different?

The tūī growled and Hatupatu finished laughing with a sigh. Hatupatu pulled a twig about the thickness of his finger from the fire. The end of the stick was black and the tip still burned orange. He blew on the stick to put it out, and he licked his forefinger and thumb and squashed the ember. He held up his hand—his finger and thumb covered in soot, and then he traced the swirls on his cheek, again leaving uneven smudges.

And, oh, to see a story transform him. Hatupatu did not just tell a story, he manifested it. The energy of it started deep in his belly, a fire that rose up through his spine, filled his chest and lifted his head. His voice became more resonant as if he spoke with the voices of generations.

'In the beginning, men would paint their faces with these patterns—they would tell everyone the history of that man, who his people were and where he belonged. But the markings were not permanent and needed to be applied every day. Mataora had married a woman from the Underworld, Niwareka. She was beautiful, and he was quick to temper. Mataora beat his wife, and she ran home to her father Uetonga. Mataora followed her to the Underworld despite the danger in doing so. Uetonga was tattooing a man when Mataora came upon him. Uetonga looked at the painted designs on the face of Mataora and shook his head. He reached out and wiped clean the cheeks of Mataora with his thumb.

'"Son-in-law," Uetonga said, "it should not be so easy to forget your family and your history. These are things that ought to be writ in blood."

'Uetonga bade the young man to lie down before him. As the chisel bit into his skin, Mataora sang so that his pain was transformed into something beautiful. So that he wouldn't offend his father-in-law.

'It is like this,' he picked up his stick again and plunged it in the ground beside him, creating divots of pattern. 'Except the sticks that are used have bone or shell or stone on them, and they move them like this'—he held his stick on an angle, its tip close to the ground. He picked up another stick with his free hand and used that to tap the tip of the first stick. Quick, sharp taps as he moved the first stick slowly around.

It looked like how the Song Makers had created their wooden carvings, chisel to wood. Did the masters of wood challenge their skills on the flesh of the living? It would seem that I was not the only creature created by the Song Makers—they created themselves as well.

'Uetonga worked pigment into the skin of Mataora, deep enough so that Mataora would never forget, so that his skin would always hold the marks. As Mataora sang, Niwareka heard his voice, and in it such beauty and pain that she sought out her husband. She followed his voice to her father's fire and saw a man whose face was covered in blood. She knew from his voice that it was Mataora; she knew from his voice the sorrow he felt, and she forgave him.'

He must have had a powerful voice, this Mataora, to make Niwareka forgive his trespass on her body, to make her consider putting herself at risk to be with him again. I had heard the voices of the Song Makers, and although they could be beautiful, they simply did not have the range or dexterity of bird song. I was, I *am*, incredulous about her reaction.

'He beat her.'

'Yes. But she forgave him. Niwareka took her husband to her house and cared for him as he healed. She fed him water, drip by drip into his mouth.'

And suddenly I saw myself in his story. I was Niwareka drip-feeding my husband. His face was unrecognisable, being swollen and bloody, but I knew his voice and his eyes. In my imagination, when the swelling subsided and the blood was washed off, it was Hatupatu who I held in my lap, not Mataora. Hatupatu and I together in my cave—husband and wife.

'And when he had healed and Niwareka washed him, the whakapapa of Mataora stood proud on his face. Mataora yearned for home. He took Niwareka from her father's realm once more. At the gate between worlds, the guardian Te Kūwatawata told the couple that the entrance to the Underworld would be sealed from the living forever. If Niwareka shed tears for her whānau, Mataora did not know as he never turned back to see.'

Why did Niwareka continue to follow a man such as Mataora? Why didn't she turn back to be embraced by her family? The man she had chosen cared little for her feelings, and somehow made her place his needs above her own. How could that be? Of course my thoughts then show how little I knew about love—I would soon learn that love like this demands sacrifice. I would learn to curl myself around his needs. I would learn to let his life shape mine.

'When Mataora returned home, his people were amazed that he had come back—come back from the Underworld, come back with his wife. They were amazed at his tā moko—the precise lines chiselled into his face. He demonstrated his newfound skill on his wife. The people watched as he tapped the design into her skin, the blood springing from the cuts in her chin. Mataora marked her as his own, their relationship to be one of pain and blood and tears. Niwareka wept for the father she had left behind in the Underworld, her crude tā moko a poor imitation of the fine work her father had gifted her husband. Each tap of the chisel separating her from her people until the day that her life left her.'

Hatupatu threw the stick into the fire, and scrubbed the patterns from the ground with his foot.

'Mataora brought tā moko to the people from the Underworld. Taking one means shutting the gate between childhood and the rest of your life. It means that you are ready.'

'Ātaahua.'

'I suppose it is, in a way.'

I shook my head and pointed at him, 'Ready. Ātaahua.'

'Well, *I* think so, but nobody else does.'

I lay my hand on my chest, 'I do.'

'Nobody *important* then.'

Did Niwareka gladly suffer such blows? Hatupatu seemed to be able to strike at my heart with very little effort at all. I should have paid more attention to it, instead of wallowing in its delicious hurt. It was a warning and a lesson that I just didn't see.

That night Hatupatu murmured in his sleep. Was he dreaming of his love or his wife? What would he say when I asked him in the morning? Perhaps he would keep it to himself, one of those private thoughts that I did not know about. I thought about where his cache of these was located in his brain. Perhaps I could tap a small hole in his head and just drain that part. Would he be happier without the memory of Ātaahua, if he just had me instead? In his dream he was smiling, and it hurt because he had never smiled at me like that.

CHAPTER ELEVEN

KUTUKUTU AHI

The story Hatupatu told warped time. I let his words mesmerise me until the constellations had climbed across the sky and the fire had died down to glowing embers. He liked to tell stories with a stick in his hand—an echo of some future tokotoko, but like him, his stick was green. He pushed the embers with its point, and it roused a lazy flame from our fire.

'And that's when I found you, Kura.'

Something akin to anger roused me and the tūī lashed to my hand from our reverie.

'*I* found.'

'Do you want to tell the story then? Our story?'

I cocked my head at him.

'I didn't think so,' he laughed, but there was no warmth to it.

'Funny?'

He sighed. 'Sometimes it's such an effort to talk to you, it gives me a headache.'

I passed him the calabash of water and he took it without acknowledgement, as if it appeared to him because he willed it.

I pointed at his head. 'Hurt?'

'It's just sometimes I'm reminded that I'm not talking to … an equal. Do you understand equal?'

'Same, same.'

'Yes, same. You and I are not the same.'

Such a ridiculous thing to say! Of course we were not the same. The tūī growled.

'I'm so sick of hearing that noise.'

And before I thought about what I was doing, I stopped pushing my thoughts and the tūī relaxed its body. The boy honestly thought that our conversations were more taxing on him; he did not know the effort to make my thoughts like a clear stream, he did not know the discomfort of the tūī to contort its voice into his language. I left Hatupatu watching over the dying fire. I walked into the cave and unwrapped the tether of the tūī from my wrist and let the bird hop from my arm to its roost. The tūī spoke to its roost mates in the pitch that is impossible for human ears to register—it sought comfort in its own tongue. Just like Hatupatu had.

I walked out of the cave. It was not until I was in the treetops that I realised I had followed his orders like a well-trained kurī. That on that day he was my master. I left Hatupatu with his aching head and climbed up to the treetops, swooping a good distance away from the cave. I let my thoughts loose, allowed them to flow out around me. And all the birds caught in my penumbra growled in unison.

CHAPTER TWELVE

AWARUA

*He underestimated me. Despite all that I had shown him—
my ability to perform his simple tests, my acquisition
of the tūī, and my ability to use it to talk to him—
Hatupatu still doubted that I was capable of many
things. He simply refused to believe me, as if I had a
reason to lie to him. Perhaps he thought every being he
came in contact with was like him—deceitful.*

We sat at the mouth of the cave one evening before it was too dark for his
eyes to see. Hatupatu had wrapped himself in a cloak covered in the red

feathers plucked from under the wings of hundreds of kākā. It was the cloak he favoured the most. Sometimes he would stroke the feathers, as if laying them straight helped to smooth his own thoughts.

'How many other people have you caught?'

'None.'

'Just me?'

'Yes.'

'I thought you must have caught a few people to have a collection of cloaks such as these. High-ranking too—but not ariki, since you do not have a kahu kurī.'

He looked at me, as if he was expecting to see some kind of change in my face. When he didn't see any, he went back to stroking the feathers on the cloak. If Hatupatu had his own tūī to talk through, I suspect it would have been growling.

'Did you sneak into a village and take these cloaks? Like you did the tūī?'

'I made.'

'I'd like to meet the woman who made this cloak—it is so fine. Not everyone can make a cloak like this you know. She must be a patupaiarehe to weave like this.'

'I made.'

'I bet she has every man in the village vying for her hand in marriage. She will make her husband such fine cloaks like no one has seen before. If I married such a woman and brought her home, I would be a chief. Hanui and Haroa themselves would flay their own kurī to make me a dog-skin cloak.' Hatupatu had told me before about his brothers and their kurī, one black and one white. It was something that he spoke of often, his brothers' dogs. He worried over it like an overgrooming bird who has plucked their breast of feathers—not in the pursuit of some parasite, but of some comfort.

'I made.'

'Such a woman—capable of making something so fine, so beautiful. She must be a thing of beauty herself.'

'I. Made.'

He smiled at me in a way that made me want to rip his head off then and there, like I was an infant that needed to be indulged. But if I'd ripped off his head I wouldn't have had the pleasure of proving him wrong, of—as you say—rubbing his nose in it.

Perhaps his interest in my handiwork ought to have raised my suspicions. Through the many miromiro minds, I had witnessed him examining the cloaks, rubbing the fibres between his fingers as if to test their smoothness, and feeling the drape of it in his hand. I had thought it a symptom of his human hands—since I acquired mine I had become fascinated with the texture of everything, the pads of my fingers sensitive to tiny changes in surface and temperature. Hatupatu was forever touching things—his hair, his skin, his clothing. He would smooth the feathers of the birds I gave him before plucking them clean. Gathering, communicating—not only with his voice but also his hands. Once I noticed this habit, I tried to emulate him during our conversations, reasoning that this conceit of human behaviour would endear me to him.

It would take at least a few days, perhaps even a week, to ready my supplies. I would gather the harakeke during the day while I was hunting, even though the season for cutting harakeke had long passed. I had thought that the Song Makers' superstition about gathering harakeke at night was because of their fear of the patupaiarehe, but I learnt later the restriction had a practical reason. The moisture of night dew or of rain can damage the plant when it is cut; so, like the diagonal cuts made to free the harvested leaves, the practice of harvesting harakeke during the long summer days preserved the heart of the plant from rot. Tying it to superstition made the restriction self-enforceable—no one would risk being taken by the fairies for the sake of a few flax leaves.

I would cut it during the day, but could not change the season. Of course I could have waited until the days lengthened again, but by then Hatupatu may have gone, either from running away or perhaps I would have learnt all that I needed from him. But it was more than the feeling that my time with him was running out. He had hurt my pride, and I wanted to show him up

as soon as possible. The feeling of impatience at seeing the look on his face—
What is funny? The look on your face—was overwhelming. There was a lesson
to be learnt.

I would make him the dog-skin cloak. The cloak that was beyond
his status as the youngest-born son. A cloak that could be borne upon
the shoulders of his eldest brother, but never by Hatupatu. He would see it
on the shoulders of his nephew or grand-nephew—it would never be passed
down his line. In normal circumstances, Hatupatu would only receive a cloak
such as that if his mother had lost all her sons save him, or if he managed a
marriage well above himself.

I would make him the dog-skin cloak. It would be the final test of me
in his grand experiment. He would watch as I turned flax and skin into a
cloak in a matter of days. He would know that my skills as a weaver outshone
the women in the village, that my hands were capable of creating such
beauty despite their appearance. I still don't want to admit to myself that
tied up in that thought was the hope that he would see *my* beauty despite
my appearance. It is a strange thing, but I had never felt as truly ugly as
when Hatupatu seemed to be repulsed by my presence. Stranger still
was my apparent need for validation from him—he was the source of my
anxiety and the only way I knew how to salve it.

I would make him the dog-skin cloak.

I had seen very few dog-skin cloaks made during my apprenticeship. It was
not taken lightly, the death of a kurī. They were useful creatures to the Song
Makers. They assisted on hunts and provided warmth and companionship to
their owners. They were fiercely loyal and smart enough to be trained. There
was enough human in their behaviour that they became beloved. But once a
kurī was killed, every part of it was used.

Kurī were relatively small, three or four could be stitched together for a
great man. If I was to make myself a cloak, I think I would need half a dozen
or more. For the cloak I intended to make Hatupatu, I would only take two—
one black, one white. I planned to cut the skins into strips and alternate the

fur, black with white, and let the muka shine through the gaps. A pattern called awarua—two rivers of dark and light. It would showcase all my skills as a weaver.

And so I spent the next week gathering and preparing my supplies. I chose the easiest jobs first, gathering the harakeke and stripping it to the muka. So often had I done this—stripping, beating, washing—that it gave me comfort. It gave me confidence. And as I worked, the familiarity of it allowed my mind to wander, to weave the cloak in my mind, so that when my hands finally twined aho with whenu I had already made the cloak many times over. The strips of skin could not be woven into the garment like the small bundles of feathers I was used to working with. Instead, I would weave a plain base for the cloak and sew the strips of skin onto it. I would use my claws to sew, punching a small hole through the skin and pushing a loop of thread through the hole. I would weave a thread through these loops to secure the stitches.

I had observed his shoulders in detail—how Hatupatu carried his right slightly higher than his left, the muscles more pronounced in his favoured arm. I calculated the number of whenu needed to curve the cloak around him, the short rows that would need to be worked to give the garment shape, so that when he wore it, the weight of it would not tug on the tie around his neck alone. And aesthetically, it would show off his broadening back and tapered waist. The strips of fur would slightly curve too, so that when it was worn the stripes would seem to be straight. Such a cloak had never been seen, could never be made by any hands other than mine. Such a cloak could lift Hatupatu from his lowly status. Such a cloak would lift me as well.

Perhaps I had too much at stake in this endeavour. Looking back on it now, I am not sure what I hoped to achieve. My obsession with the cloak had gone beyond a point of pride. It felt as though my world would be destroyed if I could not accomplish it.

His words, his words kept repeating in my mind.

She must be a thing of beauty herself.

Ātaahua.

Ātaahua.

Why did he sway me? Why did I have to prove myself to him? What did it matter if he believed me? Why did it matter—to prove that this monster, this ogress, this *thing* was capable of creating beauty?

Like I have said before, Hatupatu was a master weaver himself. And like the techniques I used in shaping a garment, his skill was invisible to the untrained eye.

    I would make him a dog-skin cloak.

I had not told Hatupatu my plans to make him a cloak. I suspect that he had forgotten our conversation about the cloaks a week before—he could not seem to hold a thought in his head for very long at all. It irked me that it didn't matter to him. The conversation was a parasite in my brain controlling everything that I was.

I waited until evening to set off for the village, just as I had done when I found the tūī.

'Where are you going?' His question stopped me. I turned and looked at him.

Did he expect me to answer him? I had let the tūī roost, but even if I had my voice, why did he expect me to tell him where I was going? It was not as if he held *me* captive.

    At least that is what I told myself.

I wasn't sure what he could see. His eyes had trouble seeing in the dark— more so when he had been staring into the bright flame. Hatupatu could be easily blinded by both dark and light. I made my gesture larger than it needed to be so that he could see it. I swept my wing out and up, and pointed my index finger to the sky.

I didn't wait for him to offer a reply, or to question me further. I flexed my feet and pushed myself up into a leap so that I was clear of our home.

If his eyes adjusted sufficiently to allow Hatupatu to see me as I scaled a tree to start my ascent into the canopy, he never told me.

I pushed off from the first treetop, cracking its top branches in my haste. As I glided from tree to tree, I could not shake the feeling of that first tree, of crushing a living thing beneath me. I had not thought of it before, the weight of me, of my corporeal being. When I first acquired my body, I was so caught up in experiencing the effects of being that I had not considered my effect on the world. I had never really questioned my *being*, the fact of my existence. Telling you this now might give you the impression that I had stopped to ponder this—but I hadn't. I continued, pushing myself up from tree branches, using their give to buoy my flight. I could think about my presence in the world whilst giving effect to it. It was, as your philosophers would call it, a thought experiment.

But for me—this branch would still be growing true.

But for me—these feathers on my cloak would still be attached to their original owners.

But for me—Hatupatu would have starved, alone in the forest.

It was a self-serving line of thought, that my presence was ultimately a positive thing. The branch would grow stronger, the feathers would last several more lifetimes as a cloak, I had saved the boy and he lived happily with me. Even then I was telling the story to suit me. I allowed myself to ignore my limitations, I allowed myself to embrace them.

I had become more human than I had intended.

The village of Hatupatu was quiet when I arrived. The Song Makers had retired to their dwellings to sleep, or mate, or to tell jokes and stories. The kurī that had followed me when I took the tūī greeted me once more. I patted its head and let it lick my claws.

You're not the kurī I'm looking for, you silly yellow thing. I pushed the thought into its mind, and it cocked its head at me. I found the gesture endearing, something that the kurī and I both had in common. I appreciated the genius of the animal, to flatter me in this way. No wonder the humans loved these kurī so. And there were many of them sleeping outside their masters' dwellings. Many that were black. Many that were white. But I passed them over—I was looking for specific dogs. The kurī *had* to be the ones that Haroa and Hanui owned, otherwise my gesture would be hollow.

I sniffed the air, trying to find the scent of the brothers, Hanui and Haroa. I thought that they would smell similar to their brother, Hatupatu, just as features between siblings seem to echo one another. When I had lived with kiwi, my sense of smell had been keen—I could smell earthworms burrowing in the soil. My sense of smell at this time, in comparison to humans, would still have been impressive, but it was not sensitive enough to sniff out the brothers' dwellings. The smell of the village was overwhelmingly Song Maker, and I hadn't known enough of them to pick up their differences from afar. The kurī beside me picked up my thoughts, but more remarkably picked up the scent. Somehow the mammal could put together the olfactory puzzle that eluded me. It sniffed the air, and then the ground, and trotted ahead of me. It turned and looked back at me as if to say, *You follow me now,* and I, with no other leads, did.

A black dog was curled up outside a dwelling, and my yellow one sniffed him in greeting. The black dog lifted its head and yawned. I crept closer to the dwelling and inhaled—I could smell it now, the tang of the familiar scent of Hatupatu, but not entirely him. I patted both dogs' heads. I wanted to be sure that the black dog would stay beside me. I should have made a tether for it myself, but how would I have explained that to Hatupatu? Instead, I hoped to find something near the whare. I found a piece of rope and tied it around the neck of the black dog so that it had no choice but to trot behind me.

The yellow dog was ahead of us, waiting outside a second dwelling. Here, a white dog slept. I thanked my yellow guide again with a pat on the head. The two dogs, the black one and the white one—I carried one under each arm as I ran into the forest. The yellow dog could not keep up with me, but I could hear its howls of disappointment.

Yellow dog, you do not want to follow me tonight. You do not want to see what these claws that you've licked will do to your litter mates.

The kurī under my arms squirmed. They were not used to being held this way. I would set them down soon enough.

Should I go into the detail of their deaths? That I tied the black one to a tree while I slit the throat of the white, and held it by the hind legs so it would bleed out, as I had seen Hatupatu do to the birds I brought him. Would you want to see that scene repeated again as I killed and bled the black dog? Do you want a description of how I slit around their ankles and down their bellies so that I could pull off their skin almost intact? That I left the mask of fur on their faces so that their lolling tongues looked like they had done on hot days, when the dogs had tried to cool themselves.

I worked on their skins away from our cave, slicing away the fat and sinew with my claws. It reminded me of preparing muka—the white of the skin revealed from under the cover of muscle.

I cracked open the dogs' skulls and scooped out their brains. These I put into a calabash bowl to take back to the fire Hatupatu had made, only a few minutes away. By the time I arrived back at our cave, Hatupatu had left the remnants of the fire and crawled into bed. There were a few embers left glowing, so I fed them with a little dried moss and kindling as I had seen Hatupatu do. I did not need much heat to coax the oil from the brains. I used my claws to stir them over the flame. It seemed to me a pity to use the kurī brains to preserve the skin. What more could I have learnt about the Song Makers from kurī eyes? What secrets were hidden behind its howl? It seemed to me to be a waste, to lose these creatures' thoughts and memories to stave off the inevitable rot of their form. But the mind would have to be sacrificed, my feat of weaving would not impress if it rotted around the shoulders of Hatupatu. I licked my claws clean, but the heat had robbed the brain of any of its thoughts. It was now just protein, fat and water.

I took the calabash back to the kurī skins and rubbed half the mixture on the pelts. I tidied the site, making sure that the skin and brain mixture was safe until the following night. I thought about burying the headless kurī carcasses, which would be a shameful waste of their bodies. I remembered that all of the kurī should be used, and how rare it was for a Song Maker to eat kurī meat. Hatupatu had told me this with the same drunken look in his eyes that kererū get thinking of karaka berries. I knew that he would relish this meat, but if I took the flesh back to our camp, the surprise would be ruined.

So I returned the dogs to their owners, imagining their delight to find such a boon when they emerged from their dwellings in an hour or so at dawn. The yellow dog had sniffed the bodies when I returned and backed away from me, its tail tucked between its legs. It seemed that kurī were as superstitious about their dead as the humans they chose to live with.

I used the length of rope I had leashed the black dog with to tie it by its hind legs and hang it in the eaves of the whare. I did not have rope for the white dog, so I left it lying across the doorway of its home.

I had said the words over their bodies, the karakia I had heard Hatupatu recite over his birds before he ate them. As I left the village, I felt happy that these two lives I had taken would surprise Hatupatu and his brothers.

Over the next couple of nights, while Hatupatu slumbered, I continued to tan the kurī hides. I stretched the skins, as I had seen the men do—holding back some of my strength so that I didn't rip them apart. Where the men had used smoothed logs to rub the skins and break down the fibres, I used my own body, rubbing the furred side of the skin against my knees until it was pliable.

I took pleasure in sinking my fingers into the fur of the skins, the soft texture delightful. I feel no shame in admitting that I took off the cloak that covered my chest and rubbed the fur against that too. Some loose hairs stuck to my skin as I rubbed, my chest speckled with black and white fur. It was so soft against my skin, so soft it made the fine muka seem rough when I put my cloak back on.

The different textures of muka and fur, the different temperatures of the warmth beneath my cloak and the chill of the night air—made my nipples harden. I was tempted, then, to make the cloak for myself. Why would I expend all this effort for Hatupatu?

Even though this exercise was more about my need to prove myself to him, it felt like the sacrifice of these two dogs, these two in particular, would go to waste if the cloak was made for anyone but him.

If I had made the cloak for myself, I would have lined the underside of it with the fur so that it would warm and comfort my skin—that would be more practical than laying it on the outside. I thought about the cloak I had designed for him, the fur stripes, light and shadow competing with one another for attention. *Attention.* That was what his cloak was for. It was designed to garner his attention.

I wonder now if I had subconsciously given Hatupatu up in the design of that cloak. It was a design to impress humans, his brothers, his parents, his village. For the cloak to be truly successful, it would need to impress more than him, more than me. Now it seems as if the cloak was a sort of prophecy—of his decision to leave me, of his destiny to become legend. Was it me who planted the idea in his mind?

It is surprising now that I had considered none of these thoughts at the time. My mind was focused on stretching the skins for smoking, on the execution of the cloak, on the look on his face. Hatupatu was asleep when I returned to our cave with the skins stretched out on frames. The fire, just as a few nights before, was ash and a few tenacious embers. This time I stoked a large fire, nurturing it from dried moss and twigs to large branches. When I had made a good base of embers—orange-hearted, white-ashed lumps—I placed green wood on top. The smoke made it difficult to keep my eyes open as I placed the framed skins on branches. I had sunk the branches in the ground near the fire pit so that the skins were held above and away from the flames.

While the skins smoked, I set up the branches for my loom in the entrance to the cave. It had always been where I set up my work, but now it served another purpose. In the morning when Hatupatu awoke, he would have to walk around me, around my work—it would be impossible to deny that

I had made *this* cloak. I had already made the tāniko for the neck of the cloak, twining aho around whenu to make niho—triangular patterns of black and white like the jagged teeth of the kurī. By the time I had my work prepared and the fire stoked, I had little more than an hour before the dawn. It would be time enough to make a good start on the cloak base, so I sat in the middle of the loom and began to weave.

The work flowed quickly in that hour. There is something about that time of night that allows my fingers to fly, as if the work is creating itself and I am but a witness to it. Just before the sun's light had penetrated the forest, the first of the dawn chorus awoke. People often wonder how it is that the birds will greet the day before the light has even changed. There is a feeling of daybreak—it is hard to describe to you. Perhaps it is as simple as sensing the turn of the earth towards the sun that the birds and I feel—it is our internal clock, as you like to say. Or changes in temperature and light that your senses are too dull to detect. That is the physical, but there is more. An emotional feeling, dare I say, a spiritual feeling. It is a mixture of longing and inevitability, no, of *certainty*. The song before the light is almost a prayer, an entreaty for the light to return.

> Darkness must inevitably arc into light.
>
> Ki te whaiao, ki te ao mārama.

It is a daily miracle, and the birds' song is partly joy that the light has returned, and partly joy that they are alive to witness it.

The dawn chorus was in full song by the time Hatupatu emerged from the cave. It was not the feeling or daybreak, nor the song of the birds that awoke him, rather it was the pressure of his full bladder. He almost stumbled over me—his eyes had not adjusted to the dim light of the morning from the dark of the cave. I'm not sure if he had opened his eyes at all, his shuffling feet had seemed to learn the way by themselves morning after morning.

Hatupatu bumped into my arm as I stretched to the beginning of my row. He stopped and rubbed his eyes, as if he was breaking the seal of sleep that was upon them.

'What are you doing?'

I gestured to my loom, the tūī still inside the cave.

His sigh was sharp and impatient. I continued my row as he stomped back into the gloom of the cave to retrieve the tūī. He tried to hand the bird to me, but I waved him off—I was busy weaving. Hatupatu looped the tether of the tūī around his upper arm so that the bird could rest upon his shoulder.

'What are you doing?'

'I make.'

Hatupatu walked around me and my loom. He peered from side to side, got on his knees and looked under my work, as if there was room for me to hide the true weaver. He did not believe his own eyes.

'You're weaving?'

'Yes.'

He seemed transfixed by my hands, all his focus was on them as I worked the muka. I slowed down my weaving so that he could see my movements— they were still faster than he had ever seen before. He was so focused that he did not notice the fire or the skins above it. The wind shifted and a little smoke from the fire wafted towards us. Hatupatu scrunched his eyes and held his forearm above them to shield them from the smoke. It was an overdramatic gesture for the amount of smoke, really. His attention shifted from me to the fire pit.

'What are those?'

'Kurī.'

Hatupatu walked to the fire, avoiding the smoke in the wind as best he could. He hesitated before touching the dog skins as if they were just a dream and his touch would shatter them.

'One black, one white. Just like ...'

'Your brothers'.'

He looked at me, even though my voice was perched on his shoulder. I held his gaze. I could weave by touch alone.

'Where did you get these?'

'I make.'

'No, whose dogs are these?'

There seemed to be anger in his voice. I was not sure why, but I felt as if I couldn't tell him where I had acquired the dogs. I thought that using these kurī would make him happy, but now I wasn't so sure. It was something that I ought to have considered.

The tūī growled.

'No. No thinking of lies. Tell me where you got these kurī.'

I cocked my head. It was strange to be accused of lying. I had never told an untruth before, nor had I a reason to. I had told him the truth and he did not believe me, but that did not make *me* a liar. I have no use for lies, not then, not now. And so I told him the truth, no matter the consequence.

'Your brothers.'

He looked from me to the furs and back again, a slow shake of his head as if he could deny it. He walked towards me, untying the bird from his shoulder and as he came near he let the tether go. The bird, feeling the tension on its leash relax, beat its wings to fly away. Had he counted on my quick reflexes to reclaim the bird, or did he not care if my voice flew away? I would have to unpick the row I was working on to smooth out the fibres I had bunched in my haste to stand and catch the tūī. Hatupatu simply walked away as I tethered the bird to one of the branches of my loom.

I assumed that he had gone to relieve his bladder as he did every morning. My weaving had been a distraction, but his body still pressed him with the need to urinate. I reasoned that his haste in leaving to his ablutions had made him release the tūī—it was not malice or revenge. I settled back to weaving, allowing myself to become absorbed in the task, the simplicity of aho and whenu creating a whole that was bigger than themselves. Each thread strengthened by the intersection with another.

The cloak was coming along quickly. I had almost reached the shoulder when I stood to place more green wood on my fire. I should have noticed that Hatupatu had not returned then. It was not as if he wasn't on my mind as I sat back down to my work. I thought of his shoulders, their breadth and musculature, as I wove rows that would hug the curve of them. He was a presence in my mind, if not present. I wove in a sort of reverie, my mind free to wander and make connections as the tūī growled at my hand. I liked the sound of it—the growl reminded me of the beginning of it all, the beginning of time reverberating through all time, a moment that is ever present. It is immortal. A hum of recognition.

I was exhausting the poor bird, so I untied it from my loom and carried it back to its roost in the cave. I wondered if, given enough time, my voice's eyes would change to suit the gloom of the cave. Perhaps in a hundred thousand generations this bird's line would evolve to have eyes like the ruru and a mind capable of interpreting my thoughts completely. Of course, the far simpler route would be for me to find my own voice.

The fire required more wood when I came out from the cave. It was then I noticed that Hatupatu had yet to return. Although I was no longer privy to his daily ablutions, I knew that he had been away far too long. I tried not to allow panic to overtake me. I tried not to allow myself to speculate whether he had finally decided to run away. The idea of him running away now seemed illogical to me—I was making him a beautiful cloak. Surely he would not leave now? I realised that Hatupatu had no idea that I was making the cloak for him. All I had said, all I could say, was *I make*. The tūī was proving to be a stupid, crude tool only capable of blurting out a couple of words at a time.

I make. I make. I make …

Still, a blunt tool if used correctly could perform what is needed. The bird only relayed what I thought, and it is my own fault that I didn't add two simple words, words easy enough for both the bird and the boy to understand.

For you.

I thought of crying out his name in the hope that he would answer me. Foolishly, I opened my own mouth, tried to connect thought to tongue, as if my urgent need to be heard would break my silence. It did not. I sniffed the air for the scent of him, moving slowly in a circle with my beak in the air. I scented his urine and faeces and followed it to its source. Hatupatu was no longer there, but I could see broken twigs and disturbed ground leading further into the forest. I scaled a tree and hopped between treetops, following the direction of his path. Away from his leavings, I could detect a hint of him on the air. I followed it as it became stronger and stronger, my feet barely having time to settle on the branches before I pushed off again. I overshot by half a dozen or so trees, and his scent dropped away. I used my wings as a brake to my momentum, and then as a rudder, turning myself around. I took the last trees slowly, checking to see if I could smell Hatupatu at each stop.

I found him.

Hatupatu was sitting under a tree on a ridge. He was looking out over the river towards his home. I climbed down from the top of the tree, branch by branch until I was almost over him. I was relieved—that he was safe, that he had not gone far. The urge to scoop him up and take him home, as I had done on the day we met, was checked by a sound, a hiccoughing intake of air, and a sigh as it was released. It was a sound I had never heard before, and it was a sound I'd never hear from Hatupatu again. It sounded as if he had been wounded. I thought that it was perhaps his lungs, but it would seem it was his heart.

From my vantage point I could not see his face, but I know now that it would have been as wet as the river he looked upon. He wiped his face with the back of his hand, and straightened his back. He breathed in—the breath a sort of stutter to begin with, finally slowing to a steady rhythm. All the while I watched him from up in the tree, confused at what was going on.

A twig snapped and Hatupatu looked up into the tree. I froze, for some reason ashamed that he might see me. Even at the best of times his eyes had difficulty with the shadows, and now his eyes were watery and red. Hatupatu did not see me—if he had he wouldn't have left the look of utter sorrow on his face. I had seen that his kind experience their emotions physically—lips pulled back over teeth for joy, eyebrows furrowed in frustration—but I had not seen an emotion possess him so completely. His eyes and nose watered, his posture bent as if his head was too heavy, his breathing laboured. His facial features looked as if gravity had suddenly become too much for them to bear.

The strange thing was, the look of him filled me with sadness too. I felt the weight of it in my own body, even though moments before there was nothing. Hatupatu looked away, and again I felt relief—I had been reprieved of his sadness. He sighed and pushed himself up to his feet. For a moment he just stood there, and I wasn't sure what I would do if he chose to walk down to that river—would I let him go and find his way home? Or would I take him back with me, his sorrow growing deeper and heavier?

Hatupatu turned his back on the river and headed back along the path he had created. I waited until he had passed me and climbed back to the canopy. There was no need for me to rush, I would overtake him easily, but something in the physical activity exorcised the sorrow Hatupatu had given me—pushing my body through the air as fast as it would go filled me with a sense of joy.

I landed at our cave before Hatupatu had walked halfway back. I retrieved the tūī from the cave and tied it to my loom. I checked the fire and added some more wood. I contrived to make it seem as if I had never left my work, as if I had never followed him. And so it was that I constructed my first lie, twining truth around fantasy.

I was weaving when he arrived back, and if he noticed my work, he didn't seem surprised at my lack of progress—it took the women in his village many weeks to complete a garment after all. I did not look up from my work, although I could see him as I had done when he had tested my intelligence. He wore his own contrivance—somewhere on his way back to our cave he had composed a mask of calm, no trace of his earlier sorrow, apart from a slight puffiness around his eyes.

Hatupatu did not sit with me straight away. He walked to the fire and pushed the wood with a stick, stoking the flames. He coughed as the smoke rose. He looked at the skins and reached out to touch the black kurī skin, his hand stroking the fur of its hind leg. He looked over his shoulder at me, his eyes watery again—although his face was neutral. I thought it must have been the smoke.

He turned his face away from me again. He pushed his shoulders down and elongated his neck, making the most of his height, although he was still much shorter than me. He walked with a confidence that he borrowed from his stance and stood over me as I worked. Still I did not look up at him. I waited for him to make the first move. I wove and he watched. He watched and I wove, neither of us willing to give up our contrivances.

Hatupatu conceded to me. I felt triumphant when he sat down in front of me, peering into my face to try and catch my eye. I let him squirm a little longer, finishing my row before I lifted my head.

'Those are my brothers' kurī?'

'Yes.'

'You've been to my village?'

'Yes.'

Hatupatu broke his gaze then. He looked to the ground in front of himself as if it held the answer to the many questions fighting in his head. He must have had many of them because it seemed to take an age for him to sort through them all, and when he finally spoke I was less than impressed with the question he had chosen.

'Why?'

Why what? Why had I taken his brothers' kurī? Why had I visited his village? The answers to those questions were surely self-evident—to make a dog-skin cloak of black and white and significance, I had to visit his village to retrieve those dogs. I cocked my head and the tūī sighed.

'Please, Kura, tell me why.'

'I make,' I said. 'For you.'

CHAPTER THIRTEEN
TŪKINO

Hatupatu was ready.

I could smell it in the air of the cave, I could see it in his body and in the times he ejaculated in his sleep.

I have been witness to many mating rituals. Birds displaying their prowess through song or flight patterns, some through their ability to create a nest for their eggs. I have heard cicada and cricket song in summer. I have seen the successful and their legacy of offspring. I have seen some die out without passing on their traits. And so it did not shock me when Hatupatu displayed his readiness to mate.

His stories became focused on women, or rather parts
of them.

'To conquer death, Māui had to go to where life began. He had to conquer
Hinenuitepō,' Hatupatu said, his hands held apart as if it was he who was
spreading the shapely smooth thighs of the goddess. Hatupatu closed his
eyes as he thought of her, and his voice caught in a moan, perhaps imagining
that it was him crushed between her thighs.

'And as she moved in her sleep, her hangutu parted,' his breathing shifted,
became heavier, 'and before him, the werewere of Hinenuitepō glistened.'
Hatupatu wet his lower lip with his tongue. Although she was not in arousal,
her labia as he described them were granite-lipped. Her sex would cut the
demi-god in two. At the thought of it, Hatupatu instinctively protected his
own ure.

His fascination was mixed with a certain amount of revulsion. He
giggled as the pīwakawaka had done in the telling of the death of Māui—
the thought of the demi-god crawling head first into the goddess was too
much for his mind to bear. The thing I found strange about the story was
that the pīwakawaka laughed at how Māui looked, that the story focused on
the insult to Māui, not to the great and powerful woman he tried to violate.

'Why funny?'

Hatupatu blinked at me—had he forgotten I was there? Was this story
for me at all?

'A woman showing a man her,' he hesitated, swallowing hard, 'her *aroaro
kino*, her *whare haunga*—it lowers him.' Hatupatu wrinkled his nose, and I
could see his eye teeth below his sneer.

It was difficult for me to understand why female genitals would be called
these nasty names. It must be confusing to have desire mixed with disgust, or
frightening—the source of life also holds death. Was it because of the folly of
Māui? That a woman's vagina is a passage to life, but also death?

*Revolting, revolting evil thing, stinking house. A place that
is dangerous for men, and yet …*

'Ātaahua, ātaahua,' he called, but it was not something he attributed to me.

I had always undressed freely in front of Hatupatu. I covered my body not from shame, but from the elements. He had never seemed interested in my body before. If he did look at me, it was always a glance before he turned away, his face flushed. Now he pretended not to look, but I could see that although he looked straight ahead his eyes were trained on me. For the first time I felt as if I ought to hold an arm across my chest to shield my breasts from his eyes. There was an aggression in his look, as if he was insulted by my nudity because it made him feel powerless. I ought to have confronted him, but I felt remarkably vulnerable despite our size difference. There was something in his gaze that dwarfed me.

I know your stories are replete with women who change to please their men, good turned bad, shrews tamed, a former way of life abandoned for love—so it should not surprise you that I too changed for that man.

I had changed into this form under the influence of the Song Makers' stories. They had made me a woman, at least in my torso, smooth human skin unpocked by feathers, and fatty rounded breasts. Hatupatu dreamed of these features. His attention, his obsession, refined these features. My breasts became fuller and sat higher on my chest. My waist narrowed and my hips curved. The down that remained on my torso from belly to thigh thinned. Vent turned to vagina and was topped with a thatch of hair.

'Ātaahua,' he said, and I knew whom I had been modelled on.

'Ātaahua,' he said, his eyes only on my body.

Hatupatu stared at his creation. He ran his hands over my breasts and belly as if he had shaped them from clay as Tāne had done with Hineahuone. The sensation of his hands on me was not entirely unpleasant, but it did surprise me that he thought he had the right to touch me. He stroked my breast and my nipple hardened as it did when touched by something new. Hatupatu held the nipple between his forefinger and thumb, rolling it slightly between them before pulling my breast towards his mouth. He closed his eyes and suckled on my breast. It seemed strange that a behaviour I had seen in infants had become erotic in adulthood. Is that why this act felt aggressive? Because he could confuse these feelings with memories of himself as a baby?

He traced around my nipple with the tip of his tongue, his cooling saliva making my breast even more sensitive. He moved his head to my other breast, cupping the first in his hand. I could feel the groan in his throat, the vibration of it on his tongue. He used his hands to touch himself, his own nipples, his belly. He took off his maro and so he stood as naked as me. His ure was erect and he used a hand to stroke up and down the length of it. I felt like I should touch him. I wanted to feel his skin on my fingertips. His eyes were still closed as I ran my hand up his chest—I could feel the sweat on his skin, his heart through his chest. It excited me to be so close to his heart that I forgot that I needed to hold my claws away from his skin, and I nicked him on his throat.

He bit into my breast, and I opened my beak in surprise, pain and pleasure. He released me and I let him push me to my knees. He spat on his hand and massaged the spit on his ure. He walked around behind me and forced himself into me.

The tūī screamed.

He held onto my hips to steady himself as he thrust, his fists full of my feathers. Once he had found a rhythm, he moved one of his hands to try to cup my breasts, but his arms were too short to accomplish this in the position I was in. I hunched my back so he could reach, but still he was a little short, pulling the bottom of my breast down towards him and barely grazing the nipple.

He moved his hand to my back, laying his palm on my spine. He pushed his hand down on my back, and I yielded for him, my chest and wings prostrate on the ground, while my hips were held up.

My beak would have broken against the ground with the force of his thrusts, so I tipped my head back. From that position I could see his face once more—his eyes were closed and he bit his lip. Sometimes he would lift his chin and groan, the sound of it coloured with both pleasure and pain. He opened his eyes and stared ahead as his movements became faster and faster. He must have lost himself in his fantasy for a moment, because when he looked down at me his repulsion made him go limp inside of me. He was reminded that I was, that I am, *this thing, this ogress, this monster.*

He had told me again and again that I was not a person. And now I understood. How could anyone treat a person that way, with so little regard? If I had been a person that would have made him monstrous.

He pulled himself out and away from me. He covered himself first with his hand and then with his discarded maro and backed away.

I stayed how I was, whakapohane—daring him to look at my hanga kino, my whare haunga, although I think those epithets were more appropriately attributed to him.

Evil thing.

Stinking house.

Did my labia glint with saliva and semen so that they looked like they were tipped in granite? I could still feel his wetness on me and in me.

'Cover yourself.' He threw a cloak at me. I stood up and stretched my back up, straightening the spine that had been hunched and prostrated for his pleasure. I turned, strong in my nakedness. My body had become a weapon. Hatupatu averted his eyes from me as I covered my body.

I could smell every part of our intercourse in the cave, his sweat, his blood and his semen. His shame.

Later, I heard the waiata of the maiden Te Akatawhia who was forced to marry Māhanga after he looked upon her sex by hiding in her latrine.

You waited for me to be exposed.

And gazed upon me.

What did you see?

Something untouched, something desired.

Something black, very black, and yet to be pierced.

I knew the anger in her words—they were kin to me. To restore her honour she had to marry her trespasser. Husband and wife. Hatupatu and I had made fire. He was the kaikōmako and I the māhoe. I understood now the metaphor and why Hatupatu had hesitated. He was afraid to empower me. He was afraid to show his weakness.

Hatupatu sat with his back turned away from me. He had wrapped himself in the kurī-skin cloak that I had fashioned for him. I inhabited the body he had fashioned for me. I reached out to touch his shoulder, but he pulled away from me as if it was me who had done him violence.

'It can't happen again.' He was arrogant enough to believe that I would yearn for him in the way that he yearned for me.

'Why?'

'Kura, it's not natural.'

Although sex was messy and awkward, I had seen enough of it to know that it was indeed natural. I tried to touch him once again, and he jerked his head in such a way that I nicked his cheek. It was the second time I had drawn blood in our relationship.

He held a hand to his cheek and looked at me with loathing in his eyes.

'It was a mistake. And it won't happen again. What if you became ...'

'What?' *More human?*

'Pregnant. I mean is it even possible? Between a human and a ...'

Ogress.

Monster.

Thing.

I looked down at my belly and placed a hand on it, moving the hand slowly around the cloak to feel the contours of my body beneath. Was it possible? Could this new body be capable of procreation? Had his imagination been strong enough to make me fertile? I doubt whether he knew the intricacies of ova and ovary—but he could imagine a place where his seed could take root. If willed, life will find a way. If it was possible, would I lay a clutch of eggs like the birds or gestate internally like a mammal? Would my breasts swell with milk for my offspring, a child of bird-woman and man? My heart sank for a moment as I imagined a child who was less like me and more like Hatupatu. Would any of my bird characteristics present themselves? A tiny beak? A few feathers? Would my child have claws and an egg tooth to rip itself from my belly at birth?

The tūī growled.

'What does that mean?' his voice sounded as panicked as if I had threatened his life. 'What do you know, Kura?'

I cocked my head at the boy, and with my hand still on my belly I walked out of the cave.

'Kura! Kura!'

His calls were tinged with rage as I climbed up a tree and into the canopy.

Was it possible?

The birds had already begun their courtship rituals and were gathering materials for their nests. I had watched them many times over the centuries—a dispassionate interest I suppose you could say. Now I watched for the signs of their quickening keenly. I felt that it was possible for this immortal to become a parent, that perhaps for the first time in my long life I had stumbled closer to mortality.

I did not know then how right I was.

In the days after Hatupatu and I had sex, I would often hold my hand on my belly as if protecting it from the world. I had seen similar behaviour in women who were hapū, but usually they were further along than I could be. Perhaps like the riroriro I could have a clutch or two in one season. If he saw me, Hatupatu would shudder with the thought of it—perhaps he was not ready to farewell his childhood after all.

He needn't have worried. I could not feel cells dividing inside of me. I could not detect the sound of a heartbeat. I did not feel the new presence of an incorporeal soul searching for a seed to latch on to. Yet, still, whenever he was around, my hand would hold my belly. You may think it was cruelty on my part to make him think I was pregnant. Perhaps the less charitable would think it a trick to keep him by my side. Believe me when I say that I did not consciously torture him. It was not one of my experiments. I think it was his own fear that moved my hand, that in the coming weeks would make my belly and breasts swell. It was his belief that made my body change. If I had lived with him any longer, perhaps the strength of his conviction would have created a being inside of me, although what manner of thing it would have been I cannot say. Could such a thing have a consciousness of its own? Or would its be a mere splinter of mine?

Hatupatu barely talked to me. He could not look me in the eye. He never allowed himself to be near me when I undressed—it would seem as if my body's power still had a hold on him.

It seemed pointless to try and talk to him, so I resumed our old routine of leaving during the day to hunt. The kererū were getting thinner after a long winter—the fruits that they would gorge themselves on were still green and hard on the trees. I caught fewer birds, mindful that now was their time to find mates.

Hatupatu was not pleased. 'It's hardly worth making a fire for these. Why did you bother?'

All the words he had for me now were complaints or insults. It seemed strange to feel nostalgic for our happy time together—it was not that long ago. His silence made it seem as if years had passed.

At night while Hatupatu slept, I amused myself by weaving or carving. I could no longer watch him sleep. I did not care what his dreams were anymore. I would take my work to the cliff overlooking the river where I had found Hatupatu crying. It filled me with hope, this site where he had spread out his sorrow, hope that one day he would feel as deeply again, that perhaps he would feel that deeply for me.

I would sneak the finished cloaks or taiaha into the cave before dawn, thinking that perhaps he wouldn't notice. But of course he did.

'What are you doing, Kura? Why are you making all these things?'

And without thought I would place my hand on my belly as if it was an answer. And I suppose from his point of view, it was. He thought I was nesting, getting ready to welcome a new life.

It is only my speculation, but I think it sickened him to think of it—a life with me and some terrible offspring. It was not his destiny—he would not be remembered as the father of monsters.

The thought of his monstrous son—for it is always a son that men dream of—robbed him of sleep. Even though he could not slumber, he dreamt. Had I asked him what his dreams were of, he would have answered—

Death.

I imagine at first he dreamt of his own death. He could take his life by driving a taiaha into the ground and impaling himself upon it. He could fashion some rope from my store of muka and hang himself in a tree. His death would send his soul to Rarohenga where he would be welcomed by his ancestors, and he would exist peacefully for a few decades or more, until the day his son died, either by the hand of a hero or of natural causes. His spirit too would enter the Underworld and seek out the father who abandoned him. Hatupatu would have to claim his son as all spirits in Rarohenga claim their whānau, and the truth of his time with me would be out.

Hatupatu knew that he had a destiny greater than dying by his own hand. If anyone should die, I think he would have reasoned, it ought to be me. If there was life growing inside of me, he would snuff it out before it separated from me, then I would carry it with me to whatever Underworld I belonged to. Hatupatu was confident that he would not see me in Rarohenga. After all, even kurī had their own realm of afterlife—who knew where a creature like myself would go? Perhaps back to the void of Te Kore, perhaps to lurk in the dark of Te Pō.

He had decided. The bird-woman must die.

Kurangaituku must die.

CHAPTER FOURTEEN

MATENGA

Tihi-ori-ori-ori

Miromiro, a bird so small that its song is heard well before the bird is ever seen. In the shadows of the forest the male's black hood of feathers disappears. Perhaps you'll see a flash of his white breast as he clings to the bark of a tree to sing again—

Tihi-ori-ori-ori

In the shadows of my cave, the miromiro disappeared and watched. Watched Hatupatu alone. Saw his lust, not for me, but for the treasures I hoarded. Saw what I was blind to. Watched and waited in the shadows.

The Song Makers would say, *Mate kanohi miromiro—to be found out by the sharp-eyed bird.* They had seen miromiro hunting the tiny insects of the forest, darting its short, sharp beak in the rivulets made by rough bark. The keen eyes of the miromiro can see even the tiny midges. Miromiro the observant. Miromiro will find you out.

A bird so small that it can be overlooked, a bird that melds with the shadows. His eyes were not as sharp as those of the miromiro. He was blinded not by love, but by greed. The small flit of the white breast of the miromiro was not caught by Hatupatu as he set about to become a hero in his people's eyes.

There were times in the aftermath of my love affair that I wished I had the eyes of the miromiro—sharp and focused on what was before me. Able to see the tiny changes in my love, the changes in his eyes and where they rested. If I had been observant, I would have seen that he was not looking at my eyes to see me, but instead he was looking at himself reflected in them. He was imagining how his people would see him, how a comely maiden would see him, when he returned home from the dead resplendent in all the treasures he had stolen. He was seeing himself.

But I was as blind as the riroriro, naive to think that he loved me. I still thought that as I hunted in the forest for the birds that Hatupatu yearned for. I still thought that when miromiro found me. I still thought that when I heard the song of the miromiro, before I was able to pick out its body from the shadows of leaves.

Tihi-ori-ori-ori.

In happier days, at least that is how *I* saw them, Hatupatu would tell me the stories his people had made about the birds in the forest, about their special place in human stories. He would point to a bird in my cave and tell me their story as he had heard it.

He told me that miromiro was the form Māui took when he visited his mother in the Underworld, the form that impressed his mortal brothers. Miromiro had accompanied Māui in his quest to conquer death by crawling into the granite-lipped vulva of Hinenuitepō. In this story, Hatupatu cast miromiro as the bird that laughed and awoke the great goddess who closed her thighs and crushed the demi-god between them. Later in the story of Pīwakawaka, Hatupatu would claim that role as the fantail's. It didn't seem to matter to Hatupatu which bird it was, that somehow these two were quite interchangeable—they were periphery, all that really mattered was that someone laughed. Hatupatu would tell me that, in his world, the presence of these birds in my home would be a sign that something terrible would happen.

Perhaps I should have paid heed to that part of his story.

The miromiro took a role in the love affairs of humans. The Song Makers said that a charm could be whispered to the miromiro and it would sing to your errant lover—

Tihi-ori-ori-ori.

Bring her home. She is lost to me.

The sweet call of the miromiro binding the intentions of love into your heart, aho around whenu.

Miromiro, a go-between, a conduit for messages between lovers separated by the forest, by lands far away. The thoughts of your lover whispered from the shadows of the forest—you cannot see your lover, but you know that he is thinking of you, calling you back to his arms.

The message miromiro delivered to me, not the longings of true love, but a love misplaced, a love corrupted by greed. This is what the refrain held for me.

Tihi-ori-ori-ori.

A warning that my trust had been misplaced. That my love had been as blind as that of the riroriro. I had harboured a cuckoo in my nest. Miromiro called me back to my home, called on me to find my errant lover.

Perhaps it would make for a better story if I pitted Hatupatu against miromiro. I could cast miromiro as jealous of the attentions that I gave

Hatupatu, that somehow miromiro loved me as a mate, as perhaps a wife. I could make miromiro more human in character, so that the message he brought me was tinged with bitter unrequited love. That we were part of a triangle. But that would be a disservice to the memory of miromiro. I was not an object of desire or need for that being. So why then did miromiro seek me out? Why not flee back to the forest if given the chance? Who had sent miromiro to me with this message of love? Whose voice did he carry?

And it may seem cruel to you that I indeed killed the messenger, but I needed its eyes—I needed to see what miromiro had seen.

It was such a small bird that I could have swallowed it whole, crushed it to death in my gullet. Instead I broke the neck of the miromiro, twisting its head with my claws to kill him quickly. Before his body caught up with his death and his heart slowed I ripped off the head, crushed the skull to suck out the brain from the eye sockets, sipping at the head as if it was a nectar-filled flower.

And with the empty skull in my hand, the bloodied body at my feet, I closed my eyes to see what miromiro had seen, to receive the real message that he had delivered to me.

I am unseen in the shadows, the black of my feathered hood blends into the recesses of my whare. I am high above every other body here—the other birds of the forest, the lizards, the bird-woman, the boy. Up here I am waiting for the pūngāwerewere to check its web for prey, unknowing that its web will soon be its own death. I have a taste for the eight-legged creature, whose many eyes are almost as good as mine.

Movement below. The boy has come back and disturbs the rest of the cave's slumber. The bird-woman follows behind him, like the shameless pīwakawaka that follow the Song Makers to feast on the insects that they disturb. She watches him, but does not see him. The bird-woman talks to the tūī, who sings the strange song of the Song Maker. The boy is sullen and seems weary despite the many hours he has slept. He is telling the bird-woman something. She has cocked her head to the side—she understands him, but he has not bothered to learn the language of the forest.

She bids him farewell. The boy does not look at her, does not reply. Instead he sits with his knees pulled up to his chest, his head down as if he has tucked it under his wing for roosting. She leaves and he lifts his head, listening to her footfalls and the swoop of her wings as she uses them to lift her steps further. When he can no longer hear the rhythm of her steps, he stands and stretches. He puts his hands on his hips and surveys the cave, nodding, his lips pulled back to reveal his teeth in that strange expression of aggressive joy that Song Makers have.

The first kill is the tūī, the white feathers at its throat curl around his squeezing fingers. He mutters something in his unintelligible language over the lifeless body.

He crushes the smaller birds in this way—hands around throat or fist crushing breastbones. He discards their bodies to the ground, necks askew and feathers ripped. The larger birds he spears—their blood drips from their perches, down his weapon and on to his hands. He is sweating with the effort and as he wipes his brow he replaces sweat for blood. And his teeth are bared further—he whoops and grunts as he kills all that lives in the cave.

The lizards are crushed under foot—he seems to mimic the heavy footfalls of the bird-woman he has tricked. And I think I've escaped this mad man, that he does not see me in the shadows, that he's forgotten that I'm here, because he is busy gathering the treasures of the Song Makers—the useless still things, the things that have no voice, no life in them. Why does he revere such things, those dead cloaks and weapons?

I keep still so that the white of my breast does not catch his eye. He clears a space amongst the dead, lays a cloak down and piles his things in the middle of it. He takes his time and folds the cloak, enveloping his treasures safely like the bird-woman's wings had enveloped him once. He ties this to his back—keeping a spear free.

And that's when he looks straight at me—his face grotesque with dried blood and his terrible open mouth. Somehow he catches me, my body trapped inside his fist. My heart beats heavily as I wait for my ribs to be crushed and my lungs to be pierced.

But his hand which had wrought such destruction only moments earlier does not squeeze the life from me. He leans in and whispers something over me—rhythmic, although I do not know what it could mean. He still has me in his hand when he leaves the cave. We are in the forest when he finally sets me free, and the urge to find the bird-woman is all consuming, even though it would be better for me to hide in the shadows once more. But I am caught in between these two—and I cannot help but fly to her.

To *me*.

I open my claws and let the head of the miromiro fall to the ground. I want to keep my eyes closed for a little bit longer, the world outside harsh and too full of light. It was not a mistake that the miromiro survived. Hatupatu sent the bird to me, its call a taunt—

Tihi-ori-ori-ori.

Through this little bird he makes it clear what he thinks of me. Makes it clear that he has no love for me.

The miromiro didn't understand his words, but I hear them clearly— *Bring her home. She has lost to me.*

I could see the emotion behind the smile that frightened the small bird—joy, triumph and arrogance. Hatupatu believed that I was too far away to harm him, believed that my love for him would stay my claws.

I was rooted to the spot out of confusion. I wasn't sure how I felt. My emotions seemed to be unstable—love and joy shifted and collided into anger and grief, creating new patterns. I felt as if they were spinning out of control—the patterns just kept merging and emerging. I was rage. I was love. I was sadness.

It was not entirely grief for the creatures he had slaughtered—I too had their blood on my hands, although those deaths were quieter, lives stolen in their sleep, so that I might share in their lives, so that I might dream. So that I might experience every moment with him, even though I was far away. I think back to those nights and wonder if he had seen me eating and if it had disgusted him, turned his heart against me.

I wanted to know what he thought. I wanted to twist off his head and sup at his brains. I wanted to feel his eyeballs pop in my mouth as my beak crushed them. I wanted to know how he saw me, how he saw the world. I wanted to know if there was ever love between us or if I had lived all that time as a fool.

I already knew the answer.

If only my body was as sleek as it had been before the Song Makers had arrived, I could have launched myself into the air and flown down to catch him. I cursed the Song Makers for what they had done to me. I cursed Hatupatu for making me more human during the time we had spent together—his daydreams of beautiful wāhine had made my breasts round and full, nipped in my waist, made my limbs thinner and less powerful. My bones had become ground dwelling and dense, my wings almost like those of the kiwi—remnants of flight. Now instead of gliding through the air with ease, I used my wings to boost my stride, elongating the distance between each step, coasting so that I could cover long distances without tiring.

My first step towards him crushed the miromiro into the forest floor. The spread of my toes allowed me to find traction in the slippery forest litter. I flexed my toes and pushed off as if I could take flight, flapped my wings open so that they could catch whatever breath of wind there was. I found a rhythm of wings and feet—pushing off and landing swiftly yet softly. I reserved my strength for when I was near him, for the inevitable chase.

The thought of the chase excited me. Although the time I spent with him had weakened me, I was still stronger than a mere boy. I still stood taller than him, I still had my beak and my claws. And my eyes had been opened. I could see Hatupatu for what he really was—prey. I wondered what his mind would taste like, what experiences I could render from his brain: what it is like to be a human fledgling, to spend so much time in a nest, to fall in love …

And the patterns shifted again, and I felt immense sadness. All I wanted was to hold him again, to hear his laugh, his stories. I wanted to forgive him and welcome him back to my cave, welcome him back to me. I wanted to eat the fermented berries of the karaka, gorge myself like a fat kererū and fall from the branches, oblivious. Oblivion. That would be welcome. Just the comforting void of Te Kore for a few moments, a few millennia, until the sadness seeped away. I slowed myself down to look for a tree, and my emotions shifted again. I was being ridiculous. Why should I have to suffer for the crimes of Hatupatu? He was the one that betrayed. He was a thief. He was a murderer. He killed for no good reason—not out of hunger or curiosity, but for pleasure. Did you not see through the eyes of the miromiro his smile, his triumph? It was Hatupatu that must fall into oblivion, not me.

And my resolve was physical. This thought was present in each footfall and wingbeat.

Hatupatu must pay. Hatupatu must pay. Hatupatu must pay.

But first I returned to my cave. I wanted to see it with my own eyes, as if I did not trust what miromiro had seen. I could smell the chaos before I entered the cave—the blood, the fear, the shit. All my treasures were gone—my voice strangled and discarded on the floor, all my weaving and carving taken. I took off the cloak I was wearing and piled the birds on top of it. I would be naked when I killed him, I would dare him to look at me—

Hanga kino—evil thing.

I carried the birds outside to the fire pit. I found the kaikōmako and māhoe and lit the fire. Once the flames had taken, I laid the birds and the cloak upon it. They created some smoke, but not enough. I ripped a branch from a tree and placed it on the fire. Now the smoke was good and thick, so when Hatupatu reached the ridge and turned back to look on my cave, he would see the smoke and know that I was on my way.

That I knew what he had done.

He wouldn't be able to resist that last look—to relish his triumph over me. I wanted to give him time to reach the top of the hill. I wanted his smug arrogance to turn sour in his stomach. I wanted to taste the fear in his brain. *She knows. Kurangaituku knows.*

And as I approached the ridge, I knew that he had seen my signal—along the path he had discarded the things that he had stolen. At first it was a fine cloak or two, a taiaha, perhaps just a few things that had slipped from his grip. But then he had shed more and more taonga. Once precious, now they just slowed him down.

I closed my eyes and pushed out a thought into the forest.

All the birds nearby stopped their own songs and for a second the forest was eerily quiet. And then it started—at least a couple of hundred of my strides away from where he ran, all the birds growled. The growl swept over and around me towards him. I climbed a tree as the wave washed over the ridge.

In the wake of the growl I heard him—breathing hard as he ran. I climbed down to the forest floor and followed the sound of him. He had shed the kurī skin cloak I made him. I picked it up, and I could smell his fear on it. I fastened the cloak around my neck and let it drop over my chest, out of the way of my hands and wings as I climbed to the treetops once more. I was perched on top of the tree that grew on the apex of the hill, waiting for Hatupatu to appear in the clearing down by the river. From there, from the rock that he would soon claim, he would be able to see me. I stretched my wings fully and braced myself against the wind at the top of the ridge. I imagined that if I flapped my wings I could make the boy run faster, and perhaps drive him into the river.

The bushline was thinning out. I saw Hatupatu emerge from the bush and run to the rock. I had worn him down—he was clumsy and slow. I stood tall and rigid in my pose, waiting for him to turn back.

Hatupatu sprinted to the large rock. He tripped on a tree root but recovered well, fear sharpening his reflexes. Hatupatu thought that he was hidden from me behind the rock. I could see him—limbs poking out from behind the rock. He lifted his head slowly, and I could see his top knot and then his head. I had him in my sights well before his eyes had even cleared the top of his rock. What was he thinking? Perhaps he thought he might be able to manipulate the truth again—talk, explain, apologise.

I stood on a treetop, my wings outstretched. I lowered my right arm and pulled the kurī skin cloak away from my hips.

Whakapohane.

Hanga kino.

Whare haunga.

I knew that he would see my insult. Hatupatu seemed to surrender. He stood up and bowed his head in submission. I should have taken it off his neck. I lowered the cloak and stretched my wings out again. The tree branch beneath me creaked as I bent my knees to power my take-off.

But when I landed on the rock, he wasn't there. It was impossible for him to have escaped without me noticing, but he wasn't there. I turned around on top of the rock—had he managed to burrow under the rock? Had a sinkhole appeared?

My feet could detect a slight vibration in the rock. I lay my head against the rock, and I could hear the rhythm of his heart. How could it be? How could he be inside the rock? I ran my hands over the surface of the rock looking for some crack, somewhere where Hatupatu could have squeezed himself in.

I laid his cloak on the rock, so he would know that I had been there. I climbed back up the hill and my tree and waited.

It was before dawn when Hatupatu appeared, emerging from the rock as if he had been part of it, as if he could change form as well as cheat death. I know you won't believe me—it is impossible in any reality except story. This story.

Hatupatu looked around as if he was disoriented and saw the cloak. He wrapped the cloak around himself and headed towards the river. I watched him, the white stripes of the kurī skins clearly visible in the dark. He underestimated me. Not only did he think that he was invisible, but he was walking. *Walking.* I wanted him to run. I wanted the fear of me coursing through him as I tore at his flesh.

I could feel dawn approaching. Soon, the first notes of the birds' chorus would start. I pushed the idea *quiet* around me. I wanted him to hear the unmistakable sound of my wings. Hatupatu ran, pulling the cloak up so it wouldn't tangle around his legs. He should have abandoned it again, but he wanted to arrive home with something of worth in his arms.

I slowed my pace behind him at a pass. I stretched my wings out so that my claws dragged across the rock, cutting the stone deep and honing the edges of my claws. Hatupatu was running on pure fear now. I could smell it on him.

Hatupatu could not resist looking back. I was close enough to grab him, but I wanted to make the chase last longer. I swiped at his face, cutting him, striping his cheek with four rows of blood and nicking the cornea of his right eye. I had marked Hatupatu, given him the tā moko he so dearly wanted. I had forced him to take responsibility. His face would bear our history for the rest of his life.

The next time I would take his throat, I'd rip his voice from his body so he couldn't say my name ever again.

He was dead. He knew this. Still he ran. I think Hatupatu wanted to die at home, on his land. The earth beneath him warmed up as he ran closer to his home. As the sun came up, the mist from the mud pools and dew also rose. The cloak was tugging at his shoulders—he held the ties together in his hand as he ran. One final leap over the mud pool Te Homo and he would be home. I would kill him then. As he leapt over the pool, he let the ties in his hand go. The cloak floated down and spread itself across the pool beneath him. Hatupatu landed clear of the mud pool and turned around to face me for the last time. I walked slowly through the mist and stopped on the other side of the pool. For a moment, we looked across the mist at each other, Hatupatu and Kurangaituku.

Blood

ran down

his face.

And yet, he lifted his chin to look at me. Defiant, as always.

I cocked my head to the side and looked down at the cloak. As I bent down, the ground beneath me gave way and I fell into the pool. The dawn chorus started that morning with a scream.

I was present for every moment of my demise. Although how I am obliged to describe it here will make you think that each step was discrete, that I had some sort of respite between my skin peeling off and my organs bursting within. The experience of it was not the neat list that follows—it was pain upon pain, overlapping or simultaneous. If you had fallen into the mud pool, I expect you would feel part of my pain, perhaps the searing of your skin and the curious sensation of your muscles stilled as they cooked. The overwhelming pain would offer you escape, you would pass out before your body was torn apart. I did not.

I was present when my eyes popped out and brain turned into puddles that ran down the raw muscle of my face. I felt each cell in my muscles swell and burst, each fibre of flesh strip from my bones as it cooked in the heat of the mud. When the flesh was gone, I felt the crack of my bones and my liquefied marrow seep out. It was pain quite unlike any other I had experienced in that body, and I collected and curated it. If death had finally come to me, I wanted to experience all of it.

The last thing I heard—the birds around me voicing my screams.

The last thing I saw—Hatupatu smiling at me.

The last thing I felt—the cell walls within me exploding.

And then—nothing.

... no Death, but Life
Augmented ...

John Milton, *Paradise Lost*, Book IX

TE WĀ NGARO

HATUPATU
AND THE
BIRD-WOMAN

This is the story that is told. It is the story of a young hero named Hatupatu and his encounter with a villainous monster, the bird-woman, Kura of the claws. It has been told so many times and by so many—each voice a thin thread on its own, but plied together they are a thick rope, resilient enough to slow even the sun. Strong enough to bind a monster in her place, perhaps forever.

The story begins in summer. The season had been mild, and the karaka, matai and miro were all fat with fruit. The kererū did not announce their presence with song; instead, the forest was filled with the sound of their wings—the soft boom as they flew from tree to tree. Brothers Hanui and Haroa had noticed the plentiful fruit as well. Both were skilled fowlers and had kept an eye on the fruiting trees in the hunting grounds that they had claimed that summer. They were excited. The last hunt at the beginning of summer, when the tūī and kākā were feeding on nectar, seemed so long ago; the brothers had the itch to go out and hunt again. They'd been waiting for the perfect conditions, relishing the planning and strategy that goes into an expedition, trying not to think of the disappointment if the plan goes awry or the elation in success. The two brothers had spent much time together in the whare mata during the hot days of summer, preparing their snares from the tough leaves of the tī.

Hatupatu was a stranger to the whare mata. He was only a few years younger than his brothers, but they were at the age when even a year seems to be a huge gap. Hatupatu had tried to follow them into the whare mata many times, but Hanui would block his way, and Haroa would say, 'Children belong outside with the women.'

Hanui and Haroa had already endured their tā moko—the mantle of adulthood chiselled into their skin. There had already been matches discussed with eligible women, families on both sides searching for desirability of allegiances as well as the young people's physical desire for one another. This would be their last hunt as brothers only; next autumn they would be husbands and, probably, fathers, just like their elder brother, Karika. The thought of their future made them excited and scared at the same time—a feeling akin to that of the hunt itself. The brothers wanted to relish this time that they had left together. They enjoyed each other's company and made a formidable hunting team, anticipating each other's movements in the forest.

They knew that one day they'd have to take their younger brother, Hatupatu, with them and that they'd have to bring him into the whare mata and teach him how to make snares and sharpen spears. But Hatupatu was such a *child*, and the brothers did not want the responsibility of looking after him—not now in the last moments of their own freedom. They would be parents soon enough.

But Hatupatu insisted. To the eyes of his brothers, he had stamped his feet and whined as he had done as a toddler and as they had done those many years ago. But their parents indulged their pōtiki, Hatupatu, and so it was that he would join his brothers' hunt for kererū.

Hanui and Haroa loved their brother; he had a great sense of humour and could find a way to make them laugh even in the most sombre situations. Hatupatu was a good storyteller,

he had a particularly strong imagination, so he was able to spin an old boring story into something new. He had a sweet voice, as sweet as the korimako that sang in the forest. Their parents had sacrificed a bird for each of their sons, but in Hatupatu it seemed as if the korimako had been reborn in his body. He was a formidable orator, twining his imagination and voice together to charm his audience, for the sweetest voice must be supported by a supple mind. The gift of oratory would be hollow without the ability to think on your feet and manipulate words to suit your purpose. But this gift left him as susceptible to stories as they were to him. As much as they loved their brother, Hanui and Haroa resented him too. Hatupatu was indulged as the youngest; he did not have the same chores that his brothers had. He did not have the same drive. He manipulated every situation, every person, to suit himself. It seemed to the brothers that they were struggling through life as though it was the thick undergrowth of the forest, suffering the scrapes of low branches as they cut their path through, and all Hatupatu had to do was follow behind them on the path that they had forged.

Worse, Hatupatu was a fast learner, and the brothers knew that he would quickly master the skills of the hunt and surpass them. And then what would they have to distinguish themselves?

They did not have to talk about it between them; Hanui and Haroa made a great team because they anticipated each other's thoughts and movements. They did not expressly agree to teach their brother humility, to show Hatupatu how sheltered he was. They just knew what they would do. And so, as the three

brothers disappeared from view of their parents' home, Hanui and Haroa loaded their bedrolls and the hue to store their catch onto their brother's back. The complaints of Hatupatu were met with laughter and slaps. Even the kurī, Moko and Tū, belonging to Hanui and Haroa, seemed to be in on it—their mouths pulled open, their tongues lolling over their canines as if they were grinning along with their masters' joke on Hatupatu. Although it was no joke. As the journey wore on and Hatupatu finally held his tongue, Hanui and Haroa congratulated themselves on the lesson that their brother had learnt—respect your elders.

But all Hatupatu had learnt was that resentment can fester beneath a placid exterior. That revenge can be exacted away from the prying eyes of those in power.

When they reached camp, their lessons for Hatupatu continued. While his brothers sat and ate the sweet dried kūmara that their mother had prepared and packed for their first night together as three in the forest, Hatupatu prepared their camp and found firewood. When he finally had a good fire going, it was dark, and the kūmara was gone. He asked for food, and a slap was the answer. Hatupatu was determined not to cry in front of his brothers. It was not the pain of the slap, although no one had ever raised a hand to him in his life; it was the shame of it—being treated by his own kin, his own brothers, as if he was a slave. He went to sleep that night with hunger and resentment gnawing at his belly.

Hatupatu knew that he was more than what they thought of him; he knew he had a place in history. He held the word *destiny* in his

mind. It was his sacred kupu. Every slight and smart was deflected by that word. It was that word that kept him going. He held onto it so tightly that it penetrated his flesh; it became part of him.

When he woke the next morning, the sun was already in the sky, and his brothers had left the camp. They had made camp in a clearing at least a couple of hours' walk from the hunting grounds—far enough away that they would not jeopardise the hunt by tainting the forest with cooked food. Hatupatu felt he was exactly between the forest and home; it would be easy to pack up his sleeping roll now and head for his village. Perhaps that is what his brothers had hoped he would do, and that thought made his mouth taste more sour than it already did from hunger. No, Hatupatu would stay. He would not run home to his mother like a child. He had a destiny to fulfil.

He tidied the campsite and found more firewood ready for that evening. Would this be how he spent his time on the hunt— excluded by his brothers, reduced to the work of women and slaves? He hoped it was just a test, and if he performed his role without complaint, without fault, his brothers would eventually see his worth. If he acted as a man, they would have to treat him as such. And if he acted as a child ...

But the child felt natural to him. The child wanted to scream and cry that this was unfair. The child was hungry and bored. The child was used to getting his own way.

Hatupatu tried to quiet the child by walking in the forest. He was still unsure of his surroundings, so he walked out from the campsite in a straight line into the dark of the canopy and sat for a

while when he felt tired. The dark of the forest offered no comfort to him. At times, it felt as if he would never catch his breath; the things that lurked in the shadows stole it from him. So, he was on his feet before his brow had fully cooled, before the sweat had ceased to roll down his back. His shins hurt, and it felt as if his ankles would snap beneath him as he followed his line back to camp as quickly as he could. In the light of the clearing, he felt foolish; his imagination had got the better of him in the dark, and he had thought he felt monsters when he knew that none existed. Worse, if his brothers knew that he had cowered in the forest like a baby, they would never teach him to hunt. The light emboldened him, and he resolved that he would explore the forest again, and he would make himself strong so that when his brothers finally took him with them, it would be as an equal. He would earn their respect and take their abuse with good humour. They were testing him. It was part of growing up and being one of them.

He would ready a fire for his brothers' return. He would find tī leaves in case they needed to repair their snares. He would clean and prepare whatever they had caught for their meal and for their store. He would accept whatever scrap of food or knowledge that would come his way. He would be stoic. He would endure.

Hanui and Haroa came back to their camp with their catch dangling from their hands: good, fat kererū that would store well and keep their whānau fed during winter's approaching days. A good hunt with plentiful, fat birds meant that they could secure their marriages. It proved that they were worthy men able to provide for their new wives and their families. And they were, although it is

tempting in this story to paint them as entirely heartless—as men who did not care for family. But they did care. They cared deeply for their whānau, especially their hōhā little brother, Hatupatu, which makes their actions against him a tragedy and something that would scar them more than they would think was possible.

But for now, the brothers felt pleased with themselves. They had had a good day snaring kererū, their camp was clean and tidy, a fire had already been laid, and their brother seemed to have accepted their authority.

Hatupatu took the kererū without complaint and strung the carcasses from their feet as his brothers instructed him to. Haroa cut the throat of the first bird to show their young brother how to bleed the catch. The blood came slowly; it had settled in the bodies during the day as they rested in a shallow trench while the brothers continued their hunt. Haroa thought that perhaps when Hatupatu had learnt sufficient respect, they could take him into the forest, and he could take the still-warm bodies from the grounds to the campsite to bleed them fresh. It made Haroa laugh to think of his haughty young brother running back and forth like a trained kurī. He bit his lip so that he wouldn't call out *Moi* to bring the dogs and his young brother to heel.

The kurī were getting under his feet as Hatupatu slit the throats of the birds. The dogs were lapping at the blood that dripped on the soil. The drips of blood stained the white head and muzzle of Moko, while it disappeared entirely into the black fur of Tū. The kurī would be the only ones feeding from the birds tonight. The brothers told Hatupatu that the birds would need

to hang for a day or so before they could be cooked or stored. Hatupatu would clean them tonight of their feathers and guts. They would all need to wait to eat their flesh.

Hatupatu plucked the birds and kept their feathers in a big pile. He thought that he would take them with him and make a gift of them to his mother. Perhaps she would weave him a kākāhu so that he would remember his first hunt. He would let these feathers cover him in a lie: that he had found success as a hunter, that his brothers let him into their fold. He would let these feathers envelop the truth, and by and by, the story would overtake the reality.

Haroa kicked dirt over the pile Hatupatu had made—the dirt marring the pure white of the breast feathers of the kererū.

'These must be kept from sight,' Haroa said. 'It will ruin the hunt if the birds see these feathers. They will flee, and our stores will be bare. Dig a trench.'

And so, his brother meant to deny Hatupatu even this— his version of reality. Hatupatu dug the trench as he was told, and he laid leaves over the top of the feathers. They would be hidden from the sight of the birds but clean enough to take home with him.

The kurī feasted on the entrails of the day's hunt, slurping in unison so that it seemed that they were just one giant black and white dog—the giant dog with two heads that people from the south told tales of. That dog would slurp the guts from humans as happily as these ate those of birds. The dogs were also given the heads of the birds—their powerful jaws crunching the skulls and mincing the meat and brains together.

After the dogs had finished their meal, they lay down next to the fire. Out here, the kurī were more valuable than Hatupatu was to his brothers. These two dogs were his brothers' favourites and skilled at hunting kiwi although they wouldn't be hunting for those birds this time. The dogs had strong, broad shoulders and stubby legs. They could chase a kiwi a short distance if it managed to escape from them. The two dogs worked together seamlessly, each anticipating the other's movements and their masters' movements too. The dogs were like the brothers' shadows, like an extension of the brothers' will. Both kurī had sired many pups. Those that showed the same aptitude as their fathers were kept and the others made fine meals, the meaty musculature being inherited by both the talented hunters and those that were not. Hatupatu hoped for a pup from one of these dogs, but their progeny were in great demand. If he asked his brothers now for a pup, they would probably give him the runt with no hope of ever being a great hunter. Much like its master.

Hatupatu patted the back leg of the black kurī, Tū. It lifted its head to Hatupatu in acknowledgement and then closed its eyes again. The dog's bushy tail thumped against his leg. It felt like this dog was his only friend although he was sure it would turn on him at its master's bidding.

Hanui and Haroa were content to let their brother be this evening. He seemed to be complying with them, obeying their orders and keeping the camp clean and well stocked. It had been the same way when they had been on their first hunt with their elder brother, Karika. It was probably the same for him when he

learnt to hunt from his uncles, who were only a few years older than him, and when the uncles had learnt from their father. It was just the way young hunters learnt; they started with the menial tasks until they could be trusted with the more complex. They learnt every part of the hunt, the rituals and the traditions. They learnt the hard work and the gnawing hunger so that this life would not be a shock to their system. Although it was less of a shock to Hanui and Haroa, they had never been as indulged as their young brother. They didn't expect to be taken to the hunt when they insisted they were ready. They waited until they were told they were ready, and then they accepted whatever role they were given.

Hatupatu seemed to understand that now. The complaints he had had the day before had stopped. He was a quick learner; they gave him that much. It had only taken a few slaps for him to know his place. Although it hurt them to raise a hand to their brother, it was better that he was slapped by them than incur the wrath of a spirit, or worse an atua, if he blundered in the forest. The forest was a dangerous place, and Hatupatu could be a rash, hot-headed boy; it was not just that he could get himself in trouble if he trampled on the rituals of the hunt, but he was also likely to get his whole village in trouble. At best, he would incur a lean hunt, and his family would have to survive on aruhe alone. At worst, an angry god could lay waste to the entire settlement or curse them for generations to come.

Was this why the brothers were moved to tell a story of the forest? A story designed to keep Hatupatu tethered to the camp

where he would be safe from the creatures lurking in the shadows for a young boy to steal and consume. They told their story as Hatupatu cleaned the birds. The limp bodies of the birds, their viscera and the drip, drip of their blood became tied up with the words of the story. The words became as bloodstained as the white head and muzzle of the kurī Moko. Hatupatu could not help but think of himself strung by the feet like the kererū—throat slit and bleeding out. But who would feast on his flesh? What creature lurked in the shadows? What terrible creature?

A giant, a monster, an ogress. The bird-woman, Kurangaituku. A hum of recognition.

She was a predator, hungering not only for the flesh of the birds but also for the flesh of men. She ripped the meat, raw and dripping with blood, from the birds with her terrible beak, feasted upon their guts and dreamt of the taste of human flesh. Those who had seen her and lived described her as a giant kōtuku. *He kōtuku rerenga tahi.* Her presence even corrupts the whakataukī, for, indeed, she was a rare sight, but not one that was welcomed.

She was unnatural—part bird, part woman. There were tales of hunters who had glimpsed her in the shadows of the forest, had seen her breasts and smooth belly as white as the face of te marama, and she had aroused more than fear.

Hanui and Haroa told their story to Hatupatu not really believing the creature their words created. They had been told the story too when they were his age, but in the years that they had been hunting here, they had not seen her. Besides, stories like this were warnings to the young, and they were about to become men and leave such fantasy behind.

Hanui and Haroa may not have believed their story, but Hatupatu did. He had felt a presence when he had walked into the forest earlier that day. There was a kind of unease in his bowels and the need to get out of the forest as soon as possible. He could not help but admire his brothers, who walked into that forest every season, who risked their lives to feed the family. He wanted to be such a man himself—able to conquer the fear that clenched at his belly.

The next day, his brothers left him alone again at camp. This time, Hatupatu had been awake when they stirred before dawn. He pretended to be asleep, and he watched which path his brothers chose, their kurī trotting beside them. Hatupatu had stayed up all night so that he could catch this moment and follow his brothers into the forest. The excitement that had kept him awake all night was waning. He was tired. Hatupatu lay on his bedroll after his brothers had left and listened to the dawn chorus. He closed his eyes for a minute, and when he opened them again, the sun was already high in the sky. Hatupatu rushed to tidy the camp as he had done the day before. He found the path his brothers had chosen hours ago and decided to follow it for as long as his nerves would allow.

Hatupatu was not sure what he was more afraid of—the bird-woman or his brothers finding him. It was probably his brothers that worried him more. The bird-woman may torture and kill him, but that would be quick. His brothers would eke out his punishment for the rest of his life. He hoped that he could sneak up on his brothers, to watch them hunt and then steal back to the camp before they noticed him.

He heard a kurī howl deep in the forest. Even though it was a familiar sound, there, in the forest shadows, it fed his fear. The story from last night, the looming trees and images of slit throats and dripping blood had coloured the howl. It made him question whether it had come from one of his brothers' beloved kurī. Why was its howl so melancholy? Had one of his brothers, or both, been caught by the giant bird-woman? Was she feeding their dogs with their guts and blood? Would she let one hang for a couple of days to feast on immediately while preserving the other in his own fat for her winter meals?

Kurangaituku lurked on the edge of his mind. Hatupatu saw her in every shadow, every twig break, every bird call. He knew that a brave man would forge forward, that a hero would come to his brothers' aid. But fear had made his feet unresponsive to his mind. His body rebelled against his will, and he was surprised and relieved to find himself rushing back to the campsite.

He told himself that it was just a story, as if a story was something frivolous. But he knew the power of story. He had used it to shape reality; he had used it to manipulate his parents to make them send him on this hunt with his brothers.

It is just a story.

Hatupatu sank down, lying his head on the ground like a child to his mother's breast. He listened to the earth, hoping to hear the heartbeat of Papatūānuku, but he could only hear his own heart. He closed his eyes to quiet his panic, but every time he did, he saw his brothers strung up in trees, their necks snapped

from the snares that the ogress caught them in. All he could hear was the drip of their blood and the kurī lapping …

And then, he could feel it—the soft tongue of a dog licking his cheek. Hatupatu opened his eyes to see the white kurī and his brother Haroa standing above him. He didn't realise how tense all his muscles had been, and now that they had relaxed, he felt light and giddy. He smiled at Haroa with relief.

'Get up you lazy hua.'

Haroa threw his catch at his little brother, who kept grinning at him. What was wrong with the boy—taking a nap when he and Hanui had been working since before sun-up? And then the kid had the gall to grin at him. Haroa gave Hatupatu a little kick in the stomach, but he still smiled, and, more disturbingly, seemed to be grateful for it.

'Get the fires started. We're hungry.'

And Hatupatu started a fire for his brothers. Haroa felt they should have been glad that he was doing what he was told, but something about it seemed wrong. Like the boy was up to something.

Hanui and Haroa feasted on the roasted kererū. They threw the meaty bones to their kurī even though the dogs had already gorged on the viscera and heads of the catch. What was left of the birds, what meat they deemed not worthy of their dogs, was given to their brother. Hatupatu ate without complaint, breaking the bones in the hope of finding a little marrow to sup on.

The brothers did not mean this diet as a punishment, nor entirely an insult. It was meant to teach the boy how to live

off bones and will alone. But although Hatupatu was glad his brothers were not dead, he could not take their treatment of him in any other way than punishment and insult.

Hanui and Haroa tasked Hatupatu with preserving their catch. They showed him how to render the fat from the kererū and how to pack its body into the hue. They showed him how to pour the fat over the bird so that the air would not spoil it. The task was sure to keep the boy busy during the day and keep him from mischief. And when they left the next day, Hatupatu was diligent: heating the birds slowly and packing them carefully before smothering them with their hot fat. Hatupatu worked despite his grumbling stomach, daring not to taste the roasting meat in case he could not control his hunger. He didn't want to disappoint his brothers; he still thought that they would relent and welcome him to the hunt soon.

When his brothers returned, the birds were stored, the camp was clean and dinner awaited them. Surely now, Hatupatu had shown them that he was humble; surely now, he had earned a meal. But his brothers yet again fed him the scraps not fit for their kurī. They thought that the silence from Hatupatu was subservience, but, in reality, it was resentment. It was the seed of revenge germinating inside him.

It had been almost a week since Hatupatu had eaten a decent meal. The hunger kept him awake at night and slowed his movements during the day. It made every part of him ache, like the hunger was eating his body from within, and it was. The worst part was that he was surrounded by food: the birds hanging to age and the birds

stored in fat. He could smell their delicious flesh on him; his pores seemed to seep with their fat. Hatupatu licked his arm and thought he could taste the birds, so he sucked on his forearm, raising his blood to the skin, which left him with round bruises on his arms.

Was it the bruises or the birds that sparked the idea? Was Hatupatu overcome by his mortal hunger so that he acted without thought—gorging himself on the birds until he came to his senses and had to find a way to cover his mistake? Or did he carefully plan it, plotting his story before ripping the sweet flesh with his teeth, letting the juice and fat from the bird coat his chin?

His story demanded sacrifice to live, so, like Māui who used his own blood for bait, Hatupatu cracked a calabash across his face, bruising his cheek and bloodying his nose. He wrestled with invisible foes, kicking dirt on the sleeping mats, pulling hair from his own head and finally he dropped, exhausted by his own exertions. His brothers were sure to believe his story. They would believe that the sky was below and the earth was above if Hatupatu told them so. Hanui and Haroa were very foolish men.

In the story that is told, his brothers find him and believe that he has been set upon and that he did his best to fight the assailants. A taua, a war party en route to a battle, had happened upon the campsite and had overcome the boy easily. Faced with such fearsome warriors, it was a miracle that Hatupatu was alive at all. In the story that is told, his brothers believed him again and again and again. In the story that is told, his brothers are finally suspicious, and one doubles back after they set out for the hunt and sees Hatupatu laughing at the foolishness of his brothers.

But these were brothers—brothers who had shared a nest, who had grown together, who had fledged together. They knew each other's faces better than their own. They knew what their younger brother was like. They questioned the story Hatupatu told, and the usually quick wit of Hatupatu failed him.

'Why didn't we see the taua?'

'The warriors have left no trail. Are they spirits and not men? There's not a single broken twig on the path.'

'Why did they spare you, brother?'

'Why do you look so smug?'

And so, in this story I tell you, the brothers of Hatupatu knew who had eaten their hard-won stores and knew who had bloodied their brother's nose and sullied their sleeping mats. Hatupatu does not laugh at his brothers' foolishness but will rue his own if he ever regains consciousness.

Hanui and Haroa did not understand why they had flown into such a rage. Perhaps it was the flimsy story their brother had come up with—that he thought them so gullible that they'd believe him. Perhaps it was because Hatupatu, despite his bloodied nose and bruising, had a smug look on his face when he told them what had 'happened'. Perhaps it was years of resentment spilling over in a few minutes. It was like they had no control over themselves. It was like they weren't even present. It was like they were listening to a story, witnessing strangers punching and kicking their brother. Even their own dogs had not recognised them and had retreated into the bush nearby, safe from the anger of their masters.

They could have let it go; the boy had only eaten a few birds, and they could have easily been replaced. He was probably sick to his stomach from gorging himself after his fast. But that strange spirit that seemed to have taken hold of them—the idea that Hatupatu must learn a lesson—moved them to punish their brother severely. And they succumbed to it, letting it possess their hands and feet and blind them to the sight of their beloved brother curled up under their blows.

The spirit that seemed to suddenly take over Hanui and Haroa left their bodies as quickly as it had arrived. The brothers recoiled from the body of Hatupatu as if they were repelled by some shift in magnetism. They sat down, panting from the exertion of the beating. The pleasure they had felt in dealing the blows had changed into deep shame. The bruises on the body and the blood on their hands were sure to condemn this hunt. They had broken the sacredness of this place by spilling the blood of Hatupatu. They would have to pack up in the morning, carry their brother home and admit to their whānau what they had done. They had sacrificed plentiful stores for the sake of a few birds. They had shown themselves to be little more than boys—unable to control their feelings of jealousy and rage. They had proved themselves unworthy to take on the mantle of adulthood. Their marriages would be delayed; their lives would be on hold. And worst, Hatupatu would have this to lord over them; he would milk every opportunity and all the sympathy that his injuries would afford him.

Hatupatu hadn't moved. Hanui caught the eye of Haroa, and Haroa moved closer to their little brother, their baby brother,

their beloved brother. The hand of Haroa hovered over Hatupatu. He was afraid that touching him would set off the rage again. Hanui moved in close to Hatupatu. He lay down so that his face was level with his little brother's, so that he could feel the breath of Hatupatu.

The face of Hatupatu was almost unrecognisable. His eyes and lips were swollen, and blood was shining on his cheeks and chin. Hanui felt no breath from his brother. He scrambled up, backing away from the boy's body. Haroa looked at Hanui in confusion and, finally, laid his hands on Hatupatu. He could feel no heartbeat; he could feel no breath.

Hidden in the bush, the kurī heard their masters' howl and replied with their own: *auau, auau, auau!*

Hanui and Haroa spent the night watching over their brother. Neither had moved him, not wanting to feel his lifeless body in their hands. Their kurī eventually crawled from the forest to sit with their masters. The black dog lay on the feet of Haroa. Haroa dug his toes into the thick fur, and each beat of the animal's heart made him feel sick, reminding him of his guilt. The sun rose, revealing the injuries wrought upon Hatupatu, and Hanui and Haroa wept for their brother again. They could not leave him that way. They needed to clean him, make him look as best they could for the journey home.

They tried to swaddle Hatupatu in his sleeping mat as if he was an infant. But Hatupatu was as stubborn in death as he had been in life. His limbs refused to move. He was frozen in the position he had died as if he continued to tell a story even if his spirit had left him.

Was it Hanui or Haroa who came up with the idea—the futility of bringing their brother's body home, of condemning themselves? Would their mother's grief be lessened by their admission of guilt? Or would she just lose three of her four sons, instead of just one?

Hatupatu had already given them the base of a story: the marauding taua that had robbed the brothers' campsite. In the story that Hanui and Haroa hatch, their young brother was set upon by a war party and killed; there was too much blood at the campsite for their brother to have survived with the little training that he had.

Yes, they were far away from camp when it happened; had they been there ... had they been there ...

The body must have been dragged away somewhere. They searched and searched but could not find Hatupatu. They wanted to bring him home, to have his bones rest with those of his ancestors, but they could not find him.

They could not find Hatupatu bundled in sleeping mats, lowered into the trench that he had himself dug and cloaked in the discarded feathers of his first hunt. So it was that Hatupatu would indeed be cloaked in the feathers of his first hunt. The brothers covered the trench with leaf litter to hide it from their eyes as they packed up the campsite. But the dogs sniffed the grave, so the brothers tied them up away from the trench until they could leave the campsite for good. The kurī stood with their heads lowered, shoulders hunched and their tails between their legs.

As they broke camp, Hanui and Haroa told each other the story again and again. They told each other the story as they headed off along the track home, and by the time they told their parents the story, it felt as if it was true.

`Hatupatu is left for dead.`

`End of story.`

At least, for most mortals. But Hatupatu ceased to be mortal long ago—dust to dust—as people are fond of saying. From your point of view, he is more akin to me than to you—a creature made up of words, thought and memory. He is no longer a man of skin, blood and viscera, but a character—mortal bones fleshed in myth.

Thus, in this story, the end of Hatupatu is really a beginning. His life until this point is a prelude, an introduction full of foreshadowing.

I am dead.

Am I dead?

`Te Pō, the darkness, is complete, oppressive.`

`The beginning and the end. Here you do not feel; you are. A thing, a nothing at once. Underneath the darkness, through the darkness, a hum. Is it potential —the start of something so huge that it will crackle through time as static on airwaves?`

`Te Pō—in the darkness listen for the hum …`

`The thing in the nothing, it is attractive; it has gravity. It is gravity, all gravity in a single point. In space. In time.`

And still the hum, the buzz of something. What was it? Perhaps Tamumukiterangi is buzzing at your ear, carrying a spirit to burrow into you instead of its maggots—the tiny life that depends on death.

Te Pō, the darkness that arcs inevitably back to light …

… and as Hatupatu opened his eyes, his mouth filled with downy feathers, and his reclaimed breath was marked by the white wisps of them as he cough coughed.

He touched his face, his limbs, his heart—still smarting from the beating, but there, pulsing with life. Hatupatu hauled himself out of the trench. Everything in his body hurt; his limbs felt stiff, and he wondered if he had slept for such a long time that he had become an old man. The campsite was empty: not just of his brothers but of everything. Why would Hanui and Haroa take their sleeping mats with them on the hunt? Why would they take the stores that were left? It was as if they had packed up and left for home, but why would they leave in the middle of the hunt? Why would they leave him behind?

Hatupatu wandered around, trying to create the scene in his mind. Here is where he had cleaned the birds, and here is where his brothers had slept. Or was it nearer to the fire pit? Where had the fire pit gone? He was sure that it had been in the centre, but there was no sign of it. The gathered wood had gone, the ashes buried. How had the world changed so quickly? What had happened to him? Why had he woken in the trench, covered in feathers? He had dreamt of Te Pō. It must have been a dream

because the only explanation is not possible. Why had he been in Te Pō? No one could visit Te Pō, only the ...

And he remembered the words that came to him in the dark, the words that seemed to define him, the words that seemed to be true:

I am dead.

Am I dead?

But now, he was back. He had escaped the embrace of Hinenuitepō, at least for now. How long was he in Te Pō? He looked for his brothers, unsure if he was wanting comfort or revenge. In the darkness things had been simple—there was no want where everything was nothing. Awake and alive, want was over-whelming—his throat was dry, his belly was empty, his bowels were full.

But the want was reassuring; it meant that he was alive. He was not some disembodied kēhua roaming the forest. But was he still a human? Even the demi-god Māui could not cheat Hinenuitepō. His heart raced. Hatupatu couldn't believe he had dared to think such a thing—that he could be ...

The cramps in his stomach cut the thought from his mind. He was human, he was sure, and he was alive. Hatupatu squatted where his brothers had laid their sleeping mats, where their heads had lain, and strained—his tūtae slow to move at first. He pushed harder, and he felt his skin tear, but at last it was loose, and his sigh was one of pain, relief and pleasure. Hatupatu held the back of his hand to his nose; the smell was overwhelming—like the shit had rotted for days in his bowels. Hatupatu stood and looked

at it. He smirked; the stinking black mess looked so much like his brothers. He didn't even bother kicking dirt over it.

His brothers had left no water or food. He smacked his swollen lips together to try and work up some saliva, but this opened the split in his bottom lip that had been fused with blood and down. He needed to drink. He needed to eat. He found a stick that had been honed, perhaps by one of his brothers, and he thought that with enough force it would pierce a bird's breast. Hatupatu took it and walked into the forest.

The hunger he could live with a while longer, but thirst was making his head muddy and his vision blurry. In a cool spot under a tree, he dug handfuls of moss from the forest floor and sucked on its moisture; it tasted earthy but was as welcome as any clear stream water. He grabbed another handful of moss, squeezed it and licked the moisture from his knuckles. He hoped that in slaking his thirst he'd staunch his strange thoughts of Te Pō. This world was the real one; of course he was human, of course he was saved. It wasn't his destiny to lie in a shallow grave, for his bones to be lost to his whānau. Defying death proved he was a hero.

Hatupatu was buoyed by the thought. A hero such as he would not die from starvation in the forest. He assumed that he must have an innate ability to hunt; all heroes are skilled in hunting and war—even if their spears are dull.

Light filtered through the leaves of the forest, making it gloomy but never completely dark. Occasionally, bigger pools of light were cast through gaps in the canopy made by fallen branches

or an entire tree. There was activity all around Hatupatu. Birds chattered and sung above him; behind him, pīwakawaka squeaked as they ate the midges disturbed by his footfall. Hatupatu tried not to think of Hinenuitepō, but the pīwakawaka kept reminding him of the story of her and Māui. The little bird had squeaked, and Māui was cut in two by the granite lined labia of Hinenuitepō, his legs crushed between hers, his head stuck within her. Hatupatu tried to banish thoughts of his own death from this journey, but the pīwakawaka just laughed at his foolishness.

It was the timelessness of the place that reminded him of Te Pō. He could have been walking a few minutes or a few hours; he couldn't tell. At home, it was easy to tell where the sun was—how much light there was left in the day. In the forest, the night could sneak up and snare him in its darkness. The timelessness went beyond the hours of the day; it seemed to Hatupatu that he could have been walking in this forest at any point in time. The forest was largely unchanged from when his grandfather had been alive and would remain so when Hatupatu had grandchildren of his own. Hatupatu thought that there would always be this forest, that there would always be birds to hunt, that this experience would be shared across generations.

In a way he was right, but not in the way that he thought.

Hatupatu found karaka seedlings. Their fruit was ripe, but he doubted whether their branches could take the weight of a fat kererū. Nearby, though, there were mature pūriri and tawa, and both were ripe with fruit and heavy with birds. He could hear the

whum whum of the wings of the kererū as they moved from branch to branch.

When the fruit was overripe and fermented, the birds were fat and slow, and some fell, drunk, from the trees. Hatupatu had no time to wait for a bird to fall from above. Squinting into the canopy, he saw the white breast feathers glinting in the green. He drew the spear up over his shoulder, used his other arm as a guide to his target and threw his stick with all the force left in his body; his bruises screamed with the effort. But Hatupatu was inexperienced; his spear fell short again and again. He wondered if he was a hero after all.

Hatupatu would not allow himself to be defeated. He continued to stalk the birds, tasting the memory of their sweet meat, but memory did not satisfy. Being so focused on the fat pigeons, he was oblivious to the rest of the forest—the pīwakawaka that still followed behind him and the creature that also hunted kererū.

He would catch a kererū. He would not die starving in the forest. Destiny was his sacred kupu. And he had held it so tightly that it had penetrated his flesh, become part of him.

We turn to his destiny, then. To ours.

A kererū swooped down from the canopy to a bush near where Hatupatu waited. Near where I waited although at this time neither Hatupatu nor I were aware of each other; we were both focused on the bird. The kererū kept feeding, out of necessity not greed—winter would soon strip the forest of food. It seemed impossible its wings could support that expansive breast. Hatupatu didn't have the skill to spear the birds above him, but

perhaps he had enough to spear one at eye level. He could hold on to the spear instead of throwing it, ramming the point through the bird. He had hoped that he could leave the first bird as an offering to Tāne Mahuta, but it seemed unlikely he would catch more than one, if, indeed, he managed to catch one at all. He would make his peace with the god later.

Should he plant his feet or keep them light, balancing on the balls of his feet like his mau rākau kaiako taught him? The pain in his calves decided it for him. He would save his strength for the lunge forward. Hatupatu breathed in as deeply as his bruised ribs allowed, trying to slow his heart and steady his hand. And then he thrust his spear and it connected.

With me.

TE WHAIAO

Though we have been separated by life, by death, by time, our wairua are bound. Two bodies of water intermingled, flowing as one. Flowing through time, through life, through death and, I allow myself to believe, love.

But is love so neglectful, so forgetful? I am consumed by you. Take everything from me, I give it freely.

`Here is my hupe.`

`Here are my roimata.`

`Here is my toto.`

But you are like a rock—unmovable. I must contort myself around the thought of you.

Can you see me now before you? A bird, a woman, a bird-woman. I opened myself up to the story; it and I are no longer separate. I have shaped it and it has shaped me. The down on my breast and belly gave way to skin. Naked from clavicle to pubis, I am exposed. I've made my heart vulnerable. The pain I feel is exquisite and overwhelming—it pulsates in time with my heart.

Am I hideous or beautiful to you? How do you see me?

`This monster.`

`This giant.`

`This ogress.`

I searched for you in the forest, lost amongst the trees. Lost amongst time. Let me wrap you in this kākahu, let me wrap you up in the world—everything here I have made for you.

My love.

My story.

Me.

I plucked my eye from its socket to give to you as a gift. A black sphere, almost perfectly round. It sat in your palm, your fingers cradling it so it did not fall. It looked like a pebble pulled from a river—glossy obsidian, with flecks of white, as if the night sky has been captured within it. Through it you have seen everything— the black, the dark, the nothingness.

You have seen the world as I have through my story. Picture me now. How do I look to you? How has your mind shaped me as I told my story? Do you recognise me as kin, calling me down from above and giving me form? Am I a mirror to you? Do you see yourself reflected in my eyes?

He kōtuku kai whakaata—a kōtuku that feeds upon its reflection.

I have fed upon you. I did not need to trap you, to sup on your mind through violence—physical or psychic—all I had to do was extend my hand to you in invitation. I opened my mind to you, and you reciprocated. I will see the world as you do.

But that is an illusion, a game we all play—the idea that any of us can truly understand what it is like to be another. That we can look upon the world with another's eyes. Even when I looked through the eyes of miromiro, I could never be fully submerged in that reality for I was always there. His mind in my mouth was never truly his.

Just as this story was never truly mine. It can only ever exist in the space between us.

It lived in the telling.

I lived in the telling.

This is me. This giant. This monster. This ogress. Through these pages, through these words, I have lived. I have ceased to be the words on this page and have become a real being, making her nest in your brain. I will lurk in the shadows of your mind—you will recall my form as your brain connects one event to another, beginning, middle and end. Each time I flash before your eyes, like the flit of a pīwakawaka following behind your steps in the forest, I grow stronger, more real. Every time you think of me, you speak of me, I become more real. Flesh and blood because you will me to be.

Through these words, these shapes drawn roughly on the ground, I whisper to you. I have borrowed your voice; I am clothed in your accent. There is power in the ability to articulate your own story. To use your own language, to use your own voice. In truth, I will never have a voice of my own—it is my nature to steal one.

The story we have shared begins and ends in a whare. A whare tapere, a house of storytelling and games. The door and the window depict Kurangaituku endlessly pursuing Hatupatu.

The whare is now filled with the things from my telling. The fine cloaks and weapons that I made are propped up against a wall. The once plain walls are now adorned with poupou punctuated with tukutuku panels. The poupou depict the images of my story—the riroriro raising the pīpīwharauroa, an ignimbrite cloud engulfing a volcano, a crack that awaits a small seed, the dogs of Hanui and Haroa and their namesakes from Rarohenga chasing each other's tails. The image of Hine split down the middle—a woman of both dawn and night, beautiful mother on one side, demon on the other,

her greenstone eyes the same no matter the guise. The bound body of Tama-o-hoi that seems to writhe before you.

The tukutuku panels are woven with the murmured chant of Tuhoto who freed Tama-o-hoi from Tarawera and the song of the miromiro—*tihi-ori-ori-ori*—a lament for a lost lover.

Look up to the ridgepole and rafters. Kōwhaiwhai swirl with soft, blue light rather than the expected kōkōwai. Are the lights that glow above you stars? The colour is too dim and blue for the stars. A hum of recognition cuts off the glow-worms' light. It is all here within this whare, my entire world.

Events slide in and out of view. The endless repetitions collide with one another and create a pattern that is reflected upon itself.

Beginning.

Middle.

End.

Middle.

Beginning.

Te Kore.

Te Pō.

Te Whaiao.

Te Pō.

Te Kore.

The idea of the whare has served its purpose. A karakia of thanks, to close the path once again.

Let this place be done.

A few words and it collapses. The door and the window panels have gone, and their openings let in the darkness rather than the light.

The thatch roof rots. Great strips are pulled away as if they are being ripped off by a fierce storm, but there is no roar of wind and the black sky above is calm.

Next, the floor beneath you gives way and there is no choice but to cling to the walls, even though we both know that they are next.

There is a choice—cling to this reality or let it go and embrace the idea of meto, of extinction, of simply not being.

The whare has gone. Here at the centre, nothing is left. No. Thing.

Ki te whaiao, ki te ao mārama.

The light, o the light that has nurtured me, that has oppressed me and defined me. The light that is me, must inevitably arc into darkness.

Te Pō.

And in the darkness I realise that I am not alone. We are many who dwell in the darkness of—

Te Pō.

The darkness is a womb—it will nurture me.

Te Pō.

And in the darkness, I listen for the hum. It is both within me and without me.

Te Pō.

The absence of light is darkness. I have perceived this. My eyes have emptied.

Te Pō.

The space that had defined my form has been replaced with darkness. I embrace it, the darkness is my comfort.

Te Pō.

The darkness is complete, oppressive. It defines and shapes my form. I push against it and it pushes back.

Te Pō.

The darkness envelops. It invades. It is me and I am darkness.

Te Pō.

And in the darkness, the hum diminishes. It is all that has been, that will be, is losing its form. Losing its will to be.

Te Pō.

This is the night that stretches on.

Te Pō.

There is a hum, a change.

The infinite void of Te Kore.

Te Kore, endless Te Kore.

Te Kore, endless Te Kore, the beginning and the end. All the things that have been and will be, but cannot manifest in—

Te Kore, endless Te Kore, the void that has no substance. I cannot perceive you. I cannot feel the weight of you. There is nothing, just Te Kore.

Te Kore, endless Te Kore, the void that stretches forever because there are no boundaries, no time. There is just Te Kore.

The darkness is everything—it is potential, it is everything that was and will be. Possibility—it may be filled, it may change, or it may remain blank.

Listen to the blank, the black, the dark. The world is dark and all that is left is darkness, a black void blankness.

Pōngerengere, dark and suffocating. Meaning has been obliterated. Seek the white spaces between the ink; let the letters and words seep into your mind. Remember all that has been written before.

All the words that have been spoken about me, written about me, bind me—their whispers encircle and define me. My name tells a story, a story that is familiar to you. My name is my story, it is me.

Kurangaituku.

LET THIS PLACE BE FILLED WITH LOVE AND BETRAYAL,

WITH DEATH AND LIFE, WITH HUMANS AND NON-HUMANS,

WITH UPHEAVAL AND CHANGE.

THESE ARE THE THINGS WE NEED FOR THE TELLING.

THESE ARE THE THINGS OF MY STORY.

In the void of time, Kurangaituku, the bird-woman, tells the story of her extraordinary life—the birds who first sang her into being, the arrival of the Song Makers and the change they brought to her world, her life with the young man Hatupatu, and her death. But death does not end a creature of imagination like Kurangaituku. In the underworlds of Rarohenga, she continues to live in the many stories she collects as she pursues what eluded her in life. This is a story of love—but is this love something that creates or destroys?

Kurangaituku is a contemporary retelling of the story of Hatupatu from the perspective of the traditional 'monster'—bird-woman Kurangaituku. For centuries, her voice has been absent from the story, and now, Kurangaituku means to claim it.

KURANGAITUKU

WHITI HEREAKA

KURANGAITUKU

First published in 2021 by Huia Publishers
39 Pipitea Street, PO Box 12280
Wellington, Aotearoa New Zealand
www.huia.co.nz

Reprinted in 2022

ISBN 978-1-77550-656-0

A catalogue record for this book is available from the National Library
of New Zealand.

Published with the assistance of

ARTS COUNCIL OF NEW ZEALAND TOI AOTEAROA

Hey you little hōhā,
keep questioning and
keep pushing boundaries.

ACKNOWLEDGEMENTS

I feel like this is a story that I have carried with me since I was a child. My whānau would spend a lot of time driving between Taupō and Rotorua, and we would always stop at Te Kōhatu o Hatupatu in Ātiamuri. I would leave my koha in the rock and shiver thinking about Hatupatu hiding there from the terrible bird-woman. Being a hōhā kid, I always wanted to know more about *her*—the bird-woman.

I acknowledge Te Rangikāheke, whose work inspired the book of Māori myths I read as a child, and the other storytellers from Te Arawa—I hope that my work can contribute in a small way to our mātauranga Māori.

I also mihi to my tīpuna and whānau.

I have been writing this novel for almost a decade, so there are many people and organisations that I am grateful to for their support over that time. Thank you to the NZSA Auckland Museum Research Grant and the very helpful librarians at the Auckland Museum in particular, who guided my initial research. To Creative New Zealand for their ongoing support, especially Haniko Te Kurapa (you can stop asking me how the novel is coming along now!). I worked on this novel during my residencies at the Michael King Writers Centre and at the Roxby Downs Community Library supported by Writers SA.

I am also a bit overwhelmed thinking about the many people whose work has inspired me or whose presence in my life unlocked a bit of this novel. Thank you to the many writers I know who have listened to me talk about this book for almost a decade and who have been, perhaps, a bit bamboozled by my jazz hands as I talk about it.

Thank you Witi Ihimaera for very gently suggesting that perhaps I was trying to write more than one book at once—you were right! You said this to me when I needed clarity, and to be honest, a boost in confidence to keep going. Ngā mihi ki a koe, e te matua.

Another special thank you to Pip Adam, a writer and reader (and human) I admire very much who very generously read this novel for me before I submitted it and let me know that my ambitious idea for the format of this novel actually worked.

Thank you to the team of people at Huia Publishers, who have been supportive and, let's be frank, patient with me! Thank you for the inciteful and incisive editing, Liz Breslin, Jane Blaikie and Bryony Walker. Ngā mihi to the reo Māori editors Kawata Teepa, Brian Morris, Pania Tahau-Hodges and Mairangimoana Te Angina who wrangled my enthusiastic but very basic understanding of te reo Māori into sentences that actually make sense! Thank you to the design team, Te Kani Price, Christine Ling and Camilla Lau; your work is consistently beautiful and does so much to support the story. Thank you Waimatua Morris, Claudia Palmer, Michaela Tapp, Brian Bargh and Eboni Waitere for taking my story from manuscript to book, from my hands into the world.

And finally, I mihi to Kurangaituku. The challenge of writing your story has tested me as an author and as a human, but I think that I am better for it. Although I remain a poor vessel for your voice, I am forever grateful for the chance to try and capture it. Forgive me my mistakes.

TE PŌ

Kurangaituku

Me, my name, my story.

All the words that have been spoken about me, written about me bind me—their whispers encircle and define me.

Where are you? I send my words to you across the void, but they just dissipate. Have I lost you forever? You are part of me, part of my soul—am I not a part of yours? Do you not feel the same yearning, the same loss when I am not near? Do you feel anything for me at all?

Auē, auē. If I could howl you would hear me across time. My love for you binds me. I cannot move or breathe without the aka, the āka cutting deeper into me. How you torture me. Does it give you pleasure?

Or am I too much for you to bear? Has my love become oppressive, weighing down upon you? You no longer want to be defined by my love. You must be free of it.

And yet it remains. It grows, despite the distance between us. Perhaps because of the distance between us. I am destroying myself so that I might be made anew by you. So that I might become a thing that you treasure, a thing that pleases you.

A sacred thing. A dark thing.

Where have you gone? I will search for you, continue to search, long after my love has rotted from the inside out and turned into something putrid. Stinking, bitter and vile.

Why must I love you more than you love me?

Sometimes the thought of you becomes so clear, the light of you so true and piercing, that it hurts me to look on you. Even if I plucked out my eyes, crushed them underfoot, I would still see you. I have let my body be torn apart, and yet the pain of loving you is greater. Because it is not requited.

Of course, you cannot love *me*. I am a monster, an ogress, a giant.

I am a liar, a thief, a murderer. I killed the birds of my flock for a hunger that was more than physical. I would suck the sweet brains from their skulls and see their life experience: the moreish over-ripe karaka berry slipping down my throat, the shrill warning call from my flock, the air squeezed out of the lungs as a claw—my claw—holds tight across my body.

Perhaps you worried I would do the same to you. Was I so transparent?

Or perhaps you saw yourself in me. The book in your hands is bloodless, yet is it not the same thing? You sup upon the experiences of others— how many lives have you tasted? Hundreds of lives and experiences to be lived and felt. A story lets you glimpse the world of the other—past, present, future—a life just waiting to be savoured. The lives I have consumed are countless. The lives you can live within stories are endless.

Through story, I gift you my sight. I let you see this world as I see it. Please do not run from me. Do not resist me. Let me in. I need to tell you this story so I can breathe again. I want to exist, at least in your mind. Because I am a creature that lives in the margins of imagination. I am a creature of thought. I am a creature that lives on the edges of words. I am a creature of dreams. I am bound and unbound in this form. I can exist in many places, in many minds, at once. But it is within yours that I yearn to be.

I am the culmination of two species' dreams. My first tīpuna were the birds who wove me into their nests and burrows, shaped their flight patterns and mating calls with the thought of me. I trilled in the day and boomed at night. And then I was, a dream made manifest by the thousands that dreamt it. A body made of will as much as it was made of atoms vibrating together.

My second tīpuna were the Song Makers. From them, I learnt the significance of the body the birds had gifted me. The Song Makers' whakataukī described me as: he kōtuku rerenga tahi; the bird who stands motionless in wait of its prey—he kōtuku kai whakaata, a bird that feeds upon its own reflection. I was kōtuku, a white heron, a marginal bird in every sense: living between water and land, a conduit between Te Rēinga and Te Ao Mārama.

A hum of recognition, he tohu.

I told myself a story about you and me. In the void you left behind, the story flourished—like the atua after the separation of Papatūānuku, the earth mother, and Ranginui, the sky father.

It lived in the telling.

I lived in the telling.

But that is telling.

And now I grieve for something that never was, something unreal, something untrue.

Ah, the truth. The tūī sings a different song to that of the kākā. But both sing the truth.

I allowed myself to believe that I could live in that story. The story of you and me. It is time for a new story. Let us breathe life into it. A story does not live until it is told. Let me tell you *this* story.

Strike from the page all that has been written before. Let the words and letters slip from your mind; pile them upon one another, obliterating their meaning—their ink bleeds into the white spaces; they become pōngerengere, dark and suffocating.

The world is dark, and all that is left is darkness, a black void blankness. It invades us, colonises us. We assimilate it until our body is no longer anything—it is part of the darkness. It is the air in our lungs, the blood in our veins, the marrow in our bones. We are in flux—the idea of us spreads out into a river, dark and suffocating. We become pōngerengere.

Te Kore,
endless Te Kore, the void that stretches forever because there are no boundaries, no time. There is just Te Kore.

Te Kore,
endless Te Kore, the void that has no substance. There is nothing to perceive. There is nothing, just Te Kore.

Te Kore,
endless Te Kore, the beginning and the end. All the things that have been and will be, but cannot manifest in—

Te Kore,
endless Te Kore.

And then the idea spreads so far that it collapses upon itself. Everything, every possible thing, is drawn together into a black sphere that can be cradled in your palm. Take it now in your hand. It is my gift to you; do not let it fall. It is lighter than you expect; it is warm, wet and yielding. It looks like glossy obsidian, flecked with white. Hold it up and see now through my eyes. Through them you see everything—the black, the dark, the nothing-ness. The entire universe has been captured within the sphere, enfolded so

tightly that enormous heat is generated. It is the heat of creation, the blank feeling its potential.

And in the infinite void of Te Kore there is a hum, a hum of recognition, a prediction of change. We have started something. It is a beginning, and in less than a second everything expands into—

Te Pō.

The darkness at last a presence, there is no longer an empty void. There is the night that stretches on.

Te Pō.

And in the darkness, the hum grows stronger. It is the hum of many voices, of infinite voices. It is all that has been, that will be, finding its form. Finding its will to be.

Particles combine and divide—the ripples of their coupling and divorce spread out and become great waves. Everything has changed.

Te Pō.

The darkness envelops. It invades. It is you and me and we are darkness.

Te Pō.

The darkness is complete, oppressive. It defines and shapes our form. It pushes down, and we push back.

Te Pō.

The darkness is our comfort, yet we continue to repulse it. The darkness that had defined our form has been replaced with space.

Te Pō.

The darkness is now an absence of light. We have perceived this. Our eyes have opened.

Te Pō.

And in the darkness, we listen for the hum. It is both within us and without us.

Te Pō.

The darkness is a womb—it has nurtured us, but we cannot stay within its confines forever.

Te Pō.

And in the darkness, we realise that we are not alone. We are many who dwell in the darkness of—

Te Pō.

The darkness, o the darkness that has nurtured us, that has oppressed us and defined us. The darkness that is us, must inevitably arc into light.

Ki te whaiao, ki te ao mārama.

A hum of recognition. Endless repetitions have created a pattern that is reflected upon itself—

Beginning.

Middle.

End.

Middle.

Beginning.

Te Kore.

Te Pō.

Te whaiao.

Te Pō.

Te Kore.

In the darkness a ruru calls. I sent her to find you—a go-between of life and death, of love lost and held. Let the ruru guide you to me—she sees all in the dark. You are not alone in the dark—is that a comfort to you? We must traverse realities to be together. But even at this distance I recognise you and my wairua calls to yours. I ache for you. Do you feel the pull towards me?

Let it pull you down to me, give in to the idea of the gravity of me. Let me be your light in the void. Let me be your centre.

Meet me here. At the centre of all that is known, all that will be.

I am asking you to cross a boundary, a boundary that was closed off to humans many centuries ago—we must trick Te Kūwatawata to open his gate. Do you trust me to lead you to this place? I will fold you within my heart, nestle you deep within my mind—you will be safe in that burrow, and I will take you with me. If you consent. Take my hand now, and we will begin.

Lie down and feel the ground beneath you—the layers of time, deep time, unfathomable time beneath you. Listen closely and you may hear the earthworms digging down and down.

It is here we build a whare from words—*of* words. A whare tapere, a house of storytelling and games. A pātaka kōrero, a storehouse of language. We will create a place where you and I will be comfortable. A place to share a story.

Our whare will be simple and symmetrical, soothing and pleasing. We strike our foundations in the light and plant our posts—four. The walls that contain you and me and our story are plain for now, but by and by they will be carved by the telling of a life—if you would call it that. Words and deeds frozen in the moment. As it is as it should be. Past, present, future —simultaneous.

On the floor, a finely woven mat. The scent of harakeke is too faint for you to detect, but to my keen senses it evokes the warm gathering days. The warp and the weft are tight; none of the blank, the black below us, shows through—not a particle. Protected from the blank, the black, you are comfortable sitting here. You are supported and yet the floor yields to you. Lie still and let my words lull you.

Look up from where you lie and let us create a roof. Thatched as they were in old times. Supporting the roof are the ridgepole and rafters, the backbone and ribs of the whare—so very like bones without kōwhaiwhai painted on them. They too are waiting for their story to begin.

And where is the heart? Who lets the whare live, keeping the rhythm? Is it you or me?

I turn my head so that I can press my forehead to yours and share your breath. I savour the touch of your lips against my cheek. Ah, if only I had lips, I would kiss you and you would know my love—at least, that is what I understand about how you love.

If only.

If only.

If only.

I pull myself away from you to create the last things our whare needs. A window and a door. I will borrow them from a whare carved by expert hands—sometime in the past, present, future; from where or when we are, it is hard to tell. Is it a memory or a dream that I borrow from? Above the window, he has carved a likeness of Hatupatu. I slide a panel across the window and shut out the great abyss of Te Pō. From afar, our whare must look so vulnerable in the vastness. How is it not crushed by the black, this idea that carries us? Take comfort in the thought that everything turns, and day is only a revolution away.

Shall I leave the door open? Upon it is a depiction of me—it is through me you are welcomed and through me that you must escape. I will leave it ajar for you.

I must perform a blessing now that the whare is whole so that we may dwell here. Water to cleanse and nourish the seeds of potential here. I take the water in my mouth and let it drip from tongue to beak to hand. Into the four corners of our whare I cast the drops to open a path. A path for those whose lives I invoke to walk, a path that we will walk as well.

Let this place be filled with the things we need for the telling—the greenstone eyes of my lover Hinenuitepō—a woman of both dawn and night, beautiful and terrible in whatever guise was forced upon her; a sting of sulphur yellow light twisting upon itself to make a rope that pulls down and down; the murmured chant that freed Tama-o-hoi from Tarawera. The ruru calls, follow her voice—it is time to begin.

Let my words be fruitful, let my words be heard, let my words sing to you.

This is my song. The song of a ridiculous creature without a voice of her own. Take pity on me, this vessel of shapes and groups that you think of as words is all I have to tell my story to you. It is an approximation. I have borrowed other voices before, poor vessels to translate my thoughts—none can come close to the true experience of my life. But I tell it to you anyway because through this story I can live again. Through this story I can be heard. Let me borrow your voice, clothe me in your accent. The voice that whispers these words to you is your own, and it is comforting. Sup upon my thoughts and let my words fill your mind until we two are as one. You and me and us.

Am I dead?

I am dead.

... I feel
The Link of Nature draw me: Flesh of Flesh,
Bone of my Bone ...

John Milton, *Paradise Lost*, Book IX

RAROHENGA

HINENUITEPŌ

I am dead.

Am I dead?

I found myself in a place that was on the edge of familiar. A lake surrounded by hills. The hills were steep, too steep to climb from the lake. Beyond these hills there were more—seemingly endless, range upon range of steep hills, like the lapping waves of the lake below. The tops of the hills were shrouded in mist, made up of the incorporeal, the dead. Though there was no sun, the hills and lake were illuminated by a gentle light, like an overcast day at the end of summer. There was no difference between night and day here, the

dull light ever present. This light was the kindest to human eyes—not too dark that they would stumble, not too bright that they would squint. I missed the darkness. I missed the stars. I missed the sunrise and set. I missed the ever-changing world.

In the beginning, I thought that perhaps this world was contained within a massive cave and the light was provided by the glow-worms that had lit my own cave. But no matter how high I drifted up, I could not find a ceiling. I could not find the glow-worms' sticky lines.

I should have recognised that place as my own kin—that reality, that light, was created by the imaginations of the spirits that came to dwell there. It was created by the stories they had listened to as children, by the stories they had told their own children, and by the stories told at their death.

I dwelt on the top of the hills to perceive the view, spreading my consciousness around the peaked ring. All around me were the spirits of Song Makers, desperately trying to keep their energy concentrated in one place, as if they were scared that to let themselves go would mean to lose themselves all together in the void. They would hold on to the idea of themselves to keep what remained of their former life intact. Some held on to the idea of their bodies—perhaps not at the time of their death but when they were at their peak. Some would repeat their name over and over again, as if the word were some sort of charm. Some whispered the name of the place *Te Rēinga*.

Down from where we incorporeal dwelt, down the hills and on the banks of the lake, there were a number of Song Makers going about the business of the living. But these were not the living. These were the spirits of Song Makers in a memory of their bodily form, living out their death for as many years as they had breathed on earth. They spent that time here, surrounded by the hills that reminded them of home. In Te Rēinga the dead would toil and wait. They waited for their years to slip past so that they might continue their journey through the Underworld, Rarohenga. They waited for their own to arrive, so that they might be welcomed properly, and so that their whānau would be reunited.

These Song Makers would play at what had once been so important to them in life—growing food that they did not eat, making shelter that they did not need, and making provisions for a winter that would never arrive. Occasionally one would stop their activity and raise their head towards the hills—some would close their eyes and move their body from side to side as if they were being pulled by some invisible rope. They would open their eyes again and in a clear voice that was amplified by the bowl of the lake, they would call to one of the incorporeal—a son, a daughter, a nephew, 'Spirit, do you belong to me?'

And one of the incorporeal on the hill would emit an emotion of acknowledgement and joy. The spirit would roll down the hill—an idea, a name suddenly given form by the recognition of another member of their family. It did not matter if the one who called had been dead for years before the spirit had arrived in Te Rēinga. Blood recognised blood and every spirit on that hill was claimed. But me.

By the time the spirit was at the foot of the hill, they transformed into an echo of their bodily selves, a spirit that could now be welcomed with touch and a hongi, although no life-breath was shared between them—it was as much a show as the activities that occupied the Song Makers who dwelt beside the lake.

I observed many of these welcomes, and the spirits all seemed to be relieved when they emerged at the foothills. All the chaos and confusion of death was put aside for the familiarity of body and task. It seemed to give them peace, to mirror their lives in their death, to be surrounded by their people. Was it a form of grieving for them? A time to mourn their own lives? Was it a comfort to be able to greet the people you love, that you had lost, or that will be lost?

I could have dwelt upon those hills forever, observing the Song Makers' spirits arrive on the hill and their transformation as they made their way down. The rhythm and ritual of it reminded me of the generations of riroriro I had watched building their nests for their chicks, and those of pīpīwharauroa. But the more I observed the ritual greeting, the more I

was filled with a kind of sadness. There was no one at the lake to greet me. I was a stranger here, as I had been in life. I was not welcome in the lives or afterlives of the Song Makers, no matter how much I tried to be.

And from sadness another emotion arose. I had not forgotten nor had I forgiven the betrayal of *my* Song Maker—I let myself feel rage at my own demise. My anger changed the sky above the tranquil lake—and all the Song Makers looked up at me, a storm in an otherwise benign day. And perhaps then I could have descended to be amongst them, because I felt the pull of their hearts, the recognition of kin—because each of them had felt what I felt then. Each of them had felt the anger of their lives slipping away from them. I could have rolled down the hill and become the manifestation of all our rage—inspiring the spirits to war amongst themselves, to tear each other apart, to stir the calmed waters.

I would like to say that it was my own conscience that stopped me, but you know me well enough to see through that lie. In Rarohenga there dwelt creatures other than the Song Makers, creatures of power, creatures who ruled the Underworld.

She did not have to raise her voice to me. She seemed not to use her power against me, although I could feel its immensity. She was not at Te Rēinga when she halted my descent down the hills—her authority and voice carried far in this world. She simply said one word—

'Quiet.'

And I was.

I was drawn to her. I pulled all aspects of myself together from the mist on the hills and focused on her presence. I found her as soon as my intention was formed, as soon as the thought took hold.

And I folded in on myself, sticky and heavy, dense and moist. No longer a thing of mist, I was a thing of earth. I became the memory of leaf litter and petrichor.

She made me. She pulled the clay from her own body to shape mine. Her clay was as rich and red as that from Kurawaka, as that from her grandmother.

She shaped me as her husband-father had shaped her mother, smoothing her hands over my form—lingering over my limbs, taking her time to perfect the folds of my labia.

She shaped me to her liking. Nothing of the bird that I was—no beak, no wings were left. My feet were wide and my toes close together, feet made for walking not gripping a branch in roost. She kissed my nostrils and ears, kissed my mouth and gave me saliva, kissed my eyes so that I could cry. She buried her tongue deep within my sex—but I was still inanimate. Finally she pressed her forehead to mine, her nose to mine, and breathed life into me—*hā!*

Tihei mauri ora!

I sneezed and opened my eyes.

'Tēnā koe, spirit.'

She had made me in her image. I was a mirror to the goddess above me. She helped me to my feet and I looked down upon the wonder she had made. My skin was smooth, free of feathers, and as red as the sky as the sun sets, not the earthy brown of the Song Makers. It seemed to glow as if my veins flowed with light rather than blood. My hair was long and hung down to my hips, long enough to cover my nakedness if I chose to. I didn't.

Her home was near the spirit path. Here, she would welcome her children back to her. Here, she would direct the spirits of the Song Makers and the spirits of the kurī to their new homes. Sometimes a spirit of the living would cross her path and she would exact a toll from them. Those that bestowed taonga would be allowed a glimpse of Te Rēinga and be able to return to their lives. Those that did not may have found themselves trapped with the spirits of kurī, unable to return to the land of the living once more.

'I have two names and many aspects, spirit. I am Hinetītama. I am Hinenuitepō.'

Ko Hinetītama koe, matawai ana te whatu i te tirohanga. You are like Hinetītama, a sight that causes the eyes to glisten.

I stared at her eyes—they reminded me of my own in life. They had no iris or pupil like the eyes of creatures who rely on light to see. Her eyes were a deep clear green, the colour of the most prized pounamu, kahurangi, except that this was living stone. Flashes of lightning lit her eyes—just as mine were like the constellations of the night sky. I could not help but to cup her cheek with my hand, and I was surprised when she did the same to me. She pulled me close to her face and kissed me, and it felt as if we were one and the same, as if I were merely an aspect of her.

I pulled away from her and put my hands to my lips. I imagined they looked as hers did—full and plumped with desire, and glistening with saliva. I traced my finger pad over my lips again as if to hold the memory of the kiss, my first. I wanted to kiss her again, but she had already turned from me and was walking away. She stopped and looked over her shoulder at me—the lightning in her eyes intense.

'Don't just stand there, spirit.'

She reached her hand back to me and I took it. I could not resist following her.

She led me to a grotto off the path. There was a small pool of water surrounded by the ferns and trees that I was familiar with in life. The plants here seemed to be perfect—no leaves were browning, the green brighter than I had ever seen before. It was as if a perfect moment in time had been preserved. I hesitated when I saw steam rising off the small pool, the memory of my death too fresh, and it infected each cell of my new body.

Hine let go of my hand. She walked slowly around the pool so that she was facing me. She looked into my eyes and smiled. She lifted a foot and pointed her toes and slowly dipped her foot into the water.

No! My mouth opened, but still I had no voice. She had taken such care with the rest of me, but wished me mute?

'You don't need a voice for me to hear you, spirit. Do you think I am actually speaking?' She smiled at me and I could feel her reaching into my mind—is this what it felt like for the tūī?

Hine stepped into the pool. She stood on a lip so that she was submerged to her knees and she opened her arms to me.

'Come.'

I walked towards her and the pool. I struggled with the desire to be with her and the memory of my death—my skin cooking and peeling from me, my muscles stiffening, the crack of my bones. Hine closed her eyes and inhaled as if the memory of my death was as sweet as the scent of mokimoki.

Hine sat on the lip, her body covered by the water.

'Come, spirit.'

I let her voice take over my will, stepping into the warm water and ignoring the screams of the past.

'Come to me.'

I stepped down further, the water covering me to my neck as I waded across to her. My hair flared out behind me like a discarded cloak floating on the surface of the pool.

Hine embraced me, pulling me closer to her so that I was sitting next to her. She kissed me again and I once again had no reckoning of time—I could have been in her arms for centuries, although when we parted it felt as if only a second had passed. She held my cheek and I pressed my face into her palm.

'I've told you my name, spirit. Will you not tell me yours?'

Kurangaituku. The name came unbidden—I hadn't realised how it had twisted around the core of me.

'And do you claim this name for yourself?'

Did I? It was perhaps the only gift that Hatupatu had given me—and the thought gave me pain.

'Kura ...,' she drew my name out slowly as she moved her hand down from my cheek, down my throat and between my breasts. She moved her hand under my breast, cupping it as lightly as she had done my cheek. She stroked it and I could not help but think of my first lover, Hatupatu. But she was not rough with my breasts—they were not pulled by her hand, my nipples were not crushed between thumb and forefinger. Her touch was as

light as the feathers that had once covered my breast, and I arched my back in response.

She kissed me and I sucked on her lower lip before she pulled away from me. 'Why are you here, Kura?'

I felt dizzy from the warmth of the water, from the warmth of her attention. How could I explain to her my presence here when I had no idea myself? The only word I could find to answer her was *Hatupatu*.

She lifted her hand to my cheek. 'Such sadness.' I realised that my face was wet not from the pool but from my own tears, the first tears I had ever shed. 'Do you mourn for him?'

No. Why would I mourn him? How could I mourn him?

'Then why do you cry?'

I could not answer the question. My body in life had never felt this way, had never responded in this way. I did not have the emotions or words to explain it.

She held my face so that I could not look anywhere but into her eyes. 'Ka heke te roimata me te hupe. Ka ea te mate.'

Yes, my tears were falling and my nose ran with mucus, but it did not feel to me as if death had been avenged.

I lifted my own hand to her; *I would not avenge myself against you.*

She narrowed her greenstone eyes at me and for a moment I thought that I had angered her—'I am not death, Kura. I am not the cause, nor the keeper of death. It was not my will that brought you here.'

Another lie, Hatupatu? *If you are not death, then who are you?*

'I am the mother who greets her children when they return to her. I am the mother who prepares them for their new state of being.' She ran her tongue along my clavicle and bit my neck.

Is this how you greet them, your children?

Hine laughed. 'I greet my children with love, love a mother has for their child. But I am still a woman and you, Kura, are not my child.'

She pulled me close to her, held me tightly to her chest, and kissed me again. I wondered if it was strange for her—her lover a reflection of herself. She knew this body intimately, it was both hers and her creation. She touched me as an experienced lover. The fumbling of Hatupatu had been amateur, but Hine was a virtuoso.

Why did you make me like you?

'I recognised myself in you.'

But I am not you.

Hine smiled at me as if she knew better than me.

What is this place?

'It is me—a place of dreams and half-remembered truths. Some of my more literal children think that it is my actual womb, that the passage they will traverse in death is the same that they travelled to life. They are correct. Some think that the womb is a metaphor, that this is an actual place beneath their world. They are correct. This place is made up of what they believe— what they all believe. And so am I.'

The woman I could see, the woman I was conversing with, was an aspect of herself.

So you will still greet your children although you are here with me?

'Yes. I am both here and everywhere,' she smiled at me. 'I believe you are the first creature I have encountered who can understand what I mean.'

I understood then what she recognised in me—we were creatures made of the same material, the imagination of others. She had created me as others had created her. She was as vulnerable as I had been to the whims of her story. Seeing myself in her eyes made her irresistible. I touched her as she had touched me, hoping to arouse the same pleasure within her.

Hine held my waist as I cupped her breasts. She slid one hand over the curve of my hip and across my belly. Her hand continued down between my legs. She plunged two of her fingers up and into me. I pushed myself down on her hand, the muscles within me pulsing as they gripped her fingers. She

pulled her hand free and my moan was one of pleasure and disappointment—if I mourned anything that day it was the presence of her within me.

She pulled away from me and smiled. She lifted herself out of the water and sat at the edge of the pool. Steam rose off her wet body as if she had fire within her, her skin seeming to shimmer in the mist. I could not stand her beauty and turned my back to her. She put her legs either side of me and drew me to her, so that my head and shoulders were between her legs. I could have leaned back and made a pillow of her, but I wanted more than comfort from her body.

I turned around, the water's resistance seeming to make my movements too slow for my impatient hunger. I knelt on the lip of the pool and reached up to kiss Hine once again. Her hair shrouded me as she leaned down for my kiss. I ran my hand down from the cheek to her breasts, emulating her soft touch. I teased her nipples with my fingers until she gasped and our lips parted. I moved my mouth to her breasts, using my tongue as softly as I had used my fingers to trace her nipple.

Hine closed her miraculous eyes and I found that my own desire was stoked by the pleasure I could give her. I wanted more. I wanted to know the core of her. I wanted to explore the place where she had given birth to mankind, the place where a demi-god had lost his quest for eternal life, the place that made men shudder with both revulsion and desire.

I pushed Hine down so that she lay on her back, her calves and feet still dipped into the warm pool. I felt as if I could remodel her with pleasure, change the peaks and valleys of her made by breast and arched back. I knelt down in the water so that my head was level with her sex. I parted her pubic hair with my hands so that her lips opened as if in bloom. I found not the granite-tipped labia Hatupatu had described to me, but moist flesh that yielded and embraced my tongue and my fingers as I explored the folds of muscle within. This was no *hanga kino*—it was not an evil thing. Nor was it *whare haunga*—it smelled musky, yet sweet, and it was as intoxicating as fermented karaka berries. I put my hand under her buttocks and tilted her pelvis, lifting her up so that I could gorge myself. I lapped at the waters of life

denied to men who would take it without asking. I too was crushed between her thighs, but unlike the demi-god I was not trespassing.

Hine pulled me up out of the water and I trailed my tongue from her clit to her navel to the hollow between her clavicles. She held me close to her chest. It heaved up and down as if she was gasping for breath, but I heard not air filling lungs, nor the beat of a heart. It was pure energy and intention that animated her body, that animated mine. We had no use of the ornaments of life in the Underworld.

I tried to stand and leave the pool, but I felt weak. I had grown accustomed to the warmth here—both from the pool and from my lover. I could have let myself dissolve into her, into this place, but the desire to be, the will that had created me in the depths of Te Kore, could not be silenced by the wonders of her body.

If only.

If only.

If only.

I do not know how long we stayed at the pool, how long we stayed in each other's embrace. Our desire for one another came easily, conversation with more difficulty. Her kiss was intoxicating to me—in the beginning, her tongue had better uses than to form words, but as I grew to love her, truly love her, I wanted more than her being. I wanted to know her mind.

I was hungry for her, I wanted to know every aspect of her. I could not be sated by her body alone. In the beginning the sensation of her fingers, her tongue, her mind penetrating me—overwhelmed my thoughts and I could think of nothing but her lips, her breasts, her puapua. Why couldn't I just give in to the pleasure? Why did I have to think that this was ...

Not enough.

She looked up at me from between my thighs—the sight of her eyes made my breath catch. She reached her hand up and I bent my head down so she could touch my face.

'Not enough, my love?' Her index finger traced my lip and I could smell me on it. I opened my mouth and sucked her fingertip.

I want …

'I know what you want, e taku ipo.' Her head was between my thighs so it was as if she spoke to the lips of my vulva, the image of *her* vulva. Is that why she made me in her image? Because she could not stand to be defined by someone else? That she could only truly love herself, or at least an image of it?

No, not only this.

I'm not sure if she heard me at all, or if she let my thoughts dissipate like the steam rising off the pool. I wonder now if my thoughts would have eventually condensed and become an annoying drip on her neck.

I want more. I want to know you.

'You know all that you need to.'

Yes, Hatupatu had told me her story. But he had lied about so many things, told stories to benefit himself. I wanted to hear it in her voice, not by a proxy. I wanted her to show me her soul. She placed one of my hands on her breast and the other between her legs.

'This is what you need to know. This is our story, Kura.'

Hine.

I pushed my fingers into her, felt my resolve ebb away with each contraction of her muscles.

No. I withdrew my hand and ignored her sigh, *I want to know that there is more than this between us.*

'Why can't you just accept this, accept us, for what it is?'

I cocked my head—an old habit from an old body.

What is this? What am I?

And old thoughts came back—his voice saying, *You're not a person, you're—*

A monster.

An ogress.

A thing.

And she turned from me as if each thought was a blow against her. 'You see, Kura. Stories are already pushing us apart.'

No. Stories will bind us together—aho twists under and over whenu.

'If I tell you my story, we will change.'

I will love you.

'Perhaps. But it will be a different love. Tainted, because in the stories that are told, I am reduced to my relationships with men. I am the daughter *of*, the wife *of*, the woman wronged *by*. Here, I am just me. Please, just accept me.'

If I could live that moment again, I would kiss her until I forgot any other need apart from her.

If only.

If only.

She looked away from me. 'If I had not been as curious as you are now, Kura, my life would have been different. Perhaps my love for Tāne would be intact, perhaps I would still yearn for his embrace.

'Before I existed, there was only one other woman, my mother Hineahuone.

'He lay with her, as the men that would spring from his line would do with their wives and mistresses. His seed found home in her womb and Hineahuone became a mother. I was born and she called me Hinetītama. As I grew from baby to infant to child to woman, I knew no other family but my mother.

'Tāne did not see me again until I was fully grown. And when he did, he was so enamoured by my beauty that he took me far away from my home and claimed me as his wife. I never saw my mother again.

'I could have lived happily with him forever. We had a passionate relationship and I bore him many sons and daughters. Our children—are the Song Makers. Our children are the many iwi of humanity.'

She paused and then looked me in the eye. 'Perhaps I should have accepted what Tāne and I had, instead of questioning it.'

It was a rebuke, a warning, but I ignored it. It is my nature to want to know. It is who I am.

More.

She sighed, and arched her back so that her breasts popped out from beneath the warm water of the pool. A distraction, a ploy to make me forget. I turned my head from the sight of her.

'You must understand that I had no need for a father as a child. That I had accepted that my family was my mother and my mother alone. Tāne was the first man I had known. The only man I had known. I did not know that my life was the result of a mother and a father. It was not until I became full with his first child that I realised that we *two* had created it.

'Still, the question of my own father was pushed from my mind as my children demanded my attention, my womb, my breast. There was little time between to think of my origins, beyond wishing that my mother was near to help me. The questions I would have asked her would have been about motherhood—how to feed a fussy child, why my breasts ached for them when they had weaned. Why would I have bothered to ask her the identity of my father?

'Yet, the question had taken root in me. Perhaps Tāne had planted it in me the first time we made love. It grew stronger each time he filled my womb, until one day I needed to know. I needed to know where I came from.

'I asked him as we watched our children. I looked at him, but he did not look at me. Later, I would interpret this as an admission of his shame, but now I think that he was giving his attention to those that mattered most to him—his children. I was just a vessel for them, a means to an end. Had he ever loved me as his child? Had he ever loved me as his wife?

'I asked him if he knew my father, and without taking his eyes off the children who wrestled and laughed in front of us, he said, "Ask the posts." It was the answer we gave to the children when we were tired of their pleading voices. It was the answer to give when there was no answer. *Ask the posts.*

'On occasion, Tāne would leave me—probably to attend to his other wives, his other children. It was not out of the ordinary for our marriage, so please do not blame my question for his absence. It was not that he was insulted by my question that he left me that day—he left as he had left me before, intending to return. Usually the needs of my children would occupy my mind, or frequently my body. But the question still nagged. Tāne probably thought that he had put the matter to rest by telling me to, *Ask the posts.* I don't know what came over me—perhaps it is from me that some of my children have become so literal—but I asked the posts. I asked, but did not expect them to answer me. But they did.'

I must have had an incredulous look on my borrowed face because she said to me, 'Do you doubt what I say? You lived your life on earth as a creature shaped by imagination, yet you don't believe in a little magic?'

I believe in you.

'You need to believe in the story, not the teller. It was you who wanted me to tell this, Kura.' Hine cocked her head to the side as I had done. It felt like she was mocking me, like it was a challenge.

I want to believe.

She shook her head. We both knew that wanting and believing were quite different things. Should I have lied to placate her? Would she carry on to placate me? We both waited for the other to say something. We had not known silence between us unless we were entwined with one another, and then that was not silent but full of sighs and moans and the sound of tongue against skin. I wanted to hear her story more than she wanted to tell it, so it was up to me to break the silence. What of a lie to oneself if the outcome gets you what you want? It is a trifle, easily forgotten—it does not mark you indelibly. It is not the start of something bigger. Is it?

I could not meet her eyes.

I believe.

Her smile was sad, a smile of defeat rather than triumph. My answer had disappointed her—she could see through my lie and it proved that I was willing to be untrue with her to get what I wanted. I suppose I could say that this was the point where the rot set in, in our relationship, if our lovemaking could be called a *relationship*, but I knew that it was when I broke away from her kiss and asked her for more.

'I'm not sure if the posts spoke aloud, but I heard them.

'*Your husband is your father, your lover is your maker.* Was it the voice of the post that I heard, or a truth that I had known but could not admit? From the first child, I knew that life needed both mother and father to be, and Tāne was the only man I had ever met. The only man on the earth.

'And once I acknowledged the truth I could not unsee it. The evidence was all around me—in his children's faces, in their bodies. They looked like their father. And I, their sister-mother, looked like him too. They were tall, had strong limbs and high foreheads and cheeks—they belonged to him before they belonged to me.

'I was foolish and naive when we lay together, but Tāne knew who I was. He was my father, and he had fashioned my mother with his own hands— since he created her too, did that make him my grandfather as well? He knew that I was his daughter, yet it is I who must carry the shame of his act.

'In the stories that my children tell of our marriage, it is me who is shamed by the identity of my father. The weight of it drove me from his arms, his house and the light into this kingdom. They say he came to beg for my return and that I chose to stay.

'It was not shame that made me run away. It was disgust. I could not bear to look at him, the man who had held me tenderly after rutting in me. The man so in love with his own image that he made it his wife. Who would do such a thing?'

Had she forgotten that she had done the same thing to me? I touched the face she had given me—the high forehead and cheeks, a copy of a copy.

'I left my children behind. I have greeted their progeny for many generations.

'Here I took a new name—Hinenuitepō, no longer a maiden of light but a woman of darkness. It is of my own choosing that I reside here. I became more than the mother of humanity. Here I shrugged off the confinements of my life on earth; I embraced the magic that had created my mother. I am not flesh like my children anymore.

'And Tāne did come to me—not that day as some stories tell it. He did not chase me across the sky to this place. Years passed before he sought me out, time enough for me to find my strength in this place, to become this place. To set the rules of this plane and to enforce them. He came to the threshold and I would not let him pass. "Father," I said, "I only allow spirits to visit my realm either in dream or in death. You must care for our children in life; in death they will return to me. Know that I will honour our children, but I cannot honour our union." He turned away from the threshold and I have not seen him again.'

He left so easily?

'What would you have him do? Try to overpower me?'

But he is a god.

'And I am the daughter of a god.'

Will Tāne come here one day?

Hine laughed. 'He is a god. He is immortal.'

I thought I was immortal too—I had lived for centuries on earth and had never experienced death. And yet …

'Here you are.'

The echoes of my death made my limbs spasm, the memory of the searing heat spreading through my cells. She gasped as she felt it too—my impossible death. It was the only time I had seen her brow clouded with doubt. 'What would it take for a god to die?'

If all his children turned away from him. If they all forgot his name. If they stop telling his stories.

'How could they forget? His trees remind them of his deeds. They are like his legs pushing up against Rangi his father. No. Tāne will never die—they tell his stories too often. He is woven into their lives. As am I.' She reached her hand to me, stroking my cheek with the back of it. 'Is that enough for you, Kura? Do you think you know me now?'

Again, it was a warning and a challenge, a chance to embrace her once again. Perhaps I should have, buried myself between breasts or thighs, continued my existence with her in that pool. But I was not sated—I wanted to know more.

Tell me about Māui.

She moved in closer to me, and in a soft voice she said, 'Why? Does the thought of a man inside me excite you?'

I pushed away from her, a wave forming between us in the warm water.

She pushed further, her voice sharp and mocking. 'Does it make you giggle like the pīwakawaka, the thought of him pushing himself into my flesh?'

I clenched my jaw. If I had closed my eyes, I knew that I would have seen the floor of my cave as my spine was pushed down. Her words were like his spit-slicked penis forced in me.

I wanted to tell her that I understood her horror, that I had been violated too. But in this conversation, I was the perpetrator—I had forced her to tell it. That I had finally recognised myself within her.

'You look horrified, Kura. Have I not behaved in the way you expected of me? Did you hope that you could comfort me? That I would play victim as well as killer? Why is the horror of the story that Māui is crushed or cut in two? Here is a man who attempted to violate me as I slept—what kind of reaction did he expect from me? What kind of reaction did you expect?'

I could not answer her. I moved towards her, the water slowing my steps. I pulled her face to mine again and kissed her, hoping that she'd kiss me back,

hoping that all would be forgiven and forgotten in our love. But Hine had been right, the words had tainted our breath with the stink of evil. Our teeth clashed, and her tongue felt heavy in my mouth.

Hanga kino.

Whare haunga.

Our lips parted and we sat a while forehead to forehead. It was not that I loved her less, we didn't fit as we had done before. It was not our differences that had undone us, but our similarities. To look at each other was a reminder of what had passed. We had ended, and it was my fault. I wanted to know all aspects of her, yet I was too weak to accept them. I stood up and climbed out of the pool, steam rising off my body.

'Please, don't leave, Kura.'

I felt as if the mists that shrouded us were becoming clear, that I was becoming clear—that the boundaries between me and Hine were defined. I did not realise that until then I felt as if my edges were smudged, as if I could bleed into her.

I could not look back at her. I knew that if I saw her beauty again I would lose my resolve. But something strange was happening to my body. I lifted my hand in front of me and my being was rising cell by cell with the mist. I seemed to be evaporating with each step I took away from her. I turned around.

What is happening?

'I no longer see myself in you.'

Hine stood up from the water and she was beautiful and terrible. Her skin glowed, her eyes flashed with lightning.

I could not help myself, Ātaahua.

She pursed her full lips and blew and I was dispersed.

CHAPTER TWO

TE WHARE O WHIRO ME TŪ

I had lost the light of Hinetītama. I let myself sink further down into Rarohenga. I could hear a deep hum—a hum of recognition—like many voices talking over each other, dozens, hundreds, thousands. The hum was coming from the darkness.

From a distance it seemed as if the darkness was pure black, but as I mingled with it I saw colours swirling together—deep blues and olive greens, browns and ochre red, and at the edges sulphur yellow. It moved like the lights of the aurora in the sky, a shimmer, a ribbon continually unfurling. And ah,

the sound and the colours were the same, each shade a different pitch of voice, a choir of colour. I let my consciousness ride the waves, I became the bands of colour, the splashes of ochre, the sting of yellow.

In the darkness the sulphur yellow, particle by particle, came together, a pinprick of yellow, then a dot, and then a line, until I could block out all the other voices and focus on its words.

'Spirit,' it whispered, 'do you seek death?'

As if it sensed my curiosity, the yellow turned into a rope to be followed, twisting further into the darkness and down. I followed the path it made. As I descended, the yellow rope disappeared—I could not use it to find my way back. It only ran in one direction.

I followed the rope down until I found where it was tethered. The sulphur yellow swirled around me, illuminating that place with the curious yellow light the world has before a thunder storm. Above me, the colours swirled and merged looking very much like storm clouds. I could hear them cackling above me.

The rope was tethered to the prow of a large upturned waka. Lashed to the prow was the body of a boy, the rope around his neck looped a few times and pulled so tight that his eyes and tongue protruded. I thought the boy was a masterpiece of a skilled carver, the wood looked as soft as flesh, the grain so fine it looked like skin, until the figurehead jerked his neck and tilted his bulging features at me.

I recoiled from him in surprise—almost joining the churning clouds above me. From within the waka I heard laughter, amplified to a boom by the chamber of the waka. I followed the laughter, avoiding the figurehead who was struggling at the prow.

'I did not take you to be such a sensitive being.' A man sat on the threshold of light and shadow formed by the upturned boat. I recognised the sulphur of his voice. He did not look up as I gathered myself under the waka. 'Are you scared of me spirit? Are you scared to meet death?'

I had no mouth for speech. Particle by particle, I pulled my words from the voices in the clouds. My new voice was disjointed and hissed with static.

I have already met death. That is why I am here.

He laughed again. 'I do not meet many spirits who have held onto their wit. The spirits I meet usually cower before me.'

Who are you?

'Who are you, spirit, who does not recognise Whiro?' He stood up and stepped into the light. He lifted his chin and smiled as he opened his arms as if he expected applause, yet he seemed to me to be an ordinary man.

Who are you?

He frowned and his smile disappeared. 'How do you not know my name? How do you not know my deeds? I am Whiro!' He shouted his name at me as if the greater volume would make me suddenly understand.

From the shadow of the waka, someone else laughed. Whiro looked over his shoulder towards the voice.

'I am Whiro!' the voice mocked him, 'I am Whiro!' From the shadow a figure stepped out. Although his form was that of a human, I recognised that he was like Hinenuitepō, larger and pulsing with supernatural power. As he stepped from the shadow I could see his eyes—it was as if they were human hearts pulsing with blood. As this man came forward, Whiro dropped his arms and bowed his head slightly.

'Do you recognise me, spirit?'

No.

Whiro bit his lip to stifle his laughter. The supernatural being looked over his shoulder at Whiro, who looked down at his feet. Whiro suppressed his laughter, but I could see that his back was shaking with the effort.

'I am Tū.' He stood as Whiro had done before, waiting for my reaction. I had none to give. 'I am Tūmatauenga, Tūkariri, Tūkaitauā and Tūmatawhāiti.' At each name he paused to give me time to supplicate before him, so that he might forgive my ignorance. I did not.

Whiro whispered to Tū, 'Try saying your names over again …'

Tū spoke over his shoulder at Whiro, 'What good would that do?'

Whiro beckoned Tū towards him and they huddled together with their backs to me.

'I'm not going to say my names again,' Tū said. 'It's embarrassing.'

'I mean, sure, it may be embarrassing that a great atua, such as yourself, must repeat yourself. But, maybe the spirit is hard of hearing.'

'Do you think?'

'It's the only plausible thing isn't it?' Whiro patted Tū on the shoulder. 'Who hasn't heard of Tūmatauenga, Tūkariri ...'

' ... Tūkaitauā, Tūmatawhāiti.' Tū nodded. 'Yes, you're quite right. Must be hard of hearing.'

'Must be. The only explanation.'

Whiro kneaded the shoulders of Tū, and Tū shook out his arms and legs as if preparing for a bout. Tū inhaled deeply and then turned around towards me again. He took a step forward and looked over his shoulder to Whiro who nodded his head up and raised his eyebrows.

Tū drew his chest up and bellowed, 'I am Tūmatauenga, Tū, Tūkariri, Tūkaitauā and Tūmatawhāiti ...'

Whiro could not hold his laughter anymore. He bent over with laughter. 'Not so cunning, Tū. Not so cunning.'

'Who are you to laugh at the god of war?'

'I'm sorry, Tū,' Whiro did not look sorry, 'but this is quite funny.'

Tū, the mighty god of war crossed his arms and pouted, 'The spirit didn't recognise you either.'

Whiro stepped forward again to address me. 'Where are you from, spirit, that you have not heard the names Tū and Whiro? We are known and feared by all children of Tāne.'

I am not a child of Tāne.

'Then whose child are you?' Tū asked.

If Hatupatu had asked this of me, the tūī would have growled with my frustration. Could anyone or anything claim me as their child? I created myself from Te Kore or from the dreams of bird and man. Tū and Whiro

watched as I swirled in front of them. I gathered so many voices to form my words, so that I might yell as they had yelled at me. My voice, legion, dwarfed them.

I AM.

No father.

No mother.

Me.

Tū smiled. 'Do you have a name?'

I do. But it is mine to keep.

'Do you not want us to know you?'

I thought of Hine, and the power she had when I knew nothing of her. In telling her story she was left vulnerable to me. Although I did not fear these two, I understood that I was in their home and perhaps they ruled this reality just as Hine had ruled hers. I wanted to keep what little power I had.

You know all that you need to.

Tū reached out and tried to crush me in his hand. What little he caught of me in his fist, trickled out from the gaps between his fingers. My laughter was shifting light above them.

'You are arrogant and insolent, spirit,' Tū said.

I am.

And Tū laughed.

Where am I?

Whiro spoke for them both, 'This is the house of Whiro and Tū.'

'Tū and Whiro.'

'It is *my* waka.'

'I am a *god*.'

It seemed to be a long-standing argument, so Whiro pressed on with his introduction. 'This is the waka I built from a tree I stole from the forest of Tāne ...' Tū whooped with laughter again and Whiro smiled with pride.

'I carved this waka with my friend Tura to explore, to go on a great voyage. Tura had little imagination and very little ambition. He thought we would explore the world above, but I wanted to claim a place for myself here. The boy you see lashed to my prow was the first victim of murder. He was helping me lash my waka and when I looked at him working, I wondered how long he would fight for his life.'

Whiro nudged Tū. Tū nodded and conjured a toki from the air, testing the sharpness of the blade against his forearm. He practised his strike as if honing his movement to the balance of the tool.

Whiro stood with his hands on his hips, rolled his eyes and sighed.

'Tū ...'

Tū held up his index finger at Whiro. He posed his body mid-strike, his torso twisted to exaggerate his physique. He nodded at Whiro. 'Continue ...'

Whiro continued, and as he spoke they play-acted the scene together.

'As the boy bent down, I threw a loop of rope around his throat and pulled.'

Tū struggled against Whiro and gasped for air. Whiro wrestled with him and seemed to pant with pleasure as much as exertion.

'He was stronger than I had thought, and so I pulled another loop of rope around the first, and pulled with both my fists, raising his feet off the ground, yet he still fought.' Whiro spoke of his murder with undisguised gratification. If he had been a mortal man, I imagine he would have grown stiff at the description.

Whiro twisted himself around so that he was back-to-back with Tū.

'To choke the life from him, I had to turn my back and pull over my shoulder. I had to bend over and carry his kicking body on my back until his legs stilled and his urine soaked me.'

Tū committed to his role completely, letting his limp body slide down off Whiro and into the puddle at the feet of Whiro.

'It was disappointing that I could not see the life fade from my first kill's eyes. I hid his body under the wood chips until I could install him at the prow. Now I get to look at his face every time I travel.'

Tū sat up, resurrected from his theatrical death.

'You are skipping over the best parts, Whiro.' The disturbing smile of Tū was mirrored by the smile of Whiro, as he relished the tale of the figurehead. 'The boy's body was discovered by his father who demanded to know what had happened to his son.'

'And I told him as I have told you, spirit.'

'Just as he told you. Whiro described the murder to the boy's father as calmly as he might have described chipping the hull out.'

'The boy's father shook with despair and rage. "How dare you!" he said. "How dare you!" And he charged at me.' Whiro raised his arm and Tū threw him his toki. Whiro caught it and struck his blow. 'I saw the life drain from my second kill.' Whiro mimed striking the father again and again. 'His skull split so easily for me.'

'Whiro feasted on the father's flesh. The first human to do so.'

I could not help but to stir at this part of the story—Whiro had achieved what I dreamed to do, feast on the mind of a human. Envy ran through me, and for a second I became dense, and the memory of my face emerged beak first from the mist.

'Ah,' Whiro said, 'we are blood of blood then, spirit? We are kin.'

I did not answer him, and so he continued.

'My waka was finished, blessed by the blood of two generations. There were whispers about the disappearance of the boy and his father. If they had asked, I would have told the villagers what had happened. I was not ashamed of my work. Tura may have heard the whispers, but he joined me anyway, at least until he made sighting of an island. I had hoped to bring Tura here with me, but he was a man who did not belong here. The boy I could bring with me—his spirit is lashed to mine.

'They say that I am the father of murder and cannibalism, that I introduced those evils to the world. They say that I am a thief who steals the spirits of men, women and children and brings them on their voyage to Rarohenga. Only the dead can sail on my waka, only the dead make the journey here.'

There was a long pause. Whiro just stood with his chin lifted, a smile cracking his face. The silence continued and Whiro twitched his eyes and brows, widening his lips as he clenched his jaw.

Tū stepped in front of Whiro, holding his arm out as if he needed to hold Whiro back. 'Greetings to you, spirit. You who claim no origin or lineage. Know that you are present before one of the original beings of existence, the son of Ranginui'—he lifted his arm and swept it above his head—'and Papatūānuku.' Tū knelt down and touched the ground beneath him.

Whiro folded his arms and sighed. Tū, still kneeling, reached out his hand to Whiro, as if asking to be supported. Whiro batted his hand away.

'What's wrong with you?' Tū hissed.

'You interrupted me.'

'But you had finished your story.'

'Had I? Had I?'

Tū looked confused. It was obvious to me that it was a trap—an attempt at starting a pointless argument. Whatever he chose to do now would be wrong.

Tū pushed himself up and addressed me. He walked behind Whiro, who still crossed his arms.

'For aeons our parents held each other in a tight embrace.' Tū hugged Whiro from behind and Whiro yelped and yielded.

'Our mother grew full with child and gave birth to us, yet our parents' embrace endured. We children lived pressed between our parents. We grew as children do, but without the space to know ourselves. We wanted more. I proposed to my brothers that we kill our parents so their arms and legs would finally unlock. My brothers rejected my idea. And so I lived between my parents, with my brothers, until the day that Tāne,' he said the name with little reverence, 'stood on his hands and pushed Rangi from Papa with his feet.'

Tū pulled himself away from Whiro.

'From then on we brothers lived in the cold light between our parents, listening to their laments for each other. Most of us stayed with our mother.

Tāne clothed her in forests, Tangaroa embraced her with his oceans. Rongo and Haumia used her fertile soils to grow kūmara and fern root. In this new world of light, my brothers had found their place. I seemed to be the only one who struggled with what to do on earth.

'But not all of us chose to live in our mother's embrace. Tāwhirimātea, the wind, chose to live with our father. He never agreed with our plan to separate our parents and it pained him to hear the cries of our parents for one another. It pained him so much that he tore his own eyes out and ripped them into tiny pieces and threw them into the sky. He howled and buffeted us from above. He would rip trees from the earth and cause great waves to crash at our mother's shore. My other brothers were reluctant to confront him. They decided that they would simply continue with their own work, repairing or replacing what Tāwhirimātea had destroyed. Or worse, they would hide from our brother and wait until his rage subsided, or until he turned his attention to another brother's realm.

'I could not let him control us like that. We had separated our parents so that we might have freedom, liberty from their oppression. I could not let a zealot terrorise the rest of us. I tried to convince my brothers of what needed to be done, but they lacked the courage to stand up against him. It was clear to me that I must sacrifice my comfort to ensure the safety and the continuation of our way of life. If my brothers would not stand with me, then I would stand for them.

'I prepared as best I could for the first battle. None of us had ever gone to war before. I had no weapons but my hands and my wits. I did not know what to expect when I called my brother down to me. He raged against me, pushing me, attempting to lay me flat. I dug my feet into our mother and pushed back at him. I made my hands into fists and pummelled his body.

'I won the battle, and it kindled a desire in me. I had found my place in this world, had found what I might grow and cultivate—war. I sought out my brothers who would not stand against Tāwhirimātea, knowing that they would be powerless compared to me. I executed each of them for their insubordination—Rongo, Haumia, Tangaroa and Tāne.'

He lifted his chin with pride. He thought that the story was one of triumph. But it seemed implausible to me—both that his brothers controlled such things, and if I could accept that, that he had defeated them. Even if I accepted his story that his brothers controlled the winds, the forests and the sea, I could not accept that he had killed them. For did not the wind continue to blow? Did not the sea continue to roll in and out on the shore? Did not the trees continue to grow? If he had truly killed his brothers then would not these things be dead too?

Taking words from the clouds to express my thoughts was just as frustrating as using the tūī. I could not seem to bring complex thoughts together. I had to use simple, clear language instead.

Tāne is dead?

Tū looked disappointed. 'An aspect of him died. Even I cannot kill a god. Not permanently. No one can.'

Not one, but many.

His brow furrowed and for a moment I could see his shared whakapapa with Hine. 'I don't know what you mean, spirit. Are you a god killer?'

No. No one here is.

Whiro stifled a laugh again and Tū looked back at him, and then towards me. 'Do you mean to challenge the god of war?'

To what?

'A battle, of course.'

To what end?

'To see who will win. To see who is stronger.'

Is that why wars are waged?

'You are a strange spirit who seems to know nothing about war. Why are you here?'

I followed the rope.

Whiro smirked. 'If you could see my anchor rope, if you are with us here, spirit, what evils did you bring to humanity?'

Evil?

'Those who find this place, or who are brought by me here, suffer from disease—either of the body or the mind. Amongst our guests are maladies, marauders, murderers and warmongers. What are you? Not human, since you are not a child of Tāne and have heard of neither of your hosts. A new sickness that has claimed the lives of humanity—a fever or a pox?'

What was I indeed? I had planned to kill a human, but had never followed through with my plan. Is it evil enough just to dream of it, to imagine the taste on your tongue? If that was true, then this waka would have been overwhelmed with spirits. It is not enough just to wish for something, one must take action to be responsible.

Perhaps I was like a disease—I had invaded the thoughts and stories, first of the birds and then of the humans, to give myself form. I fed off their attention like a parasite. I encouraged the spread of my stories so that I could sap strength from many. But none had died because of my thoughts, although I had killed beings for their thoughts. Is it evil to feed off the lives of others?

Hatupatu had called me evil, because of how I looked, and then because of how I tempted him. But he was not reacting to evil within *me*—he saw his own evil reflected in my image.

But yet, Whiro and Tū claimed that I would not have been drawn to them if I did not have evil within me. I knew what it was but pretended I didn't, allowing myself to be blind to the rage I held for the betrayal I felt. I came here because it had infected me. I came here because I wished to go into battle. It was not me who brought evil to humanity, but humanity who brought evil to my heart.

'Why are you here?' Whiro stood tall and waited my answer.

Revenge.

Both Whiro and Tū whooped with joy. 'You are kin, spirit.'

Whiro said, 'Come.'

He beckoned me as he turned and stepped into the shadow. I followed him into the darkness and found that the space he walked into was far wider and longer than the waka above had seemed. Of course this place had different rules than the world I had experienced in 'life'—just as Hinenuitepō could exist as both womb-like cave and woman, so too could this place stretch out to accommodate hordes of spirits.

There was a battle raging within the waka—men fighting men with taiaha, mere or their bare hands.

Tū smiled as we watched them, raising his voice to be heard over the battle cries. 'It is beautiful, isn't it? This is my work, my masterpiece.'

I expanded across the battle—to those below, perhaps it looked as if a storm was brewing above them. I observed many fights at once—each warrior a master at the art of war. I learnt how the body moves when striking, how quickly the feet move in parry, and how much strength it takes to choke a man to death. The warriors' deaths here seemed to be as temporary as the deaths of atua. A warrior had barely enough time to close his eyes, or fall on his back, before he was reanimated again. Even those that had limbs cut from them, or skin flayed, seemed to have no rest. Men who became meals to their foes would cry out as the flesh was torn from their limbs. Even those with no flesh at all, whose organs had been consumed or crushed into the ground, still fought—their bones held together by their desire to kill.

I mingled with the blood in the air, enjoying the taste of it, becoming infected with the madness I witnessed. I tried to concentrate myself and push my consciousness into one of the warriors. I entered him, splattering his skin with the blood I had held onto. I could not control his body and neither could he. We stood in the middle of the battlefield unable to move. Soon, the warriors around us realised that we stood paralysed. I could have left his body then, given him a chance to fight the ring of warriors that were closing in on him—but I didn't. I wanted to feel what his defeat would be like.

His body could not scream as the warriors descended on him, as his flesh and limbs were hacked. I kept his body upright as he endured blow after blow, before finally releasing him to the ground.

But no satisfaction could be had by torturing some nameless warrior. It was not his body that I wanted to inflict pain upon. I could stay here under the hull of the waka of Whiro, in the endless loop of battle, feeding my rage but never finding relief from it. I withdrew from the field, raining blood upon those who remained. They did not notice my retreat, the blood I shed mixing in with the blood already on their skin.

'What, you've had enough, spirit?' Tū asked as I gathered myself and my wits. 'Have you had your revenge?'

The fighting around me had been chaotic and senseless. The men fought for fighting's sake—enemy turned ally and ally turned enemy in the space of the blow of a mere. There was no reason, no purpose to this battle.

Why are they fighting?

'To honour me.' Tū opened his arms out as if he was embracing the entire battle—each blow inflicted on the battlefield opened on his chest in a flare of light. His skin would close over, but not before another blow flared. Instead of sapping his strength, these injuries seemed to bolster him.

This is how you feed?

'This is what sustains me.'

This pain?

'These people. What do you feed on, spirit? What sustains you?'

Whiro had been laughing as he watched the battle on the field. His grin was so big that it seemed to threaten to split his face. His eyes were opened wide as if he was afraid of missing all of the action. I noticed that the whites of his eyes were tinged with the yellow I had followed here. That if he was in the realm of the living, he would have been sure to die from whatever disease was within him. He was enjoying the insanity, growing more and more excited from the violence before him, and his eyes were saturated with yellow.

'Is it time?' Whiro asked Tū.

'I release them to you.'

Whiro opened his mouth and a stream of sulphur yellow poured from him. It clung to the ground, spreading out like fog towards the men fighting. It looked as though the men were knee deep in some poisonous river, and still it flowed from the mouth of Whiro. His eyes were losing their yellow tinge as the battlefield became choked with yellow mist.

And then the men began to fall, not from the blows of weapons but from the yellow mist they inhaled. The men coughed and shook with fever until they could stand no more. They fell on top of each other in a writhing heap and then they were still. Their bodies turned putrid quickly, the wounds they had sustained in the battle turning gangrenous, their untouched flesh rotting. When their flesh had been stripped and their bones had crumbled into the ground below, Whiro breathed in.

He inhaled the yellow mist, his chest lifting up and expanding with the volume of it. He breathed in not only the malady that had cleared the battlefield but also the fragments of bodies left behind. When he had inhaled all of the yellow mist, when it seemed as if he could hold no more air in his body, he held his breath as if savouring the taste of it—as if he was enjoying the sensation of it in his lungs and in his brain. His eyes fluttered underneath his closed eyelids as he held on, longer than I had ever seen a human go without breath. Finally he let his breath go with a *hā*, a mere sigh after the devastation it had wrought.

Are they gone?

Both Whiro and Tū shook their heads. The ground of the empty battlefield stirred. Climbing up from the dirt—fingertip to hand to arm—the warriors were rising again. Now each was whole as they pushed themselves, clawed themselves from their graves. The ones that rose first hacked at those who lingered longer beneath the ground—some had already lost limbs before they had shaken the loose earth from their eyes. They sneezed—*tihei*—a perversion of Tāne breathing life into Hineahuone. Each cried as they rose to battle again. A cry for death, not life.

Tū again stepped forward and opened his arms to his progeny. Whiro of the yellow eyes grinned as the battle began once more. I could not stand to watch this cycle again. I could not let myself be tempted to rejoin the fray. I skirted along the top of the hull, over the masters of this place, Whiro and Tū, and towards the light. I followed the curve of the hull up and down and then over the prow. The figurehead with the bulging eyes and tongue moved his head, following my movement up. If I had looked in his eyes, he probably would have begged me to loosen his bindings so that his spirit might find Te Rēinga and his loved ones.

Te Rēinga.

I thought of the hills and the lake below, the love of the relatives who called the spirits down. I need not follow a yellow path to find it, I could just will myself to be there.

And I did.

CHAPTER THREE

WHANAUNGA

Did Te Rēinga materialise before me, or did I materialise within it? I cannot be sure—its appearance to me or my appearance to it was disorientating. I imagine it felt like it might feel to wake from an unexpected deep sleep, unsure whether you have slept right through to the next day or whether only a few minutes have passed. Perhaps in those moments of confusion you ask yourself whether you still live or if you have passed on, before assuring yourself that the room is the same and that your heart still beats.

I was glad to be free of the madness of the realm of Whiro and Tū, and back to somewhere so familiar, somewhere beautiful—although to me there was also beauty in the horror of the upturned hull of the waka of Whiro, beauty in the passion and chaos of the fight, beauty in the decay of flesh. Perhaps I was kin to Whiro and Tū after all. Perhaps I had stayed too long with them, perhaps part of me stayed there.

I rolled over the tops of the hills, feeling the thoughts of the newly arrived spirits. These spirits seemed like innocents compared to the fierce warriors I had left behind. I wondered how many had been embraced by Hine before following their path here. I tried to detect her on them—her touch, her smell, but I could not find a trace of her there. I grieved that she might have withheld it from me.

I watched as the spirits below called up to their kin in the hills, watched the descent of the incorporeal, and their transformation into their past form. Such power their name had over them that the mere call of it could bind them in the memory of their former body.

And then he looked up to the hills. A man of broad shoulders, a man who carried the responsibility he had shouldered in life. A man whose face bore the scars of his escape from this giant, this monster, this ogress, this bird-woman. He recognised me as I recognised him and he called my name.

'Kurangaituku.'

Called me as he would call blood of his blood, as he would call to his beloved. We both knew that his call was one of surprise rather than one to reunite us, but the rules of that realm do not discriminate between the intentions behind the call. If a name was called then a spirit would descend. If the spirit was recognised, then it was welcomed to live by the lake.

We are entwined—aho twists over and under whenu.

I was pulled towards him, offering no resistance. Somewhere down the hill, I felt myself pull into cells, knit together into flesh. Somewhere down the hill, I had legs to carry me forward. Somewhere down the hill, my body formed,

part bird and part woman. Somewhere down the hill, my eyes had returned and I could see his face, contorted in horror.

'Kurangaituku!'

I was formed from his memory and mine—as tall as the biggest moa, my stature greater than any man who would ever live from his tribe. My legs sturdy; my clawed feet dug into the ground of the hill as I descended. Underneath shaggy feathers, the muscles of my thighs flared and lengthened with each step. I felt the weight of my breasts as I ran, the slight chill on my bare skin.

And then the tug of wind resistance as my wings returned to me, each tipped with long, thin fingers, each with sharp talons that doubled their length at least.

I AM …

… made manifest by his call to me, by the rules of this realm.

I reclaimed the body that was ripped apart by the heat of the mud pool, feeling the sensation of my body even though I knew it wasn't real flesh and blood. Still, it felt as I remembered it—the weight of my step, the resistance of air and ground against limbs, the stretch of muscle in movement.

Hatupatu was not as I remembered him. The body his spirit reclaimed was that of an older man, at least twenty years or more older than when he had spent time with me. The boy had filled out—his legs were strong and muscular, his shoulders and chest had broadened, and there was a hint of grey in his hair. His face bore more than the scar I had given him, the rest of his face carved and coloured with tā moko. My scar was left ink free, but the skin that covered my claw marks stood out, shiny and puckered in his mask. The eye that I had nicked had turned white and opaque—he looked fearsome.

He had turned to run before I had even finished my descent.

'What is it that you want, spirit?'

I want …

I thought of the miromiro sent to find me, how its lilt—*tihi-ori-ori-ori*—made me believe for a moment that he had sent his love to me, before I knew the truth.

I want …

I thought of Hine, my hands on her thighs, my tongue on her tonetone, my fingers deep in her, the pulse of her muscles as they contracted and released around my hand, and in that perfect moment I still wasn't satisfied.

I want …

I thought of my cave and the centuries that I had dwelt there, the pūrātoke and ngārara that lived with me, the manu that roosted above me, the taonga I had made and collected, the life, my life, that I had built there rent apart in just a moment.

I want …

```
The smell of his sweat, semen, blood.

The taste of his fear trailing behind him as he ran.

The sight of his smirk crumbling into a scream.
```

I want …

I want …

REVENGE.

And so I pursued Hatupatu once more.

He ran first to one of the hills that surrounded the lake, scrambling up and sliding down the sides that were too steep to climb. I had reached the flat near the lake and was lengthening my strides towards him. Dirty, with knees and palms torn and scraped by his attempted ascent, Hatupatu ran to the lake. He turned to look at me before leaping into the water.

He swam with the confidence of a person raised near water. He had strong smooth strokes and kicks and moved with an assured rhythm. As fast as I was on land, it was clear that I would be no match with him in the water. Besides, I could see no sense in following him into the lake—the water would weigh down my feathers and sink me below the water. Instead I ran around the lake to meet him on the shore at the other side, watching him as he made progress across the lake.

And then something strange happened—Hatupatu disappeared. I thought that perhaps he had dived under the water, and so I waited for him to make a reappearance when his breath ran out. I waited several minutes until I realised that in this realm, in the realm of the dead, he probably did not need to breathe as he had done on earth. I had forgotten that he, like me, was dead.

I ran on to where I thought he would land and waited there awhile too, but there was still no sign of him. There was no other choice but to follow him into the water. I stepped off the shore into the shallows. The water was neither hot nor cold, but the temperature of human blood. Tepid and comforting to those who came to bathe. I waded deeper expecting the feathers on my legs to become sodden and heavy, but like so many things in that realm, the water behaved unexpectedly. It was not like the pool I had shared with Hinenuitepō. Although I could feel the water here, although it felt wet to me—my body stayed dry. The lake was like the people who lived on its shores—representations of earth memories.

I went further out until my feet no longer touched the ground, buoyed by this phantom water. I stretched out my wings—it was the closest feeling I had of flying in my body since I first transformed into this monstrous body. I hesitated to dip my head under, the thought of my death haunting me still. I felt foolish because of this irrational thought, and then angry at myself.

What do you want, spirit?

What do you want?

I dived under the surface and was surprised to see the world above mirrored below, the light was just as bright. I looked up from the centre of the lake

and there was a dark circle in the middle of the sky, the grey clouds circling around it, and I felt its pull. I burst through the surface of the mirrored lake and flew up into the greyed skies above, moving as freely and assuredly as one who was raised in the air.

I flew towards the darkness, circling as the clouds above me circled. As I approached, I saw that the clouds had formed a wall around the darkness, a passage that curved up. I flew into the centre of it and found my feet on swirling clouds that felt as dense as the ground. I walked further into the darkness, the passage becoming tighter around me, as if it was made of contracting muscle.

I moved further into the passage. The light was dappled in the passage, the clouds it was made from swirling around me. It was cramped for a creature of my size; I had to duck my head and keep my arms tucked in.

I heard footsteps ahead of me, someone walking at a leisurely pace. Someone who thought that they had escaped again. I ran as best as I could, using my arms and hands on the walls to claw my way forward. The footsteps ahead of me stopped as if the person was listening for me. And then they picked up their pace.

`I could see him.`

`I was gaining on him.`

Hatupatu ran further down the passage where the light became muddy. I could see the tinge of sulphur yellow in the air in front of him and heard the hum—I knew where he was heading. I pushed myself to crawl faster. I could see Hatupatu ahead of me until suddenly he had disappeared again, and so had the light. This time it seemed as if a gate had closed between us.

I dropped from the ceiling and ran towards it, hoping to ram it open with my shoulder, but as I approached I saw that it was an animate barrier. On each side of the passage, like the carved pou of the Song Makers, were two entities. They stood as tall and robust as tōtara trees, so tall in the narrow passage that they seemed to need to twist themselves to fit the curves of it perfectly. Their heads faced forward, but their bodies were in profile.

Clasped together as they were, they seemed to make one great face. Their heads created the gate's eyes, their joined hands made the nose and their legs and feet the mouth. I looked for somewhere to breach them, but they filled the space entirely.

They spoke in one voice. 'You may not pass between Tuapiko and Tuwhaitiri, spirit.'

Why had they let Hatupatu pass, and not me?

Tuapiko and Tuwhaitiri seemed to be able to read my thoughts and my intentions. 'Your spirit is heavy with utu. You are clumsy with the wish for revenge.'

As if to prove their point, I attempted to ram them with my shoulder. They stood strong—I bounced off them and landed on the ground.

'Turn back, spirit, you may not pass.'

I turned my back on them. I knew where Hatupatu was headed. I had been there before. But as much as I willed myself to the waka of Whiro, I still found myself standing in this narrow passage. The hills that surrounded the lake were too steep to climb, and even if I was successful in that ascent there was range upon mountain range to traverse. In this form I had to pass these guardians to follow Hatupatu.

If I was not a match for them physically then I hoped I was mentally. These beings did not rule this realm—they were just enforcers of the rules. To get past them all I needed was the authority to do so.

I closed my eyes and thought of Hine—the power that throbbed beneath her skin, her eyes of living greenstone. I felt the shift within the memory of me and opened my eyes, now pounamu in colour and lightning streaked. I turned and faced Tuapiko and Tuwhaitiri, and pushed my will towards them.

Let me pass.

Tuapiko and Tuwhaitiri lowered their eyes to me. 'Forgive us, we did not recognise you.' They shuffled apart and I strode through them.

The muddy light of the passage merged into darkness, deep blues and olive greens, browns and ochre red and the hint of sulphur yellow, the droning hum of voice upon voice. I could not see Hatupatu in the darkness, but I continued.

Again the sulphur yellow clumped together.

Spirit, it said and I flicked my hand through it dispersing the particles in the air. I had no time for the parlour tricks of Whiro and Tū. This time the yellow followed me down.

Spirit, it said and I ignored it.

The colour swirled around me, the voice urgent.

Spirit …

I did not need the guidance of those words; I knew what I sought.

I climbed down the passage and landed on the waka of Whiro, balancing on the ridge of the hull. I walked one foot in front of the other along the length of it until I reached the figurehead on the prow. I could not tell if he recognised me—his eyes and tongue bulged in much the same way as they had done before. I cocked my head at him and considered slitting his throat, but that would not have been a mercy in this place—instead he would exist with the pain forever, his heart pumping out his blood until he ran dry, only to be revived again with full veins.

I opened my wings so I could glide down from the top of the hull.

From the shadow of the hull I heard the voice of Whiro. 'Who are you, spirit? The spirits I meet usually cower before me.'

I had neither the voice nor the inclination to answer him. I walked under the prow of the waka.

'Who are you?' Whiro boomed, but I would not cower to a fool.

Kurangaituku. I let my name wrap around me—sound and colour buffeted Whiro.

Tū laughed in the shadow and came forward.

'Do you recognise …'

I strode past them both, not wanting to waste time on their posturing. Whiro and Tū followed me into the shadow.

The smell of blood—I had forgotten the tang of metal in the scent of spilt blood. The battle continued to rage as I suppose it had done for centuries. There seemed to be more warriors than before, but it was hard to tell in the writhing mass of bodies. Although I could not spread myself over the battle as I had done before, I was tall enough to look over the heads of the fighting men.

At first I could not see Hatupatu. All the men seemed to look the same, enraged and graceful in their movements. Whiro and Tū had followed me into the waka and stood either side of me. Tū stepped forward and was about to open his arms to the warriors when I spotted Hatupatu. He was standing over the body of a man he had defeated. His arms tensed as he grabbed the fallen warrior's hair and hacked at his neck. Blood spattered him as he tore head from body. Hatupatu held his prize aloft, before throwing it onto a pile of other heads. He picked up his mere to fight again. I did not know then that in his mind he was reliving his most famous battle, that in his mind he was claiming the head of Raumati again and again.

I opened my wings, blocking Tū from his blood libation. He would not feast from this battle before I did.

'How dare you …'

I turned and looked at the god of war, and he saw the rage in my eyes. He saw that I would satisfy his hunger for conflict more than one hundred of the warriors that he had trapped in this waka.

Tū licked his lips. 'Go.'

And I stepped onto the battlefield.

For a moment the warriors were too engrossed in their own battles to see me. I stood tall with my wings at my side. I was still as they fought around me. I was waiting for Hatupatu to turn. I was waiting for him to see me.

Hatupatu had won another battle. Again he stood over the body of his fallen enemy, his face was down as he hacked the head free. He cried out in

victory as he lifted both his head and the one he had won—only to have his voice die as he saw me.

And then I struck. I opened my wings, impaling the warriors either side of me, one through the back and one through the chest. I closed my hands into fists ripping their hearts from their bodies, through spine and ribs. They fell at my feet as I crushed their hearts.

Tū sighed and groaned and laughed as I inflicted death upon death, clearing my path to Hatupatu.

Hatupatu cleared his own path, felling warriors as he escaped from me.

My feathers were saturated in blood—my wings as red as the kākahu kākā that Hatupatu once coveted. I twisted the head off one of the warriors as easily as I had done to the miromiro. I held it up to Hatupatu as he had held his prize, mocking his prowess. It almost worked. He stood his ground for a moment, a warrior intent on restoring his mana, intent on facing me in battle. This giant, this monster, this ogress.

'Kurangaituku!' he called me towards him, raising his mere above his head.

I could hear the delirious laughter of Tū behind me. 'It is glorious, glorious ...'

And then Whiro asking, 'Is it time?'

No. I would not let Whiro rob me of this moment. I turned to see him step forward, see his mouth open and the sulphur yellow pouring out. I opened my wings and pushed myself up into the air, burying the head I had ripped off with my push off. I landed next to Whiro and grabbed his cheeks with my hand, hoping to squeeze his mouth shut. His eyes bulged like his figurehead's.

'Kurangaituku wants you to stop.' Tū slurred his words like he had fed on fermented karaka berries.

I held on to the cheeks of Whiro, my claws digging into his scalp, which bled down his forehead and into his yellow eyes. I pointed towards where Hatupatu had stood moments before, but my prey had gone. I let go of Whiro as I looked for Hatupatu. The yellow mist of Whiro filled the battlefield

and men started to fall. Even as the crowd thinned from fever I could not see Hatupatu.

I alighted to the battlefield once more and walked in the yellow mist, watching men succumb to the disease of Whiro. I searched through the bodies of those that had already been ravaged, the rot setting in so that some of them fell apart in my hands. The yellow mist made it difficult to see. Where had Hatupatu gone? Was he still here amongst these men?

Whiro breathed in, sucking the yellow mist from the air, taking with it whatever remnants remained of the warriors that had fought here. I was alone on the empty battlefield. I turned to look at Whiro and Tū—although they had already feasted they looked hungry again.

I walked to where I had last seen Hatupatu as the ground stirred beneath me. From where he had stood a hand emerged from the ground. I clasped it in my own and helped the spirit up from the blood soaked dirt, but it was not him. I crushed the warrior's skull before he had lifted his torso from his grave. I pulled man after man from the ground beneath me but none were Hatupatu. He must have escaped when I tried to stop Whiro. I ran towards the stern of the waka, even though it looked as if I would not be able to stand up there as it was buried deep into the ground.

'Wait, don't leave,' I heard Tū plead. 'The battle starts anew.'

I could hear the cries of the warriors I had left behind me. I could feel their blood drying on my feathers. I ran from them until I could not run, until I had to crawl underneath the hull of the waka. I crawled until it felt as if the waka had collapsed on top of me, until it felt as if I was trapped within an egg again wishing for release.

I could not push up through the waka—I tried to punch through the hull but the wood held strong. My only choice then was down. I began to dig beneath me—the space I had crawled into was so tight that at first it felt as if I was only moving the earth one millimetre at a time. I made barely a scratch for what seemed like hours. I pushed my hands further into the ground beneath me and remembered the lake of Te Rēinga, water that was the memory of water. This was not earth as I had experienced it in life.

I was not buried here as I was after the eruption. My claws would not break against this. I did not have to wait for a crack to free me. I just had to will it.

As the thought took hold, I felt my hands push through as if I had plunged them into water. I dived head first into the puddle I had created and plunged down.

CHAPTER FOUR
AUĒ

I felt as if I was floating in water again. I looked above me, and I could see the colours of the darkness swirling—tinged with the sulphur yellow of the realm of Whiro.

The colours above were reflected in this world too, but dappled. Beneath me the colour pooled into blobs of darkness that were dark grey or brown. I could not tell; it was as if my eyes were slightly out of focus, or that I was looking through something viscous. It did seem as if I was underwater— my feathers were clean of the blood from the battlefield, and they seemed

to float. But unlike being in the water on earth, I could hear and smell. I could hear whispers; they eddied around me, rolling into me like waves. This realm smelled like petrichor, the earth after rain. It reminded me of the forest. I opened my beak and it filled with a salty taste, and it made me feel sad and heavy. I felt myself sink down a bit lower. What was this world made of?

Motivating myself to move was difficult. I swam down further towards the whispers, trying to make them out. As I swam down, the blobs of darkness became clearer. They were the floating bodies of spirits. Some floated higher than others, but all had curled themselves up, knees to chests. The whispers I heard were louder and clearer as I descended. The sound was hundreds, if not thousands, of laments for the dead.

Auē! Auē!

The word extended into a wail, the *ēēē* seemingly endless and tinged with weeping.

I swam closer to one of the suspended spirits—his eyes were shut and his mouth open as if he was crying. I swam to another, a woman this time. She held her knees to her chest, her mouth open as if she cried in mourning. But no sound came from her mouth; the laments I heard were not coming from these spirits' opened mouths. Instead the laments were entering the mouths of the spirits, the spirits swallowing the sadness. Their mouths open and greedy as pīpīwharauroa.

This world was made of the tears that had been shed for the dead, the laments and prayers of the living, and all of that grief weighed heavily on the spirits. I thought of Hinenuitepō holding me and whispering, *Ka heke te roimata me te hupe. Ka ea te mate*—and my gasp let grief both in and out.

I shut my beak. The taste of sadness I had experienced above was enough to sap my motivation. The water lower down was thick with grief—such pain would be debilitating. I could not let it distract me from my goal, from finding Hatupatu.

I watched the woman as she swallowed the mourning. As she slowly sank further and further down, she lifted her chin and opened her mouth wider.

The spirits on this level all appeared to be doing the same, as if they were greedy for the pain.

I swam amongst them and then back up, looking for Hatupatu. I found him just as he was lifting his own chin up. I reached out and opened the scars on his face anew, but blood did not rush out. Instead he rose a little in the water, as if some of the sadness had escaped him. I foolishly opened my mouth in frustration and the sadness rushed into me. None of these laments were for me, but I could feel the sadness within them. I could feel the grief of lives cut short, of the loneliness of the living.

I sank as Hatupatu sank. I felt my own chin tilt upwards waiting to be fed like a greedy pīpīwharauroa chick. I felt the sadness fill me, the salt of tears like blood pulsing in my veins.

Auē! Auē!

To close my mouth to the sadness took all of my strength, but still I had swallowed enough to lose the will to move my own limbs. I had become one of the many spirits who were sinking down and down.

The laments had been replaced with a sound that was like ripping and of something dry rubbing together.

We all sank down into blackness—it looked glossy and moved like seaweed. The black of it was cross-hatched with a little grey. This level was dry, but it still felt as if we were floating. I could not see anything but black, but the darkness had a substance to it. In some places soft, in other places harsh. I reached out and realised that I could hold the darkness in my hand.

It was hair. Cut or shorn from the heads of the mourning. I pushed through it and it clung to my limbs, wrapped around my feet like weeds. It was like digging through sand—as soon as I had displaced some of it, the void was filled with more hair. I pushed through it to find Hatupatu.

Some of the hair had formed into knots around the spirits, woven around them like Taranga had wrapped the body of her stillborn son Māui. I ripped the hair apart with my claws, letting great handfuls float away. Inside, the spirits were completely naked—stripped of any memory of clothing and

all the hair from their body. Their bodies curved into their knots so that they looked as babies might in their mothers' wombs. The knots rewove themselves with floating hair as soon as I had ripped them apart.

I could feel the hair twisting around my legs as I swam to find the pod that held Hatupatu. If I was as still as these spirits perhaps I too would have been encased in a knot of hair. I used my claws to rip through the hair, pulling myself from knot to knot until I found him. It seemed like the knots themselves were being pulled down. I ripped open a knot and found him, ripping and ripping the hair away from his face as the knot reworked itself.

We were moving down, and we were accelerating. I did not know if I had the strength to hold onto the knot of Hatupatu. I clung to the outside of it, and the hair wove around me, trapping my hands and feet and then working its way up my limbs, finally covering my head. It felt like the hair was trying to rip my feathers from me. It wrapped around each shaft and knotted itself and pulled. But it did not work—although I felt the pain of being plucked, my feathers held fast. Perhaps the hair only had power over its own kind. It loosened around me as if it rejected me, and I found myself floating above the knot of Hatupatu as it raced down.

I pushed off against the mass of hair above me, swimming down into sticky redness. The smell of iron was unmistakable, I was swimming in blood. I swam down looking for the knots of hair, but they had disappeared. The spirits now floated unfurled and naked. Their eyes were opened and their mouths closed. Their arms and legs relaxed as if each of them were floating on their backs. Slashes of light appeared on the skin of their limbs— it looked as though they were being cut. As each slash appeared, the spirits seemed to sigh with pleasure rather than pain, as if the cut released the grief they had absorbed in the worlds above.

I slashed a spirit across its chest with my claws. The cuts glowed with light and the spirit smiled at me. I slashed another one and another and every one had the same reaction. The slashes of light became more frequent and the flesh that had entrapped the spirits came free, at first in thin ribbons and then in large chunks. The flesh floated up above me making a thick

barrier, so thick that it began to push me and all of the spirits down further into this world. Below us all was light—golden and tinged at the edges with the blue of summer sky. We were all being pushed towards it.

The spirits were freeing themselves of their bodies now, pulling at tags of flesh and tugging at skin. One pulled the flesh off her forearm and hand, and for a brief moment the light underneath mimicked the flesh that had held it until it found its own form—free from the confines of flesh and bone. Those spirits who had freed themselves entirely moved towards the light and as more spirits joined them, the gravity of this world reversed—the spirits were now drawn up instead of down.

To me it felt as if I was being pushed up by the flesh and down by the light above, and the blood-like substance that I was floating in was draining away. The flesh finally pushed up against my feet. I had to bend over to keep my head below the surface—the light above seemed too bright for my eyes. But I could not avoid it forever and so I closed my eyes and broke the surface.

CHAPTER FIVE

ROHE

When I opened my eyes I found that I was standing chest deep in a slow-moving river. Above me was the vaulted ceiling of a cavern, and the river ran through it. Tied to the bank opposite me was a raft. A woman stood at the head of the raft as spirits boarded it. Her long hair was down, veiling her face. She held a pole in her hands, and I was not sure if it was to be used as a rudder or to punt. She did not look back at the spirits who were gathering—she kept her eyes forward, perhaps focused on their destination.

I walked towards the raft, the water running swiftly, but it was easy to cross. I was only a stride or two from the raft when the woman raised her pole to me.

'Ssspirid. Yu mussd sssdop,' she spoke with a hissing lisp, her words slow and slurred.

I continued to walk towards her and she lifted her pole and struck it down towards me like a taiaha. I parried away from it.

'Sspirid, yre unclean widh flesssh. I canno dake yu vrom dhiss place.'

Again I walked towards her. This time her blow met me. I was surprised by the power of it and shook my head.

'Yu muss redurn.' She used her pole to push my head, trying to push me under. I was dazed by the blow, and she managed to dip the front of my head down. Under the water I smelled iron and saw spirits rending their flesh. I grabbed her pole and heaved myself up, back into her world. We both struggled with the pole—she was trying to loosen it from my grip and I was trying to pull myself up with it. I could see that she was pulling the pole towards her with all of her strength, so I let it go. She fell backwards onto her raft, sending spirits up into the air as if they were dust. I used the time she was down to swim to the raft and pull myself onto it. She stood and threatened me with her pole again.

'Hoo ar yu do devy me, ssspirid?'

Yet another being who thought that I ought to recognise them. My body told of my frustration—my shoulders slumped and my head hung down.

The woman nudged me with her pole, but I did not respond to her. I sat on the edge of the raft, my feet dipping into the water. I let my legs relax so my feet drifted in the current of the river. She nudged me again. If she had pushed a little harder I would have fallen off the edge and let myself sink or be carried away.

'Ssspirid ...' The woman knelt down beside me, and the raft adjusted to the shift in weight. When I didn't turn to answer her, the woman sat down beside me. She unfolded her legs from beneath her, making the raft rock from side to side. She dangled her feet into the water next to mine, bird claw and

human foot both lifted and pulled by the current. She kicked her legs a little against the current and then let them relax—kick, relax, kick, relax—as if she could not stand to be pushed around by anything or anyone. We sat and watched the light rippling the surface of the water, felt the raft sink lower with each new spirit, although they did not weigh anything at all. The laws of earth are difficult to forget, even in places where they do not apply.

The spirits pooled together as they boarded, no one distinguishable from another. They had become parts of a whole.

'I mussd daake dhese ssspiridss sssoon.'

She reached a hand to me and I flinched. 'Imm sssorry for hhhidding yu. I musssd daake a virm hhand wiv sssome ssspiridss hhoo revusse duh give uuh dheeir vorms.'

So I was not the first to emerge still stuck in my body.

'Ssome ssspiridss hhhave a harr dime givving uuh dhuh idea dhad dhey ah ee'le ...' She cupped her hand under my chin and turned my head to look at her. 'Uud I ssee dhad yu ah nod a ... 'errssson.'

It was not meant as an insult, so why did I take it as one? I pulled my head from her hand and nicked her with my beak as I withdrew. The woman's face was strange—it somehow did not seem to fit her head, it seemed too big for her as if she was wearing a mask. She seemed to have trouble controlling her face—her expressions were a little off, or a little too slow, and some of her muscles twitched involuntarily. Stranger still, her skin was fully decorated with tā moko in a manner that I thought only for male Song Makers. Her face was confusing, and so without realising, I had cocked my head while looking at her.

She touched her cheek gingerly, as if her face was poisonous to the rest of her. 'Ai hussand id dhisss duh ee.' She reached her hand towards me again, 'Hhoo did dhad duh yu?'

I pulled myself away from her touch, and scrambled to my feet. A few spirits that had just boarded were knocked off the raft as I stood, pooling on the surface of the water for a moment before rising and boarding again.

I cannot say why I reacted this way to her touch. Perhaps I was wary that I might become bewitched by her as I had with Hine. This woman was as ugly as Hine was beautiful, but I knew that my feelings for Hine were more than a reaction to her looks. Hine and I had loved each other for what we recognised in one another. In this woman I sensed a life and a betrayal akin to mine— and I didn't want empathy, I still wanted revenge.

She waited for the rocking of the raft to subside before she spoke again. She did not move from where she sat, the splash of her kicking legs punctuating her speech.

'Doess my uglinesss reeulssse yu? Id reevoldsss ee. I havv nod ooked uh ai vasse sssinsse I came down hhere. Id iss onne dhing duh lossse ai 'eaudy, 'ud doo hhave id ree'aced 'y dhuh vasse oh dhuh one dhad sssdole id? Hhe daundsss ee sssdill in ai revlexxion.'

    Kick.

'I wass thuh sssisster of the sssun, and jusssd asss 'eaudivul. *Rohe dhuh 'eaudivul sssun maiden.* Avder Māui sslowed duh sssun, he dook ee asss hisss wive. I wasss duh ssspoilsss vrom 'addle I sssu'ose. I dell yu dhisss ssso yu undahsssdand dhad oursss wass nod a marriage made vrom love. I wass hisss prizzz and he wasss ai capdor.'

    Kick, kick.

She turned and looked at me over her shoulder. 'Have yu heard of ai hussband's exxxploidsss?' I nodded and she turned away from me again. 'Ai husssband wasss a demi-god, which iss do say dhad he wasssn'd much of a god ad all.' She laughed, a quiet hissing hiccough.

'Sssuch exxxploidsss—daming the sssun, vissshing duh land vrom duh sssea—dhey all dook a doll on hisss 'ody.' She turned again and pointed at her nose. 'Dhisss isss vrom when he 'oke hisss nossse do ussse hisss 'ood asss 'ait. Id never healed sdraighd and I can only 'reathe dhrough one nosssdril. Hiss ssskin iss dark and 'inkled from duh harsssh raysss of duh sssun dhad

burned him asss he held id widh hisss ropesss. Hiss ssskin isss loosse vrom ssshapessshivding from man do 'ird do man.'

Kick.

'I wasss 'eaudivul when he married ee. I dook pride in that 'eaudy. I wasss young and dhoughd dhad I would be 'eaudivul forever; id wasss whad defined me asss me. 'Erhavsss I wasss haughty, 'erhavsss I could have ssshown more deverensse do ai husssband, bud why ssshould I have ssshown ressspecd for a man who injured my ssssibling and kidnapped me?

'More dhan dhad, dhisss man did nod dessserve a wive sssuch asss ee. I wasss more 'eaudivul dhan him, yesss, but I wasss alssso ranked high above him. He had debasssed ee by kidnapping ee. I could nod defend mysself or my honour 'ysically. Duh only revenge I had at ai disss'osssal wasss emoxxional.'

KICK. Kick.

'When he lay widh ee I closssed ai eyesss and durned ai head. He would hold ai chin and dry do durn my head dowardsss him asss he rutted. "Why?" he would asssk avderwardsss. "Why do you nod look ad me?" I told him dhad hisss vasse disssgusssded ee, dhad iv I looked ad him while he wasss on dop of me dhad I would choke on ai own vomid and he would 'e ra'ing a cor'sse. He raissed hiss hand to ssdrike me, and I raissed ai cheek to ressseive it, knowing dhad he would nod mar ai 'eaudy. He walked away vrom me defeaded and I feld vicdoriousss.'

Ki!
Kick.   Kick.

'Every day, I would dry do vind a way do mock him. One day I sdood in dog exsskremend and I showed my husssband duh sssole of ai voodd—"Here isss your revlecxxion, husssband." Anodher day I vound a rodden kūmara in our pid. I lay id 'eside ee on hisss ssslee'ing mad and when ai husssband appeared I acded sssurprised—wasss he nod in bed already? I dook sssuch 'leassure in eacsh liddle jab. One mosquito bide iss annoying, hundredsss u'on hundredsss can be fadal.'

    Kick.

'He assked ee onsse iv he could have ai vasse. Id seemed a sdrange kesdion ad
duh dime—he had already daken all of ee. He already *had* ai vasse. I didn'd
realisse he meand id liderally.'

    KICK.

    KICK.

    KICK.

'He dook ai vasse asss I ssslepd—he had vound an incandaxxion do ssswa'
our vasses. I'm nod sssure iv dhis is whad he indended. 'Erhavss he dhoughd
dhad our vasses would remould dhemssselvesss on our headsss. 'Erhavsss
he god duh magic wrong. Asss yu can sssee, ai head wasss doo sssmall vor
hisss vasse—id did nod have duh 'one sssdrudjah do sssuppord id. I woke
uuh and found id divviculd do open ai eyesss, ai eyelidsss did nod ssseem
do ressss'ond do my dhoughdsss anymore. I douched ai vasse and id feld
sssdrange—dry and loossse where id onsse had been sssmoodh and daud. I
heard my hussband laugh—hisss laughder sssounded sssdrange asss dhough
id wass ssdrangled.'

    … kick.

'"Hooo iss ugly now, Rohe?" he asssked. I usssed ai vingersss do 'risse o'en ai
uncoohradive eyess. And dhen I doo laughed.'

    Her laugh now was more like a cough, as if she had expelled a
metastasised sigh.

    'Aldhough he had daken ai 'eaudy vor himssself, I could sssee dhad
he wasss nod asss 'eaudivul asss I had been. Ai vasse on hiss head had
been sssdredghed—hiss moudh pulled wide in a grimasse and hisss eyesss
were sssquinded. He wasss sssdill ugly. Uglier 'ecaussse ov whad he had
done. Id looked asss iv hisss ssskin would ssplid iv he sssmiled. I laughed
and wepd ad whad he had done. He had ruined usss both.'

    Kick. Kick.

'I asssked him do swidch usss back, 'leaded dhad I would never mock him again, dold him dhad I would look at hisss vasse when we made love. He revusssed. He would kee' my vasse no madder how ridiculousss he looked becausssse he knew ai punissshmend wass greader dhan hiss.'

Kick.

'I sssdayed in our whare dhad day. I had do learn how do condrol dhis vasse. I wepd for ai losssd 'eaudy and sssdruggled widh who I now wasss. Thisss man had deveaded ee, 'roughd ee do heel. I wasss no longer the 'eaudivul ssisssster of duh sssun. All dhad I wasss now wasss duh wive o' Māui.'

Rohe looked down at her feet, so small in the water below her.

'When he redurned dhad nighd, he revused do look at ee. He moved hiss ssslee'ing mad var vrom ee. Ssso now I was nod even hiss wive. 'Erhavvs ad bessd he would kee ee ass a ssslave and 'erhavss marry anodher 'eaudivul woman.'

Kick.

'Duh sssun rossse again. I wadched duh raysss 'ussh dhrough duh gapss in our wallss. Ai sssibling wass looking vor ee, reaching oud do douch ee. No doubd duh ssun had ssseen the new vase o' Māui. I knew dhad my hussband would nod hesssidade in mocking ai family onsse more. I wasss assshamed ad whad had been done do ee. I waided undil duh ssun wasss ssedding, undil duh ssun could nod ssee whad had been done do ee, and ran dowards ai vamily. I ran do where duh ssun ssetss, Te Uranga o te Rā. I live in duh gloam, duh murky dussk where I cannod ssee his vasse revlecded back at ee.

'I heard ov hiss deadh, crussshed and deca'daded bedween duh dhighsss of Hinenuitepō. And you mighd dhink dhad I rejoissed ad duh newsss—bud id made me sssad. Nod for hiss deadh, bud becausse he had preyed upon another sssleeping woman do ged whad he wanded. I should have ssssdopped him.'

I looked at the gathering spirits behind me. Had Māui waited on her raft? Did she recognise him when he arrived? One of these was surely Hatupatu, but stripped of his flesh and his ego I could no longer recognise him.

Rohe lifted her feet from the water and used her pole to push herself back up to standing. The raft rocked as she stood.

'I dake dhesse ssspiridss vrom ai realm do duh nexss. Dhey ar 're'ared do meed Miru. Dheir vorm reminds ee of duh ssun'ss rayss, aldhough dhey ar dimmer and cooler.' Rohe pulled the pole free from the bottom of the river and swung it around towards me—the tip of it at my throat.

'Ar yu here do claim ai realm vor yr own? Yu ressissded losssing yr body and idendidy—yu ar nod 'uman like dhesse ssspiridss. Dhese worlds ar revuge vor dhose who could nod live widhin duh sdricduresss ov realidy. Here, we can creade our own. I will nod lossse ai world again becaussse ov inaddenxxion. I will defend id from yu.'

She pushed me back with her pole. As I moved, the spirits burst and reformed around me—I was surrounded by their light and their thoughts for a moment. It was impossible to tell one from another—the light was the same, amber like honey, their thoughts an absence of want, an absence of self. Their peace made me feel angry. These spirits had lost their fight, their will to exist. They had lost themselves.

Rohe kept pushing me until I was at the edge of her raft. 'Dhiss iss ai realm. Yu may nod redurn undil yu have given uuh all yr wandsss, yr needsss and yr ambixxions. Onsse yu ar vree vrom duh burdenss of exissstensse, I will ferry yu do duh home o' Miru. Id would be bedder for yu, only I have ssseen her vasse and id is derrible. Lossse yrssself and yr mind ssso dhad Miru does nod haund yu. Yu don'd wand duh memory ov her—id is like ssshe hasss no vasse ad all, jusd a derrible, derrible void. Id made me veel dizzzzy like I would fall indo id. Go.'

She pulled her pole back slightly and used it to punch me in my chest. I was knocked back and toppled into the water.

I could see the strata of flesh beneath me, I could see the water turning a dark red deep down. I could hear the wailing far away under the water, *Auē!*

Auē! I closed my mouth to it and looked above me. I could see the shadow of the raft of Rohe—bobbing from corner to corner as she searched for any signs of my resurfacing. She must have been satisfied that I was not going to return, as I saw her thrust her pole into the water and push the raft from the bank.

I swam underneath the raft and held onto it, digging my claws into its base. Rohe did not seem to notice as she steered the raft through the river's current. The river ran fast, Rohe navigating over rapids and falls. I swung my legs up and clung to the underside with both my hands and my feet. It felt as if we were moving downwards—but to where? Rivers I had known on earth flowed towards lakes or seas—was the world of Miru an ocean?

The water slowed and Rohe navigated the raft towards a bank. I detached my feet and then my hands from her raft and let myself float beneath it for a moment. I pulled my arms back and let my wings push back against the water to swim backwards from underneath the raft. I let the top of my head surface and watched as Rohe steered her vessel back into the current and disappeared into darkness.

MIRU

This was no ocean. Rohe had brought the spirits to what seemed to be a little bay, the beach not much bigger than three of her raft lengths. I could easily cover the distance with a few strides. The bay was framed by rocky outcrops that rose like columns supporting the ceiling above. The curve of the ceiling made me sure that this world was shaped like a sphere—that if I looked to where the raft had been or gone I would only find a gently sloping wall of rock, and if I swam down I would find the same at the bottom.

Rohe had left the spirits on the shore. They still clumped together, and occasionally a sliver of light slipped from the mass on the sand.

Up from the beach, behind the dunes, I saw a whare. It seemed smaller than those I had seen during my life, but I had been in Rarohenga long enough to know that all was not as it seemed. Perhaps this whare opened up inside like the waka of Whiro, or perhaps it was a gateway to another place. Whatever it turned out to be, there was no doubt that it belonged to whoever ruled this world.

She came down from her whare, down to the dunes, and picked up the spirits that lay on the shore in her arms. Behind her, two great lizards followed. They looked like the lizards of the forest, like *all* the lizards of the forest—part kaweau, part mokomoko, part tuatara. They mostly resembled the tuatara—the crest of spines running down the head and body, but their skin was smooth like the mokomoko. The toes had claws as well as the sticky pads of the kaweau—these creatures could climb the walls if they wanted to. One was dark, shiny and black. The other was light, almost white, with diamonds of yellow on its back.

They resembled the lizards I had known except they were of a tremendous size—they followed behind their mistress, standing as tall as kurī. They were so like guard dogs that they both swivelled their heads towards me when I moved in the water.

The woman had her back to me as she gathered the spirits, but she saw her companion's reaction to the water. 'Tūtangatakino,' she said to the dark one, and 'Mokohikuwaru,' to the light, 'seek.'

The two lizards stalked down the shore as their mistress headed for her home with her bundle of spirits. Tūtangatakino and Mokohikuwaru moved together, fanning out either side of the little bay, intent on herding me out of the water. As each of them walked into the water, I swam towards them. Soon I was in water shallow enough to stand and when I did, both lizards froze. I was as much a bird of the forest as they were lizards of it. They knew the natural order of the world above—and even in these worlds of unreality, instinct is hard to shake.

I sprang from the water, using my wings to glide down near the dark one, Tūtangatakino. I was just as gigantic and monstrous as he—and he released his tail as I grabbed it. I held it, still twitching, as I turned to find Mokohikuwaru—pale enough to hide amongst the dunes, but dim-witted enough to climb the dark walls instead. I leapt up towards him, snapping my beak, and I caught his tail as he fled—both lizards running home to their mistress, Miru.

I held both tails in my hand as I climbed the dunes to her house. Miru sat on the paepae in front of her whare. Her lizards had crawled up to the maihi, one on each side above her, so still that they looked as if they were carved into the wood. Miru did not look up at me. Her skin and hair were dark, like the paru from the river flats I used to dye muka black. Her hair hung down to her waist so that when she was sitting it brushed along the top of the paepae. She was dressed in garments that were a startling white against her dark skin—a fine cloak fastened across one shoulder and a maro that fell to her knees. She was equal to me in height—larger than any Song Maker that I had seen—and had wide hands and long slim fingers that worked quickly and expertly.

In a pile next to her were the spirits she had gathered. She reached into the pile and grabbed a handful, using her fingernails to separate the spirits into strands. Her maro left her thighs naked and she rolled the strands together against her thigh, twining two or three at a time, preparing the spirits as I had prepared muka for weaving.

I dropped the lizards' tails in front of her and she looked up at me. She could have been twin to Hinenuitepō, or perhaps I was meeting another aspect of my lover. Her eyes flashed with lightning as well, but were the opaque white of cataracts. For a moment I foolishly thought she was blind, and bent down towards her to get a better look.

Miru grabbed my beak and I discovered that her hands were strong as well as nimble.

'You bring these to me? Why? As offerings?' Miru released my beak and I stumbled back.

The lizards hissed at me and stopped suddenly as I raised my head.

Miru stood and hit the maihi with her fist. 'Some kaitiaki you turned out to be. Get out of here you useless things!' The lizards crawled up to the ridgepole of the whare and disappeared along the roof. Miru bent down, picked up their tails, and threw them at the lizards as they departed. 'Take these with you!'

Miru sat down again. 'They'll just sulk for a while. They'll be back when they get hungry. Unless they eat each other's tails, I suppose.' She pulled strands out of the pile again and rolled them together. I watched her. It was comforting to see something so familiar. My hands itched to weave again.

I sat next to her and she stopped to look at me. 'Sure, make yourself at home, stranger. First you maim my pets and now you expect some hospitality?'

She looked so much like Hine in face, but in temperament they differed greatly.

'Why do you keep looking at me?'

I touched my face and reached out to hers in answer.

'I remind you of someone? What do you see in my face? My pets see kin—to them I have the face of a lizard. When Rohe arrived, I had thought that perhaps we two could converse. On her first trip here, she brought the spirits up to the whare. I stood to greet her and she dropped the bundle she was carrying. To her I looked frightening. I could not ask her—she had lost her speech, and then she ran from me. Is it her face that I wear for you?'

I shook my head at her question, *No.*

'It is someone of this place though? Someone you were fond of, since you stare at me.' I cocked my head at her, wishing I had the speech to end this guessing game.

'Not Whiro, not Tū? Perhaps that slut Hinetītama.'

Her venom surprised me and I jerked my head back.

'Friend of yours is she? "Friend" of a lot of people I hear. I refuse to call her "Hinenuitepō". There is only one mistress of the dark and it isn't that red whore. I hear she's set herself up with a whare up in her realm just like mine. It wasn't enough to claim this place as hers? She has to *copy* me as well?'

The smooth rhythm of Miru had become ragged—her twined strands lumpy and uneven. 'Before she fled down here, all of this was mine. And then she comes and opens the doors to every bloody being. At least Rohe is respectful. Do any of the others bring me tributes? No.'

I put my hand over hers to stop her rolling. She grabbed my hand and turned it over to look at my palms.

'Good smooth palms. Long fingers, and those claws! Have you ever been a weaver?'

I nodded and she split the pile of spirits between us. I teased out a few strands with my claws and rolled them together on my chest as I had done when I lived.

Miru patted my thigh, covered as it was in shaggy feathers. 'I guess you can't hitch this up can you?' And she laughed. Her laugh bounced around the cavern and I knew that I had been right about the shape of it. We were in a bubble, Miru and I, a bubble made of stone.

We sat and twined the strands of spirits together, and as they were rolled their colour changed from amber to pink. We turned one unformed pile into hanks of twined fibre, ready to weave. I wondered how Miru changed the colour from pink to the white of her garments. I had assumed she would use this fibre to make the garments she wore. When all the spirits had been processed, I followed Miru down to the shore.

'Now we wash them.'

She took the hanks in both hands and plunged them into the water. I had to taste the water—was it still salty? Was this the secret to the colour of her garments? But the water tasted fresh, and a little effervescent.

'We wash them so they are free of any impurities. We wash them clean.'

The hanks in her hands *did* change colour—but not to the white of her garments. Instead they turned a deeper pink, banded in red. I thought it was a trick of the water, or perhaps some unseen current, but the hanks seemed to be moving. When Miru lifted her hands out of the water, the hanks had turned into worms. The worms slithered over each other,

weaving themselves in and out of any gaps they could find. Some already hung from between her fingers.

She caught a few before they fell into the water. 'Not here, little ones.' She closed her hands on them as best she could and walked out of the water.

Miru climbed up the beach and the dunes quickly. 'These ones are keen to go,' she said. She dropped them in front of her whare. For a moment they just sat in a mass as they had done on the raft of Rohe. And then they wriggled apart, some heading straight down, some wiggling further off before digging themselves into the ground. From the shadows of the whare, Tūtangatakino and Mokohikuwaru appeared—they ate any too slow to escape them. I moved to stop the lizards, but Miru stopped me instead.

'It is not a tragedy that some are eaten. These are the spirits that are already free. They have moved from life to death, from afterlife to another death of sorts. These spirits have been stripped and made pure. They have learnt to be alone, they have learnt to be as one. They are now worms, noke, moving down towards meto. They will learn what it is to be extinct, what it is to no longer exist.'

I fell to my knees and pecked at a few worms, hoping that I could ingest their thoughts and feelings. But I tasted nothing but earth. I had come all this way following Hatupatu, hoping for a chance to balance our story. To avenge my own death by his hands, to satisfy utu. And now I was left here on my knees with a mouth full of dirt. I let my shoulders and head drop. I had been defeated by him again.

Miru placed her hand on my shoulder. 'Existence is difficult. These creatures only know it for a century if they are lucky. Creatures like you and me must endure it for far longer.'

Miru helped me to my feet and we sat on her paepae again. Miru looked out over her bay as she spoke.

'I have been here since the beginning, since this place was created out of Te Kore and Te Pō—since I was created out of Te Kore and Te Pō. I am not the progeny of sky and earth. I am not the seed of god and clay. I awoke

and I came to be. I did not come here to flee an errant husband, or to indulge my appetites—this has always been my existence. There was the void and then there was this place, carved out of the nothingness. There was me and then there was this form, created by the stories sung by the people above.

'They visit me because I am the daughter of Te Kore and Te Pō. They visit me to know the potential in non-existence. They have felt it all their lives—the fear of death. In me they find release from that fear, that the only freedom that is absolute is in extinction. I grant them release that I cannot grant myself.'

She put her hand on mine. 'Is it time for me, spirit? Have you come to replace me? Will I finally become noke and visit meto for myself?' Miru squeezed my hand and I looked at her face. She was smiling.

'I know that you are like me. I can see Te Pō reflected in your eyes. We are kin, sisters perhaps, to use the human term. You have come here to free me from my bondage, to free me from this form and responsibilities.'

Miru untied the cloak she was wearing and pulled it from her shoulders. She folded the cloak carefully and laid it at my feet. She stood and removed her pakimaero, folding that as carefully as she had done her cloak, and laid that at my feet as well. She stood before me, naked.

'I am ready, sister.'

But I wasn't. How could I free her from this place? Could I really end her? I had thought myself dead and then found myself here. What if Miru was wrong? That beyond here was not extinction, but another form of life? If we had crawled from the void and created ourselves perhaps we could not return there—the spark of our consciousness would mark us out. I looked at her and knew that I could not do it.

'Why do you hesitate? Is it this form that troubles you? Think of someone else.'

She closed her eyes and her form became blurry. I tried to hold on to the image of Hine, but I was finding it difficult. Was Miru able to see into my mind? How had she managed to learn that skill? If I had been able to pluck

thoughts and memories from the minds of other beings, then I would still be living in my forest. I would not have followed the path that condemned me to this Underworld. The thought of Hatupatu flashed through my mind before I could suppress it.

'Ah!' Miru sighed as if in pleasure. 'That one then.'

I watched as her face changed from that of my lover to that of my husband. Hatupatu as I remembered him in life—a lithe youth, his face freshly scarred by my claws. The only things that she couldn't change were the darkness of her skin and the colour of her eyes.

'Am I as you remember?' Miru had even found his voice from my memory. Even though I knew it was an illusion, I could feel my hatred for him igniting. I grasped the paepae with my hands, making deep grooves into it with my claws.

Miru smiled his cocky smirk at me. 'Sister. It will be a pleasure for us both. We will both find peace.'

I stood and Miru backed away from me. 'I know you want the chase,' she said before she turned towards the shore. I let her run in front of me, revelling in the feeling of the chase again. And the dimensions of reality shifted—the bay stretched further as we ran along it, perhaps it would be never-ending if we willed it. But Miru was impatient for extinction and she ran towards the water.

Miru fell face first into the water. I hauled her up by her shoulders and made her face me. The water was still shallow here—it came up to her hips as she sat.

'You want to see him die?' she said with his voice and his mouth. I placed one hand across her throat and squeezed. Her Hatupatu mask bulged, the eyes and tongue protruding like the figurehead on the waka of Whiro. She held onto my wrist, not to break my grip but to shore it up. Still she did not perish. I squeezed harder and pushed her back forcing her head under the water. I heard hissing above me. Tūtangatakino and Mokohikuwaru were

clinging to the ceiling of the cavern. *Useless guardians,* I thought. But I was just as ineffective as an assassin.

I let go of her throat and she sat up in the water. I thought that my failure would be the end of it, that she would give up—but instead she continued to egg me on.

'Is that all you have? Is your rage so impotent? No wonder he bested you—you have no creativity, no flair.'

I am ashamed that it took so little to get a rise out of me. An illusion of face and voice and I lost reason. I became this giant, this monster, this ogress. I slashed that face again, shredding both cheeks this time.

I ripped at the skin of that face, pulling off his smug expression.

Miru smiled and I ripped the lips from her face. 'Yes,' she said. 'Yes!' I pulled her jaw free and sliced off her tongue so I couldn't hear his voice anymore. Miru grabbed at my breasts, tweaking my nipples as Hatupatu had done, and I slashed down her arms from wrist to armpit. It was so satisfying, that I allowed myself to believe it was Hatupatu I was eviscerating, not Miru. She held on like the spirits who fought for Tū until every scrap of her was torn away. Beneath her flesh there was no skeleton, her form held together with will alone. We had both willed her destruction.

Her flesh lay in strips on top of the water. I walked back up to the shore and watched it wash in like seaweed after a storm. Pieces of Miru lay in a thick band along her bay. I stood and started to gather the strands, walking from one end of the bay to the other, making a bundle of her. I carried the bundle to the whare.

The lizards hissed from their place on the maihi. I banged my fist on it as their mistress had done and they scuttled away. I plucked some strands from the black pile beside me, using my claws to thin each thread before rolling them together. I worked until I had created a hank like Miru and I had done together. I took the hank to the water and held it underneath. The colour did not change, but the hank did begin to move and squirm. I took

it back to the whare as I had seen Miru do and dropped the mass on the ground. I sat down on the paepae to watch what these worms would do. From the shadows of the whare the lizards appeared again. They slunk past me and headed towards the worms to feast on their mistress. Some of her escaped to dig down as noke to meto.

And then she was gone.

CHAPTER SEVEN

HĀPAINGA

I sat and watched the spot for a while. The lizards crawled up onto the maihi—still wary of me, but sensing that I was their new mistress. For a moment I entertained the thought—that I could spend eternity there, preparing the spirits of the Song Makers for their final journey. Trapped in that unchanging stone bubble. The garments lay at my feet. All I had to do was to put them on.

I heard a splash on the shore. I lifted my head and saw Rohe and her raft. She was lifting her cargo ashore. The lizards came down from their roosts and

sat either side of me. I snapped my beak at them—they flinched, but did not run. These creatures had accepted my new role as mistress of that realm, but I couldn't.

I waited until Rohe had departed before I stood up. I went down to the shore, the lizards following behind me. I walked past the bundle of spirits and into the water. I would find a way out.

I swam until I came to a wall of rock, and inched around it trying to find a crack. I tried to simply push through the rock barrier, to imagine that it was not there, but the rock seemed to hold fast. It seemed illogical to me; without Miru, how was this facade still standing? Did she not create this world? I thought that as the new mistress of the place, that I ought to be able to bend it to *my* will. These rocks could only exist because I imagined them, this water how I imagined it to be. I had thought that the realms of Rarohenga obeyed the whims of their rulers, but there seemed to be a greater power controlling this place. Whatever it was that made this realm was stronger than my will. Those that seemed to be in power were subject to the reality of their realm, just as the spirits who passed through them were.

I swam back to shore and sat awhile next to the bundle of spirits. Was that my fate then, stuck in this realm preparing spirits to wriggle to extinction?

Good smooth palms. Long fingers, and those claws! Have you ever been a weaver?

I massaged my palm, releasing the cramp that knotted the base of my thumb. I curled and flexed the fingers on that hand as I pressed down on the mound of muscle. In the mortal realm, I would weave to focus my thoughts, *aho twists under and over whenu*, but here there was no comfort in raranga. It was the problem.

I left the pile where it lay, unable to accept the role I had been given.

It occurs to me now that this is my greatest strength and flaw—my inability to accept the role that I have been given. I have never been able to accept something as fate. I must always question, I must always feel like I have some sort of control of my path. Why do I need to question the origin of my existence? Did I create the question, or did it create me?

I would like to say that I pondered these ideas as I walked from the shore to the whare of Miru, but in honesty, I wallowed in the thought that I had once again been made a victim. I felt sad that I was stuck here. I felt angry that I had no real power, no choice, no freedom. But Miru had escaped her fate—it was only reasonable that in time I could too.

The lizards had crawled down from the maihi and were staring at the ground in front of the whare. Stupid, stupid creatures. As I approached I saw that the ground was moving, the rich black soil was coming together and forming shapes. I squatted down beside Tūtangatakino and Mokohikuwaru to get a better look. The lizards poked out their tongues, sensing a change.

A long, sharp shape lifted up from the soil. It was not until the tip of it almost touched my beak that I realised that the soil had formed a face, no longer a mirror of Hine or Hatupatu, but a mirror of my own face. Her eyes were still shut as her features became more defined. Her eyes opened— startling white against the black of her flesh. She opened her beak and for the first time I heard what my voice would sound like aloud.

'Auē! How can this be,' she screeched, like the cry of a kārearea. She lifted her head from the ground and looked around her. 'You freed me from this place. You freed me ...'

I backed away from her—she had lifted her neck and shoulders up. She rotated her right shoulder as she freed her arm from the ground. She put her hand palm down as she worked on her left arm. She dug her claws into the ground as she pushed herself up, as if she was leaving a pool of water.

'How can this be?' It was an accusation she hissed at me, and Tūtangatakino and Mokohikuwaru joined their rightful mistress.

I ran from her before she set her feet on the ground. It was not fear of Miru that made me run—but fear that I would be forever locked in a cycle of destruction with her. How many times would I rip her apart only to have her reform in front of me? The insanity of performing the same action over and over again for eternity.

I knew there was nowhere to hide from her but the water. It would be a temporary reprieve, but a reprieve nonetheless. I lifted only my eyes above

the water as I had done when I first came to this realm. Miru stood on the shore looking for me, her pets standing either side of her. I kept very still, hoping to remain hidden in the shadow. Her eyes scanned the water and I ducked down beneath the surface. It was only a matter of time before she sent the lizards into the water to find me. I heard splashes above me and assumed that they were almost upon me. I looked up to the surface and saw a large shadow—too large for either of the lizards.

Rohe had returned. I swam up to her raft and dug my claws into the bottom of it. I lifted my head and pressed it against the raft, so that I could hear what was going on above the surface of the water.

'Miru!' Rohe sounded startled and frightened. I imagined she had averted her eyes from Miru who was naked—her whole body must have been a void to Rohe, not just her face.

'Where is the spirit?' The voice of Miru was authoritative and demanding, even through its harsh screech. I wondered if Rohe heard her voice as I did.

'I havv 'roughd yu duh sssspiridsss, aldhough id sseemsss yu havv nod vinished widh duh onesss I 'roughd earlier.'

'I have *not* finished with the spirit. Where is it?'

'I do nod know whad yu 'ean. Dhey ar dhere, on duh ssshore.'

'Not those. The spirit who was intact.'

'I did nod 'ring sssuch a sssspirid.'

'It was here.'

There was a pause. I was rocked back and forth as weight shifted on the raft. The pole that Rohe held was lifted from the water.

'Miru. Yu may nod 'oard …'

'Where is it?'

'Dake dhese sssspiridss—I releassse dhem do yu. 'Ud do nod board ai ravd—I will devvend id from yu.'

Another pause, and then the raft rocked as something landed on it. I heard the pole connect and the splash as one of the lizards was thrown from the raft. I looked at its legs treading the water—white like the wake of a wave, Mokohikuwaru then.

There was another shift in weight as Rohe pushed her cargo off, letting the spirits spill and pool on the surface of the water. The water that surrounded the raft was thick with the spirits, a slick of amber-coloured light.

'What have you done?' The hiss of Miru was venomous.

'I have done whad iss demanded ov ee. I have delivered dhese ssspiritdss do yu.'

'What of the other spirit? You must have brought it. No other being can pass into this world but you.'

'I don'd kno whad yu ar dalking aboud. I havv nod verried ssuch a ssspirid here. Yr mind iss 'laying dricks on yu.'

'I did not imagine it! The spirit tore me apart—I was extinct!'

'And yed, here yu ar, Miru.' Rohe pushed off and waves made by her raft made it difficult to hear anymore. I looked back and saw Miru wading into the water, her legs looking like mine, and as she gathered the floating spirits from the water, I could see she still had my claws. Rohe pushed the raft into the current, and we moved away from Miru and her realm. Rohe navigated the raft through rapids and falls.

The current slowed and Rohe guided the raft to the bank. I detached myself from the raft and swam a short distance from it. I surfaced and watched as the spirits rose from the water and boarded the raft of Rohe. I plunged underwater again. If Rohe turned at the sound of it, all she would have seen was the ripple I left on the surface. I swam down towards the dark-red bottom of the river, towards the strata of flesh that made the riverbed. I waited until I saw where the spirits were entering through the strata of flesh and I swam towards it, widening the gap by ripping through with my claws, the ribbons of flesh floating up with the spirits that had been liberated from it. The hole I made allowed a rush of spirits through, where before only a few at a time could seep through. I looked above me—the water was thick with the light of them, and I wondered if the raft would flounder.

I pushed through the spirits into the layer of blood, swimming up and ignoring the pain as it slashed across my body. Up and up I swam despite the pull down. I grabbed handfuls of hair and wrenched my way up into the

itchy darkness. I used the knots as steps for my ascent and soon the layer of hair gave way to the layer of salty tears. The wailing now was overwhelming. It was no longer a whisper and the water was thick with spirits, many, many more than there had been before. I kept my mouth closed, shutting out the weight of the sadness around me. I used my wings and legs to keep pushing up, and when I reached the surface I could feel that the water had changed into soil, and so I used my claws to dig up, to free my head and shoulders, and to push myself into the stern of the waka of Whiro.

The realm of Whiro and Tū had changed. The space in the stern was filled with bodies. I waited until the bodies had rotted away to nothing. I waited until the cycle of battle had begun again. I crawled through the space and the ground beneath me stirred. Warriors pulled themselves up and fought and died in the cramped space. I pulled my way through the crush of them, digging through them as if they were dirt. When I finally made my way to a place where I could stand, the men beneath me were piled four or five deep. The ones who were still standing fought with new weapons—muskets, although I didn't know that at the time. They seemed to me to be magic, sticks that exploded with smoke and made a loud noise. The men stood well apart from one another—none were close enough to strike a blow. They stood in a ring, and when they raised their weapons, each pointed at the next one along like a chain. This must have been the will of Tū, such an unnatural stance for these warriors. All at once they fired at each other.

Harmless, I thought, *like the posturing of males trying to win a mate, all puffed up and booming.*

And then the ball hit. Such devastation was wrought with these new weapons—holes blown through bodies, or tops of heads removed. All of the men that had stood were now falling. The battlefield was emptied of survivors. I walked into the middle of the ring and picked up a musket from one of the warriors. Already the yellow mist had reached my knees. I looked up to where Tū and Whiro stood, but it was difficult to make them out.

'Ah! Spirit, you are too late for this battle. But you only need to wait a short while for the next.' Tū laughed.

The bodies beneath my feet were disintegrating and I was sinking down with them, their rotting flesh like mud between my toes. I raised the musket towards Tū, and pulled the trigger as I had seen the warriors do. There was no explosion of smoke, nor any sound except an impotent click. The musket was spent. I threw the useless weapon down and waded through the bones towards the rulers of the realm.

Whiro was inhaling the last of the warriors. I did not recognise him at first. He had grown corpulent since I had last seen him, his skin pockmarked and his nose and mouth swollen with bulbous growths. He had lost fingers—the stumps that were left had swollen at the ends, strangling the exposed bones which had turned black with rot. Whiro coughed and wheezed to catch his breath, his inhale a great whoop like the roar of a hakawai.

The body of Tū was covered with gaping musket wounds, there being no time for him to regenerate his flesh in between battles as he had done before.

The pain of his battle wounds made Tū giddy and delirious. His eyes widened and he became agitated as the ground stirred again. In the last battle he had lost part of his face and an ear, the flesh flapped down and rested on his shoulder, and each time he moved his head what little had been woven together ripped apart again.

'It begins! It begins!' Tū looked at me and Whiro, hoping to infect us with his enthusiasm. Whiro groaned and clutched his massive belly. I walked past them, not turning back as the muskets began to ring out.

I climbed up the hull of the waka, using my claws. At least the figurehead was unchanged—I nodded at him, his familiarity comforting after the stark changes inside the waka. It was disorienting, the changes so abrupt. How long had my journey been? To me it seemed as if only a day or two had passed, but time here was deceptive. Had it been decades or centuries of earth years?

There was the sound of sobbing around me. I thought perhaps it was a remnant from the sea of tears that still clung to me, an earworm of despair.

'Kura ...'

I heard Hine whisper, and turned around expecting to see her, but she wasn't there. Of course she wasn't there, it was all in my mind, her voice, the sobbing.

'Kura ...'

I heard her again, above me. I looked up into the murky darkness, but still could not see her. But I could hear her voice amongst the many. I jumped from the hull of the waka to the wall that surrounded the realm and climbed up towards the passage I had followed down. As I ascended, the swirls of colour above me began to form one great spiral. The ochre red separated from the blues, greens and browns above me and pooled in the centre of the storm. Slowly, the red descended towards me forming into finger tips, then a hand, then an arm. The fingers stretched out as if someone was trying to grab me. I stretched my own hand towards it. My hand was held in a tight clasp and I was pulled upwards. I held on to the wall with my other hand, feeling as if I would be torn in two before I let the wall go, and surrendered to the pull from above.

Then the hand let go of mine and I found myself once again in water. Where was I now? Back in the sea of tears? The lake at Te Rēinga?

I emerged from the pool that Hine and I had shared. Once again she had pulled me into her world. I looked around me—the pool was still fringed with ferns and trees, steam rising from the pool, still a perfect moment in time. Perhaps this world had been left untouched. Perhaps it was only the house of Whiro and Tū that was changed.

Hine stood a few paces from the pool's edge and had her back to me. Her hair fell down her back, resting at the top of her smooth, round buttocks. Her skin was as I remembered it, flawless and beautifully red. I felt embarrassed and shy—Hine had never seen what I looked like in life. She had made me beautiful and I had ruined it. I climbed from the pool and shook the water from my feathers, and Hine still did not turn. She was sobbing. I assumed she was still mourning our time together.

I wanted to embrace her, but I was afraid that she'd reject me. This giant, this monster, this ogress. Still, it pained me to hear her cry. I reached out and put my hand on her shoulder, carefully keeping the tips of my fingers up so that I didn't pierce her skin.

'Kura?'

I held my breath as she turned to me, waiting for her to register how ugly I had become. But I was not the only one who had changed since we had parted. Her waist had thickened and her breasts had flattened like she had lost her dimension. It was not just that she was no longer a maiden—it was not age that had made her this way—it was that she had lost control over her space: it seemed to encroach on her rather than her on it. Her lips were pulled out sharply like the mouth of a barracouta, her jaw jutting out into a large underbite. When she opened her mouth, I could see that from the top of it grew five fangs of obsidian, glistening and sharp.

It was me who took a step back. It was me who rejected Hine.

'You needed my story more than you wanted me. You did this.' It would seem that she also grieved her lost beauty. 'Do you see what stories have done?' Her skin glowed with heat and anger. 'They have made monsters of us both.'

I opened my mouth to explain, forgetting that I had no voice.

'That is what they made you, Kura?'

A monster, an ogress, a thing.

She held out her arms and looked down at herself. 'This is what they've made me. No longer the mother that comforts them in death, but a thing to be feared, a demon to be reviled. My embrace is no longer sought by them—it is considered evil—as if I would prey upon my own children.'

Hine walked towards the path and I followed behind her. She looked up the path and then at me. 'They choose another path now, after they die. So few of my children visit me now. The ones that do have told me that new people and new ways have come, spreading out over the land. Bringing new ways to die. Bringing new stories and their own gods. They say that the newcomers hoard land and resources. That they kill birds not to eat, but to

collect the bodies and display them. They collect many things for display, these new ones—insects, leaves, images and stories.

'They collect my children's stories to preserve them, but corrupt their telling with their own narratives. This is how I have become a monster, through their telling. And their voices carry far—they capture their words onto leaves and let them loose on the world. Their voices, their telling of *my* story, drowns out the old. Drowns out the truth.

'One day soon, this path will be abandoned. My children will find another mother to comfort them. What will become of me, when that happens? Is it better to be *this* creature than to be forgotten altogether? I do not know.'

And in that moment I saw myself within her. She was kin.

I could have wept for her then. Not because she had lost her power, but because she believed she had, that she no longer had any control of her narrative. It was not her appearance that made her unattractive, it was her resignation to defeat. Where was the Hine that defied husband, father and god? Who carved out a place for herself? Who called herself the great woman of the night, Hinenuitepō.

Ko Hinetītama koe, matawai ana te whatu i te tirohanga.

Her defeat broke my heart.

I stood on the path in front of her and held out my hand. I would pull her out as she had pulled me—we would walk this path together. But Hine shook her head.

'No.'

I held my hand out to her a moment longer, looking into those miraculous pounamu eyes, hoping that she would see me.

Take my hand, take my hand.

But she turned her face away from me. I dropped my hand to my side and my head hung low. I looked up the path again; suddenly it seemed to stretch forever. I turned and walked and never saw Hine again.

TE ARA

The path seemed long and straight, although when I turned back to look I couldn't see where I had come from, as if the past curved away from view. Ahead wasn't that much clearer. A fine dust hung in the air; it reminded me of an ash cloud after an eruption. Perhaps I thought of it this way because the light glowed lava-orange. The dust did not sting my skin or irritate my eyes—it just made the world look out of focus.

I walked and walked, hoping that this path did not simply loop back to the whare of Hine. I was not physically tired, but mentally so. I stopped walking

and sat down on the path. I leaned back and suddenly found that I was supported by something. I turned around and found that the path had ended and the posts of a gate were behind me. The world seemed to have narrowed, so that there was no way around the gate. There were no rock walls like in the world of Miru—it was as if reality simply ended either side of the path. If I pushed against it, it stretched and then repelled my touch.

The posts of the gate were taller than me and intricately carved. I recognised the figures as the rulers I had met in Rarohenga. At the very bottom of each post were worms that seemed to be crawling down towards the ground. On the left post was Tūtangatakino and on the right Mokohikuwaru. Both lizards' heads faced downwards as if they feasted upon the worms below them. Above Tūtangatakino was his mistress, Miru, preparing souls like muka. On the right, above Mokohikuwaru, waves of water were carved, and navigating her raft through waves of still waters was Rohe. She stood above the level of Miru, and the tail of Mokohikuwaru twisted around her pole. Above the depiction of Rohe and mirrored were the figures of Whiro and Tū. Whiro was on the left and was shown with rope twisted around him. Tū was on the right and held a taiaha as if he was ready to strike down whoever came along this path. Above them, on either side, were the profiles of Tuapiko and Tuwhaitiri—the gate they had formed at last was flung open. Above them, more water and the waves of hills of Te Rēinga.

Astride both the posts, rising from between them was Hine—as I remember meeting her. The carving almost captured her perfectly, although she was flattened. Her skin was smooth and red, her eye sockets fitted with pounamu. It seemed as if she looked down on me as I stood beneath her.

At the top of the gateway, between the legs of Hine, shards of sharp granite pointed down, perhaps to snare those that would try to climb over the gate rather than seek permission for it to be opened.

The gate itself was made from wood. It looked like taiaha had been lashed together, the top of the gate sharpened wood. It was a mouth then, stone teeth above and wooden below.

I pulled at the gate trying to loosen its lashings, but it held fast. As I shook the gate again I noticed that I wasn't alone. On the other side of the gate, his back to me, was a spirit. He spoke to me without turning his head, keeping his eyes firmly fixed on the path ahead of him. He spoke slowly as if he was savouring the chance to speak.

'I am Te Kūwatawata, guardian of this waharoa that separates our world from that of the living.'

What tale would this spirit tell? What trickery would I have to resort to, to pass him?

'This is a place of transition, the threshold between life and death. You must contemplate this before you make a decision. You must have the correct intention, you must abide by the correct protocol, to move from one state to the next.'

That was all? I had to make a decision? I had made the decision before I arrived at the waharoa of Te Kūwatawata. I was leaving this world and returning to my own. I waited for Te Kūwatawata to open the gate and let me pass. He did not move from his place, instead he spoke again.

'Once I allowed mortals to come and go through this gate. Some were given precious gifts from the world below to share with their families above. Thus, the world above became less wild and more civilised like our world. But the habits of the upper world are hard to break. Mataora and Niwareka, fearing that I would take their taonga, lied to me. Thus I closed the gate to mortals.'

I remembered the story that Hatupatu had told me about tā moko. He left out that part.

Te Kūwatawata had said that I had a choice, and yet the gate was closed? I was confused.

'You should turn back, spirit. This path leads only one way—from the land of the living to our land. There is nothing for you beyond this gate. Why would you want to leave this world? The world above is full of violence and evil. Our world is one of light.'

Had the gaze of Te Kūwatawata been so steadfastly ahead that he did not know what was happening in the world below? What was once a world of light was changing and yet he didn't know it?

'Turn back, turn back, spirit. Back to the world of tranquillity. You will find peace there. The road to the world above is chaotic and dangerous.'

Te Kūwatawata and his gate stood in the way of my path, but he was not denying me passage as bluntly as Tuapiko and Tuwhaitiri. Instead, he was trying to make it seem that I had a choice, and that the only choice for me was to turn back.

I looked above the gate—if I could not go around nor through it, then perhaps I could go over it? I could not see what was above the gate, if there was a barrier above it, or if reality just ended at its sides. It was probable, but from where I stood it was still unknown, it was still a chance to escape.

I dug my claws into the gate, mounting it on the left side, my toes gouging the back of Tūtangatakino and my fingertips grasping at the feet of Whiro.

'Turn back, turn back, spirit. I cannot allow you to suffer in the world above. Go back now and find peace.'

I climbed to the top of the post and was forced to crouch. The border above me crushed down. I knew it would be the same on the other side but could not leave without trying. I clung to the carving of Hinenuitepō, flattening my cheek against her lips for one last kiss. I reached the right side and my assumption had been correct—the world pressed down on me again. I climbed down the right side of the gate, gouging it as I had done the left. This waharoa demanded symmetry.

'Turn back, spirit. This is not the season for you to travel along my path. Perhaps one day I will open the gate again, but it is not today.'

I shook the gate again. I knew it wouldn't give but it seemed to be the only way to vent my frustration. I turned my back to it and let myself slide down the left post to the ground. As I came to sit, the post behind me disappeared and I fell back.

CHAPTER NINE
TAMA-O-HOI

I closed my eyes awhile. I did not want to see the dust of lava-orange swirling above me. I wished I was anywhere but on this path. Where could I turn now? I knew I hadn't been granted passage by Te Kūwatawata, instead I had been dismissed. I did not want to head back to Hine. If I kept going forward I would probably meet Te Kūwatawata again and play out the same charade.

My body felt heavy and I let it relax. It felt as if my limbs were sinking down through the ground. I opened my eyes. Where was I now? I moved my head as I lay on my back. It looked like my cave, hollowed out from rock. I sat

up a little and moved my head further around. If it was a cave I could see no entrance, the hollow extending far in front of me and far behind. It was a tunnel of some sort. The tunnel curved around as if it had been dug by a worm—the walls were almost smooth. It was made of rock, but not formed by erosion. I pushed myself up on my knees and brushed my hand on the wall. There were lines pressed in the rock, dribbles of stone from layers, as if the rock had once been liquefied. And I realised what it had once been.

I was in a lava tube, a path cut by molten rock racing to push itself out into the world. If I could have, I would have smiled—this would be my escape from Rarohenga, following the path of an ancient eruption back to my home.

I did not know which way to follow, so I simply chose a direction and started to walk. I could hear whispers down the tunnel. Perhaps I should have avoided them, whispers in that world had led me astray before. Whispers in every world have led me astray.

They were words to bind. Words to shackle. But what did they bind? I came to the end of the tunnel—there was no further path, and yet I could hear the whispers beyond. I ran my palms across the end of the tunnel, looking for some crack or fissure. There was a fine crack across the entire wall. I tried to prise it open with my claws, scratch it open as once I had tried to from my own lava cave. I expected my claws to break against the rock, instead they seemed to sink within it. I pulled them back and then fell backwards when the crack opened suddenly. It was an eye. The creature must have been massive—its eye was taller than I stood.

The eye lifted away from the end of the tunnel and I crawled through into a huge cavern. There, hanging upside down, was a creature bound by words. The words were the whispers I had heard, repeating again and again as they twisted around his body. They held him in place like ropes, binding his arms in front of him and his legs together. These words held so much magic that they could bind a giant and suspend him in the air. He hung like a pūriri moth in a cocoon—improbably suspended by just a thread of words

attached to the ceiling. He had the form of a man, but he was as big as a mountain. His skin was a ruddy brown, the colour of red scoria. The words that had him bound were golden and glowed, lighting the dull cavern. I stood where his eye had been, on a ledge. He must have contorted his neck to rest his head there. I can't imagine that it was comfortable for him to do so, but nothing about his situation was comfortable. Standing on the ledge I was level with his face so that we could see eye to eye.

'Gah,' he said, shaking the cavern and making me fall backwards, 'you are not human, even though you have the stink of them on you. Be gone, you are no use to me. You will not even satisfy my hunger.'

The words that bound him tightened as he moved his head to speak, cutting into his flesh. He roared and the cavern shook again and his binding cut deeper. He stilled his body and calmed his breath, and the bindings slackened in response. He squinted at me, trying to make sense of my form.

'What are you?' he whispered and the bindings tightened slightly. 'There is human about you, but you are not human.'

I stood and opened my arms wide to show him my wings.

'A bird and a woman. I have eaten neither. Perhaps I ought to try?'

I backed away from his mouth.

'Calm yourself, bird-woman, you are so scrawny it isn't worth the effort.'

I ventured forward a step, but kept distance between his tongue and my body.

'How did you find yourself here, bird-woman?'

I opened my beak, and stretched out my hands in a shrug to show that I had no voice.

'A bird who cannot sing? You are a ridiculous creature.' He laughed, shaking the cavern again. He laughed despite the bindings cutting into him. His laughter continued until the bindings seemed to have strangled him completely. He stopped moving and his eyes were closed. I watched him, but he did not move. I thought that his bindings had killed him. I moved closer to him to check. He was breathing but it was shallow, probably because

his bindings were still tight around him. He was unconscious, so I decided to explore the cavern while I had the chance.

The tunnel was the only way in or out at the bottom of the cavern. I looked above me, thinking that perhaps there was a vent at his feet, near the top of this mountain. The walls hugged closely to the giant's body leaving only a wingspan between flesh and stone. The walls were as smooth as those in the tunnel, moulded by lava rather than carved by water. I reached above my head and stabbed my claws into the rock face, but could not get a good grip. The answer was obvious—climb the giant instead of the walls.

I walked around to the back of his head, in case he awoke as I climbed. I took two great handfuls of his hair and pulled myself up to his scalp. His hair made it easy to traverse his skull, and I was soon sitting at the base of it. The first rung of the giant's bindings was well above me, circling the neck. Even if I stretched, the distance was at least double my height. I had to use his flesh to climb, digging my claws into his neck. His body shuddered and spasmed as I hit the nerves in his spine. I dug my claws deeper to ride out his movements, the words above me constricting the giant.

'Little gnat,' he whispered, 'why do you bite?'

I hastened my ascent now that the giant had woken. He flinched at each hold as I climbed towards his bindings. Watching how the bindings cut into his body, I assumed that they would have substance, but as I reached for the words twisting around his neck, my claws fell through them as if they were made of smoke. That close, the words melded into each other so they sounded like a continuous hiss. I had planned to use his bindings to crawl up to the top of the cavern, following them like a well-worn path through a forest. I had thought that perhaps I could rest awhile upon them, my fingers and toes already cramping from the climb.

'Stop tormenting me.'

I had no choice but to dig into his flesh to continue my climb. If I climbed down now, the giant would surely eat me.

'I had thought that you were the one who would release me. I thought it was your voice that prayed to me. But you have been sent here just to torture me. Are the words of Ngātoroirangi not punishment enough?'

His back was rounded because his hands were tied in front of him. Although I could not use the bindings as grips, the flesh that was raised and compressed around them could be used in their stead.

'Did I imagine the voice, little gnat? The pleas to the great Tama-o-hoi, bound in Ruawāhia, to free himself and visit utu upon the unbelievers—was that all in my head? Do you even exist, little gnat? Or is this a new trick of Ngātoroirangi—to send voices and gnats to make me insane? You are a wondrous illusion—I can feel you crawling across my back.' He laughed, 'And now I can hear the voice again. So clever of Ngātoroirangi to make the voice flatter me, I have grown deaf to the curses.'

The giant was delusional. The voice existed as I did—it was faint over the hiss of the bindings, but it was *real*. I crawled across his shoulder blade to his armpit, hanging onto his hair. The giant was ticklish and rocked with laughter as I found my foothold in his armpit hair.

'Please, gnat. Mercy.'

I crawled from his armpit to his triceps. The flesh beneath me moved as he tensed the muscle. He turned his great head towards me.

'It is difficult for me to see you there.'

My journey continued over his arm. I did not pause in the small gap between his arm and chest—how easy it would be to be crushed there. I climbed up to his nipple and perched upon it. Tama-o-hoi curled his neck so he could see me on his chest.

'There you are, little gnat. I am not imagining you.'

I shook my head in response.

'And the voice? Can you hear it too?'

I nodded. His smile was vast and terrifying—it would be so easy to lose my footing and disappear into that mouth. I clung to his nipple.

'I will not eat you, little gnat. You have not come to punish me. You are he tohu.'

I must have been to him like the glow-worms were to me—poor company, but company nonetheless.

'You are a strange creature—ill thought out—nature did not create you in this form. I take it humans have afflicted you with your life, as they have afflicted me with mine?'

I nodded again. His chest heaved with a sigh, and I had to dig my claws deep into his areola to keep from falling.

'I have been bound here since humans made the land above their home. Tarawera was my home and I defended it from invaders. So I ate the ones that had fallen, was that so monstrous? And so they sent their great tohunga Ngātoroirangi who had old, old magic from Hawaiki. He bound me and thrust me down into the chasm Ruawāhia and here I have been, a prisoner for centuries.'

The disembodied voice had changed—it was no longer a whisper of pleas, it was stronger. Now it commanded the bindings to loosen. They slackened a little.

'The magic of Ngātoroirangi is old and strong, it has held me for so many years. This new magic that calls to me is not as strong, but it doesn't need to be, little gnat. All I need is a small break, a loose thread.'

I reached down towards the binding across his chest, the words twisting around each other like twining rope. The twist was becoming looser—I could see a gap between the golden words. I could put my claws between them, and although I knew that my touch would not affect them, from the perspective of Tama-o-hoi it must have looked as if I had nicked them. As if I had caused them to fray.

'We are allies then, little gnat.' He laughed, and the bindings did not move to strangle him. 'What do you want?'

I turned my head up and pointed to the top of the cavern.

'You want to escape this place? Our aims align. I will be free of the curse of Ngātoroirangi. I will be free of this prison.'

The words that bound him were losing their form, their light growing dimmer. Tama-o-hoi expanded his chest and they barely held. He wriggled his arms free, rocking his body back and forth, smashing into the cavern walls. I fell from my spot on his chest, coming to rest on the ledge of his chin. Tama-o-hoi picked me up with his freed hand and placed me on the ledge by the tunnel.

'You should take shelter.'

I crouched in the mouth of the tunnel and watched the giant as he pulled the bindings from his body, at last freeing his legs. He landed heavily on his back, shaking great sheets of stone free from the cavern walls. He lay for a while staring at the bindings that hung above him. He pushed himself up, finally upright after centuries. Tama-o-hoi ripped the bindings from their anchor on the roof, making a hole in the cavern.

'I can see the stars, little gnat.' He bent down and picked me up, careful not to crush me in his hand. 'You should see them too.' He lifted me up towards the hole he had made. I could see the stars—Matariki was already rising, and I could feel the chill air of winter.

'We are freed, little gnat.' Tama-o-hoi blew me from his palm like a child blows a butterfly, 'Fly away now.'

The updraught of his breath lifted me high above the mountain and into the sky. This was my country, the rivers, the lakes and the forests. I glided over them as Tama-o-hoi ripped apart Tarawera.

... no Death, but Life
Augmented ...

John Milton, *Paradise Lost*, Book IX

TE WĀ NGARO

HATUPATU
AND THE
BIRD-WOMAN

This is the story that is told. It is the story of a young hero named Hatupatu and his encounter with a villainous monster, the bird-woman, Kura of the claws. It has been told so many times and by so many—each voice a thin thread on its own, but plied together they are a thick rope, resilient enough to slow even the sun. Strong enough to bind a monster in her place, perhaps forever.

The story begins in summer. The season had been mild, and the karaka, mataī and miro were all fat with fruit. The kererū did not announce their presence with song; instead, the forest was filled with the sound of their wings—the soft boom as they flew from tree to tree. Brothers Hanui and Haroa had noticed the plentiful fruit as well. Both were skilled fowlers and had kept an eye on the fruiting trees in the hunting grounds that they had claimed that summer. They were excited. The last hunt at the beginning of summer, when the tūī and kākā were feeding on nectar, seemed so long ago; the brothers had the itch to go out and hunt again. They'd been waiting for the perfect conditions, relishing the planning and strategy that goes into an expedition, trying not to think of the disappointment if the plan goes awry or the elation in success. The two brothers had spent much time together in the whare mata during the hot days of summer, preparing their snares from the tough leaves of the tī.

Hatupatu was a stranger to the whare mata. He was only a few years younger than his brothers, but they were at the age when even a year seems to be a huge gap. Hatupatu had tried to follow them into the whare mata many times, but Hanui would block his way, and Haroa would say, 'Children belong outside with the women.'

Hanui and Haroa had already endured their tā moko—the mantle of adulthood chiselled into their skin. There had already been matches discussed with eligible women, families on both sides searching for desirability of allegiances as well as the young people's physical desire for one another. This would be their last hunt as brothers only; next autumn they would be husbands and, probably, fathers, just like their elder brother, Karika. The thought of their future made them excited and scared at the same time—a feeling akin to that of the hunt itself. The brothers wanted to relish this time that they had left together. They enjoyed each other's company and made a formidable hunting team, anticipating each other's movements in the forest.

They knew that one day they'd have to take their younger brother, Hatupatu, with them and that they'd have to bring him into the whare mata and teach him how to make snares and sharpen spears. But Hatupatu was such a *child*, and the brothers did not want the responsibility of looking after him—not now in the last moments of their own freedom. They would be parents soon enough.

But Hatupatu insisted. To the eyes of his brothers, he had stamped his feet and whined as he had done as a toddler and as they had done those many years ago. But their parents indulged their pōtiki, Hatupatu, and so it was that he would join his brothers' hunt for kererū.

Hanui and Haroa loved their brother; he had a great sense of humour and could find a way to make them laugh even in the most sombre situations. Hatupatu was a good storyteller,

he had a particularly strong imagination, so he was able to spin an old boring story into something new. He had a sweet voice, as sweet as the korimako that sang in the forest. Their parents had sacrificed one bird for each of their sons, but in Hatupatu it seemed as if the korimako had been reborn in his body. He was a formidable orator, twining his imagination and voice together to charm his audience, for the sweetest voice must be supported by a supple mind. The gift of oratory would be hollow without the ability to think on your feet and manipulate words to suit your purpose. But this gift leaves him as susceptible to stories as they are to him. As much as they loved their brother, Hanui and Haroa resented him too. Hatupatu was indulged as the youngest; he did not have the same chores that his brothers had. He did not have the same drive. He manipulated every situation, every person, to suit himself. It seemed to the brothers that they were struggling through life as though it was the thick undergrowth of the forest, suffering the scrapes of low branches as they cut their path through, and all Hatupatu had to do was follow behind them on the path that they had forged.

Worse, Hatupatu was a fast learner, and the brothers knew that he would quickly master the skills of the hunt and surpass them. And then what would they have to distinguish themselves?

They did not have to talk about it between them; Hanui and Haroa made a great team because they anticipated each other's thoughts and movements. They did not expressly agree to teach their brother humility, to show Hatupatu how sheltered he was. They just knew what they would do. And so, as the three

brothers disappeared from view of their parents' home, Hanui and Haroa loaded their bedrolls and the hue to store their catch onto their brother's back. The complaints of Hatupatu were met with laughter and slaps. Even the kurī, Moko and Tū, belonging to Hanui and Haroa, seemed to be in on it—their mouths pulled open, their tongues lolling over their canines as if they were grinning along with their masters' joke on Hatupatu. Although it was no joke. As the journey wore on and Hatupatu finally held his tongue, Hanui and Haroa congratulated themselves on the lesson that their brother had learnt—respect your elders.

But all Hatupatu had learnt was that resentment can fester beneath a placid exterior. That revenge can be exacted away from the prying eyes of those in power.

When they reached camp, their lessons for Hatupatu continued. While his brothers sat and ate the sweet dried kūmara that their mother had prepared and packed for their first night together as three in the forest, Hatupatu prepared their camp and found firewood. When he finally had a good fire going, it was dark, and the kūmara was gone. He asked for food, and a slap was the answer. Hatupatu was determined not to cry in front of his brothers. It was not the pain of the slap, although no one had ever raised a hand to him in his life; it was the shame of it—being treated by his own kin, his own brothers, as if he was a slave. He went to sleep that night with hunger and resentment gnawing at his belly.

Hatupatu knew that he was more than what they thought of him; he knew he had a place in history. He held the word *destiny* in his

mind. It was his sacred kupu. Every slight and smart was deflected by that word. It was that word that kept him going. He held onto it so tightly that it penetrated his flesh; it became part of him.

When he woke the next morning, the sun was already in the sky, and his brothers had left the camp. They had made camp in a clearing at least a couple of hours' walk from the hunting grounds—far enough away that they would not jeopardise the hunt by tainting the forest with cooked food. Hatupatu felt he was exactly between the forest and home; it would be easy to pack up his sleeping roll now and head for his village. Perhaps that is what his brothers had hoped he would do, and that thought made his mouth taste more sour than it already did from hunger. No, Hatupatu would stay. He would not run home to his mother like a child. He had a destiny to fulfil.

He tidied the campsite and found more firewood ready for that evening. Would this be how he spent his time on the hunt—excluded by his brothers, reduced to the work of women and slaves? He hoped it was just a test, and if he performed his role without complaint, without fault, his brothers would eventually see his worth. If he acted as a man, they would have to treat him as such. And if he acted as a child ...

But the child felt natural to him. The child wanted to scream and cry that this was unfair. The child was hungry and bored. The child was used to getting his own way.

Hatupatu tried to quiet the child by walking in the forest. He was still unsure of his surroundings, so he walked out from the campsite in a straight line into the dark of the canopy and sat for a

while when he felt tired. The dark of the forest offered no comfort to him. At times, it felt as if he would never catch his breath; the things that lurked in the shadows stole it from him. So, he was on his feet before his brow had fully cooled, before the sweat had ceased to roll down his back. His shins hurt, and it felt as if his ankles would snap beneath him as he followed his line back to camp as quickly as he could. In the light of the clearing, he felt foolish; his imagination had got the better of him in the dark, and he had thought he felt monsters when he knew that none existed. Worse, if his brothers knew that he had cowered in the forest like a baby, they would never teach him to hunt. The light emboldened him, and he resolved that he would explore the forest again, and he would make himself strong so that when his brothers finally took him with them, it would be as an equal. He would earn their respect and take their abuse with good humour. They were testing him. It was part of growing up and being one of them.

He would ready a fire for his brothers' return. He would find tī leaves in case they needed to repair their snares. He would clean and prepare whatever they had caught for their meal and for their store. He would accept whatever scrap of food or knowledge that would come his way. He would be stoic. He would endure.

Hanui and Haroa came back to their camp with their catch dangling from their hands: good, fat kererū that would store well and keep their whānau fed during winter's approaching days. A good hunt with plentiful, fat birds meant that they could secure their marriages. It proved that they were worthy men able to provide for their new wives and their families. And they were, although it is

tempting in this story to paint them as entirely heartless—as men who did not care for family. But they did care. They cared deeply for their whānau, especially their hōhā little brother, Hatupatu, which makes their actions against him a tragedy and something that would scar them more than they would think was possible.

But for now, the brothers felt pleased with themselves. They had had a good day snaring kererū, their camp was clean and tidy, a fire had already been laid, and their brother seemed to have accepted their authority.

Hatupatu took the kererū without complaint and strung the carcasses from their feet as his brothers instructed him to. Haroa cut the throat of the first bird to show their young brother how to bleed the catch. The blood came slowly; it had settled in the bodies during the day as they rested in a shallow trench while the brothers continued their hunt. Haroa thought that perhaps when Hatupatu had learnt sufficient respect, they could take him into the forest, and he could take the still-warm bodies from the grounds to the campsite to bleed them fresh. It made Haroa laugh to think of his haughty young brother running back and forth like a trained kurī. He bit his lip so that he wouldn't call out *Moi* to bring the dogs and his young brother to heel.

The kurī were getting under his feet as Hatupatu slit the throats of the birds. The dogs were lapping at the blood that dripped on the soil. The drips of blood stained the white head and muzzle of Moko, while it disappeared entirely into the black fur of Tū. The kurī would be the only ones feeding from the birds tonight. The brothers told Hatupatu that the birds would

need to hang for a day or so before they could be cooked or stored. Hatupatu would clean them tonight of their feathers and guts. They would all need to wait to eat their flesh.

Hatupatu plucked the birds and kept their feathers in a big pile. He thought that he would take them with him and make a gift of them to his mother. Perhaps she would weave him a kākāhu so that he would remember his first hunt. He would let these feathers cover him in a lie: that he had found success as a hunter, that his brothers let him into their fold. He would let these feathers envelop the truth, and by and by, the story would overtake the reality.

Haroa kicked dirt over the pile Hatupatu had made—the dirt marring the pure white of the breast feathers of the kererū.

'These must be kept from sight,' Haroa said. 'It will ruin the hunt if the birds see these feathers. They will flee, and our stores will be bare. Dig a trench.'

And so, his brother meant to deny Hatupatu even this— his version of reality. Hatupatu dug the trench as he was told, and he laid leaves over the top of the feathers. They would be hidden from the sight of the birds but clean enough to take home with him.

The kurī feasted on the entrails of the day's hunt, slurping in unison so that it seemed that they were just one giant black and white dog—the giant dog with two heads that people from the south told tales of. That dog would slurp the guts from humans as happily as these ate those of birds. The dogs were also given the heads of the birds—their powerful jaws crunching the skulls and mincing the meat and brains together.

After the dogs had finished their meal, they lay down next to the fire. Out here, the kurī were more valuable than Hatupatu was to his brothers. These two dogs were his brothers' favourites and skilled at hunting kiwi although they wouldn't be hunting for those birds this time. The dogs had strong, broad shoulders and stubby legs. They could chase a kiwi a short distance if it managed to escape from them. The two dogs worked together seamlessly, each anticipating the other's movements and their masters' movements too. The dogs were like the brothers' shadows, like an extension of the brothers' will. Both kurī had sired many pups. Those that showed the same aptitude as their fathers were kept and the others made fine meals, the meaty musculature being inherited by both the talented hunters and those that were not. Hatupatu hoped for a pup from one of these dogs, but their progeny were in great demand. If he asked his brothers now for a pup, they would probably give him the runt with no hope of ever being a great hunter. Much like its master.

Hatupatu patted the back leg of the black kurī, Tū. It lifted its head to Hatupatu in acknowledgement and then closed its eyes again. The dog's bushy tail thumped against his leg. It felt like this dog was his only friend although he was sure it would turn on him at its master's bidding.

Hanui and Haroa were content to let their brother be this evening. He seemed to be complying with them, obeying their orders and keeping the camp clean and well stocked. It had been the same way when they had been on their first hunt with their elder brother, Karika. It was probably the same for him when he

learnt to hunt from his uncles, who were only a few years older than him, and when the uncles had learnt from their father. It was just the way young hunters learnt; they started with the menial tasks until they could be trusted with the more complex. They learnt every part of the hunt, the rituals and the traditions. They learnt the hard work and the gnawing hunger so that this life would not be a shock to their system. Although it was less of a shock to Hanui and Haroa, they had never been as indulged as their young brother. They didn't expect to be taken to the hunt when they insisted they were ready. They waited until they were told they were ready, and then they accepted whatever role they were given.

Hatupatu seemed to understand that now. The complaints he had had the day before had stopped. He was a quick learner; they gave him that much. It had only taken a few slaps for him to know his place. Although it hurt them to raise a hand to their brother, it was better that he was slapped by them than incur the wrath of a spirit, or worse an atua, if he blundered in the forest. The forest was a dangerous place, and Hatupatu could be a rash, hot-headed boy; it was not just that he could get himself in trouble if he trampled on the rituals of the hunt, but he was also likely to get his whole village in trouble. At best, he would incur a lean hunt, and his family would have to survive on aruhe alone. At worst, an angry god could lay waste to the entire settlement or curse them for generations to come.

Was this why the brothers were moved to tell a story of the forest? A story designed to keep Hatupatu tethered to the camp

where he would be safe from the creatures lurking in the shadows for a young boy to steal and consume. They told their story as Hatupatu cleaned the birds. The limp bodies of the birds, their viscera and the drip, drip of their blood became tied up with the words of the story. The words became as bloodstained as the white head and muzzle of the kurī Moko. Hatupatu could not help but think of himself strung by the feet like the kererū—throat slit and bleeding out. But who would feast on his flesh? What creature lurked in the shadows? What terrible creature?

A giant, a monster, an ogress. The bird-woman, Kurangaituku. A hum of recognition.

She is a predator, hungering not only for the flesh of the birds but also for the flesh of men. She rips the meat, raw and dripping with blood, from the birds with her terrible beak, feasts upon their guts and dreams of the taste of human flesh. Those who had seen her and lived described her as a giant kōtuku. *He kōtuku rerenga tahi*. Her presence even corrupts the whakataukī, for, indeed, she was a rare sight, but not one that was welcomed.

She was unnatural—part bird, part woman. There were tales of hunters who had glimpsed her in the shadows of the forest, had seen her breasts and smooth belly as white as the face of te marama, and she had aroused more than fear.

Hanui and Haroa told their story to Hatupatu not really believing the creature their words created. They had been told the story too when they were his age, but in the years that they had been hunting here, they had not seen her. Besides, stories like

this were warnings to the young, and they were about to become men and leave such fantasy behind.

Hanui and Haroa may not have believed their story, but Hatupatu did. He had felt a presence when he had walked into the forest earlier that day. There was a kind of unease in his bowels and the need to get out of the forest as soon as possible. He could not help but admire his brothers, who walked into that forest every season, who risked their lives to feed the family. He wanted to be such a man himself—able to conquer the fear that clenched at his belly.

The next day, his brothers left him alone again at camp. This time, Hatupatu had been awake when they stirred before dawn. He pretended to be asleep, and he watched which path his brothers chose, their kurī trotting beside them. Hatupatu had stayed up all night so that he could catch this moment and follow his brothers into the forest. The excitement that had kept him awake all night was waning. He was tired. Hatupatu lay on his bedroll after his brothers had left and listened to the dawn chorus. He closed his eyes for a minute, and when he opened them again, the sun was already high in the sky. Hatupatu rushed to tidy the camp as he had done the day before. He found the path his brothers had chosen hours ago and decided to follow it for as long as his nerves would allow.

Hatupatu was not sure what he was more afraid of—the bird-woman or his brothers finding him. It was probably his brothers that worried him more. The bird-woman may torture and kill him, but that would be quick. His brothers would eke out his punishment for the rest of his life. He hoped that he could sneak up on his brothers, to watch them hunt and then steal back to the camp before they noticed him.

He heard a kurī howl deep in the forest. Even though it was a familiar sound, there, in the forest shadows, it fed his fear. The story from last night, the looming trees and images of slit throats and dripping blood had coloured the howl. It made him question whether it had come from one of his brothers' beloved kurī. Why was its howl so melancholy? Had one of his brothers, or both, been caught by the giant bird-woman? Was she feeding their dogs with their guts and blood? Would she let one hang for a couple of days to feast on immediately while preserving the other in his own fat for her winter meals?

Kurangaituku lurked on the edge of his mind. Hatupatu saw her in every shadow, every twig break, every bird call. He knew that a brave man would forge forward, that a hero would come to his brothers' aid. But fear had made his feet unresponsive to his mind. His body rebelled against his will, and he was surprised and relieved to find himself rushing back to the campsite.

He told himself that it was just a story, as if a story was something frivolous. But he knew the power of story. He had used it to shape reality; he had used it to manipulate his parents to make them send him on this hunt with his brothers.

It is just a story.

Hatupatu sank down, lying his head on the ground like a child to his mother's breast. He listened to the earth, hoping to hear the heartbeat of Papatūānuku, but he could only hear his own heart. He closed his eyes to quiet his panic, but every time he did, he saw his brothers strung up in trees, their necks snapped

from the snares that the ogress caught them in. All he could hear was the drip of their blood and the kurī lapping ...

And then, he could feel it—the soft tongue of a dog licking his cheek. Hatupatu opened his eyes to see the white kurī and his brother Haroa standing above him. He didn't realise how tense all his muscles had been, and now that they had relaxed, he felt light and giddy. He smiled at Haroa with relief.

'Get up you lazy hua.'

Haroa threw his catch at his little brother, who kept grinning at him. What was wrong with the boy—taking a nap when he and Hanui had been working since before sun-up? And then the kid had the gall to grin at him. Haroa gave Hatupatu a little kick in the stomach, but he still smiled, and, more disturbingly, seemed to be grateful for it.

'Get the fires started. We're hungry.'

And Hatupatu started a fire for his brothers. Haroa felt they should have been glad that he was doing what he was told, but something about it seemed wrong. Like the boy was up to something.

Hanui and Haroa feasted on the roasted kererū. They threw the meaty bones to their kurī even though the dogs had already gorged on the viscera and heads of the catch. What was left of the birds, what meat they deemed not worthy of their dogs, was given to their brother. Hatupatu ate without complaint, breaking the bones in the hope of finding a little marrow to sup on.

The brothers did not mean this diet as a punishment, nor entirely an insult. It was meant to teach the boy how to live

off bones and will alone. But although Hatupatu was glad his brothers were not dead, he could not take their treatment of him in any other way than punishment and insult.

Hanui and Haroa tasked Hatupatu with preserving their catch. They showed him how to render the fat from the kererū and how to pack its body into the hue. They showed him how to pour the fat over the bird so that the air would not spoil it. The task was sure to keep the boy busy during the day and keep him from mischief. And when they left the next day, Hatupatu was diligent: heating the birds slowly and packing them carefully before smothering them with their hot fat. Hatupatu worked despite his grumbling stomach, daring not to taste the roasting meat in case he could not control his hunger. He didn't want to disappoint his brothers; he still thought that they would relent and welcome him to the hunt soon.

When his brothers returned, the birds were stored, the camp was clean and dinner awaited them. Surely now, Hatupatu had shown them that he was humble; surely now, he had earned a meal. But his brothers yet again fed him the scraps not fit for their kurī. They thought that the silence from Hatupatu was subservience, but, in reality, it was resentment. It was the seed of revenge germinating inside him.

It had been almost a week since Hatupatu had eaten a decent meal. The hunger kept him awake at night and slowed his movements during the day. It made every part of him ache, like the hunger was eating his body from within, and it was. The worst part was that he was surrounded by food: the birds hanging to age and the birds

stored in fat. He could smell their delicious flesh on him; his pores seemed to seep with their fat. Hatupatu licked his arm and thought he could taste the birds, so he sucked on his forearm, raising his blood to the skin, which left him with round bruises on his arms.

Was it the bruises or the birds that sparked the idea? Was Hatupatu overcome by his mortal hunger so that he acted without thought—gorging himself on the birds until he came to his senses and had to find a way to cover his mistake? Or did he carefully plan it, plotting his story before ripping the sweet flesh with his teeth, letting the juice and fat from the bird coat his chin?

His story demanded sacrifice to live, so, like Māui who used his own blood for bait, Hatupatu cracked a calabash across his face, bruising his cheek and bloodying his nose. He wrestled with invisible foes, kicking dirt on the sleeping mats, pulling hair from his own head and finally he dropped, exhausted by his own exertions. His brothers were sure to believe his story. They would believe that the sky was below and the earth was above if Hatupatu told them so. Hanui and Haroa were very foolish men.

In the story that is told, his brothers find him and believe that he has been set upon and that he did his best to fight the assailants. A taua, a war party en route to a battle, had happened upon the campsite and had overcome the boy easily. Faced with such fearsome warriors, it was a miracle that Hatupatu was alive at all. In the story that is told, his brothers believed him again and again and again. In the story that is told, his brothers are finally suspicious, and one doubles back after they set out for the hunt and sees Hatupatu laughing at the foolishness of his brothers.

But these were brothers—brothers who had shared a nest, who had grown together, who had fledged together. They knew each other's faces better than their own. They knew what their younger brother was like. They questioned the story Hatupatu told, and the usually quick wit of Hatupatu failed him.

'Why didn't we see the taua?'

'The warriors have left no trail. Are they spirits and not men? There's not a single broken twig on the path.'

'Why did they spare you, brother?'

'Why do you look so smug?'

And so, in this story I tell you, the brothers of Hatupatu knew who had eaten their hard-won stores and knew who had bloodied their brother's nose and sullied their sleeping mats. Hatupatu does not laugh at his brothers' foolishness but will rue his own if he ever regains consciousness.

Hanui and Haroa did not understand why they had flown into such a rage. Perhaps it was the flimsy story their brother had come up with—that he thought them so gullible that they'd believe him. Perhaps it was because Hatupatu, despite his bloodied nose and bruising, had a smug look on his face when he told them what had 'happened'. Perhaps it was years of resentment spilling over in a few minutes. It was like they had no control over themselves. It was like they weren't even present. It was like they were listening to a story, witnessing strangers punching and kicking their brother. Even their own dogs had not recognised them and had retreated into the bush nearby, safe from the anger of their masters.

They could have let it go; the boy had only eaten a few birds, and they could have easily been replaced. He was probably sick to his stomach from gorging himself after his fast. But that strange spirit that seemed to have taken hold of them—the idea that Hatupatu must learn a lesson—moved them to punish their brother severely. And they succumbed to it, letting it possess their hands and feet and blind them to the sight of their beloved brother curled up under their blows.

The spirit that seemed to suddenly take over Hanui and Haroa left their bodies as quickly as it had arrived. The brothers recoiled from the body of Hatupatu as if they were repelled by some shift in magnetism. They sat down, panting from the exertion of the beating. The pleasure they had felt in dealing the blows had changed into deep shame. The bruises on the body and the blood on their hands were sure to condemn this hunt. They had broken the sacredness of this place by spilling the blood of Hatupatu. They would have to pack up in the morning, carry their brother home and admit to their whānau what they had done. They had sacrificed plentiful stores for the sake of a few birds. They had shown themselves to be little more than boys—unable to control their feelings of jealousy and rage. They had proved themselves unworthy to take on the mantle of adulthood. Their marriages would be delayed; their lives would be on hold. And worst, Hatupatu would have this to lord over them; he would milk every opportunity and all the sympathy that his injuries would afford him.

Hatupatu hadn't moved. Hanui caught the eye of Haroa, and Haroa moved closer to their little brother, their baby brother,

their beloved brother. The hand of Haroa hovered over Hatupatu. He was afraid that touching him would set off the rage again. Hanui moved in close to Hatupatu. He lay down so that his face was level with his little brother's, so that he could feel the breath of Hatupatu.

The face of Hatupatu was almost unrecognisable. His eyes and lips were swollen, and blood was shining on his cheeks and chin. Hanui felt no breath from his brother. He scrambled up, backing away from the boy's body. Haroa looked at Hanui in confusion and, finally, laid his hands on Hatupatu. He could feel no heartbeat; he could feel no breath.

Hidden in the bush, the kurī heard their masters' howl and replied with their own: *auau, auau, auau!*

Hanui and Haroa spent the night watching over their brother. Neither had moved him, not wanting to feel his lifeless body in their hands. Their kurī eventually crawled from the forest to sit with their masters. The black dog lay on the feet of Haroa. Haroa dug his toes into the thick fur, and each beat of the animal's heart made him feel sick, reminding him of his guilt. The sun rose, revealing the injuries wrought upon Hatupatu, and Hanui and Haroa wept for their brother again. They could not leave him that way. They needed to clean him, make him look as best they could for the journey home.

They tried to swaddle Hatupatu in his sleeping mat as if he was an infant. But Hatupatu was as stubborn in death as he had been in life. His limbs refused to move. He was frozen in the position he had died as if he continued to tell a story even if his spirit had left him.

Was it Hanui or Haroa who came up with the idea—the futility of bringing their brother's body home, of condemning themselves? Would their mother's grief be lessened by their admission of guilt? Or would she just lose three of her four sons, instead of just one?

Hatupatu had already given them the base of a story: the marauding taua that had robbed the brothers' campsite. In the story that Hanui and Haroa hatch, their young brother was set upon by a war party and killed; there was too much blood at the campsite for their brother to have survived with the little training that he had.

Yes, they were far away from camp when it happened; had they been there ... had they been there ...

The body must have been dragged away somewhere. They searched and searched but could not find Hatupatu. They wanted to bring him home, to have his bones rest with those of his ancestors, but they could not find him.

They could not find Hatupatu bundled in sleeping mats, lowered into the trench that he had himself dug and cloaked in the discarded feathers of his first hunt. So it was that Hatupatu would indeed be cloaked in the feathers of his first hunt. The brothers covered the trench with leaf litter to hide it from their eyes as they packed up the campsite. But the dogs sniffed the grave, so the brothers tied them up away from the trench until they could leave the campsite for good. The kurī stood with their heads lowered, shoulders hunched and their tails between their legs.

As they broke camp, Hanui and Haroa told each other the story again and again. They tell each other the story as they head off along the track home, and by the time they tell their parents the story, it will feel as if it is true.

    Hatupatu is left for dead.

    End of story.

At least, for most mortals. But Hatupatu ceased to be mortal long ago—dust to dust—as people are fond of saying. From your point of view, he is more akin to me than to you—a creature made up of words, thought and memory. He is no longer a man of skin, blood and viscera, but a character—mortal bones fleshed in myth.

    Thus, in this story, the end of Hatupatu is really a beginning. His life until this point is a prelude, an introduction full of foreshadowing.

I am dead.

Am I dead?

Te Pō, the darkness, is complete, oppressive.

The beginning and the end. Here you do not feel; you are. A thing, a nothing at once. Underneath the darkness, through the darkness, a hum. Is it potential —the start of something so huge that it will crackle through time as static on airwaves?

Te Pō—in the darkness listen for the hum …

The thing in the nothing, it is attractive; it has gravity. It is gravity, all gravity in a single point. In space. In time.

*And still the hum, the buzz of something. What was
it? Perhaps Tamumukiterangi is buzzing at your ear,
carrying a spirit to burrow into you instead of its
maggots—the tiny life that depends on death.*

*Te Pō, the darkness that arcs inevitably back
to light …*

… and as Hatupatu opened his eyes, his mouth filled with downy feathers, and his reclaimed breath was marked by the white wisps of them as he cough coughed.

He touched his face, his limbs, his heart—still smarting from the beating, but there, pulsing with life. Hatupatu hauled himself out of the trench. Everything in his body hurt; his limbs felt stiff, and he wondered if he had slept for such a long time that he had become an old man. The campsite was empty: not just of his brothers but of everything. Why would Hanui and Haroa take their sleeping mats with them on the hunt? Why would they take the stores that were left? It was as if they had packed up and left for home, but why would they leave in the middle of the hunt? Why would they leave him behind?

Hatupatu wandered around, trying to create the scene in his mind. Here is where he had cleaned the birds, and here is where his brothers had slept. Or was it nearer to the fire pit? Where had the fire pit gone? He was sure that it had been in the centre, but there was no sign of it. The gathered wood had gone, the ashes buried. How had the world changed so quickly? What had happened to him? Why had he woken in the trench, covered in feathers? He had dreamt of Te Pō. It must have been a dream

because the only explanation is not possible. Why had he been in Te Pō? No one could visit Te Pō, only the …

And he remembered the words that came to him in the dark, the words that seemed to define him, the words that seemed to be true:

I am dead.

Am I dead?

But now, he was back. He had escaped the embrace of Hinenuitepō, at least for now. How long was he in Te Pō? He looked for his brothers, unsure if he was wanting comfort or revenge. In the darkness things had been simple—there was no want where everything was nothing. Awake and alive, want was overwhelming—his throat was dry, his belly was empty, his bowels were full.

But the want was reassuring; it meant that he was alive. He was not some disembodied kēhua roaming the forest. But was he still a human? Even the demi-god Māui could not cheat Hinenuitepō. His heart raced. Hatupatu couldn't believe he had dared to think such a thing—that he could be …

The cramps in his stomach cut the thought from his mind. He was human, he was sure, and he was alive. Hatupatu squatted where his brothers had laid their sleeping mats, where their heads had lain, and strained—his tūtae slow to move at first. He pushed harder, and he felt his skin tear, but at last it was loose, and his sigh was one of pain, relief and pleasure. Hatupatu held the back of his hand to his nose; the smell was overwhelming—like the shit had rotted for days in his bowels. Hatupatu stood and looked at it. He smirked; the stinking black mess looked so much like his brothers. He didn't even bother kicking dirt over it.

His brothers had left no water or food. He smacked his swollen lips together to try and work up some saliva, but this opened the split in his bottom lip that had been fused with blood and down. He needed to drink. He needed to eat. He found a stick that had been honed, perhaps by one of his brothers, and he thought that with enough force it would pierce a bird's breast. Hatupatu took it and walked into the forest.

The hunger he could live with a while longer, but thirst was making his head muddy and his vision blurry. In a cool spot under a tree, he dug handfuls of moss from the forest floor and sucked on its moisture; it tasted earthy but was as welcome as any clear stream water. He grabbed another handful of moss, squeezed it and licked the moisture from his knuckles. He hoped that in slaking his thirst he'd staunch his strange thoughts of Te Pō. This world was the real one; of course he was human, of course he was saved. It wasn't his destiny to lie in a shallow grave, for his bones to be lost to his whānau. Defying death proved he was a hero.

Hatupatu was buoyed by the thought. A hero such as he would not die from starvation in the forest. He assumed that he must have an innate ability to hunt; all heroes are skilled in hunting and war—even if their spears are dull.

Light filtered through the leaves of the forest, making it gloomy but never completely dark. Occasionally, bigger pools of light were cast through gaps in the canopy made by fallen branches or an entire tree. There was activity all around Hatupatu. Birds chattered and sung above him; behind him, pīwakawaka squeaked

as they ate the midges disturbed by his footfall. Hatupatu tried not to think of Hinenuitepō, but the pīwakawaka kept reminding him of the story of her and Māui. The little bird had squeaked, and Māui was cut in two by the granite lined labia of Hinenuitepō, his legs crushed between hers, his head stuck within her. Hatupatu tried to banish thoughts of his own death from this journey, but the pīwakawaka just laughed at his foolishness.

It was the timelessness of the place that reminded him of Te Pō. He could have been walking a few minutes or a few hours; he couldn't tell. At home, it was easy to tell where the sun was—how much light there was left in the day. In the forest, the night could sneak up and snare him in its darkness. The timelessness went beyond the hours of the day; it seemed to Hatupatu that he could have been walking in this forest at any point in time. The forest was largely unchanged from when his grandfather had been alive and would remain so when Hatupatu had grandchildren of his own. Hatupatu thought that there would always be this forest, that there would always be birds to hunt, that this experience would be shared across generations.

    In a way he was right, but not in the way that
he thought.

Hatupatu found karaka seedlings. Their fruit was ripe, but he doubted whether their branches could take the weight of a fat kererū. Nearby, though, there were mature pūriri and tawa, and both were ripe with fruit and heavy with birds. He could hear the *whum whum* of the wings of the kererū as they moved from branch to branch.

When the fruit was overripe and fermented, the birds were fat and slow, and some fell, drunk, from the trees. Hatupatu had no time to wait for a bird to fall from above. Squinting into the canopy, he saw the white breast feathers glinting in the green. He drew the spear up over his shoulder, used his other arm as a guide to his target and threw his stick with all the force left in his body; his bruises screamed with the effort. But Hatupatu was inexperienced; his spear fell short again and again. He wondered if he was a hero after all.

Hatupatu would not allow himself to be defeated. He continued to stalk the birds, tasting the memory of their sweet meat, but memory did not satisfy. Being so focused on the fat pigeons, he was oblivious to the rest of the forest—the pīwakawaka that still followed behind him and the creature that also hunted kererū.

He would catch a kererū. He would not die starving in the forest. Destiny was his sacred kupu. And he had held it so tightly that it had penetrated his flesh, become part of him.

We turn to his destiny, then. To ours.

A kererū swooped down from the canopy to a bush near where Hatupatu waited. Near where I waited although at this time neither Hatupatu nor I were aware of each other; we were both focused on the bird. The kererū kept feeding, out of necessity not greed—winter would soon strip the forest of food. It seemed impossible its wings could support that expansive breast. Hatupatu didn't have the skill to spear the birds above him, but perhaps he had enough to spear one at eye level. He could hold on to the spear instead of throwing it, ramming the point through

the bird. He had hoped that he could leave the first bird as an offering to Tāne Mahuta, but it seemed unlikely he would catch more than one, if, indeed, he managed to catch one at all. He would make his peace with the god later.

Should he plant his feet or keep them light, balancing on the balls of his feet like his mau rākau kaiako taught him? The pain in his calves decided it for him. He would save his strength for the lunge forward. Hatupatu breathed in as deeply as his bruised ribs allowed, trying to slow his heart and steady his hand. And then he thrust his spear and it connected.

With me.

TE WHAIAO

Though we have been separated by life, by death, by time, our wairua are bound. Two bodies of water intermingled, flowing as one. Flowing through time, through life, through death and, I allow myself to believe, love.

But is love so neglectful, so forgetful? I am consumed by you. Take everything from me, I give it freely.

`Here is my hupe.`

`Here are my roimata.`

`Here is my toto.`

But you are like a rock—unmovable. I must contort myself around the thought of you.

Can you see me now before you? A bird, a woman, a bird-woman. I opened myself up to the story; it and I are no longer separate. I have shaped it and it has shaped me. The down on my breast and belly gave way to skin. Naked from clavicle to pubis, I am exposed. I've made my heart vulnerable. The pain I feel is exquisite and overwhelming—it pulsates in time with my heart.

Am I hideous or beautiful to you? How do you see me?

`This monster.`

`This giant.`

`This ogress.`

I searched for you in the forest, lost amongst the trees. Lost amongst time. Let me wrap you in this kākahu, let me wrap you up in the world—everything here I have made for you.

My love.

My story.

Me.

I plucked my eye from its socket to give to you as a gift. A black sphere, almost perfectly round. It sat in your palm, your fingers cradling it so it did not fall. It looked like a pebble pulled from a river—glossy obsidian, with flecks of white, as if the night sky has been captured within it. Through it you have seen everything—the black, the dark, the nothingness.

You have seen the world as I have through my story. Picture me now. How do I look to you? How has your mind shaped me as I told my story? Do you recognise me as kin, calling me down from above and giving me form? Am I a mirror to you? Do you see yourself reflected in my eyes?

He kōtuku kai whakaata—a kōtuku that feeds upon
its reflection.

I have fed upon you. I did not need to trap you, to sup on your mind through violence—physical or psychic—all I had to do was extend my hand to you in invitation. I opened my mind to you, and you reciprocated. I will see the world as you do.

But that is an illusion, a game we all play—the idea that any of us can truly understand what it is like to be another. That we can look upon the world with another's eyes. Even when I looked through the eyes of miromiro, I could never be fully submerged in that reality for I was always there. His mind in my mouth was never truly his.

Just as this story was never truly mine. It can only ever exist in the space between us.

It lived in the telling.

I lived in the telling.

This is me. This giant. This monster. This ogress. Through these pages, through these words, I have lived. I have ceased to be the words on this page and have become a real being, making her nest in your brain. I will lurk in the shadows of your mind—you will recall my form as your brain connects one event to another, beginning, middle and end. Each time I flash before your eyes, like the flit of a pīwakawaka following behind your steps in the forest, I grow stronger, more real. Every time you think of me, you speak of me, I become more real. Flesh and blood because you will me to be.

Through these words, these shapes drawn roughly on the ground, I whisper to you. I have borrowed your voice; I am clothed in your accent. There is power in the ability to articulate your own story. To use your own language, to use your own voice. In truth, I will never have a voice of my own—it is my nature to steal one.

The story we have shared begins and ends in a whare. A whare tapere, a house of storytelling and games. The door and the window depict Kurangaituku endlessly pursuing Hatupatu.

The whare is now filled with the things from my telling. The fine cloaks and weapons that I made are propped up against a wall. The once plain walls are now adorned with poupou punctuated with tukutuku panels. The poupou depict the images of my story—the riroriro raising the pīpīwharauroa, an ignimbrite cloud engulfing a volcano, a crack that awaits a small seed, the dogs of Hanui and Haroa and their namesakes from Rarohenga chasing each other's tails. The image of Hine split down the middle—a woman of both dawn and night, beautiful mother on one side, demon on the other,

her greenstone eyes the same no matter the guise. The bound body of Tama-o-hoi that seems to writhe before you.

The tukutuku panels are woven with the murmured chant of Tuhoto who freed Tama-o-hoi from Tarawera and the song of the miromiro—*tihi-ori-ori-ori*—a lament for a lost lover.

Look up to the ridgepole and rafters. Kōwhaiwhai swirl with soft, blue light rather than the expected kōkōwai. Are the lights that glow above you stars? The colour is too dim and blue for the stars. A hum of recognition cuts off the glow-worms' light. It is all here within this whare, my entire world.

Events slide in and out of view. The endless repetitions collide with one another and create a pattern that is reflected upon itself.

Beginning.

Middle.

End.

Middle.

Beginning.

Te Kore.

Te Pō.

Te Whaiao.

Te Pō.

Te Kore.

The idea of the whare has served its purpose. A karakia of thanks, to close the path once again.

Let this place be done.

A few words and it collapses. The door and the window panels have gone, and their openings let in the darkness rather than the light.

The thatch roof rots. Great strips are pulled away as if they are being ripped off by a fierce storm, but there is no roar of wind and the black sky above is calm.

Next, the floor beneath you gives way and there is no choice but to cling to the walls, even though we both know that they are next.

There is a choice—cling to this reality or let it go and embrace the idea of meto, of extinction, of simply not being.

The whare has gone. Here at the centre, nothing is left. No. Thing.

Ki te whaiao, ki te ao mārama.

The light, o the light that has nurtured me, that has oppressed me and defined me. The light that is me, must inevitably arc into darkness.

Te Pō.

And in the darkness I realise that I am not alone. We are many who dwell in the darkness of—

Te Pō.

The darkness is a womb—it will nurture me.

Te Pō.

And in the darkness, I listen for the hum. It is both within me and without me.

Te Pō.

The absence of light is darkness. I have perceived this. My eyes have emptied.

Te Pō.

The space that had defined my form has been replaced with darkness. I embrace it, the darkness is my comfort.

Te Pō.

The darkness is complete, oppressive. It defines and shapes my form. I push against it and it pushes back.

Te Pō.

The darkness envelops. It invades. It is me and I am darkness.

Te Pō.

And in the darkness, the hum diminishes. It is all that has been, that will be, is losing its form. Losing its will to be.

Te Pō.

This is the night that stretches on.

Te Pō.

There is a hum, a change.

The infinite void of Te Kore.

Te Kore, endless Te Kore.

Te Kore, endless Te Kore, the beginning and the end. All the things that have been and will be, but cannot manifest in—

Te Kore, endless Te Kore, the void that has no substance. I cannot perceive you. I cannot feel the weight of you. There is nothing, just Te Kore.

Te Kore, endless Te Kore, the void that stretches forever because there are no boundaries, no time. There is just Te Kore.

The darkness is everything—it is potential, it is everything that was and will be. Possibility—it may be filled, it may change, or it may remain blank.

Listen to the blank, the black, the dark. The world is dark and all that is left is darkness, a black void blankness.

Pōngerengere, dark and suffocating. Meaning has been obliterated. Seek the white spaces between the ink; let the letters and words seep into your mind. Remember all that has been written before.

All the words that have been spoken about me, written about me, bind me—their whispers encircle and define me. My name tells a story, a story that is familiar to you. My name is my story, it is me.

Kurangaituku.